Harriet Elizabeth Prescott Spofford

The Amber Gods, and other Stories

Harriet Elizabeth Prescott Spofford

The Amber Gods, and other Stories

ISBN/EAN: 9783744749497

Printed in Europe, USA, Canada, Australia, Japan

Cover: Foto ©Andreas Hilbeck / pixelio.de

More available books at **www.hansebooks.com**

THE AMBER GODS

AND OTHER STORIES

BY

HARRIET ELIZABETH PRESCOTT

BOSTON
TICKNOR AND FIELDS
1863

R. S. S.

I CONSECRATE

TO YOU

IN WHOM MY FUTURE LIES

THESE MEMORIALS

OF A PAST THAT YOU HAVE SO ENDEARED.

H. E. P.

Contents.

THE AMBER GODS.

THE AMBER GODS.

STORY FIRST.

FLOWER O' THE PEACH.

E 'VE some splendid old point-lace in our family, yellow and fragrant, loose-meshed. It isn't every one has point at all; and of those who have, it isn't every one can afford to wear it. I can. Why? O, because it's in character. Besides, I admire point any way, — it's so becoming. And then, you see, this amber! Now what is in finer unison, this old point-lace, all tags and tangle and fibrous and bewildering, and this amber, to which Heaven knows how many centuries, maybe, with all their changes, brought perpetual particles of increase? I like yellow things, you see.

To begin at the beginning. My name, you're aware, is Giorgione Willoughby. Queer name for a girl! Yes; but before papa sowed his wild-oats, he was one afternoon in Fiesole, looking over Florence nestled below, when some whim took him to go into a church there, a quiet place, full of twilight and one great picture, nobody within but a girl and her little slave, — the one watching her mistress, the other saying dreadfully devout prayers on an amber rosary, and of course she didn't see him, or

did n't appear to.   After he got there, he wondered what
on earth he came for, it was so dark and poky, and he
began to feel uncomfortably,— when all of a sudden a
great ray of sunset dashed through the window, and
drowned the place in the splendor of the illumined painting.   Papa adores rich colors ; and he might have been
satiated here, except that such things make you want
more.   It was a Venus ;— no, though, it could n't have
been a Venus in a church, could it ?   Well, then, a Mag-
dalen, I guess, or a Madonna, or something.   I fancy the
man painted for himself, and christened for others.   So,
when I was born, some years afterward, papa, gratefully
remembering this dazzling little vignette of his youth, was
absurd enough to christen *me* Giorgione.   That 's how I
came by my identity ; but the folks all call me Yone,— a
baby name.

   I 'm a blonde, you know,— none of your silver-washed
things.   I would n't give a *fico* for a girl with flaxen hair ;
she might as well be a wax doll, and have her eyes moved
by a wire ; besides, they 've no souls.   I imagine they
were remnants at *our* creation, and somehow scrambled
together, and managed to get up a little life among themselves ; but it 's good for nothing, and everybody sees
through the pretence.   They 're glass chips, and brittle
shavings, slender pinkish scrids,— no name for them ;
but just you say blonde, soft and slow and rolling,— it
brings up a brilliant, golden vitality, all manner of white
and torrid magnificences, and you see me !   I 've watched
little bugs — gold rose-chafers — lie steeping in the sun,
till every atom of them must have been searched with the
warm radiance, and have felt that, when they reached
that point, I was just like them, golden all through,— not
dyed, but created.   Sunbeams like to follow me, I think.

Now, when I stand in one before this glass, infiltrated with the rich tinge, don't I look like the spirit of it just stepped out for inspection? I seem to myself like the complete incarnation of light, full, bounteous, overflowing, and I wonder at and adore anything so beautiful; and the reflection grows finer and deeper while I gaze, till I dare not do so any longer. So, without more words, I'm a golden blonde. You see me now: not too tall, — five feet four; not slight, or I could n't have such perfect roundings, such flexible moulding. Here's nothing of the spiny Diana and Pallas, but Clytie or Isis speaks in such delicious curves. It don't look like flesh and blood, does it? Can you possibly imagine it will ever change? Oh!

Now see the face, — not small, either; lips with no particular outline, but melting, and seeming as if they would stain yours, should you touch them. No matter about the rest, except the eyes. Do you meet such eyes often? You would n't open yours so, if you did. Note their color now, before the ray goes. Yellow hazel? Not a bit of it! Some folks say topaz, but they're fools. Nor sherry. There's a dark sardine base, but over it real seas of light, clear light; there is n't any positive color; and once when I was angry, I caught a glimpse of them in a mirror, and they were quite white, perfectly colorless, only luminous. I looked like a fiend, and, you may be sure, recovered my temper directly, — easiest thing in the world, when you've motive enough. You see the pupil is small, and that gives more expansion and force to the irids; but sometimes in an evening, when I'm too gay, and a true damask settles in the cheek, the pupil grows larger and crowds out the light, and under these thick brown lashes, these yellow-hazel eyes of yours, they are dusky and purple and deep with flashes,

like pansies lit by fire-flies, and then common folks call
them black. Be sure, I've never got such eyes for
nothing, any more than this hair. That is Lucrezia Bor-
gian, spun gold, and ought to take the world in its toils.
I always wear these thick, riotous curls round my temples
and face; but the great braids behind — O, I'll uncoil
them, before my toilet is over.

Probably you felt all this before, but did n't know the
secret of it. Now, the traits being brought out, you perceive nothing wanting; the thing is perfect, and you 've
a reason for it. Of course, with such an organization,
I'm not nervous. Nervous! I should as soon fancy a
dish of cream nervous. I am too rich for anything of the
kind, permeated utterly with a rare golden calm. Girls
always suggest little similitudes to me: there's that bru-
nette beauty, — don't you taste mulled wine when you see
her? and thinking of yourself, did you ever feel green
tea? and find me in a crust of wild honey, the expressed
essence of woods and flowers, with its sweet satiety? —
no, that's too cloying. I'm a deal more like Mendels-
sohn's music, — what I know of it, for I can't distinguish
tunes, — you would n't suspect it, — but full harmonies
delight me as they do a wild beast; and so I'm like a
certain adagio in B flat, that papa likes.

There, now! you 're perfectly shocked to hear me go
on so about myself; but you ought n't to be. It is n't
lawful for any one else, because praise is intrusion; but
if the rose please to open her heart to the moth, what
then? You know, too, I did n't make myself; it's no
virtue to be so fair. Louise could n't speak so of herself:
first place, because it would n't be true; next place, she
could n't, if it were; and lastly, she made her beauty by
growing a soul in her eyes, I suppose, — what you call

good. I'm not good, of course; I wouldn't give a fig to
be good. So it's not vanity. It's on a far grander scale;
a splendid selfishness, — authorized, too; and papa and
mamma brought me up to worship beauty, — and there's
the fifth commandment, you know.

Dear me! you think I'm never coming to the point.
Well, here's this rosary; — hand me the perfume-case
first, please. Don't you love heavy fragrances, faint with
sweetness, ravishing juices of odor, heliotropes, violets,
water-lilies, — powerful attars and extracts that snatch
your soul off your lips? Couldn't you live on rich
scents, if they tried to starve you? I could, or die on
them: I don't know which would be best. There!
there's the amber rosary! You need n't speak; look
at it!

Bah! is that all you've got to say? Why, observe
the thing; turn it over; hold it up to the window; count
the beads, — long, oval, like some seaweed bulbs, each an
amulet. See the tint; it's very old; like clots of sunshine, — are n't they? Now bring it near; see the carv-
ing, here corrugated, there faceted, now sculptured into
hideous, tiny, heathen gods. You did n't notice that
before! How difficult it must have been, when amber is
so friable! Here's one with a chessboard on his back,
and all his kings and queens and pawns slung round him.
Here's another with a torch, a flaming torch, its fire pouring out inverted. They are grotesque enough; — but
this, this is matchless: such a miniature woman, one hand
grasping the round rock behind, while she looks down
into some gulf, perhaps, beneath, and will let herself fall.
O, you should see *her* with a magnifying-glass! You
want to think of calm, satisfying death, a mere exhala-
tion, a voluntary slipping into another element? There it

is for you. They are all gods and goddesses. They are
all here but one; I 've lost one, the knot of all, the love
of the thing. Well! was n't it queer for a Catholic girl
to have at prayer? Don't you wonder where she got it?
Ah! but don't you wonder where I got it? I 'll tell you.

Papa came in, one day, and with great mystery commenced unrolling, and unrolling, and throwing tissue papers on the floor, and scraps of colored wool; and Lu and
I ran to him, — Lu stooping on her knees to look up, I
bending over his hands to look down. It was so mysterious! I began to suspect it was diamonds for me, but
knew I never could wear them, and was dreadfully afraid
that I was going to be tempted, when slowly, bead by
bead, came out this amber necklace. Lu fairly screamed;
as for me, I just drew breath after breath, without a word.
Of course they were for me; — I reached my hands for
them.

"Oh, wait!" said papa. "Yone or Lu?"

"Now how absurd, papa!" I exclaimed. "Such things
for Lu!"

"Why not?" asked Lu, — rather faintly, for she knew
I always carried my point.

"The idea of you in amber, Lu! It 's too foreign; no
sympathy between you!"

"Stop, stop!" said papa. "You sha'n't crowd little Lu
out of them. What do you want them for, Lu?"

"To wear," quavered Lu, — "like the balls the Roman
ladies carried for coolness."

"Well, then, you ought to have them. What do you
want them for, Yone?"

"Oh, if Lu 's going to have them, I *don't* want them."

"But give a reason, child."

"Why, to wear, too, — to look at, — to have and to

hold, for better, for worse, — to say my prayers on," for a bright idea struck me, — "to say my prayers on, like the Florence rosary." I knew that would finish the thing.

"Like the Florence rosary?" said papa, in a sleepy voice. "Why, this *is* the Florence rosary."

Of course, when we knew that, we were both more crazy to obtain it.

"Oh, sir," just fluttered Lu, "where did you get it?"

"I got it; the question is, Who's to have it?"

"I must and will, potential and imperative," I exclaimed, quite on fire. "The nonsense of the thing! Girls with lucid eyes, like shadowy shallows in quick brooks, can wear crystallizations. As for me, I can wear only concretions and growths; emeralds and all their cousins would be shockingly inharmonious on me; but you know, Lu, how I use Indian spices, and scarlet and white berries, and flowers, and little hearts and notions of beautiful copal that Rose carved for you, — and I can wear sandal-wood and ebony and pearls, and now this amber. But you, Lu, you can wear every kind of precious stone, and you may have Aunt Willoughby's rubies that she promised me; they are all in tone with you; but I must have this."

"I don't think you're right," said Louise, rather soberly. "You strip yourself of great advantages. But about the rubies, I don't want anything so flaming, so you may keep them; and I don't care at all about this. I think, sir, on the whole, they belong to Yone for her name."

"So they do," said papa. "But not to be bought off! That's my little Lu!"

And somehow Lu, who had been holding the rosary, was sitting on papa's knee, as he half knelt on the floor,

1 *

and the rosary was in my hand. And then he produced
a little kid box, and there lay, inside, a star with a thread
of gold for the forehead, circlets for wrist and throat, two
drops, and a ring.   O such beauties ! You 've never seen
them.

"The other one shall have these. Are n't you sorry,
Yone?" he said.

"Oh no indeed! I'd much rather have mine, though
these are splendid.   What are they?"

"Aqua-marina," sighed Lu, in an agony of admiration.

"Dear, dear! how did you know?"

Lu blushed, I saw, — but I was too much absorbed with
the jewels to remark it.

"Oh, they are just like that ring on your hand! You
don't want two rings alike," I said.   "Where did you get
that ring, Lu?"

But Lu had no senses for anything beyond the casket.

If you know aqua-marina, you know something that's
before every other stone in the world. Why, it is as clear
as light, white, limpid, dawn light ; sparkles slightly and
seldom ; looks like pure drops of water, sea-water, scooped
up and falling down again ; just a thought of its parent
beryl-green hovers round the edges ; and it grows more
lucent and sweet to the centre, and there you lose yourself in some dream of vast seas, a glory of unimagined
oceans ; and you say that it was crystallized to any slow
flute-like tune, each speck of it floating into file with a
musical grace, and carrying its sound with it. There !
it's very fanciful, but I'm always feeling the tune in
aqua-marina, and trying to find it, — but I should n't
know it was a tune, if I did, I suppose. How magnificent
it would be, if every atom of creation sprang up and said
its one word of abracadabra, the secret of its existence,

and fell silent again. O dear! you'd die, you know; but what a pow-wow! Then, too, in aqua-marina proper, the setting is kept out of sight, and you have the unalloyed stone with its sea-rims and its clearness and steady sweetness. It was n't the thing for Louise to wear; it belongs rather to highly nervous, excitable persons; and Lu is as calm as I, only so different! There is something more pure and simple about it than about anything else; others may flash and twinkle, but this just glows with an unvarying power, is planetary and strong. It wears the moods of the sea, too: once in a while a warm amethystine mist suffuses it like a blush; sometimes a white morning fog breathes over it: you long to get into the heart of it. That's the charm of gems, after all! You feel that they are fashioned through dissimilar processes from yourself, — that there's a mystery about them, mastering which would be like mastering a new life, like having the freedom of other stars. I give them more personality than I would a great white spirit. I like amber that way, because I know how it was made, drinking the primeval weather, resinously beading each grain of its rare wood, and dripping with a plash to filter through and around the fallen cones below. In some former state I must have been a fly embalmed in amber.

"O Lu!" I said, "this amber's just the thing for me, such a great noon creature! And as for you, you shall wear mamma's Mechlin and that aqua-marina; and you'll look like a mer-queen just issuing from the wine-dark deeps and glittering with shining water-spheres."

I never let Lu wear the point at all; she'd be ridiculous in it, — so flimsy and open and unreserved; that's for me; Mechlin, with its whiter, closer, chaster web, suits her to a T.

I must tell you, first, how this rosary came about. You know we've a million of ancestors, and one of them, my great-grandfather, was a sea-captain, and actually did bring home cargoes of slaves! But once he fetched to his wife a little islander, an Asian imp, six years old, and wilder than the wind. She spoke no word of English, and was full of short shouts and screeches, like a thing of the woods. My great-grandmother couldn't do a bit with her; she turned the house topsy-turvy, cut the noses out of the old portraits, and chewed the jewels out of the settings, killed the little home animals, spoiled the dinners, pranced in the garden with Madam Willoughby's farthingale, and royal stiff brocades rustling yards behind, — this atom of a shrimp, — or balanced herself with her heels in the air over the curb of the well, scraped up the dead leaves under one corner of the house and fired them, — a favorite occupation, — and if you left her stirring a mess in the kitchen, you met her, perhaps, perched in the china-closet and mumbling all manner of demoniacal prayers, twisting and writhing and screaming over a string of amber gods that she had brought with her and always wore. When winter came and the first snow, she was furious, perfectly mad. One might as well have had a ball of fire in the house, or chain-lightning; every nice old custom had been invaded, the ancient quiet broken into a Bedlam of outlandish sounds, and as Captain Willoughby was returning, his wife packed the sprite off with him, — to cut, rip, and tear in New Holland, if she liked, but not in New England, — and rejoiced herself that she would find that little brown skin cuddled up in her best down beds and among her lavendered sheets no more. She had learned but two words all that time, — Willoughby, and the name of the town.

You may conjecture what heavenly peace came in when the Asian went out, but there is no one to tell what havoc was wrought on board ship; in fact, if there could have been such a thing as a witch, I should believe that imp sunk them, for a stray Levantine brig picked her — still agile as a monkey — from a wreck off the Cape de Verdes and carried her into Leghorn, where she took — will you mind, if I say? — leg-bail, and escaped from durance. What happened on her wanderings I'm sure is of no consequence, till one night she turned up outside a Fiesolan villa, scorched with malaria fevers and shaken to pieces with tertian and quartan and all the rest of the agues. So, after having shaken almost to death, she decided upon getting well; all the effervescence was gone; she chose to remain with her beads in that family, a mysterious tame servant, faithful, jealous, indefatigable. But she never grew; at ninety she was of the height of a yard-stick, — and nothing could have been finer than to have a dwarf in those old palaces, you know.

In my great-grandmother's home, however, the tradition of the Asian sprite with her string of amber gods was handed down like a legend, and, no one knowing what had been, they framed many a wild picture of the Thing enchanting all her spirits from their beads about her, and calling and singing and whistling up the winds with them till storm rolled round the ship, and fierce fog and foam and drowning fell upon her capturers. But they all believed, that, snatched from the wreck into islands of Eastern archipelagoes, the vindictive child and her quieted gods might yet be found. Of course my father knew this, and when that night in the church he saw the girl saying such devout prayers on an amber rosary, with a demure black slave so tiny and so old behind her, it flashed back

on him, and he would have spoken, if, just then, the ray
had not revealed the great painting, so that he forgot all
about it, and when at last he turned, they were gone.
But my father had come back to America, had sat down
quietly in his elder brother's house, among the hills where
I am to live, and was thought to be a sedate young man
and a good match, till a freak took him that he must go
back and find that girl in Italy. How to do it, with no
clew but an amber rosary? But do it he did, — station-
ing himself against a pillar in that identical church and
watching the worshippers, and not having long to wait
before in she came, with little Asian behind. Papa isn't
in the least romantic ; he is one of those great fertilizing
temperaments, golden hair and beard, and *hazel* eyes, if
you will. He's a splendid old fellow ! It's absurd to
delight in one's father, — so bread-and-buttery, — but I
can't help it. He's far stronger than I ; none of the
little weak Italian traits that streak me, like water in
thick, sirupy wine. No, — he isn't in the least romantic, but he says he was fated to this step, and could no
more have resisted than his heart could have refused to
beat. When he spoke to the devotee, little Asian made
sundry belligerent demonstrations ; but he confronted her
with the two words she had learned here, Willoughby
and the town's name. The dwarf became livid, seemed
always after haunted by a dreadful fear of him, pursued
him with a rancorous hate, but could not hinder his marriage. — The Willoughbys are a cruel race. — Her only
revenge was to take away the amber beads, which had
long before been blessed by the Pope for her young mistress, refusing herself to accompany my mother, and de-
claring that neither should her charms ever cross the
water, — that all their blessing would be changed to

banning, and that bane would burn the bearer, should the salt-sea spray again dash round them. But when, in process of Nature, the Asian died, — having become classic through her longevity, taking length of days for length of stature, — then the rosary belonged to mamma's sister, who by and by sent it, with a parcel of other things, to papa for me. So I should have had it at all events, you see ; — papa is such a tease ! The other things were mamma's wedding-veil, that point there, which once was her mother's, and some pearls.

I was born upon the sea, in a calm, far out of sight of land, under sweltering suns ; so, you know, I 'm a cosmopolite, and have a right to all my fantasies. Not that they are fantasies, at all ; on the contrary, they are parts of my nature, and I could n't be what I am without them, or have one and not have all. Some girls go picking and scraping odds and ends of ideas together, and by the time they are thirty get quite a bundle of whims and crotchets on their backs ; but they are all at sixes and sevens, uneven and knotty like fagots, and won't lie compactly, don't belong to them, and anybody might surprise them out of them. But for me, you see, mine are harmonious ; in my veins ; I was born with them. Not that I was always what I am now. Oh, bless your heart ! plums and nectarines and luscious things that ripen and develop all their rare juices, were green once, and so was I. Awkward, tumble-about, near-sighted, till I was twenty, a real raw-head-and-bloody-bones to all society ; then mamma, who was never well in our diving-bell atmosphere, was ordered to the West Indies, and papa said it was what I needed, and I went, too, — and oh, how sea-sick ! Were you ever ? You forget all about who you are, and have a vague notion of being Universal Disease. I have heard

of a kind of myopy that is biliousness, and when I reached
the islands my sight was as clear as my skin ; all that tropical luxuriance snatched me to itself at once, recognized
me for kith and kin ; and mamma died, and I lived.   We
had accidents between wind and water, enough to have
made me considerate for others, Lu said ; but I don't see
that I'm any less careful not to have my bones spilt in
the flood than ever I was.   Slang? No, — poetry.   But
if your nature had such a wild, free tendency as mine, and
then were boxed up with proprieties and civilities from
year's end to year's end, maybe you, too, would escape
now and then in a bit of slang.

We always had a little boy to play with, Lu and I, or
rather Lu, — because, though he never took any dislike
to me, he was absurdly indifferent, while he followed Lu
about with a painful devotion.   I did n't care, did n't know ;
and as I grew up and grew awkwarder, I was the plague
of their little lives.   If Lu had been my sister instead of
my orphan cousin, as mamma was perpetually holding up
to me, I should have bothered them twenty times more ;
but when I got larger and began to be really distasteful
to his fine artistic perception, mamma had the sense to
keep me out of his way ; and he was busy at his lessons,
and did n't come so much.   But Lu just fitted him then,
from the time he daubed little adoring blotches of her face
on every barn-door and paling, till when his scrap-book
was full of her in all fancies and conceits, and he was old
enough to go away and study Art.   Then he came home
occasionally, and always saw us ; but I generally contrived,
on such occasions, to do some frightful thing that shocked
every nerve he had, and he avoided me instinctively, as he
would an electric torpedo ; but — do you believe ? — I
never had an idea of such a fact till, when sailing from

the South, so changed, I remembered things, and felt intuitively how it must have been. Shortly after I went away, he visited Europe. I had been at home a year, and now we heard he had returned; so for two years he had n't seen me. He had written a great deal to Lu, — brotherly letters they were, — he is so peculiar, — determining not to give her the least intimation of what he felt, if he did feel anything, till he was able to say all. And now he had earned for himself a certain fame, a promise of greater; his works sold; and if he pleased, he could marry. I merely presume this might have been his thought; · he never told me. A certain fame! But that 's nothing to what he will have. How can he paint gray, faint, half-alive things now? He must abound in color, — be rich, exhaustless: wild sea-sketches, — sunrise, — sunset, — mountain mists rolling in turbid crimson masses, breaking in a milky spray of vapor round lofty peaks, and letting out lonely glimpses of a melancholy moon, — South American splendors, — pomps of fruit and blossom, — all this affluence of his future life must flash from his pencils now. Not that he will paint again directly. Do you suppose it possible that I should be given him merely for a phase of wealth and light and color, and then taken, — taken, in some dreadful way, to teach him the necessary and inevitable result of such extravagant luxuriance? It makes me shiver.

It was that very noon when papa brought in the amber, that he came for the first time since his return from Europe. He had n't met Lu before. I ran, because I was in my morning wrapper. Don't you see it there, that cream-colored, undyed silk, with the dear palms and ferns swimming all over it? And half my hair was just flung into a little black net that Lu had made

me; we both had run down as we were when we heard
papa. I scampered; but *he* saw only Lu, and grasped her
hands. Then, of course, I stopped on the baluster to
look. They did n't say anything, only seemed to be
reading up for the two years in each other's eyes; but
Lu dropped her kid box, and as he stooped to pick it up,
he held it, and then took out the ring, looked at her and
smiled, and put it on his finger. The one she had
always worn was no more a mystery. He has such
little hands! they don't seem made for anything but
slender crayons and water-colors, as if oils would weigh
them down with the pigment; but there is a nervy
strength about them that could almost bend an ash.

Papa's breezy voice blew through the room next
minute, welcoming him; and then he told Lu to put up
her jewels, and order luncheon, at which, of course, the
other wanted to see the jewels nearer; and I could n't
stand that, but slipped down and walked right in, lifting
my amber, and saying, "Oh, but this is what you must
look at!"

He turned, somewhat slowly, with such a lovely indifference, and let his eyes idly drop on me. He did n't
look at the amber at all; he did n't look at me; I seemed
to fill his gaze without any action from him, for he stood
quiet and passive; my voice, too, seemed to wrap him
in a dream,—only an instant though; then I had
reached him.

"You 've not forgotten Yone," said papa, "who went
persimmon and came apricot?"

"I 've not forgotten Yone," answered he, as if half
asleep. "But who is this?"

"Who is this?" echoed papa. "Why, this is my
great West Indian magnolia, my Cleopatra in light
colors, my—"

"Hush, you silly man!"

"This is she," putting his hands on my shoulders, —
"Miss Giorgione Willoughby."

By this time he had found his manners.

"Miss Giorgione Willoughby," he said, with a cool bow, "I never knew you."

"Very well, sir," I retorted. "Now you and my father have settled the question, know my amber!" and lifting it again, it got caught in that curl.

I have good right to love my hair. What was there to do, when it snarled in deeper every minute, but for him to help me? and then, at the friction of our hands, the beads gave out slightly their pungent smell that breathes all through the Arabian Nights, you know; and the perfumed curls were brushing softly over his fingers, and I a little vexed and flushed as the blind blew back and let in the sunshine and a roistering wind; — why, it was all a pretty scene, to be felt then and remembered afterward. Lu, I believe, saw at that instant how it would be, and moved away to do as papa had asked; but no thought of it came to me.

"Well, if you can't clear the tangle," I said, "you can see the beads."

But while with delight he examined their curious fretting, he yet saw me.

I am used to admiration now, certainly; it is my food; without it I should die of inanition; but do you suppose I care any more for those who give it to me than a Chinese idol does for whoever swings incense before it? Are you devoted to your butcher and milkman? We desire only the unpossessed or unattainable, "something afar from the sphere of our sorrow." But, though unconsciously, I may have been piqued by this manner of his. It was new;

not a word, not a glance; I believed it was carelessness, and resolved — merely for the sake of conquering, I fancied, too — to change all that. By and by the beads dropped out of the curl, as if they had been possessed of mischief and had held there of themselves. He caught them.

"Here, Circe," he said.

That was the time I was so angry; for, at the second, he meant all it comprehended. He saw, I suppose, for he added at once, —

"Or what was the name of the Witch of Atlas,

'The magic circle of whose voice and eyes
All savage natures did imparadise'?"

I wonder what made me think him mocking me. Frequently since then he has called me by that word.

"I don't know much about geography," I said. "Besides, these did n't come from there. Little Asian — the imp of my name, you remember — owned them."

"Ah?" with the utmost apathy; and turning to my father, "I saw the painting that enslaved you, sir," he said.

"Yes, yes," said papa, gleefully. "And then why did n't you make me a copy?"

"Why?" Here he glanced round the room, as if he were n't thinking at all of the matter in hand. "The coloring is more than one can describe, though faded. But I don't think you would like it so much now. Moreover, sir, I cannot make copies."

I stepped towards them, quite forgetful of my pride. "Can't?" I exclaimed. "Oh, how splendid! Because then no other man comes between you and Nature; your ideal hangs before you, and special glimpses open and shut on you, glimpses which copyists never obtain."

"I don't think you are right," he said, coldly, his hands loosely crossed behind him, leaning on the corner of the mantel, and looking unconcernedly out of the window.

Was n't it provoking? I remembered myself, — and remembered, too, that I never had made a real exertion to procure anything, and it was n't worth while to begin then; besides not being my forte, — things must come to me. Just then Lu re-entered, and one of the servants brought a tray, and we had lunch. Then our visitor rose to go.

"No, no," said papa. "Stay the day out with the girls. It's May-day, and there are to be fireworks on the other bank to-night."

"Fireworks for May-day?"

"Yes, to be sure. Wait and see."

"It would be so pleasant!" pleaded Lu.

"And a band, I forgot to mention. I have an engagement myself, so you 'll excuse me; but the girls will do the honors, and I shall meet you at dinner."

So it was arranged. Papa went out. I curled up on a lounge, — for Lu would n't have liked to be left, if I had liked to leave her, — and soon, when he sat down by her quite across the room, I half shut my eyes and pretended to sleep. He began to turn over her work-basket, taking up her thimble, snipping at the thread with her scissors: I see now he was n't thinking about it, and was trying to recover what he considered a proper state of feeling, but I fancied he was very gentle and tender, though I could n't hear what they said, and I never took the trouble to listen in my life. In about five minutes I was tired of this playing 'possum, and took my observations.

What is your idea of a Louise? Mine is, — dark eyes, dark hair, decided features, pale, brown pale, with

a mole on the left cheek, — and that's Louise. Nothing
striking, but pure and clear, and growing always better.

For him, — he's not one of those cliff-like men against
whom you are blown as a feather. I don't fancy that
kind; I can stand of myself, rule myself. He is n't small,
though; no, he's tall enough, but all his frame is delicate, held to earth by nothing but the cords of a strong
will, — very little body, very much soul. He, too, is
pale, and has dark eyes, with violet darks in them. You
don't call him beautiful in the least, but you don't know
him. I call him beauty itself, and I know him thoroughly. A stranger might have thought, when I spoke
of those copals Rose carved, that Rose was some girl.
But though he has a feminine sensibility, like Correggio
or Schubert, nobody could call him womanish. "*Les
races se féminisent.*" Don't you remember Matthew
Roydon's Astrophill?

> "A sweet, attractive kind of grace,
>   A full assurance given by looks,
>   Continual comfort in a face."

I always think of that flame in an alabaster vase, when
I see him; "one sweet grace fed still with one sweet
mind"; a countenance of another sphere: that's Vaughan
Rose. It provokes me that I can't paint him myself,
without other folk's words; but you see there's no natural
image of him in me, and so I can't throw it strongly on
any canvas. As for his manners, you've seen them; —
now tell me, was there ever anything so winning when
he pleases, and always a most gracious courtesy in his
air, even when saying an insufferably uncivil thing? He
has an art, a science, of putting the unpleasant out of his
sight, ignoring or looking over it, which sometimes gives
him an absent way; and that is because he so delights in

beauty; he seems to have woven a mist over his face then, and to be shut in on his own inner loveliness; and many a woman thinks he is perfectly devoted, when, very like, he is swinging over some lonely Spanish sierra beneath the stars, or buried in noonday Brazilian forests, half stifled with the fancied breath of every gorgeous blossom of the zone. Till this time, it had been the perfection of form rather than tint that had enthralled him; he had come home with severe ideas, too severe; he needed me, you see.

But while looking at him and Lu, on that day, I did n't perceive half of this, only felt annoyed at their behavior, and let them feel that I was noticing them. There 's nothing worse than that; it 's a very upas-breath; it puts on the brakes; and of course a chill and a restraint overcame them till Mr. Dudley was announced.

" Dear! dear! " I exclaimed, getting upon my feet. " What ever shall we do, Lu? I 'm not dressed for him." And while I stood, Mr. Dudley came in.

Mr. Dudley did n't seem to mind whether I was dressed in cobweb or sheet-iron; for he directed his looks and conversation so much to Lu, that Rose came and sat on a stool before me and began to talk.

" Miss Willoughby — "

" Yone, please."

" But you are not Yone."

" Well, just as you choose. You were going to say —?"

" Merely to ask how you liked the Islands."

" Oh, well enough."

" No more? " he said. " They would n't have broken your spell so, if that had been all. Do you know, I actually believe in enchantments now?"

I was indignant, but amused in spite of myself.

"Well," he continued, "why don't you say it? How impertinent am I? You won't? Why don't you laugh, then?"

"Dear me!" I replied. "You are so much on the 'subtle-souled-psychologist' line, that there's no need of. my speaking at all."

"I can carry on all the dialogue? Then let *me* say how you liked the Islands."

"I shall do no such thing. I liked the West Indies because there is life there; because the air is a firmament of balm, and you grow in it like a flower in the sun; because the fierce heat and panting winds wake and kindle all latent color and fertilize every germ of delight that might sleep here forever. That's why I liked them; and you knew it just as well before as now."

"Yes; but I wanted to see if you knew it. So you think there is life there in that dead Atlantis."

"Life of the elements, rain, hail, fire, and snow."

"Snow thrice bolted by the northern blast, I fancy, by which time it becomes rather misty. Exaggerated snow."

"Everything there is an exaggeration. Coming here from England is like stepping out of a fog into an almost exhausted receiver; but you 've no idea what light is, till you 've been in those inland hills. You think a blue sky the perfection of bliss? When you see a white sky, a dome of colorless crystal, with purple swells of mountain heaving round you, and a wilderness in golden greens royally languid below, while stretches of a scarlet blaze, enough to ruin a weak constitution, flaunt from the rank vines that lace every thicket, — and the whole world, and you with it, seems breaking to blossom, — why, then you know what light is and can do. The very wind there by day is bright, now faint, now stinging, and makes a low wiry music through the loose sprays as if they were tense harpstrings. Nothing startles ; all is like a grand composition utterly wrought out. What a blessing it is that the blacks have been imported there, — their swarthiness is in such consonance ! " .

" No ; the native race was in better consonance. You are so enthusiastic, it is pity you ever came away."

" Not at all. I did n't know anything about it till I came back."

" But a mere animal or vegetable life is not much. What was ever done in the tropics ? "

" Almost all the world's history, — was n't it ? "

" No, indeed ; only the first, most trifling, and barbarian movements."

" At all events, you are full of blessedness in those climates, and that is the end and aim of all action ; and if Nature will do it for you, there is no need of your interference. It is much better to be than to do ; — one is strife, the other is possession."

" You mean being as the complete attainment? There is only one Being, then. All the rest of us are — "

" O dear me ! that sounds like métaphysics ! Don't ! "

" So you see, you are not full of blessedness there."

" You ought to have been born in Abelard's time, — you 've such a disputatious spirit. That 's I don't know how many times you have contradicted me to-day."

" Pardon."

" I wonder if you are so easy with all women."

" I don't know many."

" I shall watch to see if you contradict Lu this way."

" I don't need. How absorbed she is ! Mr. Dudley is interesting ' ? "

2

"I don't know. No. But then, Lu is a good girl, and he's her minister, — a Delphic oracle. She thinks the sun and moon set somewhere round Mr. Dudley. Oh! I mean to show him my amber!"

And I tossed it into Lu's lap, saying, —

"Show it to Mr. Dudley, Lu, — and ask him if it is n't divine!"

Of course, he was shocked, and would n't go into ecstasies at all; tripped on the adjective.

"There are gods enough in it to be divine," said Rose, taking it from Lu's hand and bringing it back to me. "All those very Gnostic deities who assisted at Creation. You are not afraid that the imprisoned things work their spells upon you? The oracle declares it suits your cousin best," he added, in a lower tone.

"All the oaf knows!" I responded. "I wish you'd admire it, Mr. Dudley. Mr. Rose don't like amber, — handles it like nettles."

"No," said Rose, "I don't like amber."

"He prefers aqua-marina," I continued. "Lu, produce yours!" For she had not heard him.

"Yes," said Mr. Dudley, spacing his syllables and rubbing his finger over his lip while he gazed, "every one must prefer aqua-marina."

"Nonsense! It's no better than glass. I'd as soon wear a set of window-panes. There's no expression in it. It is n't alive, like real gems."

Mr. Dudley stared. Rose laughed.

"What a vindication of amber!" he said.

He was standing now, leaning against the mantel, just as he was before lunch. Lu looked at him and smiled.

"Yone is exultant, because we both wanted the beads," she said. "I like amber as much as she."

" Nothing near so much, Lu ! "

" Why did n't you have them, then ? " asked Rose, quickly.

" Oh, they belonged to Yone ; and uncle gave me these, which I like better. Amber is warm, and smells of the earth ; but this is cool and dewy, and — "

" Smells of heaven ? " asked I, significantly.

Mr. Dudley began to fidget, for he saw no chance of finishing his exposition.

" As I was saying, Miss Louisa," he began, in a different key.

I took my beads and wound them round my wrist. " You have n't as much eye for color as a poppy-bee," I exclaimed, in a corresponding key, and looking up at Rose.

" Unjust. I was thinking then how entirely they suited you."

" Thank you. Vastly complimentary from one who ' don't like amber ' ! "

Nevertheless, you think so."

" Yes and no. Why don't you like it ? "

" You must n't ask me for my reasons. It is not merely disagreeable, but hateful."

" And you 've been beside me like a Christian all this time, and I had it ! "

" The perfume is acrid ; I associate it with the lower jaw of St. Basil the Great, styled a present of immense value, you remember, — being hard, heavy, shining like gold, the teeth yet in it, and with a smell more delightful than amber," — making a mock shudder at the word.

" Oh, it is prejudice, then."

" Not in the least. It is antipathy. Besides, the thing is unnatural ; there is no existent cause for it. A bit

that turns up on certain sands, — here at home, for aught
I know, as often as anywhere."

"Which means Nazareth. We must teach you, sir,
that there are some things at home as rare as those
abroad."

"I am taught," he said, very low, and without looking up.

"Just tell me what is amber?"

"Fossil gum."

"Can you say those words and not like it? Don't it
bring to you a magnificent picture of the pristine world,
— great seas and other skies, — a world of accentuated
crises, that sloughed off age after age, and rose fresher
from each plunge? Don't you see, or long to see, that
mysterious magic tree out of whose pores oozed this fine
solidified sunshine? What leaf did it have? what blossom? what great wind shivered its branches? Was it a
giant on a lonely coast, or thick low growth blistered in
ravines and dells? That's the witchery of amber, —
that it *has* no cause, — that all the world grew to produce
it, maybe, — died and gave no other sign, — that its
tree, which must have been beautiful, dropped all its
fruits, — and how bursting with juice must they have
been —"

"Unfortunately, coniferous."

"Be quiet. Stripped itself of all its lush luxuriance,
and left for a vestige only this little fester of its gashes."

"No, again," he once more interrupted. "I have seen
remnants of the wood and bark in a museum."

"Or has it hidden and compressed all its secret
here?" I continued, obliviously. "What if in some piece
of amber an accidental seed were sealed; we found, and
planted, and brought back the lost æons? What a glori-

ous world that must have been where even the gum was
so precious!"

"In a picture, yes. Necessary for this. But, my
dear Miss Willoughby, you convince me that the Amber
Witch founded your family," he said, having listened
with an amused face. "Loveliest amber that ever tho
sorrowing sea-birds have wept," he hummed. "There!
is n't that kind of stuff enough to make a man detest it?"

"Yes."

"And you are quite as bad in another way."

"Oh!"

"Just because, when we hold it in our hands, we hold
also that furious epoch where rioted all monsters and
poisons, — where death fecundated and life destroyed, —
where superabundance demanded such existences, no
souls, but fiercest animal fire; — just for that I hate it."

"Why, then, is it fitted for me?"

He laughed again, but replied: "The hues harmo-
nize; the substances; you both are accidents; it suits
your beauty."

So, then, it seemed I had beauty, after all.

"You mean that it harmonizes with me, because I am
a symbol of its period. If there had been women, then,
they would have been like me, — a great creature without a soul, a —"

"Pray, don't finish the sentence. I can imagine that
there is something rich and voluptuous and sating about
amber, its color, and its lustre, and its scent; but for
others, not for me. Yes, you have beauty, after all,"
turning suddenly, and withering me with his eye, —
"beauty, after all, as you did n't *say* just now. Why
don't you put some of it into —. Mr. Willoughby is in
the garden. I must go before he comes in, or he 'll

make me stay. There are some to whom you can't
say, No."

He stopped a minute, and now, without looking, —
indeed, he looked everywhere but at me, while we
talked, — made a bow as if just seating me from a waltz,
and, with his eyes and his smile on Louise all the way
down the room, went out. Did you ever know such
insolence?

Papa made Mr. Dudley stay and dine, and of course we
were almost bored to death, when in came Rose again,
stealing behind Lu's chair, and showering her in the twilight with a rain of May-flowers.

"Now you 'll have to gather them again," he said.

"Oh, how exquisite! how delicious! how I thank you!"
she exclaimed, without disturbing one, however.

"You won't touch them again? Then I must," he
added.

"No, no, Mr. Rose!" I cried. "I 'll pick them up,
and take toll."

"Don't touch them!" said Lu, "they 're so sweet!"

"Yes," he murmured lower, "they share with you. I
always said so, you remember."

"O yes! and every May-day but the last you have
brought them to me."

"Have you the trailing-arbutus there?" asked Mr.
Dudley.

"No," returned Rose.

"I thought I detected strawberries," submitted the other,
— "a pleasant odor which recalls childhood to memory."

For some noses all sweet scents are lumped in one big
strawberry; clovers, or hyacinths, or every laden air indifferently, they still sniff—strawberries. Commonplace!

"It's a sign of high birth to track strawberry-beds where no fruit is, Mr. Dudley," said I.

"Very true, Miss Willoughby. I was born pretty high up in the Green Mountains."

"And so keep your memory green?"

"Strawberries in June," said Rose, good-naturedly. "But fruit out of season is trouble out of reason, the Dream-Book says. It's May now, and these are its blossoms."

"Everybody makes such a fuss about ground-laurel!" said I. "I don't see why, I'm sure. They're never perfect. The leaf is hideous, — a stupid duenna! You get great green leaves, and the flowers all white; you get deep rosy flowers, and the leaves are all brown and bitten. They're neither one thing nor another. They're just like heliotropes, — no bloom at all, only scent. I've torn up myriads, to the ten stamens in their feathered case, to find where that smell comes from, — that is perfectly delicious, — and I never could. They are a cheat."

"Have you finished your tirade?" asked Rose, indifferently.

"I don't believe you mean so," murmured Lu. "They have a color of their own, almost human, infantine; and when you mass them, the tone is more soft and mellow than a flute. Everybody loves May-flowers."

"Just about. I despise flutes. I like bassoons."

"They are prophets of apple-blossoms."

"Which brings them at once into the culinary."

"They are not very showy," said Mr. Dudley; "but when we remember the Fathers —"

"There's nothing like them," said Rose, gently, as he knelt by Lu, slowly putting them into order; "nothing but pure, clear things; they're the fruit of snow-flakes, the

firstlings of the year. When one thinks how sweetly
they come from their warm coverts and look into this
cold, breezy sky so unshrinkingly, and from what a soil
they gather such a wealth of simple beauty, one feels
ashamed."

"Climax worthy of the useless things!" said I.

"The moment in which first we are thoroughly
ashamed, Miss Willoughby, is the sovereign one of our
life. Useless things? They are worth king and bishop.
Every year, weariness and depression melt away when
atop of the seasons' crucible boil these little bubbles.
Isn't everybody better for lavishing love? And no one
merely likes these; whoever cares at all, loves entirely.
We always take and give resemblances or sympathies
from any close connection, and so these are in their way
a type of their lovers. What virtue is in them to distil
the shadow of the great pines, that wave layer after layer
with a grave rhythm over them, into this delicate tint, I
wonder. They have so decided an individuality, — different there from hot-house belles; — fashion strips us of
our characteristics —"

"You needn't turn to me for illustration of exotics,"
said I.

He threw me a cluster, half-hidden in its green towers,
and went on, laying one by one and bringing out little
effects.

"The sweetest modesty clings to them, which Alphonse
Karr denies to the violet, so that they are almost out of
place in a drawing-room; one ought to give them there
the shelter of their large, kind leaves."

"Hemlock's the only wear," said Louise.

"Or last year's scarlet blackberry triads. Vines together," he suggested.

"But sometimes they forget their nun-like habit," she added, "put on a frolicsome mood, and clamber out and flush all the deep ruts of the carriage-road in Follymill Woods, you remember."

"Penance next year," said I.

"No, no; you are not to bring your old world into my new," objected Rose; "they're fair little Puritans, who do no penance. Perhaps they ran out so to greet the winter-worn mariners of Plymouth, and have been pursued by the love of their descendants ever since, they getting charier. Just remember how they grow. Why, you'd never suspect a flower there, till, happening to turn up a leaf, you're in the midst of harvest. You may tramp acres in vain, and within a stone's throw they've been awaiting you. There's something very charming, too, about them in this, — that when the buds are set, and at last a single blossom starts the trail, you plucking at one end of the vine, your heart's delight may touch the other a hundred miles away. Spring's telegraph. So they bind our coast with this network of flower and root."

"By no means," I asserted. "They grow in spots."

"Pshaw! I won't believe it. They're everywhere just the same, only underground preparing their little witnesses, whom they send out where most needed. You don't suppose they find much joy in the fellow-ship of brown pine pins and sad gray mosses, do you? Some folks say they don't grow away from the shore; but I've found them, I'm sorry to say, up in New Hampshire."

"Why sorry?" asked Lu.

"Oh, I like it best that they need our sea. They're eminently choice for this hour, too, when you scarcely

2*   c

gather their tint, — that tint, as if moonlight should wish to become a flower, — but their fragrance is an atmosphere all about you. How genuinely spicy it is! It's the very quintessence of those regions all whose sweetness exudes in sun-saturated balsams, — the very breath of pine woods and salt sea winds. How could it live away from the sea?"

"Why, sir," said Mr. Dudley, "you speak as if it were a creature!"

"A hard woody stem, a green robust leaf, a delicate odorous flower, Mr. Dudley, what is it all but an expression of New England character?"

"Doxology!" said I.

"Now, Miss Louise, as you have made me atone for my freedom, the task being done, let me present them in form."

"I'm sure she need n't praise them," said I.

She did n't.

"I declared people make a great fuss over them," I continued. "And you prove it. You put me in mind of a sound to be heard where one gets them, — a strange sound, like low, distant thunder, and it's nothing but the drum of a little partridge! a great song out of nothing. — Bless me! what's that?"

"Oh, the fireworks!" said Lu. And we all thronged to the windows.

"It's very good of your uncle to have them," said Rose. "What a crowd from the town! Think of the pyrotechnics among comets and aerolites some fellows may have! It's quite right, too, to make our festivals with light; it's the highest and last of all things; we never can carry our imaginations beyond light —"

"Our imaginations ought to carry us," said Lu.

"Come," I said, "you can play what pranks you please with the little May; but light is my province, my absorption; let it alone."

It grew quite dark, interrupted now and then by the glare of rockets; but at last a stream of central fire went out in a slow rain of countless violets, reflected with pale blue flashes in the river below, and then the gloom was unbroken. I saw them, in that long dim gleam, standing together at a window. Louise, her figure almost swaying as if to some inaudible music, but her face turned to him with such a steady quiet. Ah me! what a tremulous joy, what passion, and what search, lit those eyes! But you know that passion means suffering, and, tracing it in the original through its roots, you come to pathos, and still farther, to lamentation, I 've heard. But he was not looking down at her, only out and away, paler than ever in the blue light, sad and resolved. I ordered candles. ·

"Sing to me, Louise," said Rose, at length. "It is two years since I heard you."

"Sing 'What's a' the steer, kimmer,'" I said. But instead, she gave the little ballad, "And bring my love again, for he lies among the Moors."

Rose went and leaned over the piano-forte while she sang, bending, and commanding her eyes. He seemed to wish to put himself where he was before he ever left her, to awaken everything lovely in her, to bring her before him as utterly developed as she might be, — not only to afford her, but to force upon her, every chance to master him. He seemed to wish to love, I thought.

"Thank you," he said, as she ceased. "Did you choose it purposely, Louise?"

Lu sang very nicely, and, though I dare say she would rather not then, when Mr. Dudley asked for the "Vale of

Avoca," and the "Margin of Zürich's Fair Waters," she
gave them just as kindly.   Altogether, quite a damp pro-
gramme.   Then papa came in, bright and blithe, whirled
me round in a *pas de deux*, and we all very gay and hila-
rious slipped into the second of May.

Dear me! how time goes! I must hurry. — After that,
I did n't see so much of Rose; but he met Lu everywhere,
came in when I was out, and, if I returned, he went, perfectly regardless of my existence, it seemed.   They rode,
too, all round the country ; and she sat to him, though he
never filled out the sketch.   For weeks he was devoted ;
but I fancied, when I saw them, that there lingered in his
manner the same thing as on the first evening while she
sang to him.   Lu was so gay and sweet and happy that I
hardly knew her; she was always very gentle, but such a
decided body, — that's the Willoughby, her mother.   Yet
during these weeks Rose had not spoken, not formally ;
delicate and friendly kindness was all Lu could have
found, had she sought.   One night, I remember, he came
in and wanted us to go out and row with him on the river.
Lu would n't go without me.

"Will you come ?" said he, coolly, as if I were merely
necessary as a thwart or thole-pin might have been, turning and letting his eyes fall on me an instant, then snatching them off with a sparkle and flush, and such a lordly
carelessness of manner otherwise.

"Certainly not," I replied.

So they remained, and Lu began to open a bundle of
Border Ballads, which he had brought her.   The very
first one was "Whistle an' I 'll come to you, my lad."   I
laughed.   She glanced up quickly, then held it in her
hands a moment, repeated the name, and asked if he
liked it.

"Oh, yes," he said. "There could n't be a Scotch song without that rhythm better than melody, which, after all, is Beethoven's secret."

"Perhaps," said Louise. "But I shall not sing this."

"Oh, do!" he said, turning with surprise. "You don't know what an aerial, whistling little thing it is!"

"No."

"Why, Louise! There is nobody could sing it but you."

"Of good discourse, an excellent musician, and her hair shall be of what color it please God," quoted I, and in came Mr. Dudley, as he usually did when not wanted; though I've no reason to find fault with him, notwithstanding his blank treatment of me. He never took any notice, because he was in love with Lu. Rose never took any notice of me, either. But with a difference!

Lu was singularly condescending to Mr. Dudley that evening; and Rose, sitting aside, looked so very much disturbed — whether pleasantly or otherwise did n't occur to me — that I could n't help enjoying his discomfiture, and watching him through it.

Now, though I told you I was n't nervous, I never should know I had this luxurious calm, if there were nothing to measure it by; and once in a great while a perfect whirlpool seizes me, — my blood is all in turmoil, — I bubble with silent laughter, or cry with all my heart. I had been in such a strange state a good while; and now, as I surveyed Rose, it gradually grew fiercer, till I actually sprang to my feet, and exclaimed, "There! it is insupportable! I've been in the magnetic storm long enough! it is time something took it from me!" and ran out-doors.

Rose sauntered after, by and by, as if unwillingly drawn by a loadstone, and found the heavens wrapped in a rosy flame of Northern Lights. He looked as though he belonged to them, so pale and elf-like was his face then, like one bewitched.

"Papa's fireworks fade before mine," I said. "Now we can live in the woods, as Lu has been wishing; for a dry southerly wind follows this, with a blue smoke filming all the distant fields. Won't it be delicious?"

"Or rain," he replied; "I think it will rain to-morrow, — warm, full rains." And he seemed as if such a chance would dissolve him entirely.

As for me, those shifting, silent sheets of splendor abstracted all that was alien, and left me in my normal state.

"There they come!" I said, as Lu and Mr. Dudley, and some others who had entered in my absence, — gnats dancing in the beam, — stepped down towards us. "How charming for us all to sit out here!"

"How annoying, you mean," he replied, simply for contradiction.

"It has n't been warm enough before," I added.

"And Louise may take cold now," he said, as if wishing to exhibit his care for her. "Whom is she speaking with? Blarsaye? And who comes after?"

"Parti. A delightful person, — been abroad, too. You and he can have a crack about Louvres and Vaticans now, and leave Lu and Mr. Dudley to me."

Rose suddenly inspected me and then Parti, as if he preferred the crack to be with cudgels; but in a second the little blaze vanished, and he only stripped a weigelia branch of every blossom.

I wonder what made Lu behave so that night; she scarcely spoke to Rose, appeared entirely unconcerned while he hovered round her like an officious sprite, was all grace to the others and sweetness to Mr. Dudley. And Rose, oblivious of snubs, paraded his devotion, seemed determined to show his love for Lu, — as if any one cared a straw, — and took the pains to be positively rude to me. He was possessed of an odd restlessness ; a little defiance bristled his movements, an air of contrariness ; and whenever he became quiet, he seemed again like one enchanted and folded up in a dream, to break whose spell he was about to abandon efforts. He told me Life had destroyed my enchantment ; — I wonder what will destroy his. — Lu refused to sit in the garden-chair he offered, — just suffered the wreath of pink bells he gave her to hang in her hand, and by and by fall, — and when the north grew ruddier and swept the zenith with lances of light, and when it faded, and a dim cloud hazed all the stars, preserved the same equanimity, kept on the *evil* tenor of her way, and bade every one an impartial farewell at separating. She is preciously well-bred.

We hadn't remained in the garden all that time, though, — but, strolling through the gate and over the field, had reached a small grove that fringes the gully worn by Wild Fall and crossed by the railway. As we emerged from that, talking gayly, and our voices almost drowned by the dash of the little waterfall and the echo from the opposite rock, I sprang across the curving track, thinking them behind, and at the same instant a thunderous roar burst all about, a torrent of hot air whizzed and eddied over me, I fell dizzied and stunned, and the night express-train shot by like a burning arrow. Of course I was dreadfully hurt by my fall and fright, — I feel the shock now, — the blow, the stroke, — but they all stood on the little mound, from which I had sprung, like so many petrifactions: Rose, just as he had caught Louise back on firmer ground when she was about to follow me, his arm wound swiftly round her waist, yet his head thrust forward eagerly, his pale face and glowing eyes bent, not on her, but me. Still he never stirred, and poor Mr. Dudley first came to my assistance. We all drew breath at our escape, and, a little slowly, on my account, turned homeward.

"You are not bruised, Miss Willoughby?" asked Blarsaye, wakened.

"Dear Yone!" Lu said, leaving Mr. Dudley's arm, "you're so very pale! It's not pain, is it?"

"I am not conscious of any. Why should I be injured, any more than you?"

"Do you know," said Rose, *sotto voce*, turning and bending merely his head to me, "I thought I heard you scream, and that you were dead."

"And what then?"

"Nothing, but that you were lying dead and torn, and I should see you," he said, — and said as if he liked to say it, experiencing a kind of savage delight at his ability to say it.

"A pity to have disappointed you!" I answered.

"I saw it coming before you leaped," he added, as a malignant finality, and drawing nearer. "You were both on the brink. I called, but probably neither you nor Lu heard me. So I snatched her back."

Now I had been next him then.

"Jove's balance," I said, taking Parti's arm.

He turned instantly to Lu, and kept by her during the remainder of the walk, Mr. Dudley being at the other side. I was puzzled a little by Lu, as I have been a good many times since; I thought she liked Rose so much. Papa met us in the field, and there the affair must be detailed to him, and then he would have us celebrate our safety in Champagne.

"Good by, Louise," said Rose, beside her at the gate, and offering his hand, somewhat later. "I'm going away to-morrow, if it's fine."

"Going?" with involuntary surprise.

"To camp out in Maine."

"Oh, — I hope you will enjoy it."

"Would you stay long, Louise?"

"If the sketching-grounds are good."

"When I come back, you'll sing my songs? Shake hands."

She just laid a cold touch on his.

"Louise, are you offended with me?"

She looked up with so much simplicity. "Offended, Rose, with you?"

"Not offended, but frozen," I could have said. Lu is like that little sensitive-plant, shrinking into herself with stiff unconsciousness at a certain touch. But I don't think he noticed the sad tone in her voice, as she said good night; I didn't, till, the others being gone, I saw her turn after his disappearing figure, with a look that would have been despairing, but for its supplication.

The only thing Lu ever said to me about this was, —

"Don't you think Rose a little altered, Yone, since he came home?"

"Altered?"

"I have noticed it ever since you showed him your beads, that day."

"Oh! it's the amber," I said. "They are amulets, and have bound him in a thrall. You must wear them, and dissolve the charm. He's in a dream."

"What is it to be in a dream?" she asked.

"To lose thought of past or future."

She repeated my words,—"Yes, he's in a dream," she said musingly.

Rose did n't come near us for a fortnight; but he had not camped at all, as he said. It was the first stone thrown into Lu's life, and I never saw any one keep the ripples under so; but her suspicions were aroused. Finally he came in again, all as before, and I thought things might have been different, if in that fortnight Mr. Dudley had not been so assiduous; and now, to the latter's happiness, there were several ragged children and infirm old women in whom, Lu having taken them in charge, he chose to be especially interested. Lu always was housekeeper, both because it had fallen to her while mamma and I were away, and because she had an administrative faculty equal to General Jackson's; and Rose, who had frequently gone about with her, inspecting jellies and cordials and adding up her accounts, now unexpectedly found Mr. Dudley so near his former place that he disdained to resume it himself;—not entirely, because the man of course could n't be as familiar as an old playmate; but just enough to put Rose aside. He never would compete with any one; and Lu did not know how to repulse the other.

If the amulets had ravished Rose from himself, they did it at a distance, for I had not worn them since that day. — You need n't look. Thales imagined amber had a spirit; and Pliny says it is a counter-charm for sorceries. There are a great many mysterious things in the world. Are n't there any hidden relations between us and certain substances? Will you tell me something impossible?—

But he came and went about Louise, and she sung his songs, and all was going finely again, when we gave our midsummer party.

Everybody was there, of course, and we had enrapturing music. Louise wore—no matter—something of twilight purple, and begged for the amber, since it was too much for my toilette,—a double India muslin, whose snowy sheen scintillated with festoons of gorgeous green beetles' wings flaming like fiery emeralds. A family dress, my dear, and worn by my aunt before me,—only that individual must have been frightened out of her wits by it. A cruel, savage dress, very like, but ineffably gorgeous. So I wore her aqua-marina, though the other would have been better; and when I sailed in, with all the airy folds in a hoar-frost mistiness fluttering round me and the glitter of Lu's jewels,—

"Why!" said Rose, "you look like the moon in a halo."

But Lu disliked a hostess out-dressing her guests.

It was dull enough till quite late, and then I stepped out with Mr. Parti, and walked up and down a garden-path. Others were outside as well, and the last time I passed a little arbor I caught a yellow gleam of amber. Lu, of course. Who was with her? A gentleman, bending low to catch her words, holding her hand in an irresistible pressure. Not Rose, for he was flitting in beyond. Mr. Dudley. And I saw then that Lu's kindness was too great to allow her to repel him angrily; her gentle conscience let her wound no one. Had Rose seen the pantomime? Without doubt. He had been seeking her, and he found her, he thought, in Mr. Dudley's arms. After a while we went in, and, finding all smooth enough, I slipped through the balcony-window and hung over the balustrade, glad to be alone a moment. The wind, blow-

ing in, carried the gay sounds away from me, even the
music came richly muffled through the heavy curtains,
and I wished to breathe balm and calm. The moon,
round and full, was just rising, making the gloom below
more sweet. A full moon is poison to some; they shut
it out at every crevice, and do not suffer a ray to cross
them; it has a chemical or magnetic effect; it sickens
them. But I am never more free and royal than when
the subtile celerity of its magic combinations, whatever
they are, is at work. Never had I known the mere joy
of being, so intimately as to-night. The river slept soft
and mystic below the woods, the sky was full of light, the
air ripe with summer. Out of the yellow honeysuckles
that climbed around, clouds of delicious fragrance stole
and swathed me; long wafts of faint harmony gently
thrilled me. Dewy and dark and uncertain was all beyond. I, possessed with a joyousness so deep through its
contented languor as to counterfeit serenity, forgot all my
wealth of nature, my pomp of beauty, abandoned myself
to the hour.

A strain of melancholy dance-music pierced the air and
fell. I half turned my head, and my eyes met Rose. He
had been there before me, perhaps. His face white and
shining in the light, shining with a strange sweet smile
of relief, of satisfaction, of delight, his lips quivering with
unspoken words, his eyes dusky with depth after depth
of passion. How long did my eyes swim on his? I cannot tell. He never stirred; still leaned there against the
pillar, still looked down on me like a marble god. The
sudden tears dazzled my gaze, fell down my hot cheek,
and still I knelt fascinated by that smile. In that moment
I felt that he was more beautiful than the night, than
the music, than I. Then I knew that all this time, all

summer, all past summers, all my life long, I had loved him.

Some one was waiting to make his adieux; I heard my father seeking me; I parted the curtains and went in. One after one those tedious people left, the lights grew dim, and still he stayed without. I ran to the window, and, lifting the curtain, I bent forward, crying, —

" Mr. Rose! do you spend the night on the balcony ? "

Then he moved, stepped down, murmured something to my father, bowed loftily to Louise, passed me without a sign, and went out. In a moment, Lu's voice, a quick sharp exclamation, touched him; he turned, came back. She, wondering at him, had stood toying with the amber, and at last crushing the miracle of the whole, a bell-wort wrought most delicately with all the dusty pollen grained upon its anthers, crushing it between her fingers, breaking the thread, and scattering the beads upon the carpet. He stooped with her to gather them again, he took from her hand and restored to her afterward the shattered fragments of the bell-wort, he helped her disentangle the aromatic string from her falling braids, — for I kept apart, — he breathed the penetrating incense of each separate amulet, and I saw that from that hour, when every atom of his sensation was tense and vibrating, she would be associated with the loathed amber in his undefined consciousness, would be surrounded with an atmosphere of its perfume, that Lu was truly sealed from him in it, sealed into herself. Then again, saying no word, he went out.

Louise stood like one lost, — took aimlessly a few steps, — retraced them, — approached a table, — touched something, — left it.

" I am so sorry about your beads! " she said, apologetically, — when she looked up and saw me astonished, — putting the broken pieces into my hand.

"Goodness! Is that what you are fluttering about so for?"

"They can't be mended," she continued, "but I will thread them again."

"I don't care about them, I'm sick of amber," I answered consolingly. "You may have them, if you will."

"No. I must pay too great a price for them," she replied.

"Nonsense! when they break again, I'll pay you back," I said, without in the least knowing what she meant. "I didn't suppose you were too proud for a 'thank you'!"

She came and put both her arms round my neck, laid her cheek beside mine a minute, kissed me, and went up stairs. Lu always rather worshipped me.

Dressing my hair that night, Carmine, my maid, begged for the remnants of the bell-wort to "make a scent-bag with, Miss."

Next day, no Rose; it rained. But at night he came and took possession of the room, with a strange, airy gayety never seen in him before. It was so chilly, that I had heaped the wood-boughs, used in the yesterday's decorations, on the hearth, and lighted a fragrant crackling flame that danced up wildly at my touch, — for I have the faculty of fire. I sat at one side, Lu at the other, papa was holding a skein of silk for her to wind, the amber beads were twinkling in the firelight, — and when she slipped them slowly on the thread, bead after bead warmed through and through by the real blaze, they crowded the room afresh with their pungent spiciness. Papa had called Rose to take his place at the other end of the silk, and had gone out; and when Lu finished, she fastened the ends, cut the thread, Rose likening her to Atropos, and put them back into her basket. Still playing with the scissors, following down the lines of her hand, a little snap was heard.

"Oh!" said Louise, "I have broken my ring!"

"Can't it be repaired?" I asked.

"No," she returned briefly, but pleasantly, and threw the pieces into the fire.

"The hand must not be ringless," said Rose; and slipping off the ring of hers that he wore, he dropped it on the amber, then got up and threw an armful of fresh boughs upon the blaze.

So that was all done. Then Rose was gayer than before. He is one of those people to whom you must allow moods, — when their sun shines, dance, — and when their vapors rise, sit in the shadow. Every variation of the atmosphere affects him, though by no means uniformly; and so sensitive is he, that, when connected with you by any intimate *rapport*, even if but momentary, he almost divines your thoughts. He is full of perpetual surprises. I am sure he was a nightingale before he was Rose. An iridescence like sea-foam sparkled in him that evening, he laughed as lightly as the little tinkling mass-bells at every moment, and seemed to diffuse a rosy glow wherever he went in the room. Yet gayety was not his peculiar specialty, and at length he sat before the fire, and, taking Lu's scissors, commenced cutting bits of paper in profiles. Somehow they all looked strangely like and unlike Mr. Dudley. I pointed one out to Lu, and if he had needed confirmation, her changing color gave it. He only glanced at her askance, and then broke into the merriest description of his life in Rome, of which he declared he had not spoken to us yet, talking fast and laughing as gleefully as a child, and illustrating people and localities with scissors and paper as he went on, a couple of careless snips putting a whole scene before us.

The floor was well strewn with such chips, — fountains, statues, baths, and all the persons of his little drama, — when papa came in. He held an open letter, and, sitting down, read it over again. Rose fell into silence, clipping the scissors daintily in and out the white sheet through twinkling intricacies. As the design dropped out, I caught it, — a long wreath of honeysuckle-blossoms. Ah, I knew where the honeysuckles grew! Lu was humming a little tune. Rose joined, and hummed the last bars, then bade us good-night.

"Yone," said papa, "your Aunt Willoughby is very ill, — will not recover. She is my elder brother's widow; you are her heir. You must go and stay with her."

Now it was very likely that just at this time I was going away to nurse Aunt Willoughby! Moreover, illness is my very antipodes, — its nearness is invasion, — we are utterly antipathetic, — it disgusts and repels me. What sympathy can there be between my florid health, my rank redundant life, and any wasting disease of death? What more hostile than focal concentration and obscure decomposition? You see, we cannot breathe the same atmosphere. I banish the thought of such a thing from my feeling, from my memory. So I said, —

"It's impossible. I'm not going an inch to Aunt Willoughby's. Why, papa, it's more than a hundred miles, and in this weather!"

"Oh, the wind has changed."

"Then it will be too warm for such a journey."

"A new idea, Yone! Too warm for the mountains?"

"Yes, papa. I'm not going a step."

"Why, Yone, you astonish me! Your sick aunt!"

"That's the very thing. If she were well, I might, — perhaps. Sick! What can I do for her? I never go into a sick-room. I hate it. I don't know how to do a thing there. Don't say another word, papa. I can't go."

"It is out of the question to let it pass so, my dear. Here you are nursing all the invalids in town, yet —"

"Indeed, I'm not, papa. I don't know and don't care whether they're dead or alive."

"Well, then, it's Lu."

"Oh, yes, she's hospital agent for half the country."

"Then it is time that you also got a little experience."

"Don't, papa! I don't want it. I never saw anybody die, and I never mean to."

"Can't I do as well, uncle?" asked Lu.

"You, darling? Yes; but it isn't your duty."

"I thought, perhaps," she said, "you would rather Yone went."

"So I would."

"Dear papa, don't vex me! Ask anything else!"

"It is so unpleasant to Yone," Lu murmured, "that maybe I had better go. And if you've no objection, sir, I'll take the early train to-morrow."

Wasn't she an angel?

Lu was away a month. Rose came in, expressing his surprise. I said, "Othello's occupation's gone?"

"And left him room for pleasure now," he retorted.

"Which means seclusion from the world, in the society of lakes and chromes."

"Miss Willoughby," said he, turning and looking directly past me, "may I paint you?"

3   '   D

"Me? Oh, you can't."

"No; but may I try?"

"I cannot go to you."

"I will come to you."

"Do you suppose it will be like?"

"Not at all, of course. It is to be, then?"

"Oh, I've no more right than any other piece of Nature to refuse an artist a study in color."

He faced about, half pouting, as if he would go out, then returned and fixed the time.

So he painted. He generally put me into a broad beam that slanted from the top of the veiled window, and day after day he worked. Ah, what glorious days they were! how gay! how full of life! I almost feared to let him image me on canvas, do you know? I had a fancy it would lay my soul so bare to his inspection. What secrets might he searched, what depths fathomed, at such times, if men knew! I feared lest he should see me as I am, in those great masses of warm light lying before him, as I feared he saw when he said amber harmonized with me, — all being things not polarized, not organized, without centre, so to speak. But it escaped him, and he wrought on. Did he succeed? Bless you! he might as well have painted the sun; and who could do that? No; but shades and combinations that he had hardly touched or known, before, he had to lavish now; he learned more than some years might have taught him; he, who worshipped beauty, saw how thoroughly I possessed it; he has told me that through me he learned the sacredness of color. "Since he loves beauty so, why does he not love me?" I asked myself; and perhaps the feverish hope and suspense only lit up that beauty and fed it with fresh fires. Ah, the July days! Did you ever wander over barren, parched stubble-fields, and suddenly front a knot of red Turk's-cap lilies, flaring as if they had drawn all the heat and brilliance from the land into their tissues? Such were they. And if I were to grow old and gray, they would light down all my life, and I could be willing to lead a dull, grave age, looking back and remembering them, warming myself forever in their constant youth. If I had nothing to hope, they would become my whole existence. Think, then, what it will be to have all days like those!

He never satisfied himself, as he might have done, had he known me better, — and he never *shall* know me! — and used to look at me for the secret of his failure, till I laughed; then the look grew wistful, grew enamored. By and by we left the pictures. We went into the woods, warm dry woods; we stayed there from morning till night. In the burning noons, we hung suspended between two heavens, in our boat on glassy forest-pools, where now and then a shoal of white lilies rose and crowded out the under-sky. Sunsets burst like bubbles over us. When the hidden thrushes were breaking one's heart with music, and the sweet fern sent up a tropical fragrance beneath our crushing steps, we came home to rooms full of guests and my father's genial warmth. What a month it was!

One day papa went up into New Hampshire; Aunt Willoughby was dead; and one day Lu came home.

She was very pale and thin. Her eyes were hollow and purple.

"There is some mistake, Lu," I said. "It is you who are dead, instead of Aunt Willoughby."

"Do I look so wretchedly?" she asked, glancing at the mirror.

"Dreadfully! Is it all watching and grief?"

"Watching and grief," said Lu.

How melancholy her smile was! She would have crazed me in a little while, if I had minded her.

"Did you care so much for fretful, crabbed Aunt Willoughby?"

"She was very kind to me," Lu replied.

There was an odd air with her that day. She did n't go at once and get off her travelling-dress, but trifled about in a kind of expectancy, a little fever going and coming in her cheeks, and turning at any noise.

Will you believe it?—though I knew Lu had refused to marry him,—who met her at the half-way junction, saw about her luggage, and drove home with her, but Mr. Dudley, and was with us, a half-hour afterward, when Rose came in? Lu did n't turn at his step, but the little fever in her face prevented his seeing her as I had done. He shook hands with her and asked after her health, and shook hands with Mr. Dudley (who had n't been near us during her absence), and seemed to wish she should feel that he recognized without pain a connection between herself and that personage. But when he came back to me, I was perplexed again at that bewitched look in his face,—as if Lu's presence made him feel that he was in a dream, I the enchantress of that dream. It did not last long, though. And soon she saw Mr. Dudley out, and went up-stairs.

When Lu came down to the table, she had my beads in her hand again.

"I went into your room and got them, dear Yone," she said, "because I have found something to replace the broken bell-wort," and she showed us a little amber bee, black and golden. "Not so lovely as the bell-wort," she resumed, "and I must pierce it for the thread;

but it will fill the number. Was I not fortunate to find it ? "

But when at a flame she heated a long slender needle to pierce it, the little winged wonder shivered between her fingers, and under the hot steel filled the room with the honeyed smell of its dusted substance.

"Never mind," said I again. "It's a shame, though, — it was so much prettier than the bell-wort! We might have known it was too brittle. It's just as well, Lu."

The room smelt like a chancel at vespers. Rose sauntered to the window, and so down the garden, and then home.

"Yes. It cannot be helped," she said, with a smile. "But I really counted upon seeing it on the string. I'm not lucky at amber. You know little Asian said it would· bring bane to the bearer."

"Dear! dear! I had quite forgotten!" I exclaimed. "O Lu, keep it, or give it away, or something! I don't want it any longer."

"You're very vehement," she said, laughing now. "I am not afraid of your gods. Shall I wear them?"

So the rest of the summer Lu twined them round her throat, — amulets of sorcery, orbs of separation; but one night she brought them back to me. That was last night. There they lie.

The next day, in the high golden noon, Rose came. I was on the lounge in the alcove parlor, my hair half streaming out of Lu's net; but he didn't mind. The light was toned and mellow, the air soft and cool. He came and sat on the opposite side, so that he faced the wall table with its dish of white, stiflingly sweet lilies, while I looked down the drawing-room. He had brought a book, and by and by opened at the part commencing,

" Do not die, Phene." He read it through, — all that
perfect, perfect scene. From the moment when he said,

> " I overlean
> This length of hair and lustrous front — they turn
> Like an entire flower upward," —

his voice low, sustained, clear, — till he reached the line,

> " Look at the woman here with the new soul," —

till he turned the leaf and murmured,

> " Shall to produce form out of unshaped stuff
> Be art, — and, further, to evoke a soul
> From form, be nothing? This new soul is mine! " —

till then, he never glanced up. Now, with a proud grace,
he raised his head, — not to look at me, but across me,
at the lilies, to satiate himself with their odorous snowi-
ness. When he again pronounced words, his voice was
husky and vibrant; but what music dwelt in it and
seemed to prolong rather than break the silver silence,
as he echoed,

> " Some unsuspected isle in the far seas " !

How many read, to descend to a prosaic life ! how few to
meet one as rich and full beside them ! The tone grew
ever lower; he looked up slowly, fastening his glance on
mine.

> " And you are ever by me while I gaze, —
> Are in my arms as now — as now — as now ! "

he said. He swayed forward with those wild questioning
eyes, — his breath blew over my cheek; I was drawn, —
I bent; the full passion of his soul broke to being,
wrapped me with a blinding light, a glowing kiss on lingering lips, a clasp strong and tender as heaven. All
my hair fell down like a shining cloud and veiled us, the

great rolling folds in wave after wave of crisp splendor.
I drew back from that long, silent kiss, I gathered up
each gold thread of the straying tresses, blushing, defiant.
He also, he drew back. But I knew all then. I had no
need to wait longer; I had achieved. Rose loved me.
Rose had loved me from that first day. — You scarcely
hear what I say, I talk so low and fast? Well, no matter, dear, you would n't care. — For a moment that gaze
continued, then the lids fell, the face grew utterly white.
He rose, flung the book, crushed and torn, upon the floor,
went out, speaking no word to me, nor greeting Louise
in the next room. Could he have seen her? No. I,
only, had that. For, as I drew from his arm, a meteoric
crimson, shooting across the pale face bent over work
there, flashed upon me, and then a few great tears, like
sudden thunder-drops, falling slowly and wetting the
heavy fingers. The long mirror opposite her reflected
the interior of the alcove parlor. No, — he could not
have seen, he must have felt her.

I wonder whether I should have cared, if I had never
met him any more, — happy in this new consciousness.
But in the afternoon he returned, bright and eager.

"Are you so very busy, dear Yone," he said, without
noticing Lu, "that you cannot drive with me to-day?"

Busy! In five minutes I whirled down the avenue
beside him. I had not been Yone to him before. How
quiet we were! he driving on, bent forward, seeing out
and away; I leaning back, my eyes closed, and, whenever
a remembrance of that instant at noon thrilled me, a stinging blush staining my cheek. I, who had believed myself
incapable of love, till that night on the balcony, felt its
floods welling from my spirit, — who had believed myself
so completely cold, was warm to my heart's core. Again

that breath fanned me, those lips touched mine, lightly, quickly.

"Yone, my Yone!" he said. "Is it true? No dream within dream? Do you love me?"

Wistful, longing, tender eyes.

"Do I love you? I would die for you!"

Ah, me! If the July days were such, how perfect were the August and September nights! their young moon's lingering twilight, their full broad bays of silver, their interlunar season! The winds were warm about us, the whole earth seemed the wealthier for our love. We almost lived upon the river, he and I alone, — floating seaward, swimming slowly up with late tides, reaching home drenched with dew, parting in passionate silence. Once he said to me, —

"Is it because it is so much larger, more strange and beautiful, than any other love could be, that I feel guilty, Yone, — feel as if I sinned in loving you so, my great white flower?"

I ought to tell you how splendid papa was, never seemed to consider that Rose had only his art, said I had enough from Aunt Willoughby for both, we should live up there among the mountains, and set off at once to make arrangements. Lu has a wonderful tact, too, — seeing at once where her path lay. She is always so well oriented! How full of peace and bliss these two months have been! Last night Lu came in here. She brought back my amber gods, saying she had not intended to keep them, and yet loitering.

"Yone," she said at last, "I want you to tell me if you love him."

Now, as if that were any affair of hers! I looked what I thought.

"Don't be angry," she pleaded. "You and I have been sisters, have we not? and always shall be. I love you very much, dear, — more than you may believe; I only want to know if you will make him happy."

"That's according," said I, with a yawn.

She still stood before me. Her eyes said, "I have a right, — I have a right to know."

"You want me to say how much I love Vaughan Rose?" I asked, finally. "Well, listen, Lu, — so much, that, when he forgets me, — and he will, Lu, one day, — I shall die."

"Prevent his forgetting you, Yone!" she returned. "Make your soul white and clear, like his."

"No! no!" I answered. "He loves me as I am. I will never change."

Then somehow tears began to come. I didn't want to cry; I had to crowd them back behind my fingers and shut lids.

"Oh, Lu!" I said, "I cannot think what it would be to live, and he not a part of me! not for either of us to be in the world without the other!"

Then Lu's tears fell with mine, as she drew her fingers over my hair. She said she was happy, too; and to-day has been down and gathered every one, so that, when you see her, her white array will be wreathed with purple heart's-case. But I didn't tell Lu quite the truth, you must know. I don't think I should die, except to my former self, if Rose ceased to love me. I should change. Oh, I should hate him! Hate is as intense as love.

Bless me! What time can it be? There are papa and Rose walking in the garden. I turned out my maid to

3 *

find chance for all this talk; I must ring for her. There, there's my hair! silken coil after coil, full of broken lights, rippling below the knees, fine and fragrant. Who could have such hair but I? I am the last of the Willoughbys, a decayed race, and from such strong decay what blossom less gorgeous should spring?

October now. All the world swings at the top of its beauty; and those hills where we shall live, what robes of color fold them! Tawny filemot gilding the valleys, each seam and rut a scroll or arabesque, and all the year pouring out her heart's blood to flush the maples, the great empurpled granites warm with the sunshine they have drunk all summer! So I am to be married to-day, at noon. I like it best so; it is my hour. There is my veil, that regal Venice point. Fling it round you. No, you would look like a ghost in one, — Lu like a corpse. Dear me! That's the second time I've rung for Carmine. I dare say the hussy is trying on my gown. You think it strange I don't delay? Why, child, why tempt Providence? Once mine, always mine. He might wake up. No, no, I could n't have meant that! It is not possible that I have merely led him into a region of richer dyes, lapped him in this vision of color, kindled his heart to such a flame, that it may light him towards further effort. Can you believe that he will slip from me and return to one in better harmony with him? Is any one? Will he ever find himself with that love lost, this love exhausted, only his art left him? Never! *I* am his crown. See me! how singularly, gloriously beautiful! For him only! all for him! I love him! I cannot, I will not lose him! I defy all! My heart's proud pulse assures me! I defy Fate! Hush —— One, — two, — twelve o'clock. Carmine!

STORY LAST.

Astra Castra, Numen Lumen.

The click of her needles and the soft singing of the night-lamp are the only sounds breaking the stillness, the awful stillness, of this room. How the wind blows without! it must be whirling white gusty drifts through the split hills. If I were as free! Whistling round the gray gable, tearing the bleak boughs, crying faint hoarse moans down the chimneys! A wild, sad gale! There is a lull, a long breathless lull, before it soughs up again. Oh, it is like a pain! Pain! Why do I think the word? Must I suffer any more? Am I crazed with opiates? or am I dying? They are in that drawer, — laudanum, morphine, hyoscyamus, and all the drowsy sirups, — little drops, but soaring like a fog and wrapping the whole world in a dull ache with no salient sting to catch a groan on. They are so small, they might be lost in this long, dark room; why not the pain too, the point of pain, I? A long, dark room; I at one end, she at the other; the curtains drawn away from me that I may breathe. Ah, I have been stifled so long! They look down on me, all those old dead and gone faces, those portraits on the wall, — look all from their frames at me, the last term of the race, the vanishing summit of their design. A fierce weapon thrust into the world for evil has that race been, — from the great gray Willoughby, threatening with his iron eyes there, to me, the sharp apex of its suffering. A fierce, glittering blade! Why I alone singled for this curse? Rank blossom, rank decay, they answer, but falsely. I lie here, through no fault of mine, blasted by disease, the dread

with no relief. A hundred ancestors look from my walls
and see in me the centre of their lives, of all their little
splendor, of their sins and follies ; what slept in them
wakes in me. Oh, let me sleep too!

How long could I live and lose nothing? I saw my
face in the hand-glass this morning, — more lovely than
health fashioned it ; — transparent skin, bounding blood
with its fire burning behind the eye, on cheek, on lip, —
a beauty that every pang has aggravated, heightened,
sharpened, to a superb intensity, flushing, rapid, unearthly, — a brilliancy to be dreamed of.   Like a great autumn
leaf I fall, for I am dying, — dying! Yes, death finds me
more beautiful than life made me ; but have I lost nothing?
Great Heaven, I have lost all!

A fancy comes to me, that to-day was my birthday.
I have forgotten to mark time ; but if it was, I am thirty-
two years old. I remember birthdays of a child, — loving, cordial days. No one remembers to-day. Why
should they ? But I ache for a little love. Thirty-two,
— that is young to die! I am too fair, too rich, for
death! — not his fit spoil! Is there no one to save me?
no help? can I not escape? Ah, what a vain eagerness! what an idle hope! Fall back again, heart! Escape? I do not desire to.   Come, come, kind rest! I
am tired.

That cap-string has loosened now, and all this golden
cataract of hair has rushed out over the piled pillows. It
oppresses and terrifies me. If I could speak, it seems to
me that I would ask Louise to come and bind it up.
Won't she turn and see ? . . .

Have I been asleep? What is this in my hands? The
amber gods? Oh, yes ! I asked to see them again ; I like
their smell, I think. It is ten years I have had them.

They enchant; but the charm will not last; nothing will. I rubbed a little yellow smoke out of them, — a cloud that hung between him and the world, so that he saw only me, — at least — What am I dreaming of? All manner of illusions haunt me. Who said anything about ten years? I have been married ten years. Happy, then, ten years? Oh, no! One day he woke. — How close the room is! I want some air. Why don't they do something —

Once, in the pride of a fool, I fear having made some confidence, some recital of my joy to ears that never had any. Did I say I would not lose him? Did I say I could live just on the memory of that summer? I lash myself that I must remember it! that I ever loved him! When he stirred, when the mist left him, when he found a mere passion had blinded him, when he spread his easel, when he abandoned love, — was I wretched? I, too, abandoned love! — more, — I hated! All who hate are wretched. But he was bound to me! Yes, he might move restlessly, — it only clanked his chains. Did he wound me? I was cruel. He never spoke. He became artist, — ceased to be man, — was more indifferent than the cloud. He could paint me then, — and, revealed and bare, all our histories written in me, he hung me up beside my ancestors. There I hang. Come from thy frame, thou substance, and let this troubled phantom go! Come! for he gave my life to thee. In thee he shut and sealed it all, and left me as the empty husk. — Did she — that other — join us then? No! I sent for her. I meant to teach him that he was yet a man, — to open before him a gulf of anguish; but I slipped down it. Then I dogged them; they never spoke alone; I intercepted the eye's language; I withered their wintry smiles to frowns; I stifled their sighs;

I checked their breath, their motion. Idle words passed our lips; we three lived in a real world of silence, agonized mutes. She went. Summer by summer my father brought her to us. Always memory was kindled afresh, always sorrow kept smouldering. Once she came; I lay here; she has not left me since. He, — he also comes; he has soothed pain with that loveless eye, carried me in untender arms, watched calmly beside my delirious nights. He who loved beauty has learned disgust. Why should I care? I, from the slave of bald form, enlarged him to the master of gorgeous color; his blaze is my ashes. He studies me. I owe him nothing. . . .

Is it near morning? Have I dozed again? Night is long. The great hall-clock is striking, — throb after throb on the darkness. I remember, when I was a child, watching its lengthened pendulum swing as if time were its own and it measured the thread slowly, loath to part, — remember streaking its great ebony case with a little finger, misting it with a warm breath. Throb after throb, — is it going to peal forever? Stop, solemn clangor! hearts stop. Midnight.

The nurses have gone down; she sits there alone. Her bent side-face is full of pity. Now and then her head turns; the great brown eyes lift heavily, and lie on me, — heavily, — as if the sight of me pained her. Ah, in me perishes her youth! death enters her world! Besides, she loves me. I do not want her love, — I would fling it off; but I am faint, — I am impotent, — I am so cold! Not that she lives, and I die, — not that she has peace, and I tumult, — not for her voice's music, — not for her eye's lustre, — not for any charm of her womanly presence, — neither for her clear, fair soul, — nor that when the storm and winter pass and I am stiff and frozen, she smiles in the sun and leads new life, — not for all this I hate her; but because my going gives her what I lost, — because, I stepped aside, the light falls on her, — because from my despair springs her happiness. Poor fool! let her be happy, if she can! Her mother was a Willoughby! And what is a flower that blows on a grave? . . .

Why do I remember so distinctly one night alone of all my life, — one night, when we dance in the low room of a seaside cottage, — dance to Lu's singing? He leads me to her when the dance is through, brushing with his head the festooned nets that swing from the rafters, — and in at the open casement is blown a butterfly, a dead butterfly, from off the sea. She holds it compassionately, till I pin it on my dress, — the wings, twin magnificences, freckled and barred and powdered with gold, fluttering at my breath. Some one speaks with me ; she strays to the window, he follows, and they are silent. He looks far away over the gray. loneliness stretching beyond. At length he murmurs: "A brief madness makes my long misery. Louise, if the earth were dazzled aside from her constant pole-star to worship some bewildering comet, would she be more forlorn than I?"

"Dear Rose! your art remains," I hear her say.

He bends lower, that his breath may scorch her brow. "Was I wrong? Am I right?" he whispers, hurriedly. "You loved me once; you love me now, Louise, if I were free?"

"But you are not free."

She does not recoil, yet her very atmosphere repels him, while looking up with those woful eyes blanching her cheek by their gathering darkness. "And, Rose — " she sighs, then ceases abruptly, while a quiver of sudden scorn writhes spurningly down eyelid and nostril and pains the whole face.

He erects himself, then reaches his hand for the rose in her belt, glances at me, — the dead thing in my bosom rising and falling with my turbulent heart, — holds the rose to his lips, leaves her. How keen are my ears! how flushed my cheek! how eager and fierce my eyes! He approaches; I snatch the rose and tear its petals in an angry shower, and then a dim east-wind pours in and scatters my dream like flakes of foam. All dreams go; youth and hope desert me; the dark claims me. O room, surrender me! O sickness and sorrow, loose your weary hold!

It maddens me to know that the sun will shine again, the tender grass grow green, the veery sing, the crocus come. She will walk in the light and re-gather youth, and I moulder, a forgotten heap. Oh, why not all things crash to ruin with me? —

Pain, pain, pain! Where is my father? Why is he away, when they know I die? He used to hold me once; he ought to hear me when I call. He would rest me, and stroke the grief aside, — he is so strong. Where is he?

These amulets stumbling round again? Amber, amber gods, you did mischief in your day! If I clutched you hard, as Lu did once, all your spells would be broken. — It is colder than it was. I think I will go to sleep. —

What was that? How loud and resonant! It stuns me. It is too sonorous. Does sound flash? Ah! the hour. Another? How long the silver toll swims on the silent air! It is one o'clock, — a passing bell, a knell. If I were at home by the river, the tide would be turning down, down, and out to the broad, broad sea. Is it worth while to have lived?

Have I spoken? She looks at me, rises, and touches that bell-rope that always brings him. How softly he opens the door! Waiting, perhaps. Well. Ten years have not altered him much. The face is brighter, finer, — shines with the eternal youth of genius. They pause a moment; I suppose they are coming to me; but their eyes are on each other.

Why must the long, silent look with which he met her the day I got my amber strike back on me now so vindictively? I remember three looks: that, and this, and one other, — one fervid noon, a look that drank my soul, that culminated my existence. Oh, I remember! I lost it a little while ago. I have it now. You are coming? Can't you hear me? See! these costly liqueurs, these precious perfumes beside me here, if I can reach them, I will drench the coverlet in them; it shall be white and sweet as a little child's. I wish they were the great rich lilies of that day; it is too late for the baby May-flowers. You do not like amber? There the thread breaks again! the little cruel gods go tumbling down the floor! Come, lay my head on your breast! kiss my life off my lips! I am your Yone! I forgot a little while, — but I love you, Rose! Rose!

Why! I thought arms held me. How clear the space is! The wind from outdoors, rising again, must have rushed in. There is the quarter striking. How free I am! No one here? No swarm of souls about me? Oh, those two faces looked from a great mist, a moment since; I scarcely see them now. Drop, mask! I will not pick you up! Out, out into the gale! back to my elements!

So I passed out of the room, down the staircase.

E

The servants below did not see me, but the hounds crouched and whined. I paused before the great ebony clock; again the fountain broke, and it chimed the half-hour; it was half past one; another quarter, and the next time its ponderous silver hammers woke the house, it would be two. Half past one? Why, then, did not the hands move? Why cling fixed on a point five minutes before the first quarter struck? To and fro, soundless and purposeless, swung the long pendulum. And, ah! what was this thing I had become? I had done with time. Not for me the hands moved on their recurrent circle any more.

I must have died at ten minutes past one.

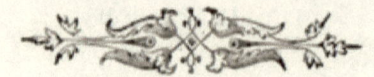

In a Cellar.

In a Cellar.

I.

IT was the day of Madame de St. Cyr's dinner, an event I never missed; for, the mistress of a mansion in the Faubourg St. Germain, there still lingered about her the exquisite grace and good-breeding peculiar to the old *régime*, that insensibly communicates itself to the guests till they move in an atmosphere of ease that constitutes the charm of home. One was always sure of meeting desirable and well-assorted people here, and a *contre-temps* was impossible. Moreover, the house was not at the command of all; and Madame de St. Cyr, with the daring strength which, when found in a woman at all, should, to be endurable, be combined with a sweet but firm restraint, rode rough-shod over the parvenus of the Empire, and was resolute enough to insulate herself even among the old *noblesse*, who, as all the world knows, insulate themselves from the rest of France. There were rare qualities in this woman, and were I to have selected one who with an even hand should carry a snuffy candle through a magazine of powder, my choice would have devolved upon her; and she would have done it.

I often looked, and not unsuccessfully, to discern what heritage her daughter had in these little affairs. Indeed, to one like myself, Delphine presented the worthier study. She wanted the airy charm of manner, the suavity and tenderness of her mother, — a deficiency easily to be pardoned in one of such delicate and extraordinary beauty. And perhaps her face was the truest index of her mind; not that it ever transparently displayed a genuine emotion, — Delphine was too well bred for that, — but the outline of her features had a keen regular precision, as if cut in a gem. Her exquisite color seldom varied, her eyes were like blue steel, she was statue-like and stony. But had one paused there, pronouncing her hard and impassive, he had committed an error. She had no great capability for passion, but she was not to be deceived; one metallic flash of her eye would cut like a sword through the whole mesh of entanglements with which you had surrounded her; and frequently, when alone with her, you perceived cool recesses in her nature, sparkling and pleasant, which jealously guarded themselves from a nearer approach. She was infinitely *spirituelle;* compared to her, Madame herself was heavy.

At the first, I had seen that Delphine must be the wife of a diplomate. What diplomate? For a time asking myself the question seriously, I decided in the negative, which did not, however, prevent Delphine from fulfilling her destiny, since there were others. She was, after all, like a draught of rich old wine, all fire and sweetness. These things were not generally seen in her; I was more favored than many; and I looked at her with pitiless perspicacious eyes. Nevertheless, I had not the least advantage; it was, in fact, between us, diamond cut diamond, — which, oddly enough, brings me back to my story.

Some years previously, I had been sent on a special mission to the government at Paris, and having finally executed it, I resigned the post, and resolved to make my residence there, since it is the only place on earth where one can live. Every morning I half expect to see the country, beyond the city, white with an encampment of the nations, who, having peacefully flocked there over night, wait till the Rue St. Honoré shall run out and greet them. It surprises me, sometimes, that those pretending to civilization are content to remain at a distance. What experience have they of life, — not to mention gayety and pleasure, but of the great purpose of life, — society? Man evidently is gregarious; Fourier's fables are founded on fact; we are nothing without our opposites, our fellows, our lights and shadows, colors, relations, combinations, our *point d'appui*, and our angle of sight. An isolated man is immensurable; he is also unpicturesque, unnatural, untrue. He is no longer the lord of Nature, animal and vegetable, — but Nature is the lord of him; the trees, skies, flowers, predominate, and he is in as bad taste as green and blue, or as an oyster in a vase of roses. The race swings naturally to clusters. It being admitted, then, that society is our normal state, where is it to be obtained in such perfection as at Paris? Show me the urbanity, the generosity in trifles, better than sacrifice, the incuriousness and freedom, the grace, and wit, and honor, that will equal such as I find here. Morality, — we were not speaking of it, — the intrusion is unnecessary; must that word with Anglo-Saxon pertinacity dog us round the world? A hollow mask, which Vice now and then lifts for a breath of air, I grant you this state may be called; but since I find the vice elsewhere, countenance my preference for the accompanying mask. But even this is vanishing; such drawing-rooms as Mme. de St. Cyr's are less and less frequent. Yet, though the delightful spell of the last century daily dissipates itself, and we are not now what we were twenty years ago, still Paris is, and will be to the end of time, for a cosmopolitan, the pivot on which the world revolves.

It was, then, as I have said, the day of Mme. de St. Cyr's dinner. Punctually at the hour, I presented myself, — for I have always esteemed it the least courtesy which a guest can render, that he should not cool his hostess's dinner.

The usual choice company waited. There was the Marquis of G., the ambassador from home; Col. Leigh, an *attaché* of that embassy; the Spanish and Belgian ministers; — all of whom, with myself, completed a diplomatic circle. There were also wits and artists, but no ladies whose beauty exceeded that of the St. Cyrs. With nearly all of this assemblage I held certain relations, so that I was immediately at ease. G. was the only one whom, perhaps, I would rather not have met, although we were the best of friends. They awaited but one, the Baron Stahl. Meanwhile Delphine stood coolly taking the measurement of the Marquis of G., while her mother entertained one and another guest with a low-toned flattery, gentle interest, or lively narration, as the case might demand.

In a country where a *coup d'état* was as easily given as a box on the ear, we all attentively watched for the arrival of one who had been sent from a neighboring empire to negotiate a loan for the tottering throne of this. Nor was expectation kept long on guard. In a moment, "His Excellency, the Baron Stahl!" was announced.

The exaggeration of his low bow to Mme. de St. Cyr, the gleam askance of his black eye, the absurd simplicity of his dress, did not particularly please me. A low forehead, straight black brows, a beardless cheek with a fine color which gave him a fictitiously youthful appearance, were the most striking traits of his face; his person was not to be found fault with; but he boldly evinced his admiration for Delphine, and with a wicked eye.

As we were introduced, he assured me, in pure English, that he had pleasure in making the acquaintance of a gentleman whose services were so distinguished.

I, in turn, assured him of my pleasure in meeting a gentleman who appreciated them.

I had arrived at the house of Mme. de St. Cyr with a load on my mind, which for four weeks had weighed there; but before I thus spoke, it was lifted and gone. I had seen the Baron Stahl before, although not previously aware of it; and now, as he bowed, talked my native tongue so smoothly, drew a glove over the handsome hand upon whose first finger shone the only incongruity of his attire, a broad gold ring, holding a gaudy red stone, — as he stood smiling and expectant before me, a sudden chain of events flashed through my mind, an instantaneous heat, like lightning, welded them into logic. A great problem was resolved. For a second, the breath seemed snatched from my lips; the next, a lighter, freer man never trod in diplomatic shoes.

I really beg your pardon, — but perhaps from long usage, it has become impossible for me to tell a straight story. It is absolutely necessary to inform you of events already transpired.

4

In the first place, then, I, at this time, possessed a valet, the pink of valets, an Englishman, — and not the less valuable to me in a foreign capital, that, notwithstanding his long residence, he was utterly unable to speak one word of French intelligibly. Reading and writing it readily, his thick tongue could master scarcely a syllable. The adroitness and perfection with which he performed the duties of his place were unsurpassable. To a certain extent I was obliged to admit him into my confidence; I was not at all in his. In dexterity and despatch he equalled the advertisements. He never condescended to don my cast-off apparel, but, disposing of it, always arrayed himself in plain but gentlemanly garments. These do not complete the list of Hay's capabilities. He speculated. Respectable tenements in London called him landlord; in the funds certain sums lay subject to his order; to a profitable farm in Hants he contemplated future retirement; and passing upon the Bourse, I have received a grave bow, and have left him in conversation with an eminent capitalist respecting consols, drafts, exchange, and other erudite mysteries, where I yet find myself in the A B C. Thus not only was my valet a free-born Briton, but a landed proprietor. If the Rothschilds blacked your boots or shaved your chin, your emotions might be akin to mine. When this man, who had an interest in the India traders, brought the hot water into my dressing-room, of a morning, the Antipodes were tributary to me. To what extent might any little irascibility of mine drive a depression in the market! and I knew, as he brushed my hat, whether stocks rose or fell. In one respect, I was essentially like our Saxon ancestors, — my servant was a villain. If I had been merely a civilian, in any purely private capacity, having leisure to attend to personal concerns in the midst of the delicate specialties intrusted to me from the cabinet at home, the possession of so inestimable a valet might have bullied me beyond endurance. As it was, I found it rather agreeable than otherwise. He was tacitly my secretary of finance.

Several years ago, a diamond of wonderful size and beauty, having wandered from the East, fell into certain imperial coffers among our Continental neighbors; and at the same time some extraordinary intelligence, essential to the existence, so to speak, of that government, reached a person there who fixed as its price this diamond. After a while he obtained it, but, judging that prudence lay in departure, took it to England, where it was purchased for an enormous sum by the Duke of —— as he will remain an unknown quantity, let us say X. There are probably not a dozen such diamonds in the world, — certainly not three in England. It rejoiced in such flowery appellatives as the Sea of Splendor, the Moon of Milk ; and, of course, those who had but parted with it under protest, as it were, determined to obtain it again at all hazards ; — they were never famous for scrupulosity. The Duke of X. was aware of this, and, for a time, the gem had lain idle, its glory muffled in a casket; but finally, on some grand occasion, a few months prior to the period of which I have spoken above, it was determined to set it in the Duchess's coronet. Accordingly, one day, it was given by her son, the Marquis of G., into the hands of their solicitor, who should deliver it to her Grace's jeweller. It lay in a small shagreen case, and before the Marquis left, the solicitor placed the case in a flat leathern box, where lay a chain of most singular workmanship, the clasp of which was deranged. This chain was very

broad, of a style known as the brick-work, but every
brick was a tiny gem, set in a delicate filagree linked
with the next, and the whole rainbowed lustrousness
moving at your will, like the scales of some gorgeous
Egyptian serpent; — the solicitor was to take this also to
the jeweller. Having laid the box in his private desk,
Ulster, his confidential clerk, locked it, while he bowed
the Marquis down. Returning immediately, the solicitor
took the flat box and drove to the jeweller's. He found
the latter so crowded with customers, it being the fash-
ionable hour, as to be unable to attend to him; he,
however, took the solicitor into his inner room, a dark
fire-proof place, and there quickly deposited the box
within a safe, which stood inside another, like a Japanese
puzzle, and the solicitor, seeing the doors double-locked
and secured, departed; the other promising to attend to
the matter on the morrow.

Early the next morning, the jeweller entered his dark
room, and proceeded to unlock the safe. This being concluded, and the inner one also thrown open, he found the
box in a last and entirely, as he had always believed, secret compartment. Anxious to see this wonder, this Eye
of Morning, and Heart of Day, he eagerly loosened the
band and unclosed the box. It was empty. There was
no chain there; the diamond was missing. The sweat
streamed from his forehead, his clothes were saturated,
he believed himself the victim of a delusion. Calling an
assistant, every article and nook in the dark room was
examined. At last, in an extremity of despair, he sent
for the solicitor, who arrived in a breath. The jeweller's
alarm hardly equalled that of the other. In his sudden
dismay, he at first forgot the circumstances and dates
relating to the affair; afterward was doubtful. The

Marquis of G. was summoned, the police called in, the
jeweller given into custody. Every breath the solicitor
continued to draw only built up his ruin. He swallowed
laudanum, but, by making it an overdose, frustrated his
own design. He was assured, on his recovery, that no
suspicion attached to him. The jeweller now asseverated
that the diamond had never been given to him; but
though the jeweller had committed perjury, this was,
nevertheless, strictly true. Of course, whoever had the
stone would not attempt to dispose of it at present, and,
though communications were opened with the general
European police, there was very little to work upon.
But by means of this last step the former possessors
became aware of its loss, and I make no doubt had their
agents abroad immediately.

Meanwhile, the case hung here, complicated and tan-
talizing, when one morning I woke in London. No
sooner had G. heard of my arrival than he called, and,
relating the affair, requested my assistance. I confess
myself to have been interested, — foolishly so, I thought
afterward; but we all have our weaknesses, and diamonds
were mine. In company with the Marquis, I waited upon
the solicitor, who entered into the few details minutely,
calling frequently upon Ulster, a young, fresh-looking
man, for corroboration. We then drove to the jeweller's
new quarters, took him, under charge of the officers, to
his place of business, where he nervously showed me
every point that could bear upon the subject, and ended
by exclaiming, that he was ruined, and all for a stone he
had never seen. I sat quietly for a few moments. It
stood, then, thus : — G. had given the thing to the solicitor, seen it put into the box, seen the box put into the
desk ; but while the confidential clerk, Ulster, locked the

desk, the solicitor waited on the Marquis to the door, —
returning, took the box, without opening it again, to the
jeweller, who, in the hurry, shut it up in his safe, also
without opening it. The case was perfectly clear. These
mysterious things are always so simple! You know now,
as well as I, who took the diamond.

I did not choose to volunteer, but assented, on being
desired. The police and I were old friends; they had so
often assisted me, that I was not afraid to pay them in
kind, and accordingly agreed to take charge of the case,
still retaining their aid, should I require it. The jeweller
was now restored to his occupation, although still sub-
jected to a rigid surveillance, and I instituted inquiries
into the recent movements of the young man Ulster. The
case seemed to me to have been very blindly conducted.
But, though all that was brought to light concerning him
in London was perfectly fair and aboveboard, it was discovered that, not long since, he had visited Paris, — on the
solicitor's business, of course, but gaining thereby an opportunity to transact any little affairs of his own. This
was fortunate; for if any one could do anything in Paris,
it was myself.

It is not often that I act as a detective. But one
homogeneous to every situation could hardly play a
pleasanter part for once. I have thought that our great
masters in theory and practice, Machiavel and Talley-
rand, were hardly more, on a large scale.

I was about to return to Paris, but resolved to call
previously on the solicitor again. He welcomed me
warmly, although my suspicions had not been imparted
to him, and, with a more cheerful heart than had lately
been habitual to him, entered into an animated conversation respecting the great case of Biter *v.* Bit, then absorb-

ing so much of the public attention, frequently addressing
Ulster, whose remarks were always pertinent, brief, and
clear.   As I sat actively discussing the topic, feeling no
more interest in it than in the end of that cigar I just cut
off, and noting exactly every look and motion of the
unfortunate youth, I recollect the curious sentiment that
filled me regarding him.   What injury had he done me,
that I should pursue him with punishment?   Me?   I am,
and every individual is, integral with the commonwealth.
It was the commonwealth he had injured.   Yet, even
then, why was I the one to administer justice ?   Why not
continue with my coffee in the morning, my kings and
cabinets and national chess at noon, my opera at night,
and let the poor devil go?   Why, but that justice is
brought home to every member of society, — that naked
duty requires no shirking of such responsibility, — that,
had I failed here, the crime might, with reason, lie at my
door and multiply, the criminal increase himself?

Very possibly you will not unite with me ; but these
little catechisms are, once in a while, indispensable, to
vindicate one's course to one's self.

This Ulster was a handsome youth ; — the rogues have
generally all the good looks.   There was nothing else
remarkable about him but his quickness ; he was perpetually on the alert ; by constant activity, the rust was
never allowed to collect on his faculties ; his sharpness
was distressing, — he appeared subject to a tense strain.
Now his quill scratched over the paper unconcernedly,
while he could join as easily in his master's conversation :
nothing seemed to preoccupy him, or he held a mind open
at every point.   It is pitiful to remember him that morning, sitting quiet, unconscious, and free, utterly in the
hands of that mighty Inquisition, the Metropolitan Police,

with its countless arms, its cells and myrmidons in the remotest corners of the Continent, — at the mercy of so merciless a monster, and momently closer involved, like some poor prey round which a spider spins its bewildering web. It was also curious to observe the sudden suspicion that darkened his face at some innocent remark, — the quick shrinking and intrenched retirement, the manifest sting and rancor, as I touched his wound with a swift flash of my slender weapon and sheathed it again, and, after the thrust, the espionage, and the relief at believing it accidental. He had many threads to gather up and hold; — little electric warnings along them must have been constantly shocking him. He did that part well enough; it was a mistake, to begin with; he needed prudence. At that time I owed this Ulster nothing; now, however, I owe him a grudge, for some of the most harassing hours of my life were occasioned me by him. But I shall not cherish enmity on that account. With so promising a beginning, he will graduate and take his degree from the loftiest altitude in his line. Hemp is a narcotic; let it bring me forgetfulness.

In Paris I found it not difficult to trace such a person, since he was both foreign and unaccustomed. It was ascertained that he had posted several letters. A person of his description had been seen to drop a letter, the superscription of which had been read by one who picked it up for him. This superscription was the address of the very person who was likely to be the agent of the former possessors of the diamond, and had attracted attention After all, — you know the Secret Force, — it was not so impossible to imagine what this letter contained, despite of its cipher. Such a person also had been met among the Jews, and at certain shops whose reputation was not of the clearest. He had called once or twice on Mme. de St. Cyr, on business relative to a vineyard adjoining her château in the Gironde, which she had sold to a wine merchant of England. I found a zest in the affair, as I pursued it.

We were now fairly at sea, but before long I found we were likely to remain there; in fact, nothing of consequence eventuated. I began to regret having taken the affair from the hands in which I had found it, and one day, it being a gala or some insatiable saint's day, I was riding, perplexed with that and other matters, and paying small attention to the passing crowd. I was vexed and mortified, and had fully decided to throw up the whole, — on such hairs do things hang, — when, suddenly turning a corner, my bridle-reins became entangled in the snaffle of another rider. I loosened them abstractedly, and not till it was necessary to bow to my strange antagonist, on parting, did I glance up. The person before me was evidently not accustomed to play the dandy; he wore his clothes ill, sat his horse worse, and was uneasy in the saddle. The unmistakable air of the *gamin* was apparent beneath the superficies of the gentleman. Conspicuous on his costume, and wound like an order of merit upon his breast, glittered a chain, *the* chain, — each tiny brick-like gem spiked with a hundred sparks, and building a fabric of sturdy probabilities with the celerity of the genii in constructing Aladdin's palace. There, a cable to haul up the treasure, was the chain; — where was the diamond? I need not tell you how I followed this young friend, with what assiduity I kept him in sight, up and down, all day long, till, weary at last of his fine sport, as I certainly was of mine, he left his steed in stall and fared on his way a-foot. Still pursuing, now I threaded quay and square,

4*

street and alley, till he disappeared in a small shop, in
one of those dark crowded lanes leading eastward from
the Pont Neuf, in the city. It was the sign of a *marchand
des armures,* and having provided myself with those per-
suasive arguments, a *sergent-de-ville* and a *gendarme,* I
entered.

A place more characteristic it would be impossible to
find. Here were piled bows of every material, ash, and
horn, and tougher fibres, with slackened strings, and
among them peered a rusty clarion and battle-axe, while
the quivers that should have accompanied lay in a distant
corner, their arrows serving to pin long, dusty, torn banners to the wall. Opposite the entrance, an archer in
bronze hung on tiptoe, and levelled a steel bow, whose
piercing *flèche* seemed sparkling with impatience to spring
from his finger and flesh itself in the heart of the intruder.
The hauberk and halberd, lance and casque, arquebuse
and sword, were suspended in friendly congeries; and
fragments of costly stuff swept from ceiling to floor,
crushed and soiled by the heaps of rusty firelocks, cut-
lasses, and gauntlets thrown upon them. In one place,
a little antique bust was half hid in the folds of some
pennon, still dyed with battle-stains; in another, scattered
treasures of Dresden and Sèvres brought the drawing-
room into the campaign; and all around bivouacked rifles,
whose polished barrels glittered full of death, — pistols, va-
riously mounted, for an insurgent at the barricades, or for
a lost millionnaire at the gaming-table, — foils, with but-
toned bluntness, — and rapiers whose even edges were
viewless as if filed into air. Destruction lay everywhere,
at the command of the owner of this place, and, had he
possessed a particle of vivacity, it would have been haz-
ardous to bow beneath his doorway. It did not, I must

say, look like a place where I should find a diamond. As the owner came forward, I determined on my plan of action.

"You have, sir," I said, handing him a bit of paper, on which were scrawled some numbers, "a diamond in your possession, of such and so many carats, size, and value, belonging to the Duke of X., and left with you by an Englishman, Mr. Arthur Ulster. You will deliver it to me, if you please."

"Monsieur!" exclaimed the man, lifting his hands, and surveying me with the widest eyes I ever saw. "A diamond! In my possession! So immense a thing! It is impossible. I have not even seen one of the kind. It is a mistake. Jacques Noailles, the vender of jewels *en gros*, second door below, must be the man. One should perceive that my business is with arms, not diamonds. I have it not; it would ruin me."

Here he paused for a reply, but, meeting none, resumed. "M. Arthur Ulster! — I have heard of no such person. I never spoke with an Englishman. Bah! I detest them! I have no dealings with them. I repeat, I have not your jewel. Do you wish anything more of me ? "

His vehemence only convinced me of the truth of my suspicions.

"These heroics are out of place," I answered. "I demand the article in question."

"Monsieur doubts me ? " he asked, with a rueful face, — "questions my word, which is incontrovertible ? " Here he clapped his hand upon a *couteau-de-chasse* lying near, but, appearing to think better of it, drew himself up, and, with a shower of nods flung at me, added, "I deny your accusation ! " I had not accused him.

"You are at too much pains to convict yourself. I charge you with nothing," I said. "But this diamond must be surrendered."

"Monsieur is mad!" he exclaimed, "mad! he dreams! Do I look like one who possesses such a trophy? Does my shop resemble a mine? Look about! See! All that is here would not bring a hundredth part of its price. I beseech Monsieur to believe me; he has mistaken the number, or has been misinformed."

"We waste words. I know this diamond is here, as well as a costly chain —"

"On my soul, on my life, on my honor," he cried, clasping his hands and turning up his eyes, "there is here nothing of the kind. I do not deal in gems. A little silk, a few weapons, a curiosity, a nicknack, comprise my stock. I have not the diamond. I do not know the thing. I am poor. I am honest. Suspicion destroys me!"

"As you will find, should I be longer troubled by your denials."

He was inflexible, and, having exhausted every artifice of innocence, wiped the tears from his eyes, — oh, these French! life is their theatre, — and remained quiet. It was getting dark. There was no gas in the place; but in the pause a distant street-lamp swung its light dimly round.

"Unless one desires to purchase, allow me to say that it is my hour for closing," he remarked, blandly, rubbing his black-bearded chin.

"My time is valuable," I returned. "It is late and dark. When your shop-boy lights up — "

"Pardon, — we do not light."

"Permit me, then, to perform that office for you. In

this blaze you may perceive my companions, whom you have not appeared to recognize."

So saying, I scratched a match upon the floor, and, as the *sergent-de-ville* and the *gendarme* advanced, threw the light of the blue spirt of sulphurous flame upon them. In a moment more the match went out, and we remained in the demi-twilight of the distant lantern. The *marchand des armures* stood petrified and aghast. Had he seen the imps of Satan in that instant, it could have had no greater effect.

"You have seen them?" I asked. "I regret to inconvenience you; but unless this diamond is produced at once, my friends will put their seal on your goods, your property will be confiscated, yourself in a dungeon. In other words, I allow you five minutes; at the close of that time you will have chosen between restitution and ruin."

He remained apparently lost in thought. He was a big, stout man, and with one blow of his powerful fist could easily have settled me. It was the last thing in his mind. At length he lifted his head, — "Rosalie!" he called.

At the word, a light foot pattered along a stone floor within, and in a moment a little woman stood in an arch raised by two steps from our own level. Carrying a candle, she descended and tripped toward him. She was not pretty, but sprightly and keen, as the perpetual attrition of life must needs make her, and wore the everlasting grisette costume, which displays the neatest of ankles, and whose cap is more becoming than wreaths of garden millinery. I am too minute, I see, but it is second nature. The two commenced a vigorous whispering amid sundry gestures and glances. Suddenly the woman turned, and, laying the prettiest of little hands on my sleeve, said, with a winning smile, —

"Is it a crime of *lèse-majesté* ?"

This was a new idea, but might be useful.

"Not yet," I said; "two minutes more, and I will not answer for the consequence."

Other whispers ensued.

"Monsieur," said the man, leaning on one arm over the counter, and looking up in my face, with the most engaging frankness, — "it is true that I have such a diamond; but it is not mine. It is left with me to be delivered to the Baron Stahl, who comes as an agent from his court for its purchase."

"Yes, — I know."

"He was to have paid me half a million francs, — not half its worth, — in trust for the person who left it, who is not M. Arthur Ulster, but Mme. de St. Cyr."

Madame de St. Cyr ! How under the sun — No, — it could not be possible. The case stood as it stood before. The rogue was in deeper water than I had thought; he had merely employed Mme. de St. Cyr. I ran this over in my mind, while I said, "Yes."

"Now, sir," I continued, "you will state the terms of this transaction."

"With pleasure. For my trouble I was myself to receive patronage and five thousand francs. The Baron is to be here directly, on other and public business. *Reine du ciel*, Monsieur ! how shall I meet him ?"

"He is powerless in Paris; your fear is idle."

"True. There were no other terms."

"Nor papers ?"

"The lady thought it safest to be without them. She took merely my receipt, which the Baron Stahl will bring to me from her before receiving this."

"I will trouble you for it now."

He bowed and shuffled away. At a glance from me, the *gendarme* slipped to the rear of the building, where three others were stationed at the two exits in that direction, to caution them of the critical moment, and returned. Ten minutes passed, — the merchant did not appear. If, after all, he had made off with it! There had been the click of a bolt, the half-stifled rattle of arms, as if a door had been opened and rapidly closed again, but nothing more.

" I will see what detains my friend," said Mademoiselle, the little woman.

We suffered her to withdraw. In a moment more a quick expostulation was to be heard.

" They are there, the *gendarmes*, my little one! I should have run, but they caught me, the villains! and replaced me in the house. *Oh, sacre!*" — and rolling this word between his teeth, he came down and laid a little box on the counter. I opened it. There was within a large, glittering, curiously-cut piece of glass. I threw it aside.

" The diamond!" I exclaimed.

" Monsieur had it," he replied, stooping to pick up the glass with every appearance of surprise and care.

" Do you mean to say you endeavored to escape with that bawble? Produce the diamond instantly, or you shall hang as high as Haman!" I roared.

Whether he knew the individual in question or not, the threat was efficient; he trembled and hesitated, and finally drew the identical shagreen case from his bosom.

" I but jested," he said. " Monsieur will witness that I relinquish it with reluctance."

" I will witness that you receive stolen goods!" I cried, in wrath.

He placed it in my hands.

"Oh!" he groaned, from the bottom of his heart, hanging his head, and laying both hands on the counter before him, — "it pains, it grieves me to part with it!"

"And the chain," I said.

"Monsieur did not demand that!"

"I demand it now."

In a moment, the chain also was given me.

"And now will Monsieur do me a favor? Will he inform me by what means he ascertained these facts?"

I glanced at the *garçon*, who had probably supplied himself with his master's finery illicitly; — he was the means; — we have some generosity; — I thought I should prefer doing him the favor, and declined.

I unclasped the shagreen case; the *sergent-de-ville* and the *gendarme* stole up and looked over my shoulder; the *garçon* drew near with round eyes; the little woman peeped across; the merchant, with tears streaming over his face, gazed as if it had been a loadstone; finally, I looked myself. There it lay, the glowing, resplendent thing! flashing in affluence of splendor, throbbing and palpitant with life, drawing all the light from the little woman's candle, from the sparkling armor around, from the steel barbs, and the distant lantern, into its bosom. It was scarcely so large as I had expected to see it, but more brilliant than anything I could conceive of. I do not believe there is another such in the world. One saw clearly that the Oriental superstition of the sex of stones was no fable; this was essentially the female of diamonds, the queen herself, the principle of life, the rejoicing receptive force. It was not radiant, as the term literally taken implies; it seemed rather to retain its wealth, — instead of emitting its glorious rays, to curl them back like the fringe of a madrepore, and lie there with redoubled quivering scintillations, a mass of white magnificence, not prismatic, but a vast milky lustre. I closed the case ; on reopening it, I could scarcely believe that the beautiful sleepless eye would again flash upon me. I did not comprehend how it could afford such perpetual richness, such sheets of lustre.

At last we compelled ourselves to be satisfied. I left the shop, dismissed my attendants, and, fresh from the contemplation of this miracle, again trod the dirty, reeking streets, crossed the bridge, with its lights, its warehouses midway, its living torrents who poured on unconscious of the beauty within their reach. The thought of their ignorance of the treasure, not a dozen yards distant, has often made me question if we all are not equally unaware of other and greater processes of life, of more perfect, sublimed, and, as it were, spiritual crystallizations going on invisibly about us. But had these been told of the thing clutched in the hand of a passer, how many of them would have known where to turn ? and we, — are we any better ?

II.

FOR a few days I carried the diamond about my person, and did not mention its recovery even to my valet, who knew that I sought it, but communicated only with the Marquis of G., who replied, that he would be in Paris on a certain day, when I could safely deliver it to him.

It was now generally rumored that the neighboring government was about to send us the Baron Stahl, ambassador concerning arrangements for a loan to maintain the sinking monarchy in supremacy at Paris, the usual synecdoche for France.

The weather being fine, I proceeded to call on Mme.
de St. Cyr. She received me in her boudoir, and on my
way thither I could not but observe the perfect quiet and
cloistered seclusion that pervaded the whole house, — the
house itself seeming only an adjunct of the still and sunny
garden, of which one caught a glimpse through the long
open hall-windows beyond. This boudoir did not differ
from others to which I have been admitted: the same
delicate shades; all the dainty appliances of Art for
beauty; the lavish profusion of *bijouterie*; and the usual
statuettes of innocence, to indicate, perhaps, the presence
of that commodity which might not be guessed at otherwise; and burning in a silver cup, a rich perfume loaded
the air with voluptuous sweetness. Through a half-open
door an inner boudoir was to be seen, which must have
been Delphine's; it looked like her; the prevailing hue
was a soft purple, or gray; a *prie-dieu*, a book-shelf, and
desk, of a dark West Indian wood, were just visible. There
was but one picture, — a sad-eyed, beautiful Fate. It was
the type of her nation. I think she worshipped it. And
how apt is misfortune to degenerate into Fate! — not that
the girl had ever experienced the former, but, dissatisfied
with life, and seeing no outlet, she accepted it stoically
and waited till it should be over. She needed to be
aroused; — the station of an *ambassadrice*, which I desired for her, might kindle the spark. There were no
flowers, no perfumes, no busts, in this ascetic place.
Delphine herself, in some faint rosy gauze, her fair hair
streaming round her, as she lay on a white-draped couch,
half-risen on one arm, while she read the morning's *feuille-
ton*, was the most perfect statuary of which a room could
boast, — illumined, as I saw her, by the gay beams that
entered at the loftily-arched window, broken only by the

flickering of the vine-leaves that clustered the curiously-latticed panes without. She resembled in kind a Nymph, just bursting from the sea; so Pallas might have posed for Aphrodite. Madame de St. Cyr received me with *empressement*, and, so doing, closed the door of this shrine. We spoke of various things, — of the court, the theatre, the weather, the world, — skating lightly round the slender edges of her secret, till finally she invited me to lunch with her in the garden. Here, on a rustic table, stood wine and a few delicacies, — while, by extending a hand, we could grasp the hanging pears and nectarines, still warm to the lip and luscious with sunshine, as we disputed possession with the envious wasp who had established a priority of claim.

"It is to be hoped," I said, sipping the *Haut-Brion*, whose fine and brittle smack contrasted rarely with the delicious juiciness of the fruit, "that you have laid in a supply of this treasure that neither moth nor rust doth corrupt, before parting with that little gem in the Gironde."

"Ah? You know, then, that I have sold it?"

"Yes," I replied. "I have the pleasure of Mr. Ulster's acquaintance."

"He arranged the terms for me," she said, with restraint, — adding, " I could almost wish now that it had not been."

This was probably true; for the sum which she hoped to receive from Ulster for standing sponsor to his jewel was possibly equal to the price of her vineyard.

"It was indispensable at the time, this sale; I thought best to hazard it on one more season. — If, after such advantages, Delphine will not marry, why — it remains to retire into the country and end our days with the barbarians!" she continued, shrugging her shoulders; "I have a house there."

"But you will not be obliged to throw us all into despair by such a step now," I replied.

She looked quickly, as if to see how nearly I had approached her citadel, — then, finding in my face no expression but a complimentary one, "No," she said, "I hope that my affairs have brightened a little. One never knows what is in store."

Before long I had assured myself that Mme. de St. Cyr was not a party to the theft, but had merely been hired by Ulster, who, discovering the state of her affairs, had not, therefore, revealed his own, — and this without in the least implying any knowledge on my part of the transaction. Ulster must have seen the necessity of leaving the business in the hands of a competent person, and Mme. de St. Cyr's financial talent was patent. There were few ladies in Paris who would have rejected the opportunity. Of these things I felt a tolerable certainty.

"We throng with foreigners," said Madame, archly, as I reached this point. "Diplomates, too. The Baron Stahl arrives in a day."

"I have heard," I responded. "You are acquainted?"

"Alas! no," she said. "I knew his father well, though he himself is not young. Indeed, the families thought once of intermarriage. But nothing has been said on the subject for many years. His Excellency, I hear, will strengthen himself at home by an alliance with the young Countess, the natural daughter of the Emperor."

"He surely will never be so imprudent as to rivet his chain by such a link!"

"It is impossible to compute the dice in those despotic countries," she rejoined, — which was pretty well, considering the freedom enjoyed by France at that period.

"It may be," I suggested, "that the Baron hopes to open this delicate subject with you yourself, Madame."

"It is unlikely," she said, sighing. "And for Delphine, should I tell her his Excellency preferred scarlet, she would infallibly wear blue. Imagine her, Monsieur, in fine scarlet, with a scarf of gold gauze, and rustling grasses in that unruly gold hair of hers! She would be divine!"

The maternal instinct as we have it here at Paris confounds me. I do not comprehend it. Here was a mother who did not particularly love her child, who would not be inconsolable at her loss, would not ruin her own complexion by care of her during illness, would send her through fire and water and every torture to secure or maintain a desirable rank, who yet would entangle herself deeply in intrigue, would not hesitate to tarnish her own reputation, and would, in fact, raise heaven and earth to — endow this child with a brilliant match. And Mme. de St. Cyr seemed to regard Delphine, still further, as a cool matter of Art.

These little confidences, moreover, are provoking. They put you yourself so entirely out of the question.

"Mlle. de St. Cyr's beauty is peerless," I said, slightly chagrined, and at a loss. "If hearts were trumps, instead of diamonds!"

"We are poor," resumed Madame, pathetically. "Delphine is not an heiress. Delphine is proud. She will not stoop to charm. Her coquetry is that of an Amazon. Her kisses are arrows. She is Medusa!" And Madame, her mother, shivered.

Here, with her hair knotted up and secured by a tiny dagger, her gauzy drapery gathered in her arm, Delphine floated down the green alley toward us, as if in a rosy cloud. But this soft aspect never could have been more widely contradicted than by the stony repose and cutting calm of her beautiful face.

"The Marquis of G.," said her mother, "he also arrives ambassador. Has he talent? Is he brilliant? Wealthy, of course, — but *gauche?*"

Therewith I sketched for them the Marquis and his surroundings.

"It is charming," said Madame. "Delphine, do you attend?"

"And why?" asked Delphine, half concealing a yawn with her dazzling hand. "It is wearisome; it matters not to me."

"But he will not go to marry himself in France," said her mother. "Oh, these English," she added, with a laugh, "yourself, Monsieur, being proof of it, will not mingle blood, lest the Channel should still flow between the little red globules! You will go? but to return shortly? You will dine with me soon? *Au revoir!*" and she gave me her hand graciously, while Delphine bowed as if I were already gone, threw herself into a garden-chair, and commenced pouring the wine on a stone for a little tame snake which came out and lapped it.

Such women as Mme. de St. Cyr have a species of magnetism about them. It is difficult to retain one's self-respect before them, — for no other reason than that one is, at the moment, absorbed into their individuality, and thinks and acts with them. Delphine must have had a strong will, and perpetual antagonism did not weaken it. As for me, Madame had, doubtless, reasons of her own for tearing aside these customary bands of reserve, — reasons which, if you do not perceive, I shall not enumerate.

"Have you met with anything further in your search, sir?" asked my valet, next morning.

"Oh, yes, Hay," I returned, in a very good humor, — "with great success. You have assisted me so much, that I am sure I owe it to you to say that I have found the diamond."

"Indeed, sir, you are very kind. I have been interested, but my assistance is not worth mentioning. I thought likely it might be, you appeared so quiet." — The cunning dog! — "How did you find it, sir, may I ask?"

I briefly related the leading facts, since he had been aware of the progress of the case to that point, — without, however, mentioning Mme. de St. Cyr's name.

"And Monsieur did not inform me!" a French valet would have cried.

"You were prudent not to mention it, sir," said Hay. "These walls must have better ears than ordinary; for a family has moved in on the first floor recently, whose actions are extremely suspicious. But is this precious affair to be seen?"

I took it from an inner pocket and displayed it, having discarded the shagreen case as inconvenient.

"His Excellency must return as he came," said I.

Hay's eyes sparkled.

"And do you carry it there, sir?" he asked, with surprise, as I restored it to my waistcoat-pocket.

"I shall take it to the bank," I said. "I do not like the responsibility."

"It is very unsafe," was the warning of this cautious fellow. "Why, sir! any of these swells, these pickpockets, might meet you, run against you, — so!" said Hay, suiting the action to the word, "and, with the little sharp knife concealed in just such a ring as this I wear, give a light tap, and there's a slit in your vest, sir, but no diamond!"—and instantly resuming his former respectful deportment, Hay handed me my gloves and stick, and smoothed my hat.

"Nonsense!" I replied, drawing on the gloves, "I should like to see the man who could be too quick for me. Any news from India, Hay?"

"None of consequence, sir. The indigo crop is said to have failed, which advances the figure of that on hand, so that one or two fortunes will be made to-day. Your hat, sir?—your lunettes? Here they are, sir."

"Good morning, Hay."

"Good morning, sir."

I descended the stairs, buttoning my gloves, paused a moment at the door to look about, and proceeded down the street, which was not more than usually thronged. At the bank I paused to assure myself that the diamond was safe. My fingers caught in a singular slit. I started. As Hay had prophesied, there was a fine longitudinal cut in my waistcoat, but the pocket was empty. My God! the thing was gone. I never can forget the blank nihility of all existence that dreadful moment when I stood fumbling for what was not. Calm as I sit here and tell of it, I vow to you a shiver courses through me at the very thought. I had circumvented Stahl only to destroy myself. The diamond was lost again. My mind flew like lightning over every chance, and a thousand started up like steel spikes to snatch the bolt. For a moment I was stunned, but, never being very subject to despair, on my recovery, which was almost at once, took every measure that could be devised. Who had touched me? Whom had I met? Through what streets had I come? In ten minutes the Prefect had the matter in hand. My injunctions were strict privacy. I sincerely hoped the mishap would not reach England; and if the diamond were not recovered before the Marquis of G. arrived, — why, there was the Seine. It is all very well to talk, — yet suicide is so French an affair, that an Englishman does not take to it naturally, and, except in November, the Seine is too cold and damp for comfort, but during that month I suppose it does not greatly differ in these respects from our own atmosphere.

A preternatural activity now possessed me. I slept none, ate little, worked immoderately. I spared no efforts, for everything was at stake. In the midst of all, G. arrived. Hay also exerted himself to the utmost; I promised him a hundred pounds, if I found it. He never told me that he said how it would be, never intruded the state of the market, never resented my irritating conduct, but watched me with narrow yet kind solicitude, and frequently offered valuable suggestions, which, however, as everything else did, led to nothing. I did not call on G., but in a week or so his card was brought up one morning to me. "Deny me," I groaned. It yet wanted a week of the day on which I had promised to deliver him the diamond. Meanwhile the Baron Stahl had reached Paris, but he still remained in private, — few had seen him.

The police were forever on the wrong track. To-day they stopped the old Comptesse du Quesne and her jewels, at the Barrière; to-morrow, with their long needles, they riddled a package of lace destined for the Duchess of X. herself; the Secret Service was doubled; and to crown all, a splendid new star of the testy Prince de Ligne was examined and proclaimed to be paste, — the Prince swearing vengeance, if he could discover the cause, — while half Paris must have been under arrest.

5   G

My own hotel was ransacked thoroughly, — Hay begging
that his traps might be included, — but nothing resulted,
and I expected nothing, for, of course, I could swear that
the stone was in my pocket when I stepped into the street.
I confess I never was nearer madness, — every word and
gesture stung me like asps, — I walked on burning coals.
Enduring all this torment, I must yet meet my daily com-
rades, eat ices at Tortoni's, stroll on the Boulevards, call
on my acquaintance, with the same equanimity as before.
I believe I was equal to it. Only by contrast with that
blessed time when Ulster and diamonds were unknown,
could I imagine my past happiness, my present wretchedness. Rather than suffer it again, I would be stretched
on the rack till every bone in my skin were broken. I
cursed Mr. Arthur Ulster every hour in the day ; myself,
as well ; and even now the word diamond sends a cold
blast to my heart. I often met my friend the *marchand
des armures.* It was his turn to triumph ; I fancied there
must be a hang-dog kind of air about me, as about
every sharp man who has been outwitted. It wanted
finally but two days of that on which I was to deliver
the diamond.

One midnight, armed with a dark lantern and a cloak,
I was traversing the streets alone, — unsuccessful, as
usual, just now solitary, and almost in despair. As I
turned a corner, two men were but scarcely visible a
step before me. It was a badly-lighted part of the town.
Unseen and noiseless I followed. They spoke in low
tones, — almost whispers ; or rather, one spoke, — the
other seemed to nod assent.

" On the day but one after to-morrow," I heard spoken
in English. Great Heavens ! was it possible ? had I
arrived at a clew ? That was the day of days for me.

"You have given it, you say, in this billet, — I wish to be exact, you see," continued the voice, — "to prevent detection, you gave it, ten minutes after it came into your hands, to the butler of Madame ——," (here the speaker stumbled on the rough pavement, and I lost the name,) "who," he continued, "will put it in the ——" (a second stumble acted like a hiccough) "cellar."

"Wine-cellar," I thought; "and what then?"

"In the ——." A third stumble was followed by a round German oath. How easy it is for me now to fill up the little blanks which that unhappy pavement caused!

"You share your receipts with this butler. On the day I obtain it," he added, and I now perceived his foreign accent, "I hand you one hundred thousand francs; afterward, monthly payments till you have received the stipulated sum. But how will this butler know me, in season to prevent a mistake? Hem! — he might give it to the other!"

My hearing had been trained to such a degree that I would have promised to catch any given dialogue of the spirits themselves, but the whisper that answered him eluded me. I caught nothing but a faint sibillation. "Your ring?" was the rejoinder. "He shall be instructed to recognize it? Very well. It is too large, — no, that will do, it fits the first finger. There is nothing more. I am under infinite obligations, sir; they shall be remembered. Adieu!"

The two parted; which should I pursue? In desperation I turned my lantern upon one, and illumined a face fresh with color, whose black eyes sparkled askance after the retreating figure, under straight black brows. In a moment more he was lost in a false *cul-de-sac*, and I found it impossible to trace the other.

I was scarcely better off than before; but it seemed to me that I had obtained something, and that now it was wisest to work this vein. " The butler of Madame ——." There were hundreds of thousands of Madames in town. I might call on all, and be as old as the Wandering Jew at the last call. The cellar. Wine-cellar, of course, — that came by a natural connection with butler, — but whose? There was one under my own abode; certainly I would explore it. Meanwhile, let us see the entertainments for Wednesday. The Prefect had a list of these. For some I found I had cards; I determined to allot a fraction of time to as many as possible; my friends in the Secret Service would divide the labor. Among others, Madame de St. Cyr gave a dinner, and, as she had been in the affair, I determined not to neglect her on this occasion, although having no definite idea of what had been, or plan of what should be done. I decided not to speak of this occurrence to Hay, since it might only bring him off some trail that he had struck.

Having been provided with keys, early on the following evening I entered the wine-cellar, and, concealed in an empty cask that would have held a dozen of me, waited for something to turn up. Really, when I think of myself, a diplomate, a courtier, a man-about-town, curled in a dusty, musty wine-barrel, I am moved with vexation and laughter. Nothing, however, turned up, — and at length I retired baffled. The next night came, — no news, no identification of my black-browed man, no success; but I felt certain that something must transpire in that cellar. I don't know why I had pitched upon that one in particular, but, at an earlier hour than on the previous night, I again donned the cask. A long time must have elapsed; dead silence filled the spacious vaults, except where now

and then some Sillery cracked the air with a quick explo-
sion, or some newer wine bubbled round the bung of its
barrel with a faint effervescence. I had no intention of
leaving this place till morning, but it suddenly appeared
like the most woful waste of time. The master of this
tremendous affair should be abroad and active; who
knew what his keen eyes might detect; what loss his
absence might occasion in this nick of time? And here
he was, shut up and locked in a wine-cellar! I began to
be very nervous; I had already, with aid, searched every
crevice of the cellar; and now I thought it would be
some consolation to discover the thief, if I never regained
the diamond. A distant clock tolled midnight. There
was a faint noise, — a mouse? — no, it was too prolonged; — nor did it sound like the fiz of Champagne; —
a great iron door was turning on its hinges; a man with
a lantern was entering; another followed, and another.
They seated themselves. In a few moments, appearing
one by one and at intervals, some thirty people were in
the cellar. Were they all to share in the proceeds of the
diamond? With what jaundiced eyes we behold things!
I myself saw all that was only through the lens of this
diamond, of which not one of these men had ever heard.
As the lantern threw its feeble glimmer on this group,
and I surveyed them through my loophole, I thought I
had never seen so wild and savage a picture, such enormous shadows, such bold outline, such a startling flash on
the face of their leader, such light retreating up the
threatening arches. More resolute brows, more determined words, more unshrinking hearts, I had not met.
In fact, I found myself in the centre of a conspiracy, a
society as vindictive as the Jacobins, as unknown and
terrible as the Marianne of to-day. I was thunderstruck,

too, at the countenances on which the light fell, — men
the loyalest in estimation, ministers and senators, million-
naires who had no reason for discontent, dandies whose
reason was supposed to be devoted to their tailors, poets
and artists of generous aspiration and suspected tendencies, and one woman, — Delphine de St. Cyr.   Their
plans were brave, their determination lofty, their con-
clave serious and fine; yet as slowly they shut up their
hopes and fears in the black masks, one man bent toward
the lantern to adjust his.   When he lifted his face before
concealing it, I recognized him also.   I had met him
frequently at the Bureau of Police; he was, I believe,
Secretary of the Secret Service.

I had no sympathy with these people.   I had sufficient
liberty myself, I was well enough satisfied with the
world, I did not care to revolutionize France; but my
heart rebelled at the mockery, as this traitor and spy,
this creature of a system by which I gained my fame,
showed his revolting face and veiled it again.   And Delphine, what had she to do with them?   One by one, as
they entered, they withdrew, and I was left alone again.
But all this was not my diamond.

Another hour elapsed.   Again the door opened, and
remained ajar.   Some one entered, whom I could not
see.   There was a pause, — then a rustle, — the door
creaked ever so little.   "Art thou there?" lisped a
shrill whisper, — a woman, as I could guess.

"My angel, it is I," was returned, a semitone lower.
She approached, he advanced, and the consequence was
a salute resonant as the smack with which a Dutch bur-
gomaster may be supposed to set down his mug.   I was
prepared for anything.   Ye gods! if it should be Delphine!   But the base suspicion was birth-strangled as

they spoke again. The conversation which now ensued between these lovers under difficulties was tender and affecting beyond expression. I had felt guilty enough when an unwilling auditor of the conspirators, — since, though one employs spies, one does not therefore act that part one's self, but on emergencies, — an unwillingness which would not, however, prevent my turning to advantage the information gained; but here, to listen to this rehearsal of woes and blisses, this *ah mon Fernand*, this aria in an area, growing momently more fervent, was too much. I overturned the cask, scrambled upon my feet, and fled from the cellar, leaving the astounded lovers to follow, while, agreeably to my instincts, and regardless of the diamond, I escaped the embarrassing predicament.

At length it grew to be noon of the appointed day. Nothing had transpired; all our labor was idle. I felt, nevertheless, more buoyant than usual, — whether because I was now to put my fate to the test, or that to-day was the one of which my black-browed man had spoken, and I therefore entertained a presentiment of good fortune, I cannot say. But when, in unexceptionable toilet, I stood on Mme. de St. Cyr's steps, my heart sunk. G. was doubtless already within, and I thought of the *marchand des armures'* exclamation, "Queen of Heaven, Monsieur! how shall I meet him!" I was plunged at once into the profoundest gloom. Why had I undertaken the business at all? This interference, this good-humor, this readiness to oblige, — it would ruin me yet! I forswore it, as Falstaff forswore honor. Why needed I to meddle in the *mêlée?* Why — But I was no catechumen. Questions were useless now. My emotions are not chronicled on my face, I flatter myself; and with my usual repose I saluted our hostess. Greeting G.

without any allusion to the diamond, the absence of which allusion he received as a point of etiquette, I was conversing with Mrs. Leigh, when the Baron Stahl was announced. I turned to look at his Excellency. A glance electrified me. There was my dark-browed man of the midnight streets. It must, then, have been concerning the diamond that I had heard him speak. His countenance, his eager glittering eye, told that to-day was as eventful to him as to me. If he were here, I could well afford to be. As he addressed me in English, my certainty was confirmed; and the instant in which I observed the ring, gaudy and coarse, upon his finger, made confirmation doubly sure. I own I was surprised that anything could induce the Baron to wear such an ornament. Here he was actually risking his reputation as a man of taste, as an exquisite, a leader of *haut ton*, a gentleman, by the detestable vulgarity of this ring. But why do I speak so of the trinket? Do I not owe it a thrill of as fine joy as I ever knew? Faith! it was not unfamiliar to me. It had been a daily sight for years. In meeting the Baron Stahl I had found the diamond.

The Baron Stahl was, then, the thief? Not at all. My valet, as of course you have been all along aware, was the thief.

My valet, moreover, was my instructor; he taught me not again to scour Cathay for what might be lying under my hand at home. Nor have I since been so acute as to overreach myself. Yet I can explain such intolerable stupidity only by remembering that when one has been in the habit of pointing his telescope at the stars, he is not apt to turn it upon pebbles at his feet.

The Marquis of G. took down Mme. de St. Cyr; Stahl preceded me, with Delphine. As we sat at table, G. was at the right, I at the left of our hostess. Next G. sat Delphine; below her, the Baron; so that we were nearly vis-a-vis. I was now as fully convinced that Mme. de St. Cyr's cellar was the one, as the day before I had been that the other was; I longed to reach it. Hay had given the stone to a butler — doubtless this — the moment of its theft; but, not being aware of Mme. de St. Cyr's previous share in the adventure, had probably not afforded her another. And thus I concluded her to be ignorant of the game we were about to play; and I imagined, with the interest that one carries into a romance, the little preliminary scene between the Baron and Madame that must have already taken place, being charmed by the cheerfulness with which she endured the loss of the promised reward.

As the Baron entered the dining-room, I saw him withdraw his glove, and move the jewelled hand across his hair while passing the solemn butler, who gave it a quick recognition; — the next moment we were seated. There were only wines on the table, clustered around a central ornament, — a bunch of tall silver rushes and flag-leaves, on whose airy tip danced fleurs-de-lis of frosted silver, a design of Delphine's, — the dishes being on side-tables, from which the guests were served as they signified their choice of the variety on their cards. Our number not being large, and the custom so informal, rendered it pleasant.

I had just finished my oysters and was pouring out a glass of Chablis, when another plate was set before the Baron.

"His Excellency has no salt," murmured the butler, — at the same time placing one beside him. A glance, at entrance, had taught me that most of the service was uni-

5 *

form; this dainty little *salière* I had noticed on the buffet, solitary, and unlike the others. What a fool had I been! Those gaps in the Baron's remarks caused by the paving-stones, how easily were they to be supplied!

"Madame?"

Madame de St. Cyr.

"The cellar?"

A salt-cellar.

How quick the flash that enlightened me while I surveyed the *salière!*

"It is exquisite! Am I never to sit at your table but some new device charms me?" I exclaimed. "Is it your design, Mademoiselle?" I said, turning to Delphine.

Delphine, who had been ice to all the Baron's advances, only curled her lip. "*Des babioles!*" she said.

"Yes, indeed!" cried Mme. de St. Cyr, extending her hand for it. "But none the less her taste. Is it not a fairy thing? A Cellini! Observe this curve, these lines! but one man could have drawn them!" — and she held it for our scrutiny. It was a tiny hand and arm of ivory, parting the foam of a wave and holding a golden shell, in which the salt seemed to have crusted itself as if in some secretest ocean-hollow. I looked at the Baron a moment; his eyes were fastened upon the *salière*, and all the color had forsaken his cheeks, — his face counted his years. The diamond was in that little shell. But how to obtain it? I had no novice to deal with; nothing but *finesse* would answer.

"Permit me to examine it?" I said. She passed it to her left hand for me to take. The butler made a step forward.

"Meanwhile, Madame," said the Baron, smiling, "I have no salt."

The instinct of hospitality prevailed; — she was about to return it. Might I do an awkward thing? Unhesitatingly. Reversing my glass, I gave my arm a wider sweep than necessary, and, as it met her hand with violence, the *salière* fell. Before it touched the floor I caught it. There was still a pinch of salt left, — nothing more.

"A thousand pardons!" I said, and restored it to the Baron.

His Excellency beheld it with dismay; it was rare to see him bend over and scrutinize it with starting eyes.

"Do you find there what Count Arnaldos begs in the song," asked Delphine, — "the secret of the sea, Monsieur?"

He handed it to the butler, observing, "I find here no — "

"Salt, Monsieur?" replied the man, who did not doubt but all had gone right, and replenished it.

Had one told me in the morning that no intricate manœuvres, but a simple blunder, would effect this, I might have met him in the Bois de Boulogne.

"We will not quarrel," said my neighbor, lightly, with reference to the popular superstition.

"Rather propitiate the offended deities by a crumb tossed over the shoulder," added I.

"Over the left?" asked the Baron, to intimate his knowledge of another idiom, together with a reproof for my *gaucherie*.

"*À gauche, — quelquefois c'est justement à droit,*" I replied.

"Salt in any pottage," said Madame, a little uneasily, "is like surprise in an individual; it brings out the flavor of every ingredient, so my cook tells me."

"It is a preventive of palsy," I remarked, as the slight trembling of my adversary's finger caught my eye.

"And I have noticed that a taste for it is peculiar to those who trace their blood," continued Madame.

"Let us, therefore, elect a deputation to those mines near Cracow," said Delphine.

"To our cousins, the slaves there?" laughed her mother.

"I must vote to lay your bill on the table, Mademoiselle," I rejoined.

"But with a *boule blanche*, Monsieur?"

"As the salt has been laid on the floor," said the Baron.

Meanwhile, as this light skirmishing proceeded, my sleeve and Mme. de St. Cyr's dress were slightly powdered, but I had not seen the diamond. The Baron, bolder than I, looked under the table, but made no discovery. I was on the point of dropping my napkin to accomplish a similar movement, when my accommodating neighbor dropped hers. To restore it, I stooped. There it lay, large and glowing, the Sea of Splendor, the Moon of Milk, the Torment of my Life, on the carpet, within half an inch of a lady's slipper. Mademoiselle de St. Cyr's foot had prevented the Baron from seeing it; now it moved and unconsciously covered it. All was as I wished. I hastily restored the napkin, and looked steadily at Delphine, — so steadily, that she perceived some meaning, as she had already suspected a game. By my sign she understood me, pressed her foot upon the stone and drew it nearer. In France we do not remain at table until unfit for a lady's society, — we rise with them. Delphine needed to drop neither napkin nor handkerchief; she composedly stooped and picked up the stone, so quickly that no one saw what it was.

"And the diamond?" said the Baron to the butler, rapidly, as he passed.

"It was in the *salière!*" whispered the astonished creature.

In the drawing-room I sought the Marquis.

"To-day I was to surrender you your property," I said ; "it is here."

"Do you know," he replied, "I thought I must have been mistaken?"

"Any of our volatile friends here might have been," I resumed ; "for us it is impossible. Concerning this, when you return to France, I will relate the incidents ; at present, there are those who will not hesitate to take life to obtain its possession. A conveyance leaves in twenty minutes ; and if I owned the diamond, it should not leave me behind. Moreover, who knows what a day may bring forth? To-morrow there may be an *émeute*. Let me restore the thing as you withdraw."

The Marquis, who is not, after all, the Lion of England, pausing a moment to transmit my words from his ear to his brain, did not afterward delay to make inquiries or adieux, but went to seek Mme. de St. Cyr and wish her good-night, on his departure from Paris. As I awaited his return, which I knew would not be immediate, Delphine left the Baron and joined me.

"You beckoned me?" she asked.

"No, I did not."

"Nevertheless, I come by your desire, I am sure."

"Mademoiselle," I said, "I am not in the custom of doing favors ; I have forsworn them. But before you return me my jewel, I risk my head and render one last one, and to you."

" Do not, Monsieur, at such price," she responded, with a slight mocking motion of her hand.

" Delphine! those resolves, last night, in the cellar, were daring, they were noble, yet they were useless."

She had not started, but a slight tremor ran over her person and vanished while I spoke.

"They will be allowed to proceed no farther,—the axe is sharpened; for the last man who adjusted his mask was a spy,—was the Secretary of the Secret Service."

Delphine could not have grown paler than was usual with her of late. She flashed her eye upon me.

" He was, it may be, Monsieur himself," she said.

" I do not claim the honor of that post."

" But you were there, nevertheless,—a spy!"

" Hush, Delphine! It would be absurd to quarrel. I was there for the recovery of this stone, having heard that it was in a cellar,—which, stupidly enough, I had insisted should be a wine-cellar."

" It was, then—"

" In a salt-cellar,—a blunder which, as you do not speak English, you cannot comprehend. I never mix with treason, and did not wish to assist at your pastimes. I speak now, that you may escape."

" If Monsieur betrays his friends, the police, why should I expect a kinder fate?"

" When I use the police, they are my servants, not my friends. I simply warn you, that, before sunrise, you will be safer travelling than sleeping,—safer next week in Vienna than in Paris."

" Thank you! And the intelligence is the price of the diamond? If I had not chanced to pick it up, my throat," and she clasped it with her fingers, " had been no slenderer than the others?"

"Delphine, will you remember, should you have occasion to do so in Vienna, that it is just possible for an Englishman to have affections, and sentiments, and, in fact, sensations? that, with him, friendship can be inviolate, and to betray it an impossibility? And even were it not, I, Mademoiselle, have not the pleasure to be classed by you as a friend."

"You err. I esteem Monsieur highly."

I was impressed by her coolness.

"Let me see if you comprehend the matter," I demanded.

"Perfectly. The arrest will be used to-night, the guillotine to-morrow."

"You will take immediate measures for flight?"

"No,—I do not see that life has value. I shall be the debtor of him who takes it."

"A large debt. Delphine, I exact a promise of you. I do not care to have endangered myself for nothing. It is not worth while to make your mother unhappy. Life is not yours to throw away. I appeal to your magnanimity."

"'Affections, sentiments, sensations!'" she quoted. "Your own danger for the affection,—it is an affair of the heart! Mme. de St. Cyr's unhappiness,—there is the sentiment. You are angry, Monsieur,—that must be the sensation."

"Delphine, I am waiting."

"Ah, well. You have mentioned Vienna,—and why? Liberals are countenanced there?"

"Not in the least. But Madame l'Ambassadrice will be countenanced."

"I do not know her."

"We are not apt to know ourselves."

"Monsieur, how idle are these cross-purposes!" she said, folding her fan.

"Delphine," I continued, taking the fan, "tell me frankly which of these two men you prefer,—the Marquis or his Excellency."

"The Marquis? He is antiphlogistic,—he is ice. Why should I freeze myself? I am frozen now,—I need fire!"

Her eyes burned as she spoke, and a faint red flushed her cheek.

"Mademoiselle, you demonstrate to me that life has yet a value to you."

"I find no fire," she said, as the flush fell away.

"The Baron?"

"I do not affect him."

"You will conquer your prejudice in Vienna."

"I do not comprehend you, Monsieur;—you speak in riddles, which I do not like."

"I will speak plainer. But first let me ask you for the diamond."

"The diamond? It is yours? How am I certified of it? I find it on the floor; you say it was in my mother's *salière;* it is her affair, not mine. No, Monsieur, I do not see that the thing is yours."

Certainly there was nothing to be done but to relate the story, which I did, carefully omitting the Baron's name. At its conclusion, she placed the prize in my hand.

"Pardon, Monsieur," she said; "without doubt you should receive it. And this agent of the government,— one could turn him like hot iron in this vice,— who was he?"

"The Baron Stahl."

All this time G. had been waiting on thorns, and, leaving her now, I approached him, displayed for an instant the treasure on my palm, and slipped it into his. It was done. I bade farewell to this Eye of Morning and Heart of Day, this thing that had caused me such pain and perplexity and pleasure, with less envy and more joy than I thought myself capable of. The relief and buoyancy that seized me, as his hand closed upon it, I shall not attempt to portray. An abdicated king was not freer.

The Marquis departed, and I, wandering round the *salon*, was next stranded upon the Baron. He was yet hardly sure of himself. We talked indifferently for a few moments, and then I ventured on the great loan. He was, as became him, not communicative, but scarcely thought it would be arranged. I then spoke of Delphine.

" She is superb ! " said the Baron, staring at her boldly.

She stood opposite, and, in her white attire on the background of the blue curtain, appeared like an impersonation of Greek genius relieved upon the blue of an Athenian heaven. Her severe and classic outline, her pallor, her downcast lids, her absorbed look, only heightened the resemblance. Her reverie seemed to end abruptly, the same red stained her cheek again, her lips curved in a proud smile, she raised her glowing eyes and observed us regarding her. At too great distance to hear our words, she quietly repaid our glances in the strength of her new decision, and then, turning, began to entertain those next her with an unwonted spirit.

" She has needed," I replied to the Baron, "but one thing, — to be aroused, to be kindled. See, it is done ! I have thought that a life of cabinets and policy might

u

achieve this, for her talent is second not even to her beauty."

"It is unhappy that both should be wasted," said the Baron. "She, of course, will never marry."

"Why not?"

"For various reasons."

"One?"

"She is poor."

"Which will not signify to your Excellency. Another?"

"She is too beautiful. One would fall in love with her. And to love one's own wife — it is ridiculous!"

"Who should know?" I asked.

"All the world would suspect and laugh."

"Let those laugh that win."

"No, — she would never do as a wife; but then as —"

"But then in France we do not insult hospitality!"

The Baron transferred his gaze to me for a moment, then tapped his snuff-box, and approached the circle round Delphine.

It was odd that we, the arch enemies of the hour, could speak without the intervention of seconds; but I hoped that the Baron's conversation might be diverting, — the Baron hoped that mine might be didactic.

They were very gay with Delphine. He leaned on the back of a chair and listened. One spoke of the new gallery of the Tuileries, and the five pavilions, — a remark which led us to architecture.

"We all build our own houses," said Delphine, at last, "and then complain that they cramp us here, and the wind blows in there, while the fault is not in the order, but in us, who increase here and shrink there without reason."

"You speak in metaphors," said the Baron.

" Precisely. A truth is often more visible veiled than nude."

" We should soon exhaust the orders," I interposed; " for who builds like his neighbor? "

" Slight variations, Monsieur! Though we take such pains to conceal the style, it is not difficult to tell the order of architecture chosen by the builders in this room. My mother, for instance, — you perceive that her pavilion would be the florid Gothic."

" Mademoiselle's is the Doric," I said.

" Has been," she murmured, with a quick glance.

" And mine, Mademoiselle? " asked the Baron, indifferently.

" Ah, Monsieur," she returned, looking serenely upon him, " when one has all the winning cards in hand and yet loses the stake, we allot him *un pavillon chinois*," — which was the polite way of dubbing him Court Fool.

The Baron's eyes fell. Vexation and alarm were visible on his contracted brow. He stood in meditation for some time. It must have been evident to him that Delphine knew of the recent occurrences, — that here in Paris she could denounce him as the agent of a felony, the participant of a theft. What might prevent it? Plainly but one thing: no woman would denounce her husband. He had scarcely contemplated this step on arrival.

The guests were again scattered in groups round the room. I examined an engraving on an adjacent table. Delphine reclined as lazily in a *fauteuil* as if her life did not hang in the balance. The Baron drew near.

" Mademoiselle," said he, " you allotted me just now a cap and bells. If two should wear it? — if I should invite another into my *pavillon chinois*? — if I should propose to complete an alliance, desired by my father, with the ancient family of St. Cyr? — if, in short, Mademoiselle, I should request you to become my wife?"

" *Eh, bien, Monsieur,* — and if you should?" I heard her coolly reply.

But it was no longer any business of mine. I rose and sought Mme. de St. Cyr, who, I thought, was slightly uneasy, perceiving some mystery to be afloat. After a few words, I retired.

Archimedes, as perhaps you have never heard, needed only a lever to move the world. Such a lever I had put into the hands of Delphine, with which she might move, not indeed the grand globe, with its multiplied attractions, relations, and affinities, but the lesser world of circumstances, of friends and enemies, the circle of hopes, fears, ambitions. There is no woman, as I believe, but could have used it.

The next day was scarcely so quiet in the city as usual. The great loan had not been negotiated. Both the Baron Stahl and the English minister had left Paris, — and there was a *coup d'état.*

But the Baron did not travel alone. There had been a ceremony at midnight in the Church of St. Sulpice, and her Excellency the Baroness Stahl, *née* de St. Cyr, accompanied him.

It is a good many years since. I have seen the diamond in the Duchess of X.'s coronet, once, when a young queen put on her royalty, — but I have never seen Delphine. The Marquis begged me to retain the chain, and I gave myself the pleasure of presenting it, through her mother, to the Baroness Stahl. I hear, that, whenever she desires to effect any cherished object which the Baron opposes, she has only to wear this chain, and effect it. It appears to possess a magical power, and its potent spell enslaves the Baron as the lamp and ring of Eastern tales enslaved the Afrites. The life she leads has aroused her. She is no longer the impassive Silence; she has found her fire. I hear of her as the charm of a brilliant court, as the soul of a nation of intrigue. Of her beauty one does not speak, but her talent is called prodigious. What impels me to ask the idle question, If it were well to save her life for this? Undoubtedly she fills a station which, in that empire, must be the summit of a woman's ambition. Delphine's Liberty was not a principle, but a dissatisfaction. The Baroness Stahl is vehement, is Imperialist, is successful. While she lives, it is on the top of the wave; when she dies — ah! what business has Death in such a world?

As I said, I have never seen Delphine since her marriage. The beautiful statuesque girl occupies a niche into which the blazing and magnificent *intrigante* cannot crowd. I do not wish to be disillusioned. She has read me a riddle, — Delphine is my Sphinx.

As for Mr. Hay, — I once said the Antipodes were tributary to me, not thinking that I should ever become tributary to the Antipodes. But such is the case; since, partly through my instrumentality, that enterprising individual has been located in their vicinity, where diamonds are not to be had for the asking, and the greatest rogue is not a Baron.

Knitting Sale-Socks.

KNITTING SALE-SOCKS.

"HE 'S took 'ith all the sym't'ms, — thet 's one thing sure! Dretful pain in hez back an' l'ins, legs feel 's ef they hed telegraph-wires inside 'em workin' fur dear life, head aches, face fevered, pulse at 2.40, awful stetch in the side, an' pressed fur breath. You guess it 's neuralogy, Lurindy? I do'no' nothing abeout yer high-flyin' names fur rheumatiz. *I* don't guess so!"

"But, Aunt Mimy, what *do* you guess?" asked mother.

"I don' guess nothin' at all, — I nigh abeout know!"

"Well, — you don't think it 's — "

"I on'y wish it mebbe the veryaloud, — I on'y wish it mebbe. But that 's tew good luck ter happen ter one o' the name. No, Miss Ruggles, I — think — it 's — the raal article at first hand."

"Goodness, Aunt Mimy! what — "

"Yes, I du; an' you 'll all hev it stret through the femily, every one; you need n't expect ter go scot-free, Emerline, 'ith all your rosy cheeks; an' you 'll all hev ter stay in canteen a month ter the least; an' ef you 're none o' yer pertected by vaticination, I reckon I — "

"Well, Aunt Mimy, if that 's your opinion, I 'll harness the filly and drive over for Dr. Sprague."

"Lor'! yer no need ter du *thet*, Miss Ruggles, — I kin kerry yer all through jest uz well uz Dr. Sprague, an' a sight better, ef the truth wuz knowed. I tuk Miss Deacon Smiler an' her hull femily through the measles an' hoopin'-cough, like a parcel o' pigs, this fall. — They *do* say Jane's in a poor way an' Nathan'l's kind o' declinin'; but, uz I know they say it jest ter spite me, I don' so much mind. You *a'n't* gwine now, be ye?"

"There's safety in a multitude of counsellors, you know, Aunt Mimy, and I think on the whole I had best."

"Wal! ef that's yer delib'rate ch'ice betwixt Dr. Sprague an' me, ye kin du ez ye like. I never force my advice on no one, 'xcept this, — I'd advise Emerline there ter throw them socks inter the fire; there'll never none o' them be fit ter sell, 'nless she wants ter spread the disease. Wal, I'm sorry yer've concluded ter hev thet old quack Sprague; never hed no more diplomy 'n me; don' b'lieve he knows cow-pox from kine, when he sees it. The poor young man's hed his last well day, I'm afeard. Good-day ter ye; say good-by fur me ter Stephen. I'll call ag'in, ef ye happen ter want any one to lay him eout."

And, staying to light her little black pipe, she jerked together the strings of her great scarlet hood, wrapped her cloak round her like a sentinel at muster, and went puffing down the hill like a steamboat.

Aunt Mimy Ruggles was n't any relation to us, I would n't have you think, though our name was Ruggles, too. Aunt Mimy used to sell herbs, and she rose from that to taking care of the sick, and so on, till once Dr. Sprague having proved that death came through her ignorance, she had to abandon some branches of her art; and she was generally roaming round the neighborhood, seeking whom she could devour in the others. And so she came into our house just at dinner-time, and mother asked her to sit by, and then mentioned Cousin Stephen, and she went up to see him, and so it was.

Now it can't be pleasant for any family to have such a thing turn up, especially if there's a pretty girl in it; and I suppose I was as pretty as the general run, at that time, — perhaps Cousin Stephen thought a trifle prettier; pink cheeks, blue eyes, and hair the color and shine of a chestnut when it bursts the burr, can't be had without one's rather pleasant-looking; and then I'm very good-natured and quick-tempered, and I've got a voice for singing, and I sing in the choir, and a'n't afraid to open my mouth. I don't look much like Lurindy, to be sure; but then Lurindy's an old maid, — as much as twenty-five, — and don't go to singing-school. — At least, these thoughts ran through my head as I watched Aunt Mimy down the hill. — Lurindy a'n't so very pretty, I continued to think, — but she's so very good, it makes up. At sewing-circle and quilting and frolics, I'm as good as any; but somehow I'm never any 'count at home; that's because Lurindy is by, at home. Well, Lurindy has a little box in her drawer, and there's a letter in it, and an old geranium-leaf, and a piece of black silk ribbon that looks too broad for anything but a sailor's necktie, and a shell. I don't know what she wants to keep such old stuff for, I'm sure.

We were none so rich, — I suppose I may as well tell the truth, that we were nearly as poor as poor can be. We'd the farm, but it's such a small one that mother and I could carry it on ourselves, with now and then a day's help or a bee, — but a bee's about as broad as it is long, — and we raised just enough to help the year out, but did n't sell. We had a cow and the filly and some sheep;

and mother sheared and carded, and Lurindy spun, — I
can't spin, it makes my head swim, — and I knit, knit
socks and sold them.   Sometimes I had needles almost
as big as a pipe-stem, and chose the coarse, uneven yarn
of the tags, and then the work went off like machinery.
Why, I can knit two pair, and sometimes three, a day,
and get just as much for them as I do for the nice ones, —
they're warm.   But when I want to knit well, as I did
the day Aunt Mimy was in, I take my best blue needles
and my fine white yarn from the long wool, and it keeps
me from daybreak till sundown to knit one pair.   I don't
know why Aunt Jemimy should have said what she did
about my socks; I'm sure Stephen hadn't been any
nearer them than he had to the cabbage-bag Lurindy was
netting, and there wasn't such a nice knitter in town as
I, everybody will tell you.   She always did seem to take
particular pleasure in hectoring and badgering me to
death.

Well, I wasn't going to be put down by Aunt Mimy,
so I made the needles fly while mother was gone for the
doctor.   By and by I heard a knock up in Stephen's
room, — I suppose he wanted something, — but Lurindy
didn't hear it, and I didn't so much want to go, so I sat
still and began to count out loud the stitches to my narrowings.   By and by he knocked again.

"Lurindy," says I, "a'n't that Steve a-knocking?"

"Yes," says she, — "why don't you go?" — for I had
been tending him a good deal that day.

"Well," says I, "there's a number of reasons; one is,
I'm just binding off my heel."

Lurindy looked at me a minute, then all at once she
smiled.

"Well, Emmy," says she, "if you like a smooth skin

more than a smooth conscience, you're welcome," — and went up-stairs herself.

I suppose I had ought to 'a' gone, and I suppose I'd ought to wanted to have gone, but somehow it was n't so much fear as that I did n't want to see Stephen himself now. So Lurindy stayed up chamber, and was there when mother and the doctor come. And the doctor said he feared Aunt Mimy was right, and nobody but mother and Lurindy must go near Stephen, (you see, he found Lurindy there,) and they must have as little communication with me as possible. And his boots creaked down the back-stairs, and then he went.

Mother came down a little while after, for some water to put on Stephen's head, which was a good deal worse, she said; and about the middle of the evening I heard her crying for me to come and help them hold him, — he was raving. I did n't go very quick; I said, " Yes, — just as soon as I've narrowed off my toe." And when at last I pushed back my chair to go, mother called in a disapproving voice, and said that they'd got along without me and I'd better go to bed.

Well, after I was in bed I began to remember all that had happened lately. Somehow my thoughts went back to the first time Cousin Stephen came to our place, when I was a real little girl, and mother'd sent me to the well and I had dropped the bucket in, and he ran straight down the green slippery stones and brought it up, laughing. Then I remembered how we'd birds-nested together, and nutted, and come home on the hay-carts, and how we'd been in every kind of fun and danger together; and how, when my new Portsmouth lawn took fire, at Martha Smith's apple-paring, he caught me right in his arms and squeezed out the fire with his own hands; and how, when

he saw once I had a notion of going with Elder Hooper's
son James, he stepped aside till I saw what a nincom Jim
Hooper was, and then he appeared as if nothing had happened, and was just as good as ever ; and how, when the
ice broke on Deacon Smith's pond, and I fell in, and the
other boys were all afraid, Steve came and saved my life
again at risk of his own ; and how he always seemed to
think the earth was n't good enough for me to walk on ;
and how I 'd wished, time and again, I might have some
way to pay him back ; and here it was, and I 'd failed
him.   Then I remembered how I 'd been to his place in
Berkshire, — a rich old farm, with an orchard that smelled
like the Spice Islands in the geography, with apples and
pears and quinces and peaches and cherries and plums, —
and how Stephen's mother, Aunt Emeline, had been as
kind to me as one's own mother could be.   But now Aunt
Emeline and Uncle 'Siah were dead, and Stephen came a
good deal oftener over the border than he 'd any right to.
To-day, he brought some of those new red-streaks, and
wanted mother to try them ; next time, they 'd made a
lot more maple-sugar on his place than he wanted ; and
next time, he thought mother's corn might need hoeing,
or it was fine weather to get the grass in : I don't know
what we should have done without him.   Then I thought
how Stephen looked, the day he was pall-bearer to Charles
Payson, who was killed sudden by a fall, — so solemn
and pale, nowise craven, but just up to the occasion, so
that, when the other girls burst out crying at sight of the
coffin and at thought of Charlie, I cried, too, — but it was
only because Stephen looked so beautiful.   Then I remembered how he looked the other day when he came,
his cheeks were so red with the wind, and his hair, those
bright curls, was all blown about, and he laughed with

the great hazel eyes he has, and showed his white
teeth; — and now his beauty would be spoiled, and
he 'd never care for me again, seeing I had n't cared
for him. And the wind began to come up; and it was
so lonesome and desolate in that little bed-room down
stairs, I felt as if we were all buried alive; and I
could n't get to sleep; and when the sleet and snow
began to rattle on the pane, I thought there was n't
any one to see me and I 'd better cry to keep it company; and so I sobbed off to dreaming at last, and woke
at sunrise and found it still snowing.

Next morning, I heard mother stepping across the
kitchen, and when I came out, she said Lurindy 'd just
gone to sleep; they 'd had a shocking night. So I went
and watered the creatures and milked Brindle, and got
mother a nice little breakfast, and made Stephen some
gruel. And then I was going to ask mother if I 'd done
so very wrong in letting Lurindy nurse Stephen, instead
of me; and then I saw she was n't thinking about that;
and besides, there did n't really seem to be any reason
why she should n't; — she was a great deal older than I,
and so it was more proper; and then Stephen had n't
ever *said* anything to me that should give me a peculiar
right to nurse him more than other folks. So I just
cleared away the things, made everything shine like a
pin, and took my knitting. I 'd no sooner got the seam
set than I was called to send something up on a contriv-
ance mother 'd rigged in the back-entry over a pulley.
And then I had to make a red flag, and find a stick, and
hang it out of the window by which there were the most
passers. Well, I did it; but I did n't hurry, — I did n't
get the flag out-till afternoon; somehow I hated to, it always seemed such a low-lived disease, and I was mortified

to acknowledge it, and I knew nobody 'd come near us for
so long, — though goodness knows I did n't want to see
anybody. Well, when that was done, Lurindy came
down, and I had to get her something to eat, and then
she went up-stairs, and mother took *her* turn for some
sleep; and there were the creatures to feed again, and
what with putting on, and taking off, and tending fires,
and doing errands, and the night's milking, and clearing
the paths, I did n't knit another stitch that day, and was
glad enough, when night came, to go to bed myself.

Well, so we went on for two or three days. I 'd got
my second sock pretty well along in that time, — just
think! half a week knitting half a sock! — and was setting the heel, when in came Aunt Mimy.

"I ain't afeard on it," says she; "don't you be skeert.
I jest stepped in ter see ef the young man wuz approachin' his eend."

"No," said I, "he is n't, any more than you are, Aunt
Mimy."

"Any more 'n I be?" she answered. "Don't you lose
yer temper, Emerline. We 're all approachin' it, but some
gits a leetle ahead; it ain't no disgrace, ez I knows on.
What yer doin' of? Knittin' sale-socks yet? and, my
gracious! still ter work on the same pair! You 'll make
yer fortin', Emerline!"

I did n't say anything, I was so provoked.

"I don' b'lieve you know heow ter take the turns w'en
yer mother a'n't by to help," she continued. "Can't ye
take up the heel? Widden ev'ry fourth. Here, let me!
You won't? Wal, I alluz knowed you wuz mighty techy,
Emerline Ruggles, but ye no need to fling away in thet
style. Neow I 'll advise ye ter let socks alone; they 're
tew intricate fur sech ez you. Mitt'ns is jest abeout

'ithin the compass uv your mind, — mitt'ns, men's single
mitt'ns, put up on needles larger 'n them o' yourn be, an'
by this rule. Seventeen reounds in the wrist, — tew an'
one 's the best seam — "

"Now, Miss Jemimy, just as if I did n't know how to
knit mittens ! "

"Wal, it seems you don't," said she, "though I don'
deny but you may know heow ter give 'em ; an' ez I alluz
like ter du w'at good I kin, I 'm gwine ter show ye."

"Show away," says I ; "but I 'll be bound, I 've knit
and sold and eaten up more mittens than ever you put
your hands in ! "

"Du tell ! I 'm glad to ha' heern you 've got such a
good digestion," says she, hunting up a piece of paper to
light her pipe. "Wal, ez I wuz sayin'," says she, "tew
an' one 's the best seam, handiest an' 'lastickest ; twenty
stetches to a needle, cast up so loose thet the fust one 's
ter one eend uv the needle an' the last ter t' other eend, —
thet gives a good pull."

"I guess your smoke will hurt Stephen's head," said I,
thinking to change her ideas.

"Oh, don't you bother abeout Stephen's head ; ef it
can 't stan' thet, 't ain't good for much. Wal, an' then
you set yer thumb an' knit plain, 'xcept a seam-stetch
each side uv yer thumb ; an' you widden tew stetches,
one each side, — s'pose ye know heow ter widden ? an'
narry ? — ev'ry third reound, tell yer 've got nineteen
stetches across yer thumb ; then ye knit, 'ithout widden-
in', a matter uv seven or eight reounds more, — you lis-
tenin', Emerline ? "

"Lor', Miss Jemimy, don't you know better than to
ask questions when I 'm counting ? Now I 've got to go
and begin all over again."

6 *

I

" Highty-tighty, Miss! You're a weak sister, ef ye can't ceount an' chat, tew. Wal, ter make a long matter short, then ye drop yer thumb onter some thread an' cast up seven stetches an' knit reound fur yer hand, an' every other time you narry them seven stetches away ter one, fur the gore."

" Dear me, Aunt Mimy! do be quiet a minute! I believe mother's a-calling."

" I'll see," said Aunt Mimy, — and she stepped to the door and listened.

" No," says she, coming back on tiptoe, — "an' you did n't think you heern any one neither. It's ruther small work fur to be foolin' an old woman. Hows'ever, I don' cherish grudges ; so, ez I wuz gwine ter say, ye knit thirty-six reounds above wheer ye dropped yer thumb, an' then ye toe off in ev'ry fifth stetch, an' du it reg'lar, Emerline; an' then take up yer thumb on tew needles, an' on t' other you pick up the stetches I told yer ter cast up, an' knit twelve reounds, an' thumb off 'ith narryin' ev'ry third —"

" Well, Miss Jemimy, I guess I shall know how to knit mittens, now!"

" Ef ye don't, 't ain't my fault. When you've fastened off the eends, you roll 'em up in a damp towel, an' press 'em 'ith a middlin' warm iron on the wrong side. There!"

After this, Miss Mimy smoked awhile in silence, satisfied and gratified. At last she knocked the ashes out of her pipe.

" Wal," says she, " I must be onter my feet. I'd liked ter seen yer ma, but I won't disturb her, an' you can du ez well. Yer ma promised me a mess o' tea, an' I guess I may ez well take it neow ez any day."

"Why, Miss Mimy," said I, "there a'n't above four or five messes left, and we can't get any more till I sell my socks."

"Wal, never mind, then, you can le' me take one, an' mebbe I kin make up the rest at Miss Smilers's."

So I went into the pantry to get it, and Aunt Mimy followed me, of course.

"Them's nice-lookin' apples," said she. "Come from Stephen's place? Poor young man, he won't never want 'em! S'pose he won't hev no objection ter my tryin' a dozen," — and she dropped that number into her great pocket.

"Nice-lookin' butter, tew," said she. "Own churnin'? Wal, you *kin* du sunthin', Emerline. W'en I wuz a heousekeeper, I used ter keep the femily in butter an' sell enough to Miss Smith, — she thet wuz Mary Breown — ter buy our shoes, all off uv one ceow. S'pose I take this pat?"

I was kind of dumfoundered at first; I forgot Aunt Mimy was the biggest beggar in Rockingham County.

"No," says I, as soon as I got my breath, "I sha'n't suppose any such thing. You're as well able to make your butter as I am to make it for you."

"Wal, Emerline Ruggles! I alluz knowed you wus close ez the bark uv a tree; it's jest yer father's narrer-contracted sperrit; you don' favor yer ma a speck. She's ez free ez water."

"If mother's a mind to give away her eye-teeth, it don't follow that I should," said I; "and I won't give you another atom; and you just clear out!"

"Wal, you kin keep yer butter, sence you're so sot on it, an' I'll take a leetle dust o' pork instead."

"Let's see you take it!" said I.

"I guess I'll speak 'ith yer ma. I shall git a consider'ble bigger piece, though I don't like ter add t' 'er
steps."

"Now look here, Miss Mimy," says I, — "if you'll
promise not to ask for another thing, and to go right
away, I'll get you a piece of pork."

So I went down cellar, and fished round in the pork-
barrel and found quite a respectable piece. Coming up,
just as my head got level with the floor, what should I
see but Miss Jemimy pour all the sugar into her bag and
whip the bowl back on the shelf, and turn round and face
me as innocent as Moses in the bulrushes. After she had
taken the pork, she looked round a minute and said, —

"Wal, arter all, I nigh upon forgot my arrant. Here's
a letter they giv' me for Lurindy, at the post-office;
ev'rybody else's afeard ter come up here." And by
and by she brought it up from under all she'd stowed
away there. "Thet jest leaves room," says she.

"For what?" says I.

"Fur tew or three uv them eggs."

I put them into her bag and said, "Now you remember your promise, Aunt Mimy!"

"Lor' sakes!" says she, "you're in a mighty herry ter
git me off. Neow you've got all you kin out uv me, the
letter, 'n' the mitt'ns, I may go, may I? I niver see a
young gal so furrard 'ith her elders in all my born days!
I think Stephen Lee's well quit uv ye, fur my part, ef he
hed to die ter du it. I don't 'xpect ye ter thank me fur
w'at instruction I gi'n ye; — there's some folks I niver
du 'xpect nothin' from; you can't make a silk pus out uv
a sow's ear. W'at ye got thet red flag out the keepin'-
room winder fur? 'Cause Lurindy's nussin' Stephen?
Wal, good-day!"

And so Aunt Mimy disappeared, and the pat of butter with her.

I called Lurindy and gave her the letter, and after a little while I heard my name, and Lurindy was sitting on the top of the stairs with her head on her knees, and mother was leaning over the banisters. Pretty soon Lurindy lifted up her head, and I saw she had been crying, and between the two I made out that Lurindy 'd been engaged a good while to John Talbot, who sailed out of Salem on long voyages to India and China; and that now he 'd come home, sick with a fever, and was lying at the house of his aunt, who was n't well herself; and as he 'd given all his money to help a shipmate in trouble, she could n't hire him a nurse, and there he was; and, finally, she 'd consider it a great favor, if Lurindy would come down and help her.

Now Lurindy 'd have gone at once, only she 'd been about Stephen, so that she 'd certainly carry the contagion, and might be taken sick herself, as soon as she arrived; and mother could n't go and take care of John, for the same reason; and there was nobody but me. Lurindy had a half-eagle that John had given her once to keep; and I got a little bundle together and took all the precautions Dr. Sprague advised; and he drove me off in his sleigh, and said, as he was going about sixteen miles to see a patient, he 'd put me on the cars at the nearest station. Well, he stopped a minute at the post-office, and when he came out he had another letter for Lurindy. I took it, and, after a moment, concluded I 'd better read it.

"What are you about?" says the doctor; "your name is n't Lurindy, is it?"

"I wish it was," says I, "and then I should n't be here."

"Oh! you're sorry to leave Stephen?" says he. "Well, you can comfort yourself with reflecting that Lurindy's a great deal the best nurse."

As if that was any comfort! If Lurinda was the best nurse, she'd ought to have had the privilege of taking care of her own lover, and not of other folks's. Besides, for all I knew, Stephen would be dead before ever I came back, and here I was going away and leaving him! Well, I didn't feel so very bright; so I read the letter. The doctor asked me what ailed John Talbot. I thought, if I told him that Miss Jane Talbot wrote now so that Lurindy shouldn't come, and that he was sick just as Stephen was, he wouldn't let me go. So I said I supposed he'd burnt his mouth, like the man in the South, eating cold pudding and porridge; men always cried out at a scratch. And he said, "Oh, do they?" and laughed.

After about two hours' driving, there came a scream as if all the panthers in Coos County were let loose to yell, and directly we stopped at a little place where a red flag was hung out. I asked the doctor if they'd got the small-pox here, too; but before he could answer, the thunder running along the ground deafened me, and in a minute he had put me inside the cars and was off.

I was determined I wouldn't appear green before so many folks, though I'd never seen the cars before; so I took my seat, and paid my fare to Old Salem, and looked about me. Pretty soon a woman came bustling in from somewhere, and took the seat beside me. There she fidgeted round so that I thought I should have flown.

"Miss," says she, at length, "will you close your window? I never travel with a window open; my health's delicate."

I tried to shut it, but it wouldn't go up or down, till a

gentleman put out his cane and touched it, and down it slid, like Signor Blitz. It did seem as if everything about the cars went by miracle. I thanked him, but I found afterward it would have been more polite not to have spoken. After that woman had done everything she could think of to plague and annoy the whole neighborhood, she got out at Ipswich, and somebody met her that looked just like our sheriff; and I should n't be a bit surprised to hear that she 'd gone to jail. When she got out, somebody else got in, and took the same seat.

"Miss," says she, "will you have the goodness to open your window ? this air is stifling."

And she did everything that the other woman did n't do. When she found I would n't talk, she turned to the young gentleman and lady that sat opposite, and that looked as if there was a great deal too much company in the cars, and found they would n't talk either, and at last she caught the conductor and made him talk.

All this while we were swooping over the country in the most terrific manner. I thought how frightened mother and Lurindy 'd be, if they should see me. It was no use trying to count the cattle or watch the fences, and the birch-trees danced rigadoons enough to make one dizzy, and we dashed through everybody's back-yard, and ran so close up to the kitchens that we could have seen what they had for dinner, if we had stayed long enough ; and finally I made up my mind that the engine had run away with the driver, and John Talbot would never have me to tend him ; and I began to wonder, as I saw the sparks and cinders and great clouds of steam and smoke, if those tornadoes that smash round so out West in the newspapers were n't just passenger-trains, like us, off the track, when all at once it grew as dark as midnight.

"Now," says I to myself, "it's certain. They've run the thing into the ground. However, we can't go long now."

And just as I was thinking about Korah and his troop, I remembered what the Doctor had told me about Salem Tunnel, and it began to grow lighter, and we began to go slower, and I picked up my wits and looked about me again. I had only time to notice that the young gentleman and lady looked very much relieved, and to shake my shawl from the clutch of the woman beside me, when we stopped at Salem, safe and sound.

I had a good deal of trouble to find Miss Talbot's house, but find it I did; and the first thing she gave me was a scolding for coming, thinking I was Lurindy, and her tongue wasn't much cooler when she found I wasn't; and then finally she said, as long as I was there, I might stay; and I went right up to see John, and a sight he was!

It was about three months I stayed and took the greater part of the care of him. Sometimes in the midnight, when he was quite beside himself, and dreaming out loud, it was about as good as a story-book to hear him. He told me of some great Indian cities where there were men in white, with skins swarthier than old red Guinea gold, and with great shawls all wrought in palm-leaves of gold and crimson bound on their heads, who could sink a ship with their lacs of rupees; and of islands where the shores came down to the water's edge and unrolled like a green ribbon, and brooks came sparkling down behind them, and great trees hung above like banners, and beautiful women came off on rafts and skiffs loaded with fruit, — the islands set like jewels on the back of the sea, and the sky covered them with light and hung above them bluer than the hang-

ings of the Tabernacle, and they sent long rivers of spice
out on the air to entice the sailor back, — islands where
night never came. Sometimes, when he talked on so, I
remembered that I'd felt rather touched up when I found
that Lurindy 'd had a sweetheart all this time, and mother
knew it, and they'd never told me, and I wondered how
it happened. Now it came across me, that, quite a number of years before, Lurindy had gone to Salem and
worked in the mills. She did n't stay long, because it
did n't agree with her, — the neighbors said, because she
was lazy. Lurindy lazy, indeed! There a'n't one of us
knows how to spell the first syllable of that word. But
that's where she must have got acquainted with John
Talbot. He'd been up at our place, too; but I was over
to Aunt Emeline's, it seems. But one night, about this
time, I thought he was dying, he'd got so very low; and
I thought how dreadful it was for Lurindy never to see
him again, and how it was all my selfish fault, and how
maybe he would n't 'a' died, if he'd had her to have taken
care of him; and I suppose no convicted felon ever endured more remorse than I did, sitting and watching that
dying man all that long and lonely night. But with the
morning he was better, — they always are a great deal
worse when they are getting well from it; he laughed
when the doctor came, and said he guessed he'd weathered that gale; and by and by he got well.

He meant to have gone up and seen Lurindy, after all,
but his ship was ready for sea just as he was; and I
thought it was about as well, for he was n't looking his
prettiest. And so he declared I was the neatest little
trimmer that ever trod water, and he believed he should
know a Ruggles by the cut of her jib, (I wonder if he'd
have known Aunt Mimy,) and if ever he went master,

he 'd name his ship for me, and call it the Sister of Charity. And he kissed me on both cheeks, and looked serious enough when he sent his love to Lurindy, and went
away; and no sooner was he gone than Miss Talbot said
I 'd better have the doctor myself; and I did n't sit up
again for about three weeks.

All this time I had n't heard a word from home, and,
for all I knew, Stephen might be dead and buried. I
did n't feel so very light-hearted, you may be sure, when
one day Miss Talbot brought me a letter. It was from
mother, and it seemed Stephen 'd only had a bad fever,
and had been up and gone home for more than a week.
So I wrote back, as soon as I could, all about John, and
how he 'd gone to sea again, and how Miss Talbot, who
set sights by John, was rather lonely, and I thought I 'd
keep her company a little longer, and try a spell in the
mills, seeing that our neighbors did n't think a girl had
been properly accomplished till she 'd had a term or two in
the factory. The fact was, I did n't want to go home just
then; I thought, maybe, if I waited a bit, my face would
get back to looking as it used to. So I worked in the
piece-room, light work and good pay, sent mother and
Lurindy part of my wages, and paid my board to Miss
Talbot. She 'd become quite attached to me, and I to
her, for all she was such an old-maidish thing; but I 'd
got to thinking an old maid was n't such a very bad thing,
after all. Fourth of July came at last, and the mills were
closed, and I went with some of the other girls on an ex-
cursion down the harbor; and when I got home, Miss
Talbot told me my Cousin Stephen had been down to see
me, and had been obliged to go home in the last train.
I wondered why Stephen did n't stay, and then it flashed
upon me that she 'd told him all about it, and he did n't

want to see me afterwards. I knew mother and Lurindy suspected why I did n't come home, and now, thinks I, they *know ;* but I asked no questions.

When September came, I saw it was n't any use delaying, and I might as well go back to knitting sale-socks then as any time. However, I did n't go till October. You need n't think I 'd stayed away from the farm all that time, while the tender things were opening, the tiny top-heavy beans pushing up, the garden-sarse greening, the little grass-blades two and two, — while all the young creatures were coming forward, the chickens breaking the shell, and the gosling-storm brewing and dealing destruction, — while the strawberries were growing ripe and red up in the high field, and the hay and clover were getting in, — you need n't think I 'd stayed from all that had been pleasant in my life, without many a good heart-ache; and when at last I saw the dear old gray house again, all weather-beaten and homely, standing there with its well-sweep among the elms, I fairly cried. Mother and Lurindy ran out to meet me, when they saw the stage stop, and after we got into the house it seemed as if they would never get done kissing me. And mother stirred round and made hot cream-biscuits for tea, and got the best china, and we sat up till nigh midnight, talking, and I had to tell everything John did and said and thought and looked, over and over again.

By and by I unpacked my trunk, and there was a little parcel in the bottom of it, and I pulled it up.

"There, Lurindy," says I, "John told me to tell you to have your wedding-dress ready against he came home, — he 's gone mate, — and here it is." And I unrolled the neatest brown silk you ever saw, just fit for Lurindy, she 's so pale and genteel, and threw it into her lap. I 'd stayed the other month to get enough to buy it.

The first thing Lurindy did, by way of thanks, was to burst into tears and declare she never could take it, that she never should marry now; and the more I urged her, the more she cried. But at last she said she'd accept it conditionally,— and the condition was, I should be married when she was.

"Well," says I, "agreed,— if you'll provide the necessary article; because I can't very well marry my shadow, and I don't know any one else that would be fool enough to have such a little fright."

At that Lurindy felt all the worse, and it took all the spirits I had to build up hers and mother's. I suppose I was sorry to see they felt so bad, (and they had n't meant that I should,) because it gave the finishing stroke to my conviction; and after I was in bed, I grew sorrier still; and if I cried, 't was n't on account of myself, but I saw how Lurindy 'd always feel self-accused, though she had n't ought to, whenever she looked at me, and how all her life she 'd feel my scarred face like a weight on her happiness, and think I owed it to John, and how intolerable such an obligation, though it was only a fancied one, would be; and I saw, too, that it all came from my not going up-stairs that first time when Stephen knocked,— because if I had, I should have been there when the doctor came, and Lurindy 'd have gone to have taken care of John herself, and it would have been her face that was ruined instead of mine; and though it was a great deal better that it should be mine, still she 'd have been easier in her mind;— and so thinking and worrying, I fell asleep.

Next day was baking-day, and Stephen was coming in the afternoon, and it was almost five o'clock when we got cleared away, and I went up-stairs to change my dress.

I thought 't was n't any use to trim myself out in bows and ruffles now, so I just put on my brown gingham and a white linen collar; but Lurindy came and tied a pink ribbon at my throat, and fixed my hair herself, and looked down and said, —

" Well, I don't see but you 're about as pretty as ever you was."

That almost finished me; but I contrived to laugh, and got down-stairs. Mother 'd run over to the village to get some yarn to knit up, for she 'd used all our own wool. It was getting dark, and I had just brought in another log, and hung the kettle on the crane. The log had n't taken fire yet, and there was only a light glimmer, from the coals, on the ceiling. I heard the back-door latch click, and thought it was mother, and commenced humming in the middle of a tune, as if I 'd been humming the rest and had just reached that part; but the figure standing there was a sight too tall for mother.

" Oh, Stephen," says I, — and my heart jumped in my throat, but I just swallowed it down, and thanked Heaven that the evening was so dark, — " is that you?"

" Yes," says he, stepping forward, and putting out his hands, and making as if he would kiss me. Just for a minute I hung back, then I went and gave him my hand in a careless way.

" Yes," says he; " and I can't say that you seem so very glad to see me."

" Oh, yes," I answered, " I am glad. Did you drive over?"

" Well," says he, " maybe you are; but I should call it a mighty cool reception, after almost a year's absence. However, I suppose it 's the best manners not to show any cordiality; you 've had a chance to learn more politeness down at Salem than we have up here in the country."

I was a little struck up by Stephen's running on so, — he was generally so quiet, and said so little, and then in such short sentences. But in a minute I reckoned he thought I was nervous, and was trying to put me at my ease, — and he knew of old that the best way to do that was to rouse my temper.

"I ha'n't seen anybody at Salem better mannered 'n mother and Lurindy," said I.

"Come home for Thanksgiving?" asked Stephen, hanging up his coat.

I kept still a minute, for I could n't for the life of me see what I had to give thanks for. Then it came over me what a cheery, comfortable home this was, and how Stephen would always be my kind, warm-hearted friend, and how thankful I ought to be that my life had been spared, and that I was useful, that I 'd made such good friends as I had down to Salem, and that I was n't soured against all mankind on account of my misfortune.

"Yes, Stephen," says I, "I 've come home for Thanksgiving; and I have a great deal to give thanks for."

"So have I," said he.

"Stephen," says I, "I don't exactly know, but I should n't wonder if I 'd had a change of heart."

"Don't know of anybody that needed it less," says Stephen, warming his hands. "However, if it makes you any more comfortable, I sha'n't object; except the part of it that belongs to me, — I sha'n't have that changed."

The fire 'd begun to brighten now, and the room was red and pleasant-looking; still I knew he could n't see me plainly, and I waited a minute, and lingered round,

pretending I was doing this and the other, which I was n't ;
I hated to break the old way of things ; and then I took
the tongs and blew a coal and lighted the dip and held it
up, as if I was looking for something. Pretty soon I
found it ; it was a skein of linen thread I was going to
wind for Lurindy. Then I got the swifts and came and
sat down in front of the candle.

"There," says I, "the swifts is broken. What shall
I do?"

"I'll hold the thread, if that's your trouble," says
Stephen, and came and sat opposite to me while I
wound.

I wondered whether he was looking at me, but I did n't
durst look up,—and then I could n't, if my life had depended upon it. At last we came to the end ; then I
managed to get a glance edgeways. He had n't been
looking at all, I don't believe, till that very moment,
when he raised his eyes.

"Are folks always so sober, when they've had a change
of heart?" he asked, with his pleasant smile.

"They are, when they've had a change of face," I was
going to say ; but just then mother came in with her
bundle of yarn, and Lurindy came down, and there was
such a deal of welcoming and talking, that I slipped
round and laid the table, and had the tea made before
they thought of it. I'd about made up my mind now
that Stephen would act as if nothing had happened, and
pretend to like me just the same, because he was so ten-
der-hearted and could n't bear to hurt my feelings nor
anybody's ; and I'd made up my mind, too, that, as soon
as he gave me a chance, I'd tell him I was set against
marriage : leastwise, I would n't have him, because I
would n't have any man marry me out of pity ; and the

more I cared for him, the more I could n't hamper an ugly face on him forever. So, you see, I had quite resolved, that, cost me what it would, I 'd say " No," if Stephen asked me. Well, it 's a very good thing to make resolutions ; but it 's a great deal better to break them, sometimes.

Having come to my conclusions, I grew as merry as any of them. And when mother put two spoons into Stephen's cup, I told him he was going to have a present. And he said he guessed he knew what it was ; and I said it must be a mitten, I 'd heard that Martha Smith had taken to knitting lately ; and he confounded Martha Smith. Mother and Lurindy were very busy talking about the yarn, and how Mr. Fisher wänted the next socks knit ; and Stephen asked me what that dish was beside me. I said, it was lemon-tart, and the top-crust was made of kisses, and would he have some ? And he said, he did n't care for anybody's kisses but mine, and he believed he would n't. And I told him the receipt of this came from the Queen's own kitchen. And he said, he did n't know that the Queen of England was any better than the Queen of Hearts. Then I said, I supposed he remembered how the latter lady was served by the Knave of Hearts in " Mother Goose " ? And he replied that he was n't going to be Jack-at-a-pinch for anybody. And so on, till mother finished tea.

After tea, I sat up to the table and ended some barley-trimming that I 'd just learned how to make ; and as the little kernels came tumbling out from under my fingers, Stephen sat beside and watched them as if it was a field of barley, growing, reaped, and threshed under his eyes. By and by I finished it ; and then, rummaging round in the table-drawer, I found the sock that I was knitting, waiting at the very stitch where I left it, 'most a year ago.

"Well, if that is n't lucky!" said I. And I sat down on a stool by the fireside, determined to finish that sock that night; and no sooner had I set the needles to dancing, like those in the fairy-story, than open came the kitchen-door again, and in, out of the dark, stepped Aunt Mimy.

"Good-evenin', Miss Ruggles!" says she. "Heow d' ye du, Emerline? hope yer gwine ter stay ter hum a spell. Why, Stephen, 's this you? Quite a femily-party, I declare fur 't! Wal, Miss Ruggles, I got kind o' tired settin' in the dark, an', ez I looked out an' see the dips blazin' in yer winder, thinks I, I 'll jest run up an' see w'at 's ter pay."

"Why, there 's ouly one dip," says Lurindy.

"Wal, that 's better 'n none," answered Miss Mimy.

I had enough of the old Adam left in me to be riled at her way of begging as much as ever I was; but I saw that Stephen was amused; he had n't ever happened to be round, when Aunt Mimy was at her tricks.

"No, Miss Ruggles," continued she, " I thank the Lord I ha'n't got a complainin' sperrit, an' hed jest ez lieves see by my neighbor's dip ez my own, an', mebbe ye 'll say, a sight lieveser."

And then Miss Mimy pulled out a stocking without beginning or end, and began to knit as fast as she could rattle, after she 'd fixed one needle in a chicken-bone, and pinned the chicken-bone to her side.

"Wal, Emerline," says she, "I s'pose ye 've got so grand down ter the mills, thet, w'at 'ith yer looms an' machines an' tic-doloreux, ye won't hev nothin' ter say ter the old way uv knittin' socks."

7   J

"Does this look like it, Aunt Mimy?" says I, shaking my needles by way of answer. "I'm going to finish this pair to-night."

"Oh," says she, "you be, be you? Wal, ef I don't e'en-a'most vum it's the same one! ef ye ha'n't been nigh abeout a hull year a-knittin' one pair uv socks!"

"How do you know they're the same pair?" asked I.

"By a mark I see you sot in 'em ter the top, ef ye want ter know, afore I thought it would be hangin' by the eyelids the rest uv yer days. Wal, I never 'xpected ye 'd be much help ter yer mother; ye 're tew fond uv hikin' reound the village."

"Indeed, Miss Mimy," said Lurindy, kind of indignant, "she 's always been the greatest help to mother."

"I don't know how I should have made both ends meet this year, if it had n't been for her wages," said mother.

Stephen was whittling Miss Mimy's portrait on the end of a stick, and laughing. I was provoked with mother and Lurindy for answering the thing, and was just going to speak up, when I caught Stephen's eye, and thought better of it. Pretty soon Aunt Mimy produced a bundle of herbs from her pocket, and laid them on the table.

"Oh, thank you, Aunt Jemimy," says mother. "Pennyroyal and catnip 's always acceptable."

"Yes," said Aunt Mimy. "An' I 'll take my pay in some uv yer dried apples. Heow much does Fisher give fur socks, Miss Ruggles?" she asked, directly.

"Fifty cents and I find, — fifteen and he finds."

"An' ye take it out uv the store? Varry reasonable. I wuz thinkin' uv tryin' my han' myself; — business 's ruther dull, folks onkimmon well this fall. Heow many strings yer gwine ter give me fur the yarbs?"

Then mother went up garret to get the apples and

spread the herbs to dry, and Lurindy wanted some different needles, and went after her. Stephen 'd just
heaped the fire, and the big blaze was tumbling up
the chimney, and Miss Mimy lowered her head and
looked over her great horn-bowed spectacles at me.

"Wal, Emerline Ruggles," says she, after a while, going back to her work, "you 've lost all *your* pink cheeks!"

I suppose it took me rather sudden, for all at once a
tear sprung and fell right down my work. I saw it glis-
tening on the bright needles a minute, and then my eyes
filmed so that I felt there was more coming, and I bent
down to the fire and made believe count my narrowings.
After all, Aunt Mimy was kind of privileged by everybody to say what she pleased. But Stephen did n't do as
every one did, always.

"Emmie's beauty was n't all in her pink cheeks, Miss
Mimy," I heard him say, as I went into the back-entry to
ask mother to bring down the mate of my sock.

"Wal, wherever it was, there 's precious little of it
left!" said she, angry at being took up, which maybe
she never was before in her life.

"You don't agree with her friends," said he, cutting in
the stick the great mole on the side of her nose; "*they*
all think she 's got more than ever she had."

Mother tossed me down the mate, and I went back.

"Young folks," says Aunt Mimy, after two or three
minutes' silence, "did ye ever hear tell o' 'Miah Kemp?"

"Any connection of old Parson Kemp in the other
parish?" asked Stephen.

"Yes," said Aunt Mimy, — "his brother. Wal, w'en
I wuz a young gal, livin' ter hum, — my father wuz ez
wealthy ez any farmer thereabouts, ye know, — I used
to keep company 'ith 'Miah Kemp. 'Miah was a stun-

mason, the best there wuz in the deestrik, an' the harn-
somest boy there tew, — though I say it thet should n't
say it, — he hed close-curlin' black hair, an' an arm it
done ye good to lean on. Wal, one spring night, — I
mind it well, — we wuz walkin' deown the lane together,
an' the wind wuz blowin', the laylocks wuz in bloom, an'
all over-head the lane wuz rustlin' 'ith the great purple
plumes in the moonlight, an' the air wuz sweeter 'ith their
breath than any air I 've ever taken sence, an' ez we wuz
walkin', 'Miah wuz askin' me fur ter fix eour weddin'-day.
Wal, w'en he left me at the bars, I agreed we 'd be mer-
ried the fifteenth day uv July comin', an' I walked hum ;
an' I mind heow I wondered ef Eve wuz so happy in
Paradise, or ef Paradise wuz half so beautiful ez thet
scented lane.   The nex' mornin', ez I wuz milkin', the
ccow tuk fright an' begun ter cut up, an' she cut up so
thet I run an' she arter me, — an' the long an' the short
uv it wuz thet she tossed me, an' w'en they got me up
they foun' I hed n't but one eye. Wal, uv course, my
looks wuz sp'iled, — fur I 'd been ez pretty 'z Emerline
wuz, — you wuz pretty once, Emerline, — an' I sent
'Miah Kemp word I 'd hev no more ter du 'ith him nor
any one else neow. 'Miah he come ter see me ; but I
wuz detarmined, an' I stuck ter my word. He did an'
said everything thet mortal man could, — that he loved
me better 'n ever, an' thet 't would be the death uv him,
an' tuk on dreful. But w'en he 'd got through, I giv'
him the same answer, though betwixt ourselves it ormost
broke my heart ter say it.   I kep' a stiff upper-lip, an' he
grew desp'rate, an' tuk all sorts uv dangerous jobs, blastin'
rocks an' haulin' stuns. One night, — 't wuz jest a year
from the night I 'd walked 'ith him in thet lane, — I wuz
stan'in' by the door, an' all ter once I heerd a noise an'

crash ez ef all the thunderbolts in the Almighty's hand
hed fallen together, an' I run deown the lane an' met the
men bringin' up sunthin' on an old door. They hed been
blastin' Elder Payson's rock, half-way deown the new
well, an' the mine hed n't worked, an' 'Miah 'd gone
deown ter see w'at wuz in it; an' jest ez he got up
ag'in, off it went, an' here he wuz 'ith a great splinter
in his chist, — ef the rest uv it wuz him. They could n't
kerry him no furder, an' sot him deown; an' there wuz
all the trees a-wavin' overhead ag'in, an' all the sweet
scents a-beatin' abeout the air, jest uz it wuz a year ago
w'en he parted from me so strong an' whole an' harnsome;
all the fleowers wuz a-blossomin', all the winds wuz blowin',
an' this lump uv torn flesh an' broken bones wuz 'Miah.
I laid deown on the grass beside him, an' put my lips close
to hisn, an' I could feel the breath jest stirrin' between;
an' the doctor came an' said 't warn't no use; an' they
threw a blanket over us, an' there I laid tell the sun rose
an' sparkled in the dew an' the green leaves an' the purple bunches, an' the air came frolickin' fresh an' sweet
abeout us; an' though I 'd knowed it long, layin' thére in
the dark, neow I see fur sartain thet there warn't no
breath on them stiff lips, an' the forehead was cold uz the
stuns beneath us, an' the eyes wuz fixed an' glazed in
thet las' look uv love an' tortur' an' reproach thet he giv'
me. They say I went distracted; an' I *du* b'lieve I 've
be'n cracked ever sence."

Here Aunt Mimy, who had told her whole story without moving a muscle, commenced rocking violently back
and forth.

"I don't often remember all this," says she, after a
little, "but las' spring it flushed over me; an' w'en I
heerd heow Emerline 'd be'n sick, — I hear a gre't

many things ye do'no' nothin' abeout, children, — I thought I 'd tell her, fust time I see her."

" What made you think of it last spring?" asked Stephen.

" The laylocks wuz in bloom," said Miss Mimy, — "the laylocks wuz in bloom."

Just then mother came down with the apples, and some dip-candles, and a basket of broken victuals; and Miss Mimy tied her cloak and said she believed she must be going. And Stephen went and got his hat and coat, and said, —

" Miss Mimy, would n't you like a little company to help you carry your bundles? Come, Emmie, get your shawl."

So I ran and put on my things, and Stephen and I went home with Aunt Mimy.

" Emmie," says Stephen, as we were coming back, and he 'd got hold of my hand in his, where I 'd taken his arm. " what do you think of Aunt Mimy now?"

" Oh," says I, " I 'm sorry I 've ever been sharp with her."

" I don't know," said Stephen. " 'T a'n't in human nature not to pity her; but then she brought her own trouble on herself, you see."

" Yes," said I.

"I don't know how to blast rocks," says Stephen, when we 'd walked a little while without saying anything, — " but I suppose there is something as desperate that I can do."

" Oh, you need n't go to threatening me !" thinks I; and, true enough, he had n't any need to.

" Emmie," says he, " if you say 'No,' when I ask you to have me, I sha'n't ask you again."

"Well?" says I, after a step or two, seeing he did n't speak.

"Well?" says he.

"I can't say 'Yes' or 'No' either, till you ask me," said I.

He stopped under the starlight and looked in my eyes.

"Emmie," says he, "did you ever doubt that I loved you?"

"Once I thought you did," said I; "but it's different now."

"I *do* love you," said he, "and you know it."

"Me, Stephen?" said I, — "with my face like a speckled sparrow's-egg?"

"Yes, you," said he; and he bent down and kissed me, and then we walked on.

By and by Stephen said, When would I come and be the life of his house and the light of his eyes? That was rather a speech for Stephen; and I said, I would go whenever he wanted me. And then we went home very comfortably, and Stephen told mother it was all right, and mother and Lurindy did what they'd got very much in the habit of doing, — cried; and I said I should think I was going to be buried, instead of married; and Stephen took my knitting-work away, and said, as I had knit all our trouble and all our joy into that thing, he meant to keep it just as it was; and that was the end of my knitting sale-socks.

I suppose, now I've told you so far, you'd maybe like to know the rest. Well, Lurindy and John were married Thanksgiving morning; and just as they moved aside, Stephen and I stepped up and took John and Aunt Mimy rather by surprise by being married too.

"Wal," says Aunt Mimy, "ef ever you hang eout an-

other red flag, 't won't be because Lurindy's nussin' Stephen!'"

I don't suppose there's a happier little woman in the
State than me. I should like to see her, if there is. I
go over home pretty often, and Aunt Mimy makes just
as much of my baby — I've named him John — as
mother does; and that's enough to ruin any child that
was n't a cherub born. And Miss Mimy always has a
bottle of some new nostrum of her own stilling every time
she sees any of us; we've got enough to swim a ship, on
the top-shelf of the pantry to-day, if it was all put together.
As for Stephen, there he comes now through the huckle-
berry-pasture, with the baby on his arm; he seems to
think there never was a baby before; and sometimes —
Stephen's such a home-body — I'm tempted to think
that maybe I have married my own shadow, after all.
However, I would n't have it other than it is. Lurindy,
she lives at home the most of the time; and once in a
while, when Stephen and mother and I and she are all
together, and as gay as larks, and the baby is creeping
round, swallowing pins and hooks and eyes as if they
were blueberries, and the fire is burning, and the kettle
singing, and the hearth swept clean, it seems as if heaven
had actually come down, or we'd all gone up without
waiting for our robes; it seems as if it was altogether too
much happiness for one family. And I've made Stephen
take a paper on purpose to watch the ship-news; for John
sails captain of a fruiter to the Mediterranean, and, sure
enough, its little gilt figure-head that goes dipping in the
foam is nothing else than the Sister of Charity.

CIRCUMSTANCE.

7 *

CIRCUMSTANCE.

SHE had remained, during all that day, with a sick neighbor, — those eastern wilds of Maine in that epoch frequently making neighbors and miles synonymous, — and so busy had she been with care and sympathy that she did not at first observe the approaching night. But finally the level rays, reddening the snow, threw their gleam upon the wall, and, hastily donning cloak and hood, she bade her friends farewell and sallied forth on her return. Home lay some three miles distant, across a copse, a meadow, and a piece of woods, — the woods being a fringe on the skirts of the great forests that stretch far away into the North. That home was one of a dozen log-houses lying a few furlongs apart from each other, with their half-cleared demesnes separating them at the rear from a wilderness untrodden save by stealthy native or deadly panther tribes.

She was in a nowise exalted frame of spirit, — on the contrary, rather depressed by the pain she had witnessed and the fatigue she had endured ; but in certain temperaments such a condition throws open the mental pores, so to speak, and renders one receptive of every influence. Through the little copse she walked slowly, with her cloak folded about her, lingering to imbibe the sense of shelter, the sunset filtered in purple through the mist of woven spray and twig, the companionship of growth not sufficiently dense to band against her, the sweet home-feeling of a young and tender wintry wood. It was therefore just on the edge of the evening that she emerged from the place and began to cross the meadow-land. At one hand lay the forest to which her path wound; at the other the evening star hung over a tide of failing orange that slowly slipped down the earth's broad side to sadden other hemispheres with sweet regret. Walking rapidly now, and with her eyes wide-open, she distinctly saw in the air before her what was not there a moment ago, a winding-sheet, — cold, white, and ghastly, waved by the likeness of four wan hands, — that rose with a long inflation, and fell in rigid folds, while a voice, shaping itself from the hollowness above, spectral and melancholy, sighed, — "The Lord have mercy on the people! The Lord have mercy on the people!" Three times the sheet with its corpse-covering outline waved beneath the pale hands, and the voice, awful in its solemn and mysterious depth, sighed, "The Lord have mercy on the people!" Then all was gone, the place was clear again, the gray sky was obstructed by no deathly blot; she looked about her, shook her shoulders decidedly, and, pulling on her hood, went forward once more.

She might have been a little frightened by such an apparition, if she had led a life of less reality than frontier settlers are apt to lead; but dealing with hard fact does not engender a flimsy habit of mind, and this woman was too sincere and earnest in her character, and too happy in her situation, to be thrown by antagonism, merely, upon superstitious fancies and chimeras of the second-sight.

She did not even believe herself subject to an hallucination, but smiled simply, a little vexed that her thought could have framed such a glamour from the day's occurrences, and not sorry to lift the bough of the warder of the woods and enter and disappear in their sombre path. If she had been imaginative, she would have hesitated at her first step into a region whose dangers were not visionary; but I suppose that the thought of a little child at home would conquer that propensity in the most habituated. So, biting a bit of spicy birch, she went along. Now and then she came to a gap where the trees had been partially felled, and here she found that the lingering twilight was explained by that peculiar and perhaps electric film which sometimes sheathes the sky in diffused light for many hours before a brilliant aurora. Suddenly, a swift shadow, like the fabulous flying-dragon, writhed through the air before her, and she felt herself instantly seized and borne aloft. It was that wild beast — the most savage and serpentine and subtle and fearless of our latitudes — known by hunters as the Indian Devil, and he held her in his clutches on the broad floor of a swinging fir-bough. His long sharp claws were caught in her clothing, he worried them sagaciously a little, then, finding that ineffectual to free them, he commenced licking her bare arm with his rasping tongue and pouring over her the wide streams of his hot, fœtid breath. So quick had this flashing action been that the woman had had no time for alarm; moreover, she was not of the screaming kind: but now, as she felt him endeavoring to disentangle his claws, and the horrid sense of her fate smote her, and she saw instinctively the fierce plunge of those weapons, the long strips of living flesh torn from her bones, the agony, the quivering disgust, itself a worse agony, —

while by her side, and holding her in his great lithe embrace, the monster crouched, his white tusks whetting and gnashing, his eyes glaring through all the darkness like balls of red fire, — a shriek, that rang in every forest hollow, that startled every winter-housed thing, that stirred and woke the least needle of the tasselled pines, tore through her lips. A moment afterward, the beast left the arm, once white, now crimson, and looked up alertly.

She did not think at this instant to call upon God. She called upon her husband. It seemed to her that she had but one friend in the world ; that was he ; and again the cry, loud, clear, prolonged, echoed through the woods. It was not the shriek that disturbed the creature at his relish ; he was not born in the woods to be scared of an owl, you know ; what then ? It must have been the echo, most musical, most resonant, repeated and yet repeated, dying with long sighs of sweet sound, vibrated from rock to river and back again from depth to depth of cave and cliff. Her thought flew after it ; she knew, that, even if her husband heard it, he yet could not reach her in time ; she saw that while the beast listened he would not gnaw, — and this she *felt* directly, when the rough, sharp, and multiplied stings of his tongue retouched her arm. Again her lips opened by instinct, but the sound that issued thence came by reason. She had heard that music charmed wild beasts, — just this point between life and death intensified every faculty, — and when she opened her lips the third time, it was not for shrieking, but for singing.

A little thread of melody stole out, a rill of tremulous motion ; it was the cradle-song with which she rocked her baby ; — how could she sing that ? And then she remembered the baby sleeping rosily on the long settee before the fire, — the father cleaning his gun, with one foot on the green wooden rundle, — the merry light from the chimney dancing out and through the room, on the rafters of the ceiling with their tassels of onions and herbs, on the log walls painted with lichens and festooned with apples, on the king's-arm slung across the shelf with the old pirate's-cutlass, on the snow-pile of the bed, and on the great brass clock, — dancing, too, and lingering on the baby, with his fringed-gentian eyes, his chubby fists clenched on the pillow, and his fine breezy hair fanning with the motion of his father's foot. All this struck her in one, and made a sob of her breath, and she ceased.

Immediately the long red tongue thrust forth again. Before it touched, a song sprang to her lips, a wild sea-song, such as some sailor might be singing far out on trackless blue water that night, the shrouds whistling with frost and the sheets glued in ice, — a song with the wind in its burden and the spray in its chorus. The monster raised his head and flared the fiery eyeballs upon her, then fretted the imprisoned claws a moment and was quiet; only the breath like the vapor from some hell-pit still swathed her. Her voice, at first faint and fearful, gradually lost its quaver, grew under her control and subject to her modulation; it rose on long swells, it fell in subtile cadences, now and then its tones pealed out like bells from distant belfries on fresh sonorous mornings. She sung the song through, and, wondering lest his name of Indian Devil were not his true name, and if he would not detect her, she repeated it. Once or twice now, indeed, the beast stirred uneasily, turned, and made the bough sway at his movement. As she ended, he snapped his jaws together, and tore away the fettered member, curling it under him with a snarl, — when she burst into

the gayest reel that ever answered a fiddle-bow. How
many a time she had heard her husband play it on the
homely fiddle made by himself from birch and cherry-
wood! how many a time she had seen it danced on the
floor of their one room, to the patter of wooden clogs and
the rustle of homespun petticoat! how many a time she
had danced it herself!—and did she not remember once,
as they joined clasps for eight-hands-round, how it had
lent its gay, bright measure to her life? And here she
was singing it alone, in the forest, at midnight, to a
wild beast! As she sent her voice trilling up and down
its quick oscillations between joy and pain, the creature
who grasped her uncurled his paw and scratched the bark
from the bough; she must vary the spell; and her voice
spun leaping along the projecting points of tune of a hornpipe. Still singing, she felt herself twisted about with a
low growl and a lifting of the red lip from the glittering
teeth; she broke the hornpipe's thread, and commenced
unravelling a lighter, livelier thing, an Irish jig. Up and
down and round about her voice flew, the beast threw
back his head so that the diabolical face fronted hers, and
the torrent of his breath prepared her for his feast as the
anaconda slimes his prey. Franticly she darted from
tune to tune; his restless movements followed her. She
tired herself with dancing and vivid national airs, growing
feverish and singing spasmodically as she felt her horrid
tomb yawning wider. Touching in this manner all the
slogan and keen clan cries, the beast moved again, but
only to lay the disengaged paw across her with heavy
satisfaction. She did not dare to pause; through the
clear cold air, the frosty starlight, she sang. If there
were yet any tremor in the tone, it was not fear,—she
had learned the secret of sound at last; nor could it be

chill, — far too high a fever throbbed her pulses; it was nothing but the thought of the log-house and of what might be passing within it. She fancied the baby stirring in his sleep and moving his pretty lips, — her husband rising and opening the door, looking out after her, and wondering at her absence. She fancied the light pouring through the chink and then shut in again with all the safety and comfort and joy, her husband taking down the fiddle and playing lightly with his head inclined, playing while she sang, while she sang for her life to an Indian Devil. Then she knew he was fumbling for and finding some shining fragment and scoring it down the yellowing hair, and unconsciously her voice forsook the wild war-tunes and drifted into the half-gay, half-melancholy Rosin the Bow.

Suddenly she woke pierced with a pang, and the daggered tooth penetrating her flesh; — dreaming of safety, she had ceased singing and lost it. The beast had regained the use of all his limbs, and now, standing and raising his back, bristling and foaming, with sounds that would have been like hisses but for their deep and fearful sonority, he withdrew step by step toward the trunk of the tree, still with his flaming balls upon her. She was all at once free, on one end of the bough, twenty feet from the ground. She did not measure the distance, but rose to drop herself down, careless of any death, so that it were not this. Instantly, as if he scanned her thoughts, the creature bounded forward with a yell and caught her again in his dreadful hold. It might be that he was not greatly famished; for, as she suddenly flung up her voice again, he settled himself composedly on the bough, still clasping her with invincible pressure to his rough, ravenous breast, and listening in a fascination to the sad,

K

strange U-la-lu that now moaned forth in loud, hollow tones above him. He half closed his eyes, and sleepily reopened and shut them again.

What rending pains were close at hand! Death! and what a death! worse than any other that is to be named! Water, be it cold or warm, that which buoys up blue ice-fields, or which bathes tropical coasts with currents of balmy bliss, is yet a gentle conqueror, kisses as it kills, and draws you down gently through darkening fathoms to its heart. Death at the sword is the festival of trumpet and bugle and banner, with glory ringing out around you and distant hearts thrilling through yours. No gnawing disease can bring such hideous end as this; for that is a fiend bred of your own flesh, and this — is it a fiend, this living lump of appetites? What dread comes with the thought of perishing in flames! but fire, let it leap and hiss never so hotly, is something too remote, too alien, to inspire us with such loathly horror as a wild beast; if it have a life, that life is too utterly beyond our comprehension. Fire is not half ourselves; as it devours, arouses neither hatred nor disgust; is not to be known by the strength of our lower natures let loose; does not drip our blood into our faces from foaming chaps, nor mouth nor slaver above us with vitality. Let us be ended by fire, and we are ashes, for the winds to bear, the leaves to cover; let us be ended by wild beasts, and the base, cursed thing howls with us forever through the forest. All this she felt as she charmed him, and what force it lent to her song God knows. If her voice should fail! If the damp and cold should give her any fatal hoarseness! If all the silent powers of the forest did not conspire to help her! The dark, hollow night rose indifferently over her; the wide, cold air breathed rudely past her, lifted her wet hair and blew it down again; the great boughs swung with a ponderous strength, now and then clashed their iron lengths together and shook off a sparkle of icy spears or some long-lain weight of snow from their heavy shadows. The green depths were utterly cold and silent and stern. These beautiful haunts that all the summer were hers and rejoiced to share with her their bounty, these heavens that had yielded their largess, these stems that had thrust their blossoms into her hands, all these friends of three moons ago forgot her now and knew her no longer.

Feeling her desolation, wild, melancholy, forsaken songs rose thereon from that frightful aerie, — weeping, wailing tunes, that sob among the people from age to age, and overflow with otherwise unexpressed sadness, — all rude, mournful ballads, — old tearful strains, that Shakespeare heard the vagrants sing, and that rise and fall like the wind and tide, — sailor-songs, to be heard only in lone mid-watches beneath the moon and stars, — ghastly rhyming romances, such as that famous one of the Lady Margaret, when

> " She slipped on her gown of green
> A piece below the knee, —
> And 't was all a long cold winter's night
> A dead corse followed she."

Still the beast lay with closed eyes, yet never relaxing his grasp. Once a half-whine of enjoyment escaped him, — he fawned his fearful head upon her; once he scored her cheek with his tongue: savage caresses that hurt like wounds. How weary she was! and yet how terribly awake! How fuller and fuller of dismay grew the knowledge that she was only prolonging her anguish and playing with death! How appalling the thought that with her voice ceased her existence! Yet she could not sing forever; her throat was dry and hard; her very breath was a pain; her mouth was hotter than any desert-worn pilgrim's; — if she could but drop upon her burning tongue one atom of the ice that glittered about her! — but both of her arms were pinioned in the giant's vice. She remembered the winding-sheet, and for the first time in her life shivered with spiritual fear. Was it hers? She asked herself, as she sang, what sins she had committed, what life she had led, to find her punishment so soon and in these pangs, — and then she sought eagerly for some reason why her husband was not up and abroad to find her. He failed her, — her one sole hope in life; and without being aware of it, her voice forsook the songs of suffering and sorrow for old Covenanting hymns, — hymns with which her mother had lulled her, which the class-leader pitched in the chimney-corners, — grand and sweet Methodist hymns, brimming with melody and with all fantastic involutions of tune to suit that ecstatic worship, — hymns full of the beauty of holiness, steadfast, relying, sanctified by the salvation they had lent to those in worse extremity than hers, — for they had found themselves in the grasp of hell, while she was but in the jaws of death. Out of this strange music, peculiar to one character of faith, and than which there is none more beautiful in its degree nor owning a more potent sway of sound, her voice soared into the glorified chants of churches. What to her was death by cold or famine or wild beasts? "Though He slay me, yet will I trust in him," she sang. High and clear through the frore fair night, the level moonbeams splintering in the wood, the scarce glints of stars in the shadowy roof of branches, these sacred anthems rose, — rose as a hope from despair, as some snowy spray of flower-bells from blackest mould.

Was she not in God's hands? Did not the world swing at his will? If this were in his great plan of providence, was it not best, and should she not accept it?

"He is the Lord our God; his judgments are in all the earth."

Oh, sublime faith of our fathers, where utter self-sacrifice alone was true love, the fragrance of whose unrequired subjection was pleasanter than that of golden censers swung in purple-vapored chancels!

Never ceasing in the rhythm of her thoughts, articulated in music as they thronged, the memory of her first communion flashed over her. Again she was in that distant place on that sweet spring morning. Again the congregation rustled out, and the few remained, and she trembled to find herself among them. How well she remembered the devout, quiet faces, too accustomed to the sacred feast to glow with their inner joy! how well the snowy linen at the altar, the silver vessels slowly and silently shifting! and as the cup approached and passed, how the sense of delicious perfume stole in and heightened the transport of her prayer, and she had seemed, looking up through the windows where the sky soared blue in constant freshness, to feel all heaven's balms dripping from the portals, and to scent the lilies of eternal peace! Perhaps another would not have felt so much ecstasy as satisfaction on that occasion; but it is a true, if a later disciple, who has said, "The Lord bestoweth his blessings there, where he findeth the vessels empty."

"And does it need the walls of a church to renew my communion?" she asked. "Does not every moment stand a temple four-square to God? And in that morning, with its buoyant sunlight, was I any dearer to the Heart of the World than now? — 'My beloved is mine, and I am his,'" she sang over and over again, with all varied inflection and profuse tune. How gently all the winter-wrapt things bent toward her then! into what relation with her had they grown! how this common dependence was the spell of their intimacy! how at one with Nature had she become! how all the night and the silence and the forest seemed to hold its breath, and to send its soul up to God in her singing! It was no longer despondency, that singing. It was neither prayer nor petition. She had left imploring, "How long wilt thou forget me, O Lord? Lighten mine eyes, lest I sleep the sleep of death! For in death there is no remembrance of thee," — with countless other such fragments of supplication. She cried rather, "Yea, though I walk through the valley of the shadow of death, I will fear no evil: for thou art with me; thy rod and thy staff, they comfort me," — and lingered, and repeated, and sang again, "I shall be satisfied, when I awake, with thy likeness."

Then she thought of the Great Deliverance, when he drew her up out of many waters, and the flashing old psalm pealed forth triumphantly : —

> " The Lord descended from above,
>   and bow'd the heavens hie:
> And underneath his feet he cast
>   the darknesse of the skie.
> On cherubs and on cherubins
>   full royally he road:
> And on the wings of all the winds
>   came flying all abroad."

She forgot how recently, and with what a strange pity for her own shapeless form that was to be, she had quaintly sung, —

> " O lovely appearance of death!
>   What sight upon earth is so fair?
> Not all the gay pageants that breathe
>   Can with a dead body compare!"

She remembered instead, — "In thy presence is fulness of joy; at thy right hand there are pleasures forevermore. God will redeem my soul from the power of the grave : for he shall receive me. He will swallow up death in victory." Not once now did she say, " Lord, how long wilt thou look on; rescue my soul from their destructions, my darling from the lions," — for she knew that the young lions roar after their prey and seek their meat from God. " O Lord, thou preservest man and beast!" she said.

She had no comfort or consolation in this season, such as sustained the Christian martyrs in the amphitheatre. She was not dying for her faith ; there were no palms in heaven for her to wave ; but how many a time had she declared, — "I had rather be a doorkeeper in the house of my God, than to dwell in the tents of wickedness!" And as the broad rays here and there broke through the dense covert of shade and lay in rivers of lustre on crystal sheathing and frozen fretting of trunk and limb and on the great spaces of refraction, they builded up visibly that house, the shining city on the hill, and singing, "Beautiful for situation, the joy of the whole earth, is Mount Zion, on the sides of the North, the city of the Great King," her vision climbed to that higher picture where the angel shows the dazzling thing, the holy Jerusalem descending out of heaven from God, with its splendid battlements and gates of pearls, and its foundations, the eleventh a jacinth, the twelfth an amethyst, — with its great white throne, and the rainbow round about it, in sight like unto an emerald : "And there shall be no night there, — for the Lord God giveth them light," she sang.

What whisper of dawn now rustled through the wilderness ? How the night was passing ! And still the beast

crouched upon the bough, changing only the posture of
his head, that again he might command her with those
charmed eyes; — half their fire was gone; she could almost have released herself from his custody; yet, had she
stirred, no one knows what malevolent instinct might have
dominated anew.   But of that she did not dream; long
ago stripped of any expectation, she was experiencing in
her divine rapture how mystically true it is that "he that
dwelleth in the secret place of the Most High shall abide
under the shadow of the Almighty."

Slow clarion cries now wound from the distance as
the cocks caught the intelligence of day and re-echoed
it faintly from farm to farm, — sleepy sentinels of night,
sounding the foe's invasion, and translating that dim intu-
ition to ringing notes of warning.   Still she chanted on.
A remote crash of brushwood told of some other beast on
his depredations, or some night-belated traveller groping
his way through the narrow path.   Still she chanted on.
The far, faint echoes of the chanticleers died into distance,
the crashing of the branches grew nearer.   No wild beast
that, but a man's step, — a man's form in the moonlight,
stalwart and strong, — on one arm slept a little child, in
the other hand he held his gun.   Still she chanted on.

Perhaps, when her husband last looked forth, he was
half ashamed to find what a fear he felt for her.   He
knew she would never leave the child so long but for
some direst need, — and yet he may have laughed at himself, as he lifted and wrapped it with awkward care, and,
loading his gun and strapping on his horn, opened the
door again and closed it behind him, going out and plunging into the darkness and dangers of the forest.   He was
more singularly alarmed than he would have been willing
to acknowledge; as he had sat with his bow hovering

over the strings, he had half believed to hear her voice mingling gayly with the instrument, till he paused and listened if she were not about to lift the latch and enter. As he drew nearer the heart of the forest, that intimation of melody seemed to grow more actual, to take body and breath, to come and go on long swells and ebbs of the night-breeze, to increase with tune and words, till a strange shrill singing grew ever clearer, and, as he stepped into an open space of moonbeams, far up in the branches, rocked by the wind, and singing, "How beautiful upon the mountains are the feet of him that bringeth good tidings, that publisheth peace," he saw his wife, — his wife, — but, great God in heaven! how? Some mad exclamation escaped him, but without diverting her. The child knew the singing voice, though never heard before in that unearthly key, and turned toward it through the veiling dreams. With a celerity almost instantaneous, it lay, in the twinkling of an eye, on the ground at the father's feet, while his gun was raised to his shoulder and levelled at the monster covering his wife with shaggy form and flaming gaze, — his wife so ghastly white, so rigid, so stained with blood, her eyes so fixedly bent above, and her lips, that had indurated into the chiselled pallor of marble, parted only with that flood of solemn song.

I do not know if it were the mother-instinct that for a moment lowered her eyes, — those eyes, so lately riveted on heaven, now suddenly seeing all life-long bliss possible. A thrill of joy pierced and shivered through her like a weapon, her voice trembled in its course, her glance lost its steady strength, fever-flushes chased each other over her face, yet she never once ceased chanting. She was quite aware, that, if her husband shot now, the ball must

8

pierce her body before reaching any vital part of the
beast, — and yet better that death, by his hand, than the
other.   But this her husband also knew, and he remained
motionless, just covering the creature with the sight.   He
dared not fire, lest some wound not mortal should break
the spell exercised by her voice, and the beast, enraged
with pain, should rend her in atoms ; moreover, the light
was too uncertain for his aim.   So he waited.   Now and
then he examined his gun to see if the damp were in-
juring its charge, now and then he wiped the great drops
from his forehead.   Again the cocks crowed with the
passing hour, — the last time they were heard on that
night.   Cheerful home sound then, how full of safety and
all comfort and rest it seemed ! what sweet morning incidents of sparkling fire and sunshine, of gay household
bustle, shining dresser, and cooing baby, of steaming
cattle in the yard, and brimming milk-pails at the door !
what pleasant voices ! what laughter ! what security !
and here —

Now, as she sang on in the slow, endless, infinite moments, the fervent vision of God's peace was gone.   Just
as the grave had lost its sting, she was snatched back
again into the arms of earthly hope.   In vain she tried
to sing, " There remaineth a rest for the people of God,"
— her eyes trembled on her husband's, and she could
only think of him, and of the child, and of happiness that
yet might be, but with what a dreadful gulf of doubt between ! She shuddered now in the suspense ; all calm
forsook her ; she was tortured with dissolving heats or
frozen with icy blasts ; her face contracted, growing small
and pinched ; her voice was hoarse and sharp, — every
tone cut like a knife, — the notes became heavy to lift, —
withheld by some hostile pressure, — impossible.   One

gasp, a convulsive effort, and there was silence, — she had lost her voice.

The beast made a sluggish movement, — stretched and fawned like one awaking, — then, as if he would have yet more of the enchantment, stirred her slightly with his muzzle. As he did so, a sidelong hint of the man standing below with the raised gun smote him; he sprung round furiously, and, seizing his prey, was about to leap into some unknown airy den of the topmost branches now waving to the slow dawn. The late moon had rounded through the sky so that her gleam at last fell full upon the bough with fairy frosting; the wintry morning light did not yet penetrate the gloom. The woman, suspended in mid-air an instant, cast only one agonized glance beneath, — but across and through it, ere the lids could fall, shot a withering sheet of flame, — a rifle-crack, half-heard, was lost in the terrible yell of desperation that bounded after it and filled her ears with savage echoes, and in the wide arc of some eternal descent she was falling; — but the beast fell under her.

I think that the moment following must have been too sacred for us, and perhaps the three have no special interest again till they issue from the shadows of the wilderness upon the white hills that skirt their home. The father carries the child hushed again into slumber, the mother follows with no such feeble step as might be anticipated. It is not time for reaction, — the tension not yet relaxed, the nerves still vibrant, she seems to herself like some one newly made; the night was a dream; the present stamped upon her in deep satisfaction, neither weighed nor compared with the past; if she has the careful tricks of former habit, it is as an automaton; and as they slowly climb the steep under the clear gray vault and the paling morning star, and as she stops to gather a spray of the red-rose berries or a feathery tuft of dead grasses for the chimney-piece of the log-house, or a handful of brown cones for the child's play, — of these quiet, happy folk you would scarcely dream how lately they had stolen from under the banner and encampment of the great King Death. The husband proceeds a step or two in advance; the wife lingers over a singular foot-print in the snow, stoops and examines it, then looks up with a hurried word. Her husband stands alone on the hill, his arms folded across the babe, his gun fallen, — stands defined as a silhouette against the pallid sky. What is there in their home, lying below and yellowing in the light, to fix him with such a stare? She springs to his side. There is no home there. The log-house, the barns, the neighboring farms, the fences, are all blotted out and mingled in one smoking ruin. Desolation and death were indeed there, and beneficence and life in the forest. Tomahawk and scalping-knife, descending during that night, had left behind them only this work of their accomplished hatred and one subtle foot-print in the snow.

For the rest, — the world was all before them, where to choose.

DESERT SANDS.

DESERT SANDS.

IT is one of my bad habits to paint so long as the mask of Proteus, which hangs just under my ceiling, smiles; with the darkness the angles fall differently, and it frowns. But always when the day fails, when the gold has reddened and deepened and vanished in purple, when the air is interfused with a soft voluptuous sense that I feel as I might a new tint, be it mauve or fuchsine, when this coolness streams over my burning lids, when I scent the sweet-brier's ineffable fragrance wantoning through the place, always when this moment comes — for which the world was made — I throw down my brushes, and without pausing to clean my palette, go out.

I speak in the present — sad wretch! I, who live only in the days that are gone. It is all past, all past, with me now. Alas! and yet again alas! I paint no more.

Why am I less omnipotent than those demigods? When the curse fell for one and heaven was blank, did numbers cease to flow? When all sound was hushed on the ear of the other, did harmonies any the less build up their great vaults in air and melodies cease to blow through them? And I —

It should be that hour now; this sweet-brier that pranks

my window gives all its breath to the damp night-wind;
it is that which steals memory, and makes the lost mine
once more.   Always, at this hour, when I went out, it was
to see her that I went.   Eos, I called her, because I liked
then to deck her in all fancies, to think of her as a bright
and morning star.   But loveliness like hers needed no
phrases of mine, — that skin, where the delicate dyes
mingled as on the apple-blossom; those eyes, bluer than
the violet planet!   All that, indeed, was much, but when
it withered, her power would be the same; she was like
the lilies of eternal peace.

I did not know I loved her, if, certainly, I ever loved
her, — too selfish, even, to know myself.   But there are
seasons when all youth's blood riots in the frame and blossoms on the cheek, when the heaven-given instincts stir in
the veins, — and the spring that sends the sap along the
bough, sent me restlessness and longing for my part.

That night then, as many a night before, I went to Eos.
She was singing in some upper room, but came down at
my demand, and sang to me.   Then her sister brought in
lights; and Charley had a ship to rig.   How gay we
were, with what names we christened her, how she served
as a skeleton on which to hang all sea legends, how we enriched her with lore of the Armada and the flags of old
heroic battle-ships, how perfectly we equipped her, and
how we ran her little pennon at half-mast when her skip-
per was sent to his pillow!   At last her father rose and
folded up his paper.

" Eos," said he, " it is time to go to bed."

" Eos," said I, " good-night."

She came out with me, and down the little garden.   We
waited at the gate a moment, perhaps to penetrate ourselves with the sweet-brier's perfume, the night, and the

summer stars. I had told her that I was going away shortly.

"For long?" she had asked.

"Forever," I had answered.

Then a pause; in it I listened to the crickets singing, the leaves rustling.

"I shall walk," I added, "that is the way to surprise Nature in her hiding-places. I shall camp one night on hemlock boughs, and the next on a ledge above the clouds. I shall learn the cipher that hides the inner spell of forests and hills and sheets of falling rivers; see much, and take as I go. It will be a life almost new, as cheery as those bas-reliefs where, at every breath, you expect the pipes to blow, the flowers to fall."

"Yes," I continued, after a while, "all my pictures have sold. I have earned too much money this year. Now I shall not begin another till November, and to this old country town I shall return no more."

She did not reply. Indeed, to my speeches she frequently made no answer, but now I felt her silence like a reproach.

"And what have you to say to that?" I asked at length.

"Nothing but good-by," she said.

"Good-by? good-by?" I repeated. "I have not thought of that. I cannot say good-by to you, Eos. I will not travel to a region without sunshine, blue sky, and universal air; without darkness and stillness and fragrance and you. You must go with me, Eos."

So Eos went with me.

I am one of those who have no right to marriage-vows, in whom self-love excludes love, who find home so thoroughly in all the wide beauty of the world that they do not need one hearth, and a woman sitting by it. I said to myself, I cannot serve two masters. I did not know that in serving Eos I served God.

Of what use is regret? will it restore? Let me only remember, remember those passionate seasons when I absorbed another life into mine, and remember with savage joy and celerity.

That summer we journeyed as I had intended, except that when I walked she rode by my side. Sometimes when I climbed a crag, she waited for me at its base; again, I sketched some bold play of cloud shadows over wide intervals, and then fleeing forward to become part of the scene —

> " More fleet she skimmed the plains
> Than she whose elfin courser springs
> By night to eery warblings,
> When all the glimmering moorland rings
> To jingling bridle-reins."

Yet always she came circling back to me, like the moth to its flame. She was blithe as birds at dawn, airier than glancing foam-flakes are; she took like a prism all the white rays of happiness into her bosom, and sparkled them out in rainbows on those about her. When the autumn came, we went into a country ripe with color, while the year set like the sun. All this time my art had been in abeyance, I had found that life was something different from my thought; Eos was my wife, this summer I was a bridegroom, for a brief three months, at least, I loved as I was loved. One day I opened my easel, chalked my sketch, and then went out alone. Returning, I held clearly the thing that I would paint, the fine, keen drawing, the clarity of tint, the strength of color; I took my brushes and worked. The next day and another I did the same; nothing came of it; the old inspiration failed, my hand was powerless, my secret lost, my fancy dead. I said, Life has been too rich, it has impoverished art; that shall cease. That did cease.

In the evening, as I stood at the window, silent and resolved, Eos came and crept again into my arms; I suffered her to remain, but I did not tighten my clasp, give her kiss or caress, or call her by any new endearing name. It was hard at first, that once it was hard, afterwards it cost me no such effort, and became habit. It is true that now and then, when south winds blew, when some divine day melted in heaven, youth and love returned to me, my heart expanded in their warmth, passion wrapped me in its cloud, and I sought Eos. She was always there, she never swerved from following me. Before the close, such days only plunged me deeper in the intoxication of their own beauty, only bent me more earnestly to my purpose. It may be that I should have suffered her to help me, that she should have mounted with me step for step; but she could not, she kept me at her level. I was right, I knew that I was right; when I had attained, I should have turned to her again. She was not strong enough to wait, and so the game was lost.

In November, we went to the city. I said to her, "One must not be niggardly. You shall go home awhile now, they have never been so long parted from you before. I can spare you."

Perhaps, but for that last sentence she would not have gone. As it was, she hesitated, and seemed to forebode evil. Then I lost no time in putting myself at work. But before the third week of her absence I found that all was useless without her. I needed her, she must be about me, she must, in fact, give all and receive nothing. I brought her back.

On arriving at her father's house that evening, I could not but contrast the cheer with the forlorn place I had left, — for then I was not rich, — the crimson shadows, the sparkling firelight; they had a warm welcome for me, for they knew nothing of my conduct, and, indeed, what was there to know, I asked myself; Eos was not unhappy, she had a woman's quick perception, saw its necessity, and adapted herself to it. Once in the evening, when we were alone a moment, she came and said:

"I did not expect you. I am surprised. I thought you could spare me."

"No," I replied, "I cannot have you away. Eos, you are my sun, the light in which I live. How *did* I live before I knew you, love?"

She laid her cheek upon my arm, the dumb caress touched me, and I stroked her hair; so rare had any expression on my part become, that the least now thrilled her with a timid joy, I think.

"Do you know," said she, "I had begun to feel as if it were all a dream, to fancy that the little glimpse of different life, this summer's snatch of delight, was something I had slept through, that I was not your wife, at all, but just Eos here at home."

I started; that must not be; least of all, now that her cousin Alain was here again, he whose relationship allowed a brother's freedom with her, and who, by his quick eye and traveller-instinct, would tell at a glance how things lay.

"Ah?" I said lightly, "has it reached that, — Eos at home away from me? But you *are* my wife, you know, and to-morrow we will go."

"No," she said, lifting her head, "to-morrow I shall not go. I wish to stay a day longer."

" Eos with a will of her own ?" I replied now, amused at the phenomenon. "I have half the mind to indulge it, and see where the caprice ends."

Just then Alain entered. I kept my arm round Eos till she withdrew and took her work. Alain found some charts and began to examine them; he would shortly leave for Algiers, to join his father's regiment there, for on one side he was of French extraction, and the knowledge of the dangers and monotonies in the life he was henceforward to lead caused every one's manners to wear an additional air of kindness in his regard. As I looked at him now, I acknowledged that his was the most faultless face I had ever seen; had I been a figure painter, I could have asked no greater boon than perpetual companionship with such beauty; as it was, to have seen him once was to have seen him too often. He had that air of easy command, that gracious coolness which carries everything before it. I saw at once that through my error all was in train for a catastrophe. We would go to-morrow, I thought; not an instant would we delay; no wonder she wished to stay; this man, with his seducing graces, could win a saint from heaven, — and it was not heaven from which Eos was to be won. Then I became aware that I was possessed of jealousy. I had hoped such a possibility was over, and could scarcely remember the time in which I had been so utterly displeased with myself. In revenge, I was on the point of allowing her the desired day; the wounded fiend turned in my heart at the thought, and whispered, In that day, watch! I strangled it with a death-grip.

" Eos," I said, " I have business in the next town, and you have two days more at home."

But had my life depended thereon, I could not hinder

myself from hastening through my affairs, and back again.
Still, however, I did not immediately seek the house, but
returned there only after a long walk undertaken to sub-
due this last spark of the heart's rebellion.   It wanted yet
an hour to sunset ; I turned the handle of the parlor-door
and entered noiselessly.   An easel stood beside the window, before it, with stick and palette, sat my wife; Alain
was by her side.

"Will he be pleased?" asked she.   "It is finished, but
is it fine?"

I stole behind them, and looked at the canvas : a cliff,
yet blue in heavy night-shadows, was rent apart, and in
the rift a brook — a thread of limpid water — crept down
and curled from reach to reach to lose itself in dimness ; a
tuft of long bearded grass, half-guessed, bent forward and
shook its awns in a wind; a young birch shivered with
the tremors of its perpetual joy, half-way up on the other
side ; and in a sky of dark and tender twilight, the morning star hung, and tricked her beams in the stream below.
For an instant I could not detect the faults; nothing that
I had done equalled it.

"It is perfect !" I exclaimed.

Eos started, sprang to her feet, and hid her face in my
cloak.   Alain grasped my hand.

"You are noble, Ruy Diaz!" said he (for so they often
travestied the first syllable of my name), "I beg your for-
giveness for having feared your surprise would not be so
agreeable.   You humble me!"

I bent back Eos's head and kissed the blushing forehead
for reply.   Nevertheless, he was wrong.   I was not pleased.
I did not love Art well enough to give my wife to it; I did
not want a rival in her; above all, I could not have her sacred name on everybody's lips.   She was mine, not theirs.

Had I kept her apart and hidden, veiling her when she
went out, always accompanying her, scarcely suffering
her existence to be known, now to hear other men discuss
her merits and demerits and slime her with their praise?
What an enigma I present to my own understanding! I
loved her only as a part of myself. I allowed her no integral life.

" No fault to find?" asked Eos at length.

" Oh, yes," I answered, "doubtless there are plenty. I
could tell you there is no composition, color crude, sentiment too intense. But to what use?"

" To improve me."

" Well, and if I do not wish to improve you, sweet?
Whose picture is this?"

" It is mine," said Alain, entrenched in his former suspicion. " She has given it to me."

" And what do you design to do with it, may I ask?"

" Certainly. I shall exhibit it at Dash and Blank's."

" I shall be extremely displeased at any such course."

" So I thought," said Alain, dryly.

" But you are mistaken. Nothing can give me greater
pleasure than this discovery. I am rejoiced to find in my
wife a kindred soul; genius gives her new links to me, art
seals her mine indeed, she is nearer and dearer because
of this immortal flame in her spirit. I am glad, darling,"
I said, folding her closer, " and is not my joy enough?"

" It is enough!" said Eos fervently, clinging to me.

And so the picture was never shown.

That evening, as Eos busied herself with her needles
and her skeins of brilliant worsteds, and Alain was intent
upon his charts again, I drew near the table and took up
a little book of French sentiment, that bore his pencillings.

" What balderdash!" I exclaimed; " any woman could

have told him better.   Eos, what is it that a woman loves
best in a man?"

"His selfishness," said Alain, without looking up.

"No," replied Eos, "not exactly, not at all.   But a
certain self-poise, something that convicts her of the fact
that he can do without her."

"And is that what you find in me?" I asked.

"Could you do without me?" she replied, archly, and
with the smile that, when she was happy enough to shed
it, always brought me to her feet.   I could reply only
with my gaze; never had I been so conscious of my love
as at that moment, of my need of her, of her grace, her
sweetness, her perfection; my whole soul trembled in my
eyes to meet her own.   She must have been aware, and
yet she refused to look up, and bent but the lower over
her needles.   Alain rose and left the room for dividers.
I resolved to lift those mutinous lids and gain the glance
that was surely beneath.   For a moment she remained
motionless, then slowly raised her head and suffered me
to see that tears streamed over the face.   Instantly I was
beside her.

"Eos," I exclaimed, "what is it?"

She dropped the work and threw her arms about me.

"Oh, I fear that you *could* do without me, I know that
you could!   I already oppress you!   I wish I were dead!"
she cried, sobbing convulsively.

"Darling," I murmured, "in the day you died, I, too,
should cease to live."

Still she clasped me, still wept.

"What shall I do, Eos," I asked, "to convince you how
dear you are?"

"Only forgive me now," she murmured, with fresh grief.

I heard Alain's step.   "You are weak and nervous," I

said, as I felt myself shaken with the violence of her emotion. "You have applied too closely of late. And, Eos, —
I do not wish to grieve you, but you must control yourself. Such outbursts, such vehemence, are not at all to
my taste."

At the word, she rebounded like a steel spring, and
hardly was she in her seat before Alain re-entered.

The next day, remembrance of the last evening's disturbance effaced, we returned to the city. For four
months I worked breathlessly; every day when Eos had
finished her little household cares, she came and sat near
me; is it strange that the work was beautiful, when so
constantly she sent her soul into it? In the evenings we
went out, down the damp streets — snow or rain or whistling east — shooting along the slippery pavements, she
and I together, in the light of flaring gas and the great
squares of color, amethyst, ruby, and emerald, spread from
the chemists' windows. Sometimes I left her for a club,
or a play, sometimes we both needed music. I had my
aim in the world; I was reaching it. Whether I were
happy or not did not occur to me, whether Eos were
happy or not I did not pause to ask. It was then that I
first saw Vespasia.

One February morning Eos had not yet come in, some
one mounted the stair and knocked: it was a footman with
the card of Mrs. Dean Vivian. Immediately on his departure, another step followed, and Mrs. Dean Vivian herself entered.

She was an imposing woman, not so much through
height as proportion, neither in the splendor of her array — though that was considerable, and was necessary
to such a face — so completely as in the grace which rendered it, unlike that of so many women, merely an ac-
cessory.

" If I may command your time, Mr. Sydney," said a voice that I could compare to nothing but the mellow sweetness of a too-ripe pear, as her skin to the soft and smooth gold-brown of the *beurré*, illumined as it was by the sinister contrast of eyes wearing the lustre and almost the tint of emeralds. " If I may command your time, Mr. Sydney," and the smile that always accompanied her words broke up the face into vivid beauty, " I wish to examine your portfolios and to order a pendant for your ' Mist on the Meadows,' which I lately purchased."

" My time is at Mrs. Vivian's service for an hour, after that I regret an engagement," I stated, for it is always best to meet such imperious dames on their own ground. The manner had the desired effect.

" Perhaps, then, another day would be more opportune," she said.

" Not at all," I replied, wheeling a rack toward her. " Be seated, and allow me." She sank into a chair, sweeping her violet draperies about her, and turned the sheets.

" An effect of Kearsarge in cloud," I said rapidly. " Rainbows in Pemigewasset valley, — Spray at Apple-dore, — Montmorenci seen from — "

" Yes," said she, detaining it, " that is well arrested ; curled in foam, a fleece upon the azure. Why do you not elaborate it ? "

" Some day I may." I opened another portfolio. " These are studies," I added, " attempts at sentiment rather than scenery. I have fused and inwrought them with the spirit of the line which they illustrate. God's own profound : the melancholy main : Ariel fetching dew by midnight from the still-vexed Bermoothes."

Mrs. Vivian surveyed each with the swift eye of a connoisseur, noted its points, and passed to the next. Soon she leaned back in her chair, and folded her hands. " Ah, well," said she, " you would certainly play the showman till I went, if permitted."

" Excuse me. I am merely condensing your time, madam," I responded.

" Oh, I thank you there; but I knew the artist well enough before, and in his works. It seemed to me that I should like to make acquaintance with the individual. Am I too presuming?"

" I can assure Mrs. Vivian that only as the artist should I repay her trouble," I answered, sincerely enough, for my experience taught me that I had already, in theory, ab-jured my human side.

" We shall see," she replied, so coolly that I was nettled.

" And it is only as the artist that I care to be known," I added.

" Making headway famously," she exclaimed, with a low laugh. " Ah, Mr. Sydney, I always succeed! If portraiture were your branch, I should sit to you for a child of the sun, — I am East Indian by birth — as it is, I shall be your guest continually while my picture pro-ceeds, and you must be mine when it is hung. Are such orders, such visitors, unwarrantable?"

" Such orders are frequent enough, such visitors rare."

" I see you can be genial, on occasion. That gives me heart to beg your company at dinner next week; some beautiful women, some sparkling wits, some poets and men of your sib."

" It is impossible, thank you. I cannot infringe upon my rule even for such enticement."

Here Mrs. Vivian rose and sailed slowly about the

room, scrutinizing its arrangements; pulling aside a fragment of gold brocade that hung from the arm of an
antique and swept the floor, she extended her long arm,
brought out an object from its screen, and inspected it.

It was a spot of swamp where the rhodora grows in
leafless bloom, and the purple blossoms crowding the
place danced on the tips of their long stems like a swarm
of brilliant insects late lit from southern gales, waving
their antennæ, rustling their wings, eager and tremulous
for fresh flight. It bore as motto, written in delicate
characters beneath, the line:

"In May, when sea-winds pierced our solitudes."

"I must have it!" she exclaimed. "It is dainty and
matchless, — quite out of your style. Is the price fixed,
Mr. Sydney?"

"It has no price, madam."

"But you will arrange one? Pray don't hesitate."
And she named enormous sums.

"The thing is a trifle," I replied, "not worth a fraction
of what you mention. Nevertheless, I cannot part with
it."

"But my heart is set upon it. Pardon me — I am
rich."

"You are not rich enough to buy it."

"Then it is of value to you, — not your handiwork,
perhaps? Whose then? May I ask the artist's name?
Who painted this exquisite bit?"

I was more annoyed than I could express, dropped my
palette and pencils with a clang, stooped to collect them,
and then, as she still paused for a reply, gave one:

"My wife."

"Ah! — I had heard — I was scarcely aware — " and
here she ceased, in order to examine the picture anew.

Mrs. Vivian owed her usual success, as many others do, to a want of delicacy.

"Well, sir," said she, "your wife can paint you another; as for me —" and she held it arm's length while gazing.

I took the picture from her hand, as if she had wished to relinquish it, and restored it to its former place. She shrugged her shoulders slightly.

"I shall see that wife, Mr. Sydney, never fear, and engage her good services on my own behalf. In what seclusion she is cloistered. Is she from Stamboul? Do you keep a seraglio? . . . . Then you will not dine with me?" she added, rising, and fixing the glittering eyes upon me.

"I deplore my inability."

"Which means that you could if you chose." She paused a moment before my easel, and adventurously raised the curtain. "Shall I tell you what satisfaction I find in your work?" she said. "If one must link Emerson's sentences with chains of their own logic, and if Shakespeare leaves always room for your imagination, some painters possess the same great quality. In wondering at the boldness of your effects, I remember how Beethoven 'permitted' consecutive fifths."

She dropped the curtain and moved on.

"I shall do myself the honor of calling upon Mrs. Sydney, shortly," she continued, as a work-basket caught her eye.

"I thank you, but Mrs. Sydney does not receive calls," I replied.

She laughed, and the flash of white teeth completed her extremes of color. At the door she paused to disturb a pile of pencil-drawings.

"Wood-scenes? Illustrations?" she said. "Ah, Byron's Dream, I see. You comprehend so various manners, from fresco to missal! Have you ever seen a missal, by the way?"

"Never."

"No? I have one, a gorgeous little thing, the work of Attavante, the Florentine. I shall have pleasure in placing it at your disposal." And resting her perfectly gloved hand in mine a moment, she bowed, smiled, and was gone."

In the afternoon I received a parcel with Mrs. Dean Vivian's compliments. It was the missal, in a case of carved sandal-wood. Within was written, in faded ink: Vespasia — Rome, — and a date of some ten years before. She was then probably far my senior, and while looking at it, it seemed to me that my morning's guest had been some creature of the old Latin reign, and that the seal dropped from her chatelain had its device — *Væ Victis* — in her native tongue.

To the surprise of Eos, I left everything for the examination of this treasure — its arabesques, its floral wealth, its grotesque and brilliant fancies, its colors that defied time. At length I put it in my pocket and went out. I walked far; it was impossible to return till the mood that was on me should be past. I could not keep my thoughts away from the superb thing that had that morning filled my vision — from the serpentine grace, the splendid hues, the daring, dazzling manner; it was new, and fascinated like a vision of Lamia. I might have thought that my over-wrought fancy had belied me, but the casket of spicy wood that enclosed the precious fardel lay under my hand, and was actual. This woman seemed to me some Oriental creature of fire and strength, and not in herself so much as in her suggestion, I was charmed. All 'the old Eastern dream of my youth — picture of palm-tree and desert — wrapped me at remembrance of her. When I returned home, at twilight, Eos was sleeping in a chair by the grate; a book had slipped from her hand to the floor; it was the Arabian Nights. I took it; and as I read by the flickering flame awhile, the spell grew deeper; I saw Damascus's gardens of delight, Cairo's streets of grottoed shadow, the stainless sky of Philoë, the Nile, mystery of mysteries. I wondered how I had endured life with this pale phantom of a woman; I cursed the dense and crowded air. The sting was upon me; henceforth though I lingered, my tent was struck.

Day followed day now, and yet I achieved nothing. Eos saw that some trouble oppressed me; she could not become sweeter than before, but she made me feel her sweetness more, and she lavished such vital force as she possessed in counteracting the fatal influence; but what spell, what magnetism, could so feeble a nature exercise against the all-potent one of that jewel-eyed enchantress? She endeavored to soothe me with her quiet, to cheer me with her sunshine; she sang to me almost constantly, since frequently, when my sense of color became involved, fine tints, clear contrasts, rich combinations, unrolled themselves to my thought at her singing-voice. She twined fresh vines about the casts; she brought in her camellia-bush, mooned and cresseted with spotless blossom; she heaped vase and shell with mounds of snowy bloom: the only odor, that faintly distilled from some pure and dewy-cool moss-rose. It was all in vain. The first time I went to Vespasia's, the house reeked with the insidious perfume of a daphné-tree. . . . . .

Vespasia came also to me. She begged me not to cease work, and found herself a seat. I obeyed; for beneath her eyes I felt a power not my own flow through my fingers and enrich my canvas. While I worked, I recognized her will, her magic, as she reclined in the low chair behind me ; I submitted to her ordination, to the influx of foreign force ; my creations grew instinct with loveliness, the color spilled ripe and profuse from my pencil. A door opened, and Eos, unaware, stepped down. I hesitated, looked at her, and thought of St. Lucia bearing light to the blind ; my line faltered, my hand remained palsied, as it were : so might a Madonna confront the Venus of Titian. She welcomed the other in distant courtesy, but continued standing by the easel, firm, mild, and with, so to say, a gentle diffusive influence ; they were antagonists, and Vespasia retreated.

Vespasia came to my studio no more, but not once or twice only did I seek her, it became a constant custom. Every evening I was her guest, by her side I heard all choice music, her lips persuaded with honeyed eloquence, her presence was a cup of intoxication, she was an adept in all ravishing arts. Did I then love her ? No ; I loved Eos as far as I could love at all ; but Vespasia's boundless beauty, with its strange tone, her luxurious habit, her sumptuous surroundings, her prodigality of spirit and person and array, were like some rich oil that fed the flame of my genius till nothing seemed impossible to me. But for the other — did she keep watch and wait ? did her cheek grow pale, her eye restless ? did she gather greater quiet and more enduring patience ? In all this weary while, what became of Eos ?

One night I was with Vespasia at the opera. She was magnificent ; she was very gay, I fancy, also ; but though I kept my gaze fixed on her, I listened only to the music. As the curtain fell on the first act of Der Freyschütz, her eyes flashed for an instant toward the opposite portion of the house, and then I saw that she was exerting all her charms to retain my attention. Following a furtive glance thrown again at the same point, I met that of Eos. She was white and radiant, her eyes darkened and glittering. Beside her sat Alain. I excused myself for a few moments, and joined her.

" Eos?" I said. "And here? I left you at home, I thought."

" Certainly you did," said Alain, in a low tone, before she could reply. " I arrived in your absence, and saw that the first thing she needed was diversion ; and the next, a journey, which I hope to be able to persuade her to take, and to take in the direction of her old home."

I bent across Eos, so that none but he could hear me :

" M. Duchênecœur knows, perhaps, the price of such interference?" I murmured.

"And always meets his obligations," was the reply, with an indignant glance.

I offered Eos my hand, she rose, and we stepped into a coach at the vestibule. I did not suffer her to sit aloof, but held her in my arms, cheek to cheek. Perhaps I thought she understood me, perhaps I did not care. I left her in the studio, re-entered the coach, drove furiously back, and rejoined Vespasia as the curtain rose again. I was more disturbed than I wished should appear. I was half aware that some dream was broken, but turned and composed myself anew, like one who wished to continue it. Perhaps nothing could have aroused my attention, and therefore calmed me, sooner than the terrible diablerie of this drama, while its music was like a soothing hand on weary eyelids. I was again in the atmosphere of this regal woman, again breathing

9   M

her magic, stilled in her affluence ; again at the breath of horn and flute, with the chord of braided harmony — all soft and grateful color swathed me. I went home with Vespasia; others were there, the rooms were ringing, I stood shrouded in a curtain and looking out. There were the pavements wet with spring rain and shining in the light. There was a woman with her shawl wrapped closely about her, leaning against the lamp-post, her white face bent upward and covering the window with such a gaze as that with which a tigress protects her young ; she had no significance for me, — I was wrapped, remotely, in a mist of bewilderment and sense. Then the others went, the lights fell, there was only a luminous blush in the place from behind rosy transparencies. Vespasia floated on toward me ; I left the curtain, and sat at her feet.

"Do you remember," said she, "how the Fay Vivien bound Merlin?"

I did not reply, too involved in the enjoyment of delicious fancy. Her arm was upon my shoulder ; I was conscious of her form bending above me, of the bunch of geraniums and lemon-leaves that blazed upon her bosom and loaded the air with superabundant sweetness, of her breath sweeping my cheek. I heard a voice that seemed to issue from a cloud in one swift murmur :

"Sydney, do you love me?"

A thorn of the sweetbrier bud which I had taken from Eos stung my hand. I did not look at Vespasia, but rose and walked from the room, from the house, out into cool night air, sleet, and wind, and freedom.

Reaching home, I sought Eos. She was neither in the studio nor elsewhere ; she was not to be found. A wild suspicion crossed me, — I leaped down the stairs to the door; something lay under the shadows of the porch, head drooping, arm outflung; it was she. I carried her in and summoned assistance. She was in a heavy stupor; with the morning, in high fever. Standing by her bedside, I did not remember our words of the evening before, when Alain entered.

"Too late, as I feared," he said impetuously. "You succeed beyond my anticipations. I thought you had only broken her heart, and it seems you have taken her life!"

I could not care, just then, for anything he might say "Hush!" was all I answered.

He looked about the room; its appointments were chaste and costly enough. "Yes," he murmured, "you become opulent, or hold the talisman to be so. Your work commands enormous amounts; one stroke of the brush fills the purse —— but all your gold is coined from her heart's blood!"

"It has not been at my option to do other than I have done," I replied, somewhat moved.

He laughed in his low-mocking way. "They are all alike," he muttered; "from Attila to Sydney, they are all the scourge of God, the instruments."

I put my hand upon his shoulder and pointed at the door. I was roused, and my eyes must have flamed.

He glanced back at Eos, and turned. "No," he said, "I shall remain; she is almost my sister, she will need me, too."

"She needs no one," I exclaimed in the same suppressed tone; "she has me."

"She will not have you long, the fit will pass, and revert to your oil-tubes and pencils," he replied coolly. "Well, — I will stoop so much and ask it: let me stay."

So he stayed. She was ill long; so soon as delirium and danger were past, I resumed my painting; I had orders to fill, and ideas to elaborate. I was fortunate beyond thought; I had never so nearly brought my performance to the level of my conception. Weeks passed swiftly, the night went, the summer was upon us. Alain, who, it may be, began to see that any other than the course which I had pursued was impossible with me, remitted his hostility. More faithful and careful than a watch-dog, he followed Eos, wheeled her sofa into the studio, lifted and held her that she might see me work, recounted to her incidents of my fame, sang to her, read to her, ransacked the markets for dainty fruits — pomegranates from Florida, granadillas, all glowing and gorgeous infiltrations of tropical sweetness and wealth. When the twilight came, at close of our wedding-day, I took her in my arms and walked with her till she slept. Alain, meanwhile, neglected none of his studies; he read us his father's letters, and his conversation, when best pleased, was chiefly of his future home in the East. At the word, all the old fire flashed up in my veins, again the desert-mania, the pyramids, the eternal sands.

At last Alain bade us farewell for years; he was to take the Arabia. Eos was restored, and on the day of his departure, we went into the country by the sea-shore Worn with watching and close application, my eyes troubled me, and Eos, in the hours when sketching was abandoned, read aloud; the book she happened on was Eothen; as she proceeded, the fascination became like the eye of the basilisk, drawing me eastward; I bade her exchange it, and she found Vathek; she repeated to me Fatima, and she sang to me a strange German

Song of Sand. When I walked by the shore, again the imperious longing seized me; my fancy travelled along this vast level of calm seas to find the loneliness it coveted, but not the fertilizing heat, the languor, the wild strange life; — bitter salt and cold was the sea. The desire rose unbidden perpetually, it lingered against my wish, it became morbid, and goaded me like the gadfly of Io. I was not ready for extended travel yet. America I recognized as the prime school of landscape; I had a principle in the thing, and wished to drain the cup at my lips ere turning to the lees of that drained centuries ago; moreover, I feared lest originality should vanish before the overpowering vitality of that old land, and I fall into mere worship. So, after a time, we went back to the city, and so for three years I plodded on. It was not like the weary plodding of others, there was never failure, always satisfaction, always an interior and intense joy, a joy over the beauty that was in the universe, and my mastery thereof, that was a perennial intoxication of triumph. Thus these three years were a season of ideal revelry; at their close I possessed myself in more strength than ever heretofore, and yet the earth revealed to me her secrets. Still, while I wore deeper and deeper the grooves of my orbit, Eos waited on me pale and patient as a satellite, — other than so, she saw I did not need her; she spoke little, she smiled only on me, at my day and night absences she made no word of remonstrance, she allowed me to find pleasure where I might, convinced that all was but the nutritive compost required to bring the germs of thought into blossom on my canvas; she became impervious to jealousy; once, capable of anger — albeit, angry as a dove's wing makes lightning — such a thing could no longer strike a spark from her sensation;

no indifference, or neglect, or wrong, wrung from her complaint, all suffering had found its ebullition in the night preceding her illness: she was Eos still, but without the spirit.   There grew in her eyes that look of desolation to be found in those of so many a tutelary saint; I remembered when they were bluer than snow-shadows, and sparkled with perpetual sunshine.

It was the third summer since Alain had left us; we went to the mountains this year, and with Eos at my hand, I ranged them again.   There was hardly a crevice in their old seamed sides which I did not know.   I knew where the black bear kept his den, and where the snakes coiled, and hissed, and bred; in the clouds upon their summits I had been wrapped, in their valleys stifled.   It was a different life that I wanted, a different race of men from these stolid mountaineers; I wearied of the pastoral — the shining armaments of war, the spear, and the bit, were flashing ever before me — my mind made pictures that this cold North could never realize.

One day, at dinner, there were some fresh arrivals, and, in the course of making acquaintance, the conversation became personal.

"That reminds me," said one.   "Do you know Mrs. Vivian?"

"Dean Vivian's widow?"

"I suppose so, somebody's widow; wealthy, superb, eyes like broken bottle-glass."

"Oh, — very well."

"You know, then, that she has left Europe?"

"I was not aware that she had been there.   When will she arrive?"

"I believe the passage is not long from Marseilles to Alexandria.   She will *never* arrive in America, she has forsworn it, and returns to the East."

"Indeed! That is a great loss."

"Yes, in some respects. It is better, on the other hand, to have every object fulfil its destiny; hers was not in civilization. She always appeared, in my object-glass, like some savage thing panting with restraint: one of those desert-creatures, full of wary, feline instincts, ready to throw off mask and sheathe claws in the desired prey. Ah, sir?" turning to me.

"Not at all," I replied, "she seemed to me eminently human. I fancied there had been Roman women like her."

"Impossible! That is because you misapprehend, and are led astray by her name. I remembered, when I used to see her, the beautiful Ghoul whom the Arabian prince married unawares, the genie and great fairy with woman-faces and ophidian extremities. Yes, her very gait, if you ever noticed, was not like that of most stately females, it was sinuous or sidelong, never attaining any mark by a straight line; and, upon my soul! it would not be hard to take the rustle of her silks for hissing. Just imagine the transformation as Keats has done. See the

'Gordian shape of dazzling hue,
Vermilion-spotted, golden, green, and blue,
Striped like a zebra, freckled like a pard,
Eyed like a peacock, and all crimson barred
And full of silver moons, that as she breathes
Dissolve, or brighter shine.'

The very Serpent, slipping among the arid sparkling wastes of sand; I expect yet to see some of her victims set their heel upon her head. Well, it is gratifying to have any substance acknowledge its magnet, and Mrs. Vivian takes to the sun rarely. It allows hope that, by and by, all the extraneous will filter off, and leave

only, in a millennial world, the pure ore, that is to say,
you and I, sir, and little madam here!" With which he
bowed to his wife, and built a ditch and glacis in her salt-
cellar, while waiting for dessert.

"After such a harangue, my dear," said the lady,
"your auditory will suspect you of being one of the
victims."

"I shall disown the 'soft impeachment.' My auditory
know my specialty; I do not paint pictures, I paint characters."

"It is not Mrs. Vivian's character so much as her
personal suggestions, that you have sketched," I interposed.

"And they *are* her character precisely, taking the
parallax into account. You know, sir, that the way to
see a star best is not to look at it directly."

Here Eos rose, and I was glad to follow. We wandered all the afternoon, and came at length upon a wet spot
where the scarlet cardinals grew. As I plucked and Eos
twined them in her hat, I looked up the great rock that
towered behind, and put my hand upon its stained face,
unheated by all the August sun. I surveyed the narrow
valley, the unyielding barrier of mountains that enclosed
me, the pale sky that stretched cold and thin above me;
I gathered another handful of the cardinals, and thought
of great African lilies, of skies brimmed with inexhaustible azure that contrast with the angles of a tent gives violet
tinges deep as the lees of claret. I felt oppressed by the
great dumb life crowding upon me, I wished to push the
gigantic flanks aside, I longed for a sparkle, a rush; solid
and heavy and immobile, I desired the slight and capricious
and rapid; shut so that my very thoughts met with re-
bound and struck again my own breast, I would have given

half my life for a gallop over long flat sands. The table-
talk, with its hints of the Orient, had fanned the embers
to a flame; my blood seemed to pour like some fierce
torrent against my pulse; at each glance that sought to
reach a distance, the hills opposed their opaque wall;
included and restrained, I felt myself in prison with all
their weight on my soul. My heart beat in my throat,
I drew my breath like fire.

"Eos," I said, "I shall go to the East."

"I thought you would," was all she replied, gathering
up the reins.

"There is nothing left me here," I continued; "the
great rivers, prairies, everglades, I have sucked them all
dry. I may go on with endless repetitions till we die.
Besides, they have no storied sanctity, the pyramids do
not begin nor the blameless Ethiops end them. My eye
craves leagues of interminable extent and stillness, distant
air tremulous above burning lands, where vast stretches
are compressed in one indefinable line as sky and earth
meet, light intense and overflowing with positive vitality,
— strong enough to sting faint eyes to death. I am
weary of undulations, heights that I can overtop, intervals
whose boundaries I know, — I long for level immeasura-
bility. It cannot be a thought of Elephantine caverns
or ruined lauras, temple, or sphinx; it is the wide horizon,
the fathomless azure, the limitless sand, — heat, and languor, and life. I am in fetters!" I exclaimed. "Invention smothered, expression checked, I cannot breathe
this air; I must go, Eos, I must go!"

"Yes," said Eos; "but it is so long."

"So long! What lengthens our time there more than
here?"

"Then I, also — can I go?"

9 *

" Can ?   Must !   After all, Eos, it is to paint that I go
to the East — and without you ?   I might as well paint
without daylight."

" But your heats, your languors, — I shall die, — I am
not strong ; I nearly dissolved in Florida, you know."

When had Eos objected to any project so urged by me,
before, and objected on such grounds ?   I turned and took
her bridle.

" You were thinking of Vespasia," I said.   " *I* was not.
I never cared for the woman, but for her influences.   Her
East is far beyond, moreover ; swarthier skies are there,
and its shores are laved by more southern seas.   It is
unlikely that we shall meet.   Yet fancy, Eos ! if we
should, how splendid the picture : white dromedaries, and
red saddle-cloths, and the face of Vespasia, from her airy
throne, flashing by us in the wilderness.   So the Enchantress Queen Labe might journey from the secret Nile
Source to the city of great Magiana !"

Eos touched her little mountain pony with the switch,
and then bent her head as she subdued his curvetting.
That was not effected at once, and we proceeded home in
silence.

Swift and deft beyond all other women, she completed
our preparations in season for the next steamer ; and
suddenly, one day, all my dreams were accomplished, for
we touched the shores of Africa.

We remained, during the winter, for purposes of re-
search and acclimation, within the precincts of the old
historic town — alien and fantastic — that received us.   I
wished, also, to take the plains in their utmost ardor ;
meanwhile, I was not idle.   With the spring, we obtained
a convoy and began our Arab life.   When my foot

touched the stirrup, when my horse first bounded beneath
my heel, when some city — whose strange, sweet name
savored of dates, and palm-wine, and 'lucent syrops tinct
with cinnamon' — veiled itself behind us, and leagues
and leagues away and around spread the glimmering
sheets, when I beheld that deep line of perpetual flight
whose profound color amassed that of so many horizons,
when for the first time I found the life I had sought, —
the bivouac, the siesta, the journeying by early stars, —
far from experiencing the exhilaration I had foreseen, I
felt myself utterly satisfied and at rest. But, in truth, so
far from rest, the state in which I was resembled that
swift revolution of bodies where they appear to be
motionless: it was the very acme of unrest. Nothing
surprised me in all that was so new; my very array
occasioned me no hinderance, it seemed as if I had never
worn another, picturesque and varied in all gay shades,
effeminate and light as wrappings of air; accustomed to
and demanding luxury, the simplicity of this life became
at once mine, the primitive manners charmed me, the
coarse fare contented me. In the night, the Arabs
circled round the dying fire made groups where *chiaro-
oscuro* could do no more; in the day we crossed the track
of some kindred party, or exchanged salutes with a
parcel of French chasseurs, or encountered the great
half-yearly caravan, defiling straight along the pathless
waste, resplendent in arms, gorgeous in color, fluttering
in fringe and scarf and banner, and snatching the breath
from the lips with its clamor, and swiftness, and grace.
Sometimes many successive halts were made near wells
of fresh sweet water, or at other times the provision,
tepid and rank, carried in the skins, sufficed us for days;
to me, even this was almost welcome, and joyfully remem-

bered as a portion of the wild delight of the life. Eos,
pillowed and canopied aloft on her mattress, uttered no
complaint when perishing of thirst, never murmured at
the heat or the jolting gait of her camel; she retreated farther under her coverings, and when the cry ran along the
line, leaned forth feebly in the hot quiet to draw strength
from the yet distant oasis whose palm-plume was cut upon
the azure like a gem. Later, with the softness, the sudden
nights that fell without twilight, the stars that hung great
and glowing from their vaults of crystalline darkness, in
the gloom, the coolness, the shelter of tamarisk-thicket
and breath of rose-laurel, she became refreshed and
enlivened, and appeared, once more, airy and light-hearted
as when in youth. How should I have known that in
that dreadful sun, those scorching winds, she suffered so?
She never told me, and my own keen enjoyment flushed
me too fully to allow perception of any pain in the world.

Thus we journeyed. We halted in strange cities of
the desert, till then unguessed; we took up our march
again from ruins over which the restless sand had blown
for centuries; all the way began to assume a new aspect,
vague, unnatural, almost demoniacal. As we went, the
great monumental camels, lost from wandering tribes,
strange sad beasts that seem the relics of some primeval
era, came and surveyed us, standing gaunt and stolid and
stony and starved between us and the sky; the little sala-
manders twisted and slipped among the burning sands;
hot exhalations rose and maddened the animals; the sirocco played fearful fantasies in our brains; the flying
lines, the alluring distances, buried themselves in mocking mirage, the watercourses became dry, the sun
withered the eye that looked abroad, the summer heats
beset us.

Our guides, who regarded everything as a matter of
course, sought shelter and sleep. Eos, every limb flaccid,
every nerve unstrung, drooped weaker and fainter, with
no word, at last, even for me, — with imperceptible breath,
and nothing but a fluttering pulse to tell the life within
her. When the night came, all retook courage. As for
me, I did not need it: I was in a state of inexhaustible
well-being, I was bathed in the lustre of these overflowing heavens, I drank the divine melancholy of infinite
distance, I was penetrated with warmth and satiated
with light.

One day, just before the noon halt, there suddenly rose
upon our vision a small caravan, rose from no one knew
where, since in the desert, owing perhaps to space, such
sights' come and go like ephemera. It consisted of a
pack-camel whose driver urged it along at intervals with
a peculiarly shrill song, and following, an Arab horseman,
the trappings of purple and burnished silver glowing in
the sun, and a dun-colored dromedary. From a seat of
sumptuous cushions high embossed on the latter, a figure,
all in white, bent, lifted aside its veil, and a face, golden
in the noonlight, and with the sinister contrast of emerald
eyes, flashed upon me. It was the face of Vespasia.
The whole passed at a rapid pace, and became lost in the
depths of the desert. Shortly afterward, we paused, and
the little bivouac slept silent in siesta. While they rested,
I had been sketching, for I allowed nothing to escape me,
neither the hooded viper with his angry hue, in the patch
of grass, nor the scorpion writhing from sight, nor an
ostrich flying before the wind of his speed with all his
plumes spread and dancing. At last I entered the tent
and lay down. For a moment I pressed my hand upon
my eyes, a sudden darkness, edged with splendor, fol-

lowed, then shooting gleams and rings and fiery spires. I opened them in the soft demi-shade of the tent; the light was intolerable. I was alarmed.

"Eos," I said, "I can scarcely see, I am dazzled. We must remain encamped here till I recover; it would not be pleasant to be left in the dark, you know," and I laughed as I spoke.

Eos lifted her languid head, put back the hair, brought her dressing-case nearer after an effort, and wetting a handkerchief in some cool-ointment there, crept toward me and bound it about my eyes. Then she drew my head upon her bosom, and I fell asleep. When I awoke, it was with a sharp exclamation and then a laugh. My difficulty had vanished with rest. I saw Eos near the lifted hangings, and Alain bending over me. He had been with us in the winter, and had counted upon meeting us frequently during our travel. He was out with skirmishers, in pursuit of fragments of certain rebellious tribes. They lingered and took the evening meal with us.

Alain was no longer genial; on the contrary, as sardonic as I had ever at any time seen him, and now and then giving way to a biting sentence. At length his companions gave notice of departure. Alain rose and bade Eos good-night; I stepped outside with him.

"You are at your old tricks again!" said he abruptly, as we stood alone a moment. I did not understand him. "Eos is dying now in good earnest."

I was startled, and then remembered his habit. "Eos experiences lassitude from the heat," I replied, "nothing more. I have nearly finished my studies; we shall return, and all will be well."

Slightly soothed by my calmness, "Heaven grant it!" said he. "She is thinner than a shadow, in this accursed land where there are no shadows! She is transparent. I have not seen such pallor in a living countenance. Her eyes are more luminous, with the trace of those great blue half-circles below them, than these porcelain heavens. Yes, she is dying, I say!" he continued with more vehemence, "not only of heat and weariness, but of suppression! This aptitude, this power, this whatever you choose to call it, genius or inspiration, for which you refuse her utterance, this has produced a spiritual asphyxia. She had better be an Arab woman and live her life! You have killed her, but no one can hang you for it!" Before I could reply, he strode to his horse, mounted, and fled like an arrow to rejoin his fellows.

At the tent-door stood Eos; I took her in my arms and wandered up and down the place, once a green island in the sea of sand, now parched and withered. I told her of my success, I talked of what swayed my thoughts, I bade her have yet a few days' patience. Perhaps the sight of Alain had reanimated her, perhaps my unusual treatment; she slipped, at length, from my grasp and walked beside me and grew gay; now she ran a few paces in advance, now came back and hung over my hand; she sang broken tunes, bits of homesick airs, twittering and chirping, as I said, like a bird at dawn.

"Alain has teased you," said she at length. "He thinks me ill, I know; but I am perfectly well, only tired. And seeing Alain was like going home."

"We will go soon, Eos; you shall be there before the last harebells are faded, for what would the year be unless I saw their blue deepen the blue of your eyes? The grapes over your mother's arbor will just have purpled to your gathering,—do you remember once when you rubbed the bloom off the bunches that their skins might shine like Copts? I wonder if the honeysuckle by the south window is dead yet; its berries should be the color of chalcedony by this time; your mother used—"

"Don't speak of home!" cried Eos, bursting into a sudden passion of tears, clinging to me and speaking through her sobs. "Don't speak of home! Of those days! It breaks my heart to think of them!"

"Eos!" I said in surprise, "do you regret it so unhappily?"

"No, no, I am not unhappy! I am most blest, because you love me better than you ever did before; but once in a while all that rises, and I perish with longing."

"Dear child," I said, smoothing the fair, flying hair from her forehead, "you shall go to-morrow, if you will. I can easily find you escort, and then remain till my work is done, without you."

"Could you?" asked Eos, drying her tears. "But I could not; where you are is my home always. I am sorry I have been so naughty,—a hindering little thing, a weak and silly little wife!"

We lingered in silence a moment, to breathe the soft warm night, to feel the gentle air sighing in the tamarisks, to see the great jewelry of heaven that every night spread its brilliant net above the desert,—sapphire and chrysolite and ruby and beryl. As we went in, Eos pointed with her white finger at one star, just above the horizon, red as a drop of blood ready to fall.

Early, under the awfully white sheen of a desert moon, the tents were struck, and we were on our way again. There was all the awakening cheer of the morning,—the neighing horses, protesting camels, the stir of equipage, tintinnabulation of bells, and cries of Arabs. The heavens bleached, a stain like that from some ruddy and enormous blossom dyed the east, the shadows lengthened, rosy light welled up and filled the great hollow of the sky; there were no clouds, no pomp, nothing but intense lustre and overpowering heat.

I had gradually fallen behind the others, as here and there appeared subjects for my pencil, and had lost them entirely from view, since I liked much to find myself so unimpeded and utterly alone, trusting the instinct of my horse to recover the train on occasion. Nothing could equal the profound hush; it seemed as if the vast extent of stillness swallowed every noise into itself, as the sea closes over dross.

While this thought passed through my mind, my horse suddenly pricked his ears and quivered under my hand, throwing back his head with swollen nostril and clustered veins, and rolling a fiery eyeball about; he appeared to listen intently, standing crisp-maned, and with the stiffened muscular action of a bronze. In a moment, I heard a long low note winding from the right — a signal of alarm. I touched him with the spur, folded my implements as we went, and galloped in its direction.

The train had already ceased progress, and had encircled the women in a hollow square. Sheik Ibrahim, meeting me, assured me that there were indisputable signs of an enemy, that he had suspected it for two or three days, but judged that the presence of the French, within such short distance, would be a sufficient safeguard, and therefore had said nothing. I remonstrated with him on his posture of defence, urging that it invited attack. He replied it was well known that bands hostile to his own tribe patrolled the desert, and it was singular we had already met none of sufficient force to assail us, and that I should soon see if his precautions were vain.

N

Far from terror, I found Eos exhilarated and trembling with excitement; her hand lay in mine like ice, and her eyes were fixed on a distant and increasing point. My glance followed hers, and before long I could plainly detect the glitter of spear-heads, the flash of sunshine on mounted weapons, floating pennons, and a mingled splendor of color, while a strangely discordant yet thrilling music announced no peaceful errand. Our horsemen pranced up and down the line, their eyes sparkling, their scarfs streaming, with difficulty restraining themselves from hurling a shower of spears at their assailants.

An hour's waiting, and they were near enough to exchange defiance; a lance leaped out and fell at my feet; then, without a word's warning, a volley of musketry, and the impetuous charge. For a moment, all thought of defence abandoned me, as I found myself in the midst of the *mêlée*, with its great, leaping steeds, its tossing kaftans, its purple and scarlet and gold, its irate motion and gesture and shrilling trumpet-peals, its flaming eyes, and the one lithe figure that flashed to and fro, mercurial and savage, among the swords, ever insinuating nearer, — in the next, a blind instinct seized me, and the warlike fury.

I do not know how the little battle fell; our enemy exceeded us thrice; I can easily imagine that their certainty of victory already dashed us with defeat. I shook a hand from my shoulder, felt it again, turned and saw Eos, who had slipped from her nest, grasping a rusty old yataghan, and replete with spirit.

"Alain!" she cried, "Alain!"

And deliverance, with the French tirailleurs, was upon us. The hostile party swerved, broke precipitately and fled; the lithe figure, which I had remarked before, alone wheeled back upon us in a wide detour, poised suddenly in its career, and leaning on one stirrup from the saddle, dashed aside white burnous and violet turban-scarf, and, under the meteor of the uplifted sword-blade, I caught again that sinister dazzle of blazing leopard eyes. I had but time to fling Eos behind me when the blow descended and sheared a portion of her dress. As instantly the balance was restored, and the figure swept on, but not before I saw the long gleam of a tirailleur's polished barrel raised in the sun, and swiftly as it fled a swifter foe fled after. I shut my eyes, but I must have felt the bound, the reel, the headlong plunge, the dragging stirrup, till a second shot felled the horse with its rider.

"Yes," said Alain, a little later, when he joined us, "the very tribe we hunt! Well routed, too."

"Among them, effendi," said Ibrahim, "was an adventuress, who certainly purchased their favor with immense treasure. Their defeat is no less than a miracle of God, a blow for charging in mad noon at command of a woman! Dogs, and sons of dogs! God willed it; she lies there dead!"

Tender to the friend, inexorable to the enemy, with the one savage trait of his nature, Alain extended his hand to Eos.

"You can set your heel upon her head!" he said.

Eos flung him a glance like the blue light shed from the swallow's wing, and clung unreasonably to me.

I wonder now why she loved me, why, rather, she did not hate me! I had occasioned her only distress, I gave her no joy, no rest. Too sure it is that human attractions and repulsions are as invisible as potent.

This affair in nowise hurried our movements; we felt, henceforth, much safer, like those who have suffered a contagious illness to be suffered but once. I lingered farther from the camp, prolonged our stages, wrought up the hints afforded me, tried my effects in the face of what they sought to accomplish, imbibed the warmth and radiance like a fruit of the tropics, and felt myself constantly more affluent. But while I made such revelry of every day, to Eos they brought torture ; the reaction from the enthusiasm and shocks of the fray prostrated her, the heats still wrung away her vitality, the very sands became loathsome in her eyes ; lifted from one arm to another, she had that horror of touching them with her foot that one has of treading on a grave ; she seemed to fear, perpetually, the sight of those jewel-eyes, that trailing viscous length, those splendid dyes, sliding among the golden grains, — frequently she seemed fascinated and forced to seek for them ; the skirmish was every night re-enacted in her dreams ; she woke with the curve of the descending weapon and the glare of that envenomed gaze before her face, her sleep was a shivering nightmare, — finally, she ceased to sleep at all. But all these things I never thought of then, — blinder than now. And so my slow murder was accomplishing.

At length the summer was over, the term of Sheik Ibrahim's service expired, I turned my back upon the desert, — not forever, as I hoped, — bade farewell to these fierce rays that had ravished me from myself, to this feast of lustre, to these long lines that shared the grandeur of infinity ; I awoke from my debauch of light, I left the great solace of sun and solitude and space and silence. I threaded again the dark, narrow bazaars, and again, with Eos, found myself on level calms of blue water ; and thus, as it were, by gentle gradations came back to my old life.

At sea, Eos lay upon the deck, placid and peaceful, yet motionless; but people were always sick at sea, I said. Once at home, and reinstated in our old ways, I looked for her recovery, and looked in vain; it became necessary to regard her as a confirmed invalid. That is the case with all American women, I said. I found her attendance, then missed her unfailing services that I had never recognized, and wondered if I could not anticipate my own wants. She lay, during the greater portion of the day, on a couch at the lower window of the room where I painted, and now I worked with a will and energy I had never known before. I rose at daybreak to contemplate my progress; I scarcely allowed myself time for my daily food; I took no recreation: it was recreation enough, it was complete joy, thus to reproduce the only summer, I declared, in which I had ever lived. I combined, and eliminated, and heightened, there was no strength possible to my palette which I did not demand, I exhausted the secrets of my art, my eyes grew heated with fixed labor, my breath, itself, paused on my lips. Eos, as intent as I, watched its growth with a fever in her cheek, and, in her feeble way, grew blithe at any powerful success. She used to follow me with her glance; now and then, yet seldom, she beckoned me to leave all and kiss her, she was so weak that she scarcely ever attempted to walk; except to carry her from room to room, to obey her rare requests, I was too absorbed to be more than remotely sensible of her existence. But she — she seemed to concentrate the love of long life into those few months. Once, when my sight was fatigued, I sat and shaded it with my hand; she thought me confused in color, and remembered her old remedy, rose, reached the piano, and slowly unwound a chain of clear, fine chords, a rill of melody stealing through them to be lost in closing chords finer and sweeter, the rich sediment that had remained in her memory from some imposing Mass. The sound, so unusual now, startled me.

"Eos !" I exclaimed, "what has happened? Are you well?"

"You know the wick flashes up when the flame is extinguished, if the day is to be fine to-morrow," she said, and laughed.

Then her face grew still, her eye wistful, she staggered and fell, and I bore her to the couch again.

So the winter skimmed away, it grew to be late in the spring, and I could look forward to the completion of my work. I did not think, then, of its pompous parade, its triumphal march from town to town, of its throng of lovers, of its world-wide fame; I saw and felt only its beauty, and needed no other recompense. There lay the desert before me again, its one moment of dawn, when the sands blanched, the skies blenched, and the opposite quarter dreamed of rosy suffusion to cast it again yet more faintly on the white dromedary and the white-wrapped Arab beside him. They, and their long pallid shadows falling from the east, alone taught me the ineffable solitude and hush; beyond them, I found again the lengthening lines, the hints of fuller light, slow and fine detail, desert compressed within desert, space and immensity daringly shut on a canvas. There was the sparkle of the sterile stretch, the wide air emptied of its torrid stings, the eternal calm and peace — the melancholy for one, the rapture for another. There was the soul of summer shed, older and more mysterious and sadder than the sea, fresh made with every morn in vigor and hope, — the work was worth its price!

One day I waited merely for the artisans with the frame. I went gayly and sat down on Eos's couch. I took her in my arms, — she was lighter than any child, — laid her head on my shoulder, and talked to her a few moments of my hopes and certainties. Then we were silent. She lifted her hand and placed it on my forehead.

"How glad I am that you love me as you do," she said. "Other love might regard me as a separate thing, seek my ease or pleasure aside, but you have made and felt me a part of yourself. I am glad, darling, and I thank God for you!"

She lifted her still beautiful head and pressed her lips to mine, long, fervently, and as if she wished I should drink the last drops of her life, — then sank back.

I heard the men on the stairs. I dropped her among her cushions, drew the screen, and admitted them. That was soon done. Then there were a few touches yet to be given, some delicate strokes, a shadow to deepen, a light to intensify, and the radiant thing stood perfect before me.

"Eos, my work is ended!" I cried. "There is nothing more to do!"

I stepped back; I scanned it intently; I turned, bewildered; and, at a sharp sting, drew my fingers down my lids. At the touch, a spear, as of some Northern Light, leapt across my vision, then murk darkness, and creeping over that, my picture, the sands of the desert, forever and forever stretched before my eyes.

"Who has drawn the shades?" I asked. "Have I worked till night? Eos, are you here?"

I moved forward, the bell from a neighboring church-tower struck the hour of noon, my hand passed through the open window and clutched empty air, groped back again and lay on features bathed in vapid chill.

Truly, there was nothing more to do, — in all my life long, nothing more to do! Night had fallen at noon. I was blind, and Eos was dead.

Midsummer and May.

10

Midsummer and May.

I.

ROBABLY you never saw such a superb creature, — if that word, creature, does not endow her with too much life : a Semiramis, without the profligacy, — an Isis, without the worship, — a Sphinx, yes, a Sphinx, with her desert, who long ago despaired of having one come to read her riddle, strong, calm, patient perhaps. In this respect she seemed to own no redundant life, just enough to eke along existence, — not living, but waiting.

I say, all this would have been one's impression ; and one's impression would have been incorrect.

I really cannot state her age ; and having attained to years of discretion, it is not of such consequence as it is often supposed to be, whether one be twenty or sixty. You would have been confident, that, living to count her hundreds, she would only have bloomed with more immortal freshness ; but such a thought would not have occurred to you at all, if you had not already felt that she was no longer young, — she possessed so perfectly that certain self-reliance, self-understanding, *aplomb*, into which little folk crystallize at an early age, but which is not to be found with those whose identities are cast in a larger mould, until they have passed through periods of fuller experience.

That Mrs. Laudersdale was the technical magnificent woman, I need not reiterate. I wish I knew some name gorgeous enough in sound and association for that given her at christening; but I don't. It is my opinion that she was born Mrs. Laudersdale, that her coral-and-bell was marked Mrs. Laudersdale, and that her name stands golden-lettered on the recording angel's leaf simply as Mrs. Laudersdale. It is naturally to be inferred, then, that there was a Mr. Laudersdale. There was. But not by any means a person of consequence, you assume? Why, yes, of some, — to one individual at least. Mrs. Laudersdale was so weak as to regard him with complacency; she loved — adored her husband. Let me have the justice to say that no one suspected her of it. Of course, then, Mr. Roger Raleigh had no business to fall in love with her.

Well, — but he did.

At the time when Mrs. Laudersdale had become somewhat more than a reigning beauty, and held her sceptre with such apparent indifference that she seemed about abandoning it forever, she no longer dazzled with unventured combinations of colors and materials in dress. She wore most frequently, at this epoch, black velvet that suppled about her well-asserted contours; and the very trail of her skirt was unlike another woman's, for it coiled and bristled after her with a life and motion of its own, like a serpent. Her hair, of too dead a black for gloss or glister, was always adorned with a nasturtium-vine, whose vivid flames seemed like some personal emanation, and whose odor, acrid and single, dispersed a character about her; and the only ornaments she condescended to assume

were of Etruscan gold, severely simple in design, elabo-
rately intricate in workmanship. It is evident she was a
poet in costume, and had at last *en règle* acquired a manner. But thirteen years ago she apparelled herself otherwise, and thirteen years ago it was that Mr. Roger Raleigh
fell in love with her. This is how it was.

Among the many lakes in New Hampshire, there is one
of extreme beauty, — a broad, shadowy water, some nine
miles in length, with steep, thickly wooded banks, and
here and there, as if moored on its calm surface, an island
fit for the Bower of Bliss. At one spot along its shore
was, and still is, an old country-house, formerly used as a
hotel, but whose patrons, always pleasure-seekers from the
neighboring towns, had been drawn away by the erection
of a more modern and satisfactory place of entertainment
at the other extremity of the lake, and it had now been
for many years closed. There were no dwellings of any
kind in its vicinity, so that it reigned over a solitude of a
half-dozen miles in every direction. Once in a while the
gay visitors in the more prosperous regions stretched their
sails and skimmed along till they saw its white porticos
and piazzas gleaming faintly up among the trees; once
in a while a belated traveller tied his horse at the gate,
and sought admittance in vain, at the empty house, of the
shadows who may have kept it. It was not pleasant to
see so goodly a mansion falling to ruin for want of fit oc-
cupancy, truly; and just as the walls had grown gray with
rain and time, the chimneys choked and the casements
shrunken, a merry company of friends and families, from
another portion of the country, consolidated themselves
into a society for the pursuit of happiness, rented the old
place, put in carpenters and masons and glaziers, and,
when the last tenants vacated the premises, took posses-

sion in state themselves. Care and responsibility were
not theirs; the matron and her servants alone received
such guests; the long summer-days were to come and
go with them as joyously as with Bacchus and his
crew.

Behold the party domesticated a fortnight at the Bawn,
as it was afterward dubbed. Mr. Laudersdale had returned to New York that morning, and his wife had not
been met since. Now, at about five o'clock, her white
robe floated past the door, and she was seen moving up
and down the long piazza and humming a faint little tune
to herself. Just then a flock of young women, married
and single, fluttered through door and windows to join
her; and just then Mrs. Laudersdale stepped down from
the end of the piazza and floated up the garden-path and
into the woods that skirted the lake-shore and stretched
far back and away. Thus abandoned, the others turned
their attention to the expanse before and below them; and
one or two made their way down to the brink, unhooked a
boat, ventured in, and, lifting the single pair of oars, were
soon laboring gayly out and creating havoc on the placid
waters.

As Mrs. Laudersdale continued to walk, the path which
she followed slowly descended to the pebbly rim, rich in
open spaces, slopes of verdure just gilding in the declin-
ing sun, and coverts of cool, deep shadow. As she advanced leisurely, involved in pleasant fancy, something
caught her eye, an unusual object, certainly, lying in a
duskier recess; she drew nearer and hung a moment
above it. Some fallen statue among rank Roman growth,
some marble semblance of a young god, overlaced with a
vine and plunged in tall ferns and beaded grasses? And
she, bending there, — was it Diana and Endymion over

again, Psyche and Eros? Ah, no! — simply Mrs. Laudersdale and Roger Raleigh.   Only while one might have
counted sixty did she linger to take the real beauty of the
scene : the youth, adopted as it were, to Nature's heart
by the clustering growth that sprang up rebounding under
the careless weight that crushed it ; an attitude of complete and unconscious grace, — one arm thrown out beneath the head, the other listlessly fallen down his side,
while the hand still detained the straw hat ; the profile,
by no means classic, but in strong relief, the dark hair
blowing in the gentle wind, the flush of sleep that went
and came almost perceptibly with the breath, and the
sunbeam that slanting round suddenly suffused the whole.
"Pretty boy!" thought Mrs. Laudersdale.   Beautiful
picture!" and she flitted on.   But Roger Raleigh was
not a boy, although sleep, that gives back, to all, stray
glimpses of their primal nature, endowed him peculiarly
with a look of childlike innocence unknown to his waking
hours.

Startled, perhaps, by the intruding step, for it was no
light one, a squirrel leaped from the bough to the grass,
and, leaping, woke the sleeper.   He himself now unper-
ceived, saw a vision in return, — this woman, young and
rare, this queenly, perfect thing, floating on and vanishing
among the trees.   Whence had she come, and who was
she ? And hereupon he remembered the old Bawn and
its occupants.   Had she seen him ? Unlikely ; but yet,
unimportant as it was, it remained an interesting and
open question in his mind.   Bringing down the hair so
ruffled in the idle breeze, he crowded his hat over it with
a determined air, half ran, half tumbled, down the bank,
sprang into his boat, and, shaking out a sail, went flirting
over the lake as fast as the wind could carry him.   Leav-

ing a long, straight, shining wake behind him, Mr. Roger
Raleigh skimmed along the skin of ripples, and, in order
to avoid a sound of shrill voices, skirted the angle of an
island, and found himself deceived by the echo and in the
midst of them.

Mrs. McLean, Miss Helen Heath, and Miss Mary
Purcell, who had embarked with a single pair of oars,
were now shipwrecked on the waters wide, as Helen
said; for one of their means of progress, she declared,
had been snatched by the roaring waves and was floating
in the trough of the sea, just beyond their reach. None
of the number being acquainted with the process of scull-
ing, they considered it imperative to secure the truant
tool, unless they wished to perish floating about unseen;
and having weighed the expediency of rigging Helen into
a jury-mast, they were now using their endeavors to regain the oar, — Mary Purcell whirling them about like a
maelström with the remaining one, and Mrs. McLean
with her two hands grasping Helen's garments, while the
latter half stood in the boat and half lay recumbent on the
lake, tipping, slipping, dipping, till her head resembled a
mermaid's; while they all three filled the air with more
exclaim, shrieking, and laughter than could have been
effected by a large-lunged mob.

"Bedlam let loose," thought the intruder, "or all the
Naiads up for a frolic?" And as he shot by, a hush fell
upon the noisy group, — Helen pausing and erecting herself from her ablutions, Mary's frantic efforts sending them
as a broadside upon the Arrow and nearly capsizing it, and
Mrs. McLean, ceasing merriment, staring from both her
eyes, and saying nothing. Mr. Raleigh seized the oar in
passing, and directly afterward had placed it in Helen's
hands. Receiving it with a profusion of thanks, she

seated herself and bent to its use. But, looking back in
a few seconds, Mr. Raleigh observed that the exhausted
rowers had made scarcely a yard's distance. He had no
inclination for gallantry, his eyes and thoughts were full
of his late vision in the woods, he wished to reach home
and dream ; but in a moment he was again beside them,
had taken their painter with a bow and an easy sentence,
but neither with *empressement* nor heightened color, and,
changing his course, was lending them a portion of the
Arrow's swiftness in flight towards the Bawn. It seemed
as if the old place sent its ghosts out to him this afternoon.
Bearing close upon the flat landing-rock, and hooking the
painter therein, he sheered off, lifting his hat, and was
gone.

"Roger! Roger Raleigh!" cried Mrs. McLean, from
the shore, "come back!"

Obeying her with an air of puzzled surprise, the person so unceremoniously addressed was immediately beside
her again.

"A cool proceeding, sir!" said she, extending both her
hands. "How long would you know your Cousin Kate
to be here, and refuse to spare her an hour?"

"Upon my honor," said her cousin, bending very low
over the hands, "I but this moment learn her presence
in my neighborhood."

"Ah, sir! and what becomes of my note sealed with
sky-blue wax and despatched to you ten days ago?"

"It is true such a note lies on my table at this moment, and it is still sealed with sky-blue wax."

"And still unread?"

"You will not force me to confess such delinquency?"

"And still unread?"

"Ten thousand pardons! Shall I go home and read

10*   o

it?" And herewith the saucy indifference of his face became evident, as he raised it.

"No. But is that the way to serve a lady's communications? Fie, for a gallant! I must take you in hand. These are your New Hampshire customs?"

"'O Kate, nice customs curtsy to nice kings!'"

"So I've heard, when curtsying was in fashion; but that is out of date, together with a good many other nice things, — caring for one's friends, for instance. Why don't you ask how all your uncles and aunts are, sir?"

"How are all my uncles and aunts, Miss?"

"Oh, don't you know? I thought you did n't. There's another billet, enclosing a bit of pasteboard, lying on your table now unopened too, I'll warrant. Don't you read any of your letters?"

"Alphabetical or epistolary?"

"Answer properly, yes or no."

"No."

"Why?"

"I know no one that has authority to write to me, as half a reason."

"Thank you, for one, sir. And what becomes of your Uncle Reuben?"

"Not included in the category."

"Then you're not aware that I've changed my estate? You don't know my name now, do you?"

> "'Bonny Kate, and sometimes Kate the curst,
> But Kate, the prettiest Kate in Christendom.'"

"Nonsense! What an exasperating boy! Just the same as ever! Well, it explains itself. Here comes a recent property unto me appertaining. McLean! My husband, Mr. John McLean, — my cousin, Mr. Roger Raleigh."

The new-comer was one of those "sterling men" always to be relied on, generally to be respected, and safely and appropriately leading society and subscription-lists. He was not very imaginative, and he understood at a glance as much of the other as he ever would understand. And the other, feeling instantly that only coin of the king's stamp would pass current here, turned his own counter royal side up, and met his host with genuine cordiality. Shortly afterward, Mrs. McLean withdrew for an improvement in her toilet, and soon returning, found them comparing notes as to the condition of the country, tender bonds of the Union, and relative merits of rival candidates, for all which neither of them cared a straw.

"How do you find me, sir?" she asked of her cousin.

"Radiant, rosy, and rarely arrayed."

"I see that your affections are to be won, and I proceed accordingly, by making myself charming, in the first place. And now, will you be cheered, but not inebriated, here under the trees, in company with dainty cheese-cakes compounded by these hands, and jelly of Helen Heath's moulding, and automatic trifles that caught an ordaining glimpse of Mrs. Laudersdale's eye and rushed madly together to become almond-pasty?"

"With a method in their madness, I hope."

"Yes, all the almonds not on one side."

"In company with cheese-cakes, jelly, and pasty, simply, — I should have claret and crackers at home, Capua willing. Will it pay?"

"You shall have Port here, when Mrs. Laudersdale comes."

"Not old enough to be crusty yet, Kate," said her husband.

" Very good, for you, John ! "

" Mrs. Laudersdale is your housekeeper ? " asked her
cousin.

" Mrs. Laudersdale ?   That is rich !   But I should
never dare to tell her.   Our housekeeper ?   Our cyno-
sure !   She is our argent-lidded Persian Girl, — our se-
rene, imperial Eleänore ; —

> ' Whene'er she moves,
> The Samian Here rises, and she speaks
> A Memnon smitten with the morning sun.' "

" Oh, indeed !   And this is a conventicle of young mat-
rimonial victims to practise cookery in seclusion, upon
which I have blundered ? "

" If the fancy pleases you, yes.   There they are."

And hereon followed a series of necessary introductions.

Mr. Roger Raleigh sat with both arms leaning on the
table before him, and wondering which of the ladies, half
whose names he had not heard, was the Samian Here, —
if any of them were, — and if, — and if, —— and here Mr.
Roger Raleigh's reflections went wandering back to the
lake-side path and its vision.   Not inopportunely at this
moment, a white garment, which, it is unnecessary to say,
he had long ago seen advancing, fluttered down the opposite path, and she herself approached.

" Ah !   *Al fresco ?* " said the pleasantest voice in the
world.

" And is n't it charming ? " asked Mrs. McLean.   " Imagine us with tables spread outside the door in Fifth Avenue, in Chestnut Street, or on the Common ! "

" Even then the arabesque would be wanting," said
she, trailing a long branch of the wild grape-vine, with
its pale and delicately fragrant blooms, along the snowy
board.   " Are the cheese-cakes a success, Mrs. McLean ?

I did n't dine, and am famished. — I see that you have
at last heard from your cousin," she added, in an undertone.

"Yes; let me pre — Roger!"

Quickly frustrating any such presentation, Mr. Roger
Raleigh half turned, and, bowing, said, —

"I believe I have had the pleasure of meeting Mrs.
Laudersdale before."

Her haughtiness would have frozen any one else. She
bent with the least possible inclination, and sat down upon
a stump that immediately became a throne. He resumed
his former position, and drummed lightly on the table,
while waiting to be served. In less complete repose than
she had previously seen him, Mrs. Laudersdale now examined anew the individual before her.

Not by any means tall she found him, but having the
square shoulders and broad chest which give, in so much
greater a degree than mere height, an impression of
strength, — a frame agile and compact, with that easy
carriage of the head and that rapid movement so de-
ceptively increasing the stature. The face, too, was
probably what, if not informed by a singularly clean
and fine soul, would, in the lapse of years, become
gross, — the skin of a clear olive, which had slightly
flushed as he addressed herself, but not when speaking
to other strangers, — kept beardless, and rather square in
contour; the mouth not small, but keenly cut, like marble,
and always quivering before he spoke, as if the lightning
of his thought ran thither naturally to seek spontaneous
expression; teeth white; chin cleft; nose of the unclas-
sified order, rather long, the curve opposite to aquiline,
and saved from sharpness by nostrils that dilated with a
pulse of their own, as those of very proud and sensitive

people are apt to do ; a wide, low forehead crowned with
dark hair, long and fine ; heavy brows that overhung
deep-set eyes of lightest hazel, but endowed by shadow
with a power that no eye of gypsy-black ever swayed for
an instant.   His whole countenance reminded you of
nothing so much as of the young heroes of the French
Revolution, for whom irregular features and sallow cheeks
were transmuted into brilliant and singular beauty.   It
wore an inwrapped air, and, with all its mobility, was a
mask.   He very seldom raised the lids, and his pallor,
though owning more of the golden touch of the sun, was
as dazzling as Mrs. Laudersdale's own.

Mrs. Laudersdale scarcely observed, — she felt ; and
probably she saw nothing but the general impression of
what I have been telling you.

"Tea, Roger ?" asked Mrs. McLean.

"Green, I thank you, and strong."

Rising to receive it, he continued his course till it naturally brought him before Mrs. Laudersdale.   Pausing
deliberately and sipping the pungent tonic, he at last
looked up, and said, —

"Well, you are offended ?"

"Then you were awake when I stayed to look at you?"
she asked, in reply ; for curiosity is a solvent.

"Then you *did* stay and look at me ?   That is exactly
what I wished to know.   How did I look, Belphœbe ?"

"Out of his eyes, tell him," said Helen Heath, in
passing.

"They were not open," responded Mrs. Laudersdale.
"And I cannot tell how you saw me."

"I saw you as Virgil saw his mother, — I mean Æneas,
— as the goddesses are always known, you remember, in
departure."

Mrs. Laudersdale felt a weight on her lids beneath his glance, and rose to approach the table.

"Allow me," said Mr. Raleigh, taking her plate and bringing it back directly with a wafery slice of bread and a quaking tumulus of fragrant jelly.

Mrs. Laudersdale laughed, though perhaps scarcely pleased with him.

"How did you know my tastes so well?" she asked.

"Since they are not mine," he replied. "Of course you eat jelly, because it is no trouble; you choose your bread thin for the same reason; likewise you would find a glass of that suave, rich cream delicious. Among all motions, you prefer smooth sailing; and I'll venture to say that you sleep in down all summer."

Mrs. Laudersdale looked up in slow and still astonishment; but Mr. Raleigh was already pouring out the glass of cream.

"I've no doubt you would like to have me sweeten it," said he, offering it to her; "but I will not humor such ascetic tendencies. I never approved of flagellation."

And as he spoke, he was gone to break ground for a flirtation with Helen Heath.

Helen Heath appeared to be one of those gay, not-to-be-heart-broken damsels who can drink forever of this dangerous and exhilarating cup without showing symptoms of intoxication. Young men who have nothing worse to do with their time gravitate naturally and unawares toward them for amusement, and spin out the thread till they reach its end without expectation, without surprise, without regret, without occasion for remorse. Mr. Raleigh could not have been more unfortunate than he was in meeting her, since it gave him reason and excuse henceforth for visiting the Bawn at all seasons.

The table was at last removed, the dew began to fall, Mrs. Laudersdale shivered and withdrew toward the house.

" *Incessu patet dea,*" Mr. Raleigh remembered.

Somewhat later, he started from his seat, bade them all good-night, ran gayly down the bank, and shoved off from shore. And shortly after, Mrs. Laudersdale, looking from her window, saw, for an instant, a single firefly hovering over the dark lake. It was Mr. Roger Raleigh's distant lantern, as, stretched at ease, he turned the slow leaves of a Froissart, and suffered the Arrow to drift as it would across the night.

The next morning Mrs. Laudersdale descended, as usual, to the breakfast-table, at an hour when all the rest had concluded their repast. Miss Helen Heath alone remained, trifling with the tea-cups, and singing little exercises.

" Quite an acquisition, Mrs. Laudersdale ! " said she.

" What ? " said the other, languidly, leaning one arm on the table and looking about for any appetizing edible. " What is an acquisition ? "

" You mean who. Mr. Raleigh, of course. But is n't it the queerest thing in the world, up here in this savage district, to light upon a gentleman ? "

" Is this a savage district ? And is Mr. Raleigh a gentleman ? "

" Is he ? I never saw his match."

" Nor I."

" What ! don't you find him so ? a thorough gentleman ? "

" I don't know what a thorough gentleman is, I dare say," assented Mrs. Laudersdale, indifferently, with no spirit for repartee, breaking an egg and putting it down, crumbling a roll, and finally attacking a biscuit but gradually raising the siege, yawning, and leaning back in her chair.

"You poor thing!" said Helen. "You are starving to death. What shall I get for you? I have influence in the kitchens. Does marmalade, to spread your muffins, present any attractions? or shall I beg for rusks? or what do you say to doughnuts? there are doughnuts in this closet; crullers and milk are nice for breakfast."

And in a few minutes Helen had rifled a shelf of sufficient temptations to overcome Mrs. Laudersdale's abstinence.

"After all," said she then, " you did n't answer my question."

"What question?"

"If it were n't odd to meet Mr. Raleigh here."

"I don't know," said Mrs. Laudersdale.

"Dear! Mary Purcell takes as much interest. She said he was impertinent, made her talk too much, and made fun of her."

"Very likely."

"You are as aggravating as he! If you had anything to do except to look divinely, we 'd quarrel. I thought I had a nice bit of entertaining news for you."

"Is that your trouble? I should be sorry to oppress you with it longer. Pray, tell it."

"Will it entertain you?"

"It won't bore *you*."

"I don't know that I *will* tell it on such terms. However, I — must talk. Well, then. I have not been dreaming by daylight, but up and improving my opportunities. Partly from himself, and partly from Kate, and partly from the matron here, I have made the following discoveries. Mr. Roger Raleigh has left some very gay cities, and crossed some parallels of latitude, to exile himself in this wilderness of ice and snow, — that's what you and I vote it, whether the trees are green and the sun shines, or not ; and I don't see what bewitched mother to adopt such a suicidal plan as coming here to be buried alive. He, that is, Mr. Raleigh, to join my ends, has lived here for five years ; and as he came when he was twenty, he is consequently about my age now, — I should n't wonder if a trifle older than you. He came here because an immense estate was bequeathed him on the condition that he should occupy this corner of it during one half of every year from his twenty-first to his thirty-first. He has chosen to occupy it during the entire year, running down now and then to have a little music or see a little painting. Sometimes a parcel of his friends, — he never was at college, has n't any chums, and has educated himself by all manner of out-of-the-way dodges, — sometimes these friends, odd specimens, old music-masters, rambling artists, seedy tutors, fencers, boxers, hunters, clowns, all light down together, and then the neighborhood rings with this precious covey ; the rest of the year, may-be, he don't see an individual. One result of this isolation is, that freaks which would be very strange escapades in other people with him are mere commonplaces. Sometimes he goes over to the city there, and roams round like a lost soul seeking for its body ; sometimes he goes up a hundred miles or two, takes a guide and handles the mountains ; and, except in the accidents at such times, he has n't seen a woman since he came."

"That accounts," said Mrs. Laudersdale.

"Yes. But just think what a life !"

"He would n't stay, if he did n't like," replied Mrs. Laudersdale, to whom the words poverty and riches conveyed not the least idea.

"I don't know. He has an uncle, of whom he is very fond, in India," continued Helen, — "an unfortunate kind of man, with whom everything goes wrong, and who is always taking fevers; and once or twice Mr. Raleigh has started to go and take care of him, and lose the whole estate by the means. He intends to endow him, I believe, by and by, after the thing is at his disposal. This uncle kept him at school, when he was an orphan in different circumstances, at a Jesuit institution; and he and Miss Kent were always quarrelling over him, and she thought she had tied up her property nicely out of old Reuben Raleigh's way. It will be nuts, if he ever accepts his nephew's proposed present. The best of it all is, that, if he breaks the condition, — there's no accounting for the caprices of wills, — part of it goes to a needy institution, and part of it inalienably to Mrs. McLean, who — "

"Is an institution, too."

"Who is not needy. There, is n't that a pretty little *conte*?"

"Very," said Mrs. Laudersdale, having listened with increasing interest. "But, Helen, you'll be a gossip, if you go on and prosper."

"Why, my dear child! He'll be over here every day, now; and do you suppose I'm going to flirt with any one, when I don't know his antecedents? There he is now!"

And as Mrs. Laudersdale turned, she saw Mr. Raleigh standing composedly in the doorway and surveying them. She bade him good-morning, coolly enough, while Helen began searching the grounds of the teacups, rather uncertain how much of her recital might have met his ears.

"Turning teacups, Gypsy Helen, and telling fates, all to no audience, and with no cross on your palm?" asked the guest.

"So you ignore Mrs. Laudersdale?"

"Not at all; you were n't looking at her cup, — if she has one. Will you have the morning paper?" he asked of that lady, who, receiving it, leisurely unfolded and glanced over its extent.

"Where's my Cousin Kate?" then demanded Mr. Raleigh of Helen, having regarded this performance.

"Gone shopping in town."

"Her vocation. For the day?"

"No, — it is time for their return now. When you hear wheels —"

"I hear them"; and he strolled to the window. "You should have said, when I heard tongues; Medes and Elamites and the dwellers in Mesopotamia were less cheerful. A very pretty team. So she took her conjugal appurtenance with her?"

"And left her cousinly impertinence behind her," retorted a gay voice from his elbow.

"Ah, Kate! are you there? It's not a moment since I saw you 'coming from the town.' A pretty hostess, you! I arrive on your invitation to pass the day —"

"But I did n't expect you before the sun."

"To pass the day, and find you absent and the breakfast-table not cleared away."

"My dear Roger, we have not quite taken our habits yet. As soon as the country air shall have wakened and made over Helen and Mrs. Laudersdale, you will find us ready for company at daybreak."

"What a passion for 'company'! I shall not be surprised some day to receive cards for your death-bed."

"Friends and relatives invited to attend? No, Roger, you must n't be naughty. You shall receive cards for my dinner-party before we go, if you won't come without; for we have innumerable friends in town already."

"Happy woman!"

"What's that? A newspaper? A newspaper! How McLean will chuckle!" And she seized the sheet which Mrs. Laudersdale had abandoned in sweeping from the room.

"Is there a Mr. Laudersdale? Where is he?" asked Mr. Raleigh, as he leaned against the window.

"Who?" asked his cousin, deep in a paragraph.

"Mr. Laudersdale. Where is he?"

"Oh! between his four planks, I suppose," she replied, thinking of the Sound-boat's berth, which probably contained the gentleman designated.

"Between his four planks," repeated Mr. Raleigh, in a musing tone, something shocked by her apparent levity, entirely misinterpreting her, and to this little accident owing nearly thirteen years' unhappiness.

"She must have married early," he continued.

"Oh, fabulously early," replied Mrs. McLean, between the lines she read. "She is Creole, I believe. She is perfect. The women are as infatuated about her as the men. Here's Helen Heath been dawdling round the table all the morning for the sake of chatting to her while she breakfasts. I don't know why, I'm sure; the woman's charming, but she's too lazy even to talk. McLean! Another flurry in France."

And after shaking hands with Mr. Raleigh, that worthy seized the proffered paper and vanished behind it, leaving to his wife the entertainment of her cousin, which duty she seemed by no means in haste to assume, preferring to remain and vex her husband with a thousand little teasing arts. Meanwhile Mr. Raleigh proceeded to take that office upon himself, by crossing the hall, exploring the parlors, examining the manuscript commonplace-volumes, and finally by sketching on a leaf of his pocket-book Mrs. Laudersdale, at the other end of the piazza, half-swinging in the vines through which broad sunbeams poured, while Helen Heath was singing and several other ladies were busying themselves with books and needlework in her vicinity.

"Ah, Mr. Raleigh!" said Helen Heath, as he put up the pocket-book and drew near, — "Mrs. Laudersdale and I have been wondering how you amuse yourself up here; and I make my discovery. You study animated nature; that is to say, you draw Mrs. Laudersdale and me."

"Mistaken, Miss Helen. I draw only Mrs. Laudersdale; and do you call that animated nature?"

"I wish you would draw Mrs. Laudersdale *out.*"

At this point Mrs. Laudersdale *fell* out; but, without otherwise stirring from his position than by moving an apparently careless arm, Mr. Raleigh caught and restored her to her balance, as lightly as if he had brushed a floating gossamer from the air to his finger. For the first time, perhaps, in her life, a carnation blossomed an instant in her cheek, then all was as before, — only two of the party felt on that instant that in some mysterious manner their relations with each other were entirely changed.

"But what *is* it that you do with yourself?" persisted Helen. "Tell us, that we may do likewise."

"Will you come and see?" he asked, — his eyes, however, on Mrs. Laudersdale. "Will you come in away from the lake to the brooks, and hang among the alders, and angle, dreaming, all day long? Or will you rise at dead of night and go out on the lake with me and watch field after field of white lilies flash open as the sun touches them with his spear? Or will you lie during still noons up among the farmers' fields where myriad bandrol corn-poppies flaunt over your head, and stain your finger-tips with the red berries that hang like globes of light in the palace-gardens of mites and midges, soaking yourself in hot sunshine and south-winds and heavy aromatic earth-scents?"

"Come!" said Mrs. Laudersdale, rising earnestly, like one in an eager dream.

"It is plain that you are in training for a poet," said Helen Heath, laughing, to Mr. Raleigh. "Well, when will you take us? Are the lilies in bloom? Shall we go to-morrow morning?"

"I don't know that I shall take you at all, Miss Helen; — river-lilies might suit you best; but these queens of the lakes, the great, calm pond-lilies, creatures of quiet and white radiance, — I have seen only one head that possessed enough of the genuine East-Indian repose to be crowned with them."

"You like repose," said Mrs. Laudersdale. "But what is it?"

"Repose is strength, — life that develops from within, and feels itself, and has no need of effort. Repose is inherent security."

"Goodness!" exclaimed Helen. "Article first in a *new* dictionary, — encyclopædia, I should say. You worship, but you don't possess your god, for you look at this moment like a shaft in the bow; and here comes an archer to give it flight."

" Where are you going, Kate ? " said her cousin.

" To pick strawberries in the garden. Want to come ? "

The three could do no better than accept her invitation. The good ladies might stare as they could after Mrs. Laudersdale, and wonder what sudden sprite had possessed her, since for neither man nor woman of the numerous party had she hitherto condescended to lift an unwonted eyelid; what they would have said to have seen her plunged in a strawberry-bed, gathering handfuls and raining them drop by drop into Helen Heath's mouth, to silence her while she herself might talk, — her own fingers tipped with more sanguine shade than their native rose, her eyes full of the noon sparkle, and her lips parted with laughter, — we cannot say. Roger Raleigh forgot to move, to speak, to think, as he watched her. But in the midst of this brilliant and novel gayety of hers, there was still a dignity to make one feel that she had by no means abandoned her regal purple, but merely adorned it with profuse golden flourishes.

At dinner that day, Helen begged to know if there were not a great many routes in the vicinity practicable only on horseback, and thought she had attained her end when Mr. Raleigh put his horses and his escort at the service of herself and Mrs. Laudersdale during their stay.

" During our stay ! " said Mrs. Laudersdale. " That reminds me that we are to go away ! "

" Pleasantly, certainly. When snows fall and storms pipe, the Bawn is an ice-house," said he.

After noon, the remainder of the day was interspersed with light thunder-showers, rendering tea on the grass again impossible ; they passed the steaming cups, therefore, as they sat on the piazza curtained with dripping woodbine. The glitter of the drops in the sunset light, a jewelled scintillation, was caught in Mrs. Laudersdale's eyes, and some unconscious excitement fanned a faint color to and fro on her cheek. At last the moon rose; the whole party, regardless of wet slippers, sauntered with Mr. Raleigh to the shore, where the little Arrow hung balancing on her restraining cord. Mrs. Laudersdale stepped in, Mr. Raleigh followed, took up an oar, and pushed out, both standing, and drifting slowly for a few rods' distance; then Mr. Raleigh made the shore again, assisted her out, and shot impatiently away alone. The waters shone like white fire in the wake he cut, great shadows fell through them where island and wood intercepted the broad ascending light, and Mrs. Laudersdale's gay laugh rung across them as the space grew,—a sweet, rich laugh, that all the spirits of the depths caught and played with like a rare beam that transiently illumined their shadowy silent haunts.

The next day, and the next, and so for a fortnight, Mr. Roger Raleigh presented himself with the breakfast-urn at the Bawn, tarried during sunshine, slipped home by starlight across the lake. Every day Mrs. Laudersdale was more brilliant, and flashed with a cheery merriment like harmless summer-lightnings. One night, as he pushed away from the bank, he said,—

" *Au revoir* for five hours."

" For five hours?" said Mrs. Laudersdale.

" For five hours."

" At half past three in the night?"

" In the morning."

" And what brings you here at dead of dark? "

" The lilies and the dawn."

" Indeed! And whom do you expect to find?"

" You and Miss Helen."

11   P

"Well, summer and freedom are here; I am ready for all fates, all deeds of valor, vigils among the rest. We will await you at half past three in the morning. Helen, we must sleep at high-pressure, soundly, crowding all we can on the square inch of time. *Au revoir.*"

A shadow stood on the piazza, in the semi-darkness, at the appointed hour; two other shadows flitted forward to meet it, and silently down the bank, into the boat, and out upon the lonely glimmering reaches of the water. Nobody spoke; the midnight capture of no fort was ever effected with more phantom-like noiselessness than now went to surprise the Vestals of the Lake; only as two hands touched for an instant, a strange thrill, like fire, quivered through each and tore them apart more swiftly than two winds might cross each other's course. Helen Heath was drowsy and half-nodding in the bow, nodding with the more ease that it was still so dark and that Mr. Raleigh's back was toward her. Mrs. Laudersdale reclined in the stern. Mr. Raleigh once in a while sent them far along with a strong stroke, then only an occasional plash broke the charm of perfect stillness. Ever and anon they passed under the lee of some island, and the heavy air grew full of idle night-sweetness; the waning moon with all its sad and alien power hung low, — dun, malign, and distant, a coppery blotch on the rich darkness of heaven. They floated slowly, still; now and then she dipped a hand into the cool current; now and then he drew in his oars, and, bending forward, dipped his hand with hers. The stars retreated in a pallid veil that dimmed their beams, faint lights streamed up the sky, — the dark yet clear and delicious. They paused motionless in the shelter of a steep rock; over them a wild vine hung and swayed its long wreaths in the water, a sweet-brier starred with fragrant sleeping buds climbed and twisted, and tufts of ribbon-grass fell forward and streamed in the indolent ripple; beneath them the lake, lucid as some dark crystal, sheeted with olive transparence a bottom of yellow sand; here a bream poised on slowly waving fins, as if dreaming of motion, or a perch flashed its red fin from one hollow to another. The shadow lifted a degree, the eye penetrated to farther regions; a bird piped warily, then freely, a second and third answered, a fourth took up the tale, blue-jay and thrush, cat-bird and bobolink; wings began to dart about them, the world to rustle overhead, near and far the dark prime grew instinct with sound, the shores and heavens blew out gales of melody, the air broke up in music. He lifted his oars silently; she caught the sweet-brier, and, lightly shaking it, a rain of dew-drops dashed with deepest perfume sprinkled them; they moved on. A thin mist breathed from the lake, steamed round the boat, and lay like a white coverlet upon the water; a light wind sprang up and blew it in long rags and ribbons, lifted, and torn, and streaming, out of sight. All the air was pearly, the sky opaline, the water now crisply emblazoned with a dark and splendid jewelry, — the paved work of a sapphire; a rosy fleece sailed across their heads, some furnace glowed in the east behind the trees, long beams fell resplendently through and lay beside vast shadows, the giant firs stood black and intense against a red and risen sun; they trailed with one oar through a pad of buds all-unaware of change, stole from the overhanging thickets through a high-walled pass, where, on the open lake, the broad, silent, yellow light crept from bloom to bloom and awoke them with a touch. How perfectly they put off sleep! with what a queenly calm displayed their spotless

snow, their priceless gold, and shed abroad their matchless
scent! He twined his finger round a slippery serpent-
stem, turned the crimson underside of the floating pavilion, and brought up a waxen wonder from its throne to
hang like a star in the black braids on her temple. An
hour's harvesting among the nymphs, in this rich atmosphere of another world, and with a loaded boat they
turned to shore again.

"Smothered in sweets!" exclaimed Mr. Raleigh, as he
sprang out, and woke Helen Heath, where, slipped down
upon the floor of the boat, her head fallen on her arms,
she had lain half asleep. They were the first words
spoken during the morning, and in such situations silence
is dangerous.

When the rest of the family descended to breakfast,
they found the pictures framed in wreaths of lilies, great
floats of them in hall and parlor, and the table laden with
flat dishes where with coiled stems they crowded, a white,
magnificent throng. Mr. Raleigh still lingered, and,
while Mrs. Laudersdale and Helen renewed their toilets,
had busied himself in weaving a crown of these and
another of poppy-leaves, hanging the one on Mrs. Laudersdale's head, as she entered refreshed, snowy, and fragrant herself, and the sleep-giving things on Helen's, —
the latter avenging herself by surveying her companion's
adornment, and, as she adjusted the bloom-gray leaves of
her own, inquiring if olives grew pickled.

Nothing could be more airy and blithe than were Mrs.
Lauderdale's spirits all that morning, — bubbles dancing
on a brook, nor foam-sparkle of rosy Champagne. She
related their adventures with graphic swiftness, and im-
provised dangers and escapes with such a reckless disre-
gard of truth that Mr. Raleigh was forced to come to the

rescue with more startling improbabilities than they would have encountered in the Enchanted Forest.

The red dawn brought its rain, and before they rose from table the sunshine withdrew and large drops began to patter in good earnest. Mr. Raleigh, who had generally suffered others to entertain him, now, as Mrs. McLean ushered the whole company into the sewing-room, seemed spurred by gayety and brilliance, and to bring into employ all those secrets through which he had ever annihilated time. For a while devoting himself to the elder dames, he won the heart of one by a laborious invention of a million varicolored angles to a square barley-corn of worsted-work, involved Mrs. McLean's crocheting in an inextricable labyrinth as he endeavored to afford her some requisite conchological assistance, and turned with three strokes a very absurd drawing of Mrs. Laudersdale's into a splendid caricature. Having made himself thus generally useful, he now proceeded to make himself generally agreeable; went with all necessary gravity through a series of complicate dancing-steps with Miss Heath; begged Miss Purcell, who was longing to cry over her novel, to allow him to read for her, since he saw that she was trying her eyes, and therewith made *fiasco* of a page of delicious dolor; and being challenged to chess by a third, declared that was child's play, and dominos was the game for science, — whereon, having seated a circle at that absorbing sport, he deserted for a meerschaum and the gentlemen, and in company with Captain Purcell, Mr. McLean, and the rest, rolled up from the hall, below, wreaths of smoke, bursts of laughter, and finally chimes of those concordant voices with which gentlemen talk politics, and, even when agreeing infamously, become vociferant and high-colored.

It was after lunch that Mrs. Laudersdale, having grown weary of the needle-women's thread of discourse, left the sewing-room and proceeded toward her own apartment. Just as she crossed the head of the staircase, the hall-door was flung open, admitting a gleeful blast of the boisterous gale, and an object that, puffing and blowing like a sad-hued dolphin, and shaking like a Newfoundland, appeared at first to be the famous South West Wind, Esq., in proper person, — whose once sumptuous array clung to his form, and whose face and hands, shining as coal, rolled off the rain like a bronze.

"Bless my heart, Capua!" cried Mr. Raleigh, removing the stem from his lips; "how came you here?"

"Lors, Massa, it's only me," said Capua.

"So I see," replied his master, restoring the pipe to its former position. "How did you come?"

"'Bout swimmed, I 'spect," answered Capua, grounding a chuckle on a reef of ivory. "'T a'n't no fish-story, dat!"

"Well, what brings you?"

"Naughty Nan, — she had n't been out —"

"Do you mean to say, you rascal! that you've taken Nan out on such a day? and round the lake, too, I'll warrant?" asked Mr. Raleigh, with some excitement.

"Jes' dat; an' round de lake, ob course; we could n' come acrost."

"You've ruined her, then —"

"Bress you, Massa, she won't ketch no cold, — she! Smokes like a beaver now; came like streak o' lightnin'."

"You may as well swim her back, — and where we can all see the sport, too."

"But —"

"No buts about it, Capua," insisted his master, with mock gravity, the stem between his teeth.

" 'Spect I'd better rub her down, now I'se here, an' wait 'll it holds up a bit, Mass' Roger?" urged Capua, coaxingly.

"Do as you're bid!" ejaculated his master; which, evidently, from long habit, meant, Do as you please.

Mrs. Laudersdale and Helen Heath had crept down the stairs during this dialogue, and now stood interested spectators of the scene. Mrs. McLean came running down behind them.

"Forgotten me, Capua?" said she.

"Lors, Miss Kate!" he replied, scraping his foot and pulling off his hat, — "Cap never f'gets his friends, though you've growed. How d'ye do, Miss Kate?"

"Nicely, thank you. And how's your wife?"

"My wife? Well, she's 'bout beat out. Massa Roger 'n I, we buried her; finer funeral dan Massa Roger's own mother, Miss Kate, dat was!"

"Poor fellow! I'm so sorry!" began Mrs. McLean, consolingly.

"Well, Miss Kate, you know some folks is easier spared 'n others. Some tongues sharper 'n others. Alwes liked to gib a hot temper time to cool, 's Massa says."

"And how do *you* do, Capua?"

"Pretty well, Miss Kate; leastways, I'se well enough, — a'n't so pretty."

"*What* is his name?" whispered Helen.

" 'Annible, Missis," said the attentive Capua, whose eyes had been for some time oscillating with indecision between Helen Heath and Mrs. Laudersdale. "Hannibal Raleigh 's my name; though Massa alwes call me Cap," he added, insinuatingly, — which, by the way, "Massa" never had been known to do.

"And are you always going to stay and take care of Master Roger?"

" 'Spect I shall. Lors, Miss Kate, he 's more bother to me 'n all my work, — dat boy ! "

" That will do, Capua," said his master ; " you may go." And therewith Capua scuffled away.

" Well, Roger, what does this mean ? " asked Mrs. Mc-Lean, as the door closed.

" It means that Capua, having been dying of curiosity, has resolved to die game, and therefore takes matters into his own hands, and arrives to inspect my conduct and my company."

" Ah, I see. He trembles for his sceptre."

" Miss Heath," said Mr. McLean, rallyingly, " you received a great many of the sable shafts."

" A Saint Sebastiana," said his wife.

" Saint Sebastian died of his wounds. Not I," said Helen.

" Let me tell you, Miss Helen," said Mr. Raleigh, " that Capua is a connoisseur, and his *dictum* is worth all flatteries. If he had only been with us this morning!"

" You have teased me so much about that, Mr. Raleigh, that I have half a mind never to go with you on another expedition."

" Make no rash vows. I was just thinking what fine company you would be when trouting. The most enchanting quiet is required then, you are aware."

" Oh ! when shall we go trouting ? "

" We ? It was only half a mind, then ! We will go to-morrow, wind and weather agreeing."

" And what must I do ? "

" You must keep still, stand in the shadow, and fish upstream."

At this point, Capua put his head inside the door again.

" What is it?" asked Mr. Raleigh.

" Forgot to say, Massa," replied Capua, rolling his eyes fearfully, and still hesitating, and half-closing the door, and then looking back.

" Well, Capua?"

" Mass' Raleigh, your house done been burned up!" said Capua, at last, jerking back his head, as if afraid of losing it.

" Ah? And what did you do with — "

" Oh, eberyting safe an' sound. 'T a'n't dat house; 't a'n't dis yer house Massa lib in; — Massa's *sparrer-*house. Reckoned I 'd better come and 'form him."

" Is that all?" asked his master, who was accustomed to Capua's method of breaking ill news.

" Now, Mass' Roger, don't you go to being pervoked an' flyin' into one ob dese yer tempers! It 's all distinguished now. Ole Cap did n't want to shock his young massa, so thought 't warn't de wisest way to tell him 't warn't de sparrer-house, either, at first. 'Twas de inside ob de libery, if he *must* know de troof; wet an' smutty dar now, mebbe, but no fire."

" Why not? What made the fire go out?" asked Mr. Raleigh, composedly.

" Well, two reasons," replied Capua, rolling a glance over the company; — " one was dis chile's exertions; an' t'other fact, on account ob wich de flames was checked, was because dere warn't no more to burn. Hi!"

" Capua, take Nan, and don't let me see your face again, till I send for it!" said his master, now slightly irate.

" Massa's nigger alwes mind him," was the dutiful response.

Mrs. Laudersdale's handkerchief fell at that moment

from the hand that hung over the balustrade. Capua darted to restore it.

"Bress her pretty eyes!" said he. "Ole Cap see's fur into a millstone as any one!" and vanished through the doorway.

"I beg your pardon," said Mr. Raleigh, turning to Mrs. Laudersdale. "He has refused to leave me, and I must indulge him too much, and my sins fall on the head of the nearest passer. He appears to have a constitutional inability to comprehend this absence of punishment. His immunity is so painful to him that I sometimes fancy him to be homesick for a lashing. In fact, all those Burdens of the Book of Isaiah, which his people carry on their backs, are dust in his balance. The sorrows that have darkened the brows of his race touch no electric chord in him. Capua is not a representative man. He is only the dry-nurse of my failings. Ah, welladay! Now if I do not hasten home, Kate, I shall find a conflagration of the whole house there before me."

And making quick adieux, — while Mrs. Laudersdale jested about tempting the raging waters, and the dinner-bell was ringing, and Helen singing,

> " Come o'er the stream, Charlie, dear Charlie, brave Charlie!
> Come o'er the stream, Charlie, and dine wi' McLean!"

he opened the door, suffered a patch of blue sky to be seen, and the segment of an afternoon rainbow, shut it, and was gone.

Early again the next morning, Mr. Raleigh sought the Bawn, followed this time by Capua, who was determined not to lose any ground once made, and who now carried the rods, bait, and other paraphernalia.

"Powerful pretty woman, dat, Massa!" said he, as

through the open doors a voice was heard gayly exclaiming and answering.

"Which one, Capua?" asked his master.

"A'n't no t'orrer," was his reply; "leastwise, a'n't no 'count, — good for nott'n. Now *she*, — pity she a'n't single, Massa, — should say she 'd lived where sun was plenty and had laid up heaps in her heart."

Here Mrs. Laudersdale came out, and shortly afterward Helen and three or four others. In reply to their questions, Mr. Raleigh stated that the preceding day's disaster had been occasioned by a meerschaum, and had merely charred a table with its superficies of papers and pamphlets, which Capua had chosen to magnify for his own purposes; and the asssemblage immediately turned its course inland and toward the brooks. The two who led soon distanced the rest, Capua trudging respectfully behind and keeping them in sight. Here, as they brushed along through the woods, they delayed in order to examine a partridge's nest, to tree a squirrel, to gather some strange wild-flower opening at their approach. Here on the banks they watched the bitterns rise and sail heavily away, and finally in silence commenced the genuine sport.

"Nonsense!" said Helen Heath, meaningly, as Mrs. Laudersdale, when the others joined them, displayed her first capture. "Is that all you 've caught?"

Mrs. Laudersdale drew in another for reply.

"How absurd!" said Helen. "Here a month ago you were the dearest and most helpless of mortals, and now you are doing everything!"

The other opened her eyes a moment, and then laughed.

"Hush!" said she.

"Shs! shs!" echoed Capua, making an infinite hubbub himself.

Silence accordingly reigned and produced a string fit
for the Sultan's kitchen, — of all the number, Mrs. Laudersdale adding by far the majority, — possibly because
her shining prey found destination in the same basket
with Mr. Raleigh's, — possibly because, as Helen had in-
timated, a sudden deftness had bewitched her fingers, so
that neither dropping rod nor tangling reel detained her
for an instant.

"Our lines have fallen in pleasant places," said Helen,
as they took at last their homeward path ; "and what a
shame ! not an adventure yet ! "

Mrs. McLean hung on Mr. Raleigh's arm as they went,
— for she had taken a whim and feared to see her cousin
in the fangs of a coquette; by which means Helen became the companion of Captain Purcell and his daughter,
and Mrs. Laudersdale kept lightly in advance, leading a
gambol with the greyhound that Capua had added to the
party, and presenting in one person, as she went springing
from knoll to knoll along the bank, now in sunshine, now
in shade, lifting the green boughs or sweeping them aside,
a succession of the vivid figures of some antique and pro-
cessional frieze. Suddenly, with a quick cry, she disappeared, and Helen had her adventure. Mr. Raleigh
darted forward, while the hound came frisking back ;
yet, when he found her fainting in the hollow, stood
with stolid immobility until Capua snatched her up and
carried her along in his arms, leaving his master to reflect
how many times such swarthy servitors might have borne
her, as a child, through her island groves. And thus the
party, somewhat sobered, resumed their march again.
But in the discovery that he had not dared to lift her
in his arms, he who took such liberties with every one, —
that, lying under her semblance of death, she had inspired

him with a certain awe, that he had suddenly found this
woman to be an object somewhat sacred, — in this discovery Mr. Raleigh learned not a little. And it would not,
perhaps, be an untrue surmise that he found therein as
much of pain as of any other emotion; since all the experiences and passions of life must share the phenomena
of the great fact itself whose pulse beats through them;
and if to love unawares be to dwell like a child in the region of thoughtless and innocent bliss, in attaining man-
hood all the sadness which is to be eliminated from life
becomes apparent, and bliss henceforth must be sought
and earned. From that day, then, Mr. Raleigh with difficulty retained his former habits, prevented any eagerness
of manner, maintained a cautious vigilance, and in so doing he again became aware that the easy *insouciance* with
which he addressed all other women had long been lost
toward Mrs. Laudersdale, or, if yet existing, had become
like the light and tender play of any lingering summer-
wind in the tress upon her brow.

Mrs. Laudersdale's ankle having been injured by her
fall, and Mrs. McLean having taken a cold, the two invalids now became during a week and a day the auditory
for all quips and pranks that Miss Heath and Mr. Raleigh
could devise. And on the event of their convalescence,
the Lord of Misrule himself seemed to have ordained the
course of affairs, with a swarming crew of all the imps
and mischiefs ever hatched. Mr. Raleigh and Capua
went and came with boat-loads of gorgeous stuff from
across the lake, a little old man appeared on the spot in
answer to a flight of telegrams, machinery and scenery
rose like exhalations, music was brought from the city,
all the availables of the family were to be found in garden, closet, house-top, conning hieroglyphical pages, and

the whole chaotic confusion takes final shape and resolves
into a little Spanish Masque, to which kings and queens
have once listened in courtly state, and which now unrolls
its resplendent pageant before the eyes of Mrs. Laudersdale, translating her, as it were, into another planet, where
familiar faces in pompous entablature look out upon her
from a whirl of light and color, and familiar voices utter
stately sentences in some honeyed unknown tongue.   And
finally, when the glittering parade finishes, and the strange
groups, in their costly raiment, throng out for dancing, she
herself gives her hand to some Prince of the pageantry,
who does her homage, and, sealing the fact of her restora-
tion, swims once round the room in a mist of harmony, and
afterward sits by his side, captive to his will, and subject
to his enchantment, while

> " All night had the roses heard
>   The flute, violin, bassoon,
> All night had the casement jessamine stirred
>   With the dancers dancing in tune,
> Till a silence fell with the waking bird
>   And a hush with the setting moon."

This little episode of illness and recovery having been
thus duly celebrated, the masqueraders again forswore
roofs and spent long days in distant junketing throughout
the woods ; the horses, too, were brought into requisition,
and a flock of boats kept forever on the wing.   And
meanwhile, as Helen Heath said, — she then least of all
comprehending the real drama of that summer, — Mrs.
Laudersdale had taught them how the Greek animated
his statue.

" And how was that ? " asked Mr. Raleigh.

" He took it out-doors, I fancy, and called the winds to
curl about it.   He set its feet in morning-dew, he let in
light and shade through green dancing leaves above it, he

gave it glimpses of moon and star, he taught the forest-birds to chirp and whistle in its ear, and finally he steeped it in sunshine."

" Sunshine, then was the vivifying stroke ? "

Helen nodded.

" You are mistaken," said he ; " the man never found a soul in his work till he put his own there first."

" I always wonder," remarked Mrs. Laudersdale here, " that every artist, in brooding over his marble, adding, touching, bringing out effects, does not end by loving it, — absorbingly, because so beautiful to him, — despairingly, because to him forever silent."

" You need n't wonder anything about it," said Helen, mischievously. " All that you have to do is to make the most of your sunshine."

Mr. McLean, struck with some sudden thought, inspected the three as they stood in a blaze of the midsummer noon, then crossed over to his little wife, drew her arm in his, and held it with cautious imprisonment. The other wife did as she was bidden, and made the most of her sunshine.

If, on first acquaintance, Mrs. Laudersdale had fascinated by her repose, her tropical languor, her latent fire, the charm was none the less, when, turning, it became one dazzle of animation, of careless freedom, of swift and easy grace. Nor, unfamiliar as were such traits, did they seem at all foreign to her, but rather, when once donned, never to have been absent ; as if, indeed, she had always been this royal creature, this woman bright and winning as some warm, rich summer's day. The fire that sleeps in marble never flashes and informs the whole mass so fully ; if a pearl — lazy growth and accretion of amorphous life — should fuse and form again in sparkling crystals, the miracle would be less. And with what complete unconsciousness had she stepped from passive to positive existence, and found this new state to be as sweet and strange as any child has found it! Long a wife, she had known, nevertheless, nothing but quiet custom or indifference, and had dreamed of love only as the dark and silent side of the moon might dream of light. Now she grew and unfolded in the warmth of this season, like a blossom perfumed and splendid. Sunbeams seemed to lance themselves out of heaven and splinter about her. She queened it over demesnes of sprite-like revelry; the life they led was sylvan; at their *fêtes* the sun assisted. The summer held to her lips a glass whose rosy effervescence, whose fleeting foam, whose tingling spirit exhaled a subtile madness of joy,—a draught whose lees were despair. So nearly had she been destitute of emotion hitherto that she had scarcely a right to be classed with humanity; now, indeed, she would win that right. Not only her character, but her beauty, became another thing under all this largess; one remembered the very Persian rose, in looking at her, and thought of gardens amid whose clouds of rich perfume the nightingales sang all night long; her manner, too, became strangely gracious, and a sweetness lingered after her presence, delicate and fine as the drop of honey in some flower's nectary. So she woke from her icy trance; but, alas! what had wakened her?

The summer was passing. Every day the garden-scenes of Watteau became vivid and real; every evening Venice was made possible, when shadowy barks slipped down dusk tides, freighted with song and laughter, and snatches of guitar-tinkling; and when some sudden torch, that for an instant had summoned with its red fire all

fierce lights and strong glooms, dipped, hissed, and
quenched below, and, a fantastic flotilla, they passed on
into the broad brilliance of a rising moon, all Middle-Age
mythology rose and wafted them back into the obscurity.
It was a life too fine for every day, fare too rich for
health; they must be exotics who did not wither in such
hot-house air. It was rapidly becoming unnatural. They
performed in the daylight stray clarified bits from
Fletcher or Molière, drama of an era over-ripe; they
sang only from an old book of madrigals; their very
reading was fragmentary, — now an emasculated Boc-
caccio, then a curdling phantasm of Poe's, and after some
such scenic horror as the "Red Death" Helen Heath
dashed off the Pesther Waltzes.

If, finally, on one of the last August-nights, we had
passed, Asmodeus-like, over the roofs, looking down we
should have seen three things. First, that Mrs. Laudersdale slept like any innocent dreamer, and, wrapped with
white moonlight, in her long and flowing outline, in her
imperceptible breath, resembling some perfect statue that
we fancy to be instinct with suspended life. Next, that
Mr. Raleigh did not sleep at all, but absorbed himself, to
the entire disturbance of Capua's slumbers, in the rapture
of reproducing, as he could, the turbulent passion and joy
of souls larger than his own. And, lastly, that Mrs.
McLean woke with visions of burglars before her eyes,
to find her pillow deserted and her husband sitting at a
writing-table.

"How startled I was!" she exclaimed. "What are
you doing, dear?"

"Writing to Laudersdale," he said, in reply.

"Why, what for? — what can you be writing to him
for?"

Q

"I think it best he should come and take his wife off my hands."

"How absurd! how contemptible! how all you husbands band together like a parcel of slaveholders, and hunt down each other's runaways!"

Mr. McLean laughed.

"Now, John, you 're not making mischief?"

"No, child, I am preventing it." And therewith the worthy man, dropping the wax on the envelope, imprinted it with a Scotch crest, and put out the light. "That's off my mind!" said he.

At last September came; a few more weeks, and they would separate, perhaps, to the four corners of the earth. Mr. Raleigh arrived one afternoon at the Bawn, and finding no one to welcome him, — that is to say, Mrs. Laudersdale had gone out, and Helen Heath was invisible, — he betook himself to a solitary stroll, and, by a short cut through the woods, to the highway, and just before emerging from the green shadows he met Mrs. Laudersdale.

"Whither now, Wandering Willie?" said she; for, singularly enough, they seemed to avoid speaking each other's name in direct address, using always some title suggested by their reading or singing, or some sportive impromptu.

"I am going to take the road."

"Like a gallant highwayman?" And without more ado, and naturally enough, she accompanied him.

The conversation, this afternoon, was sufficiently insignificant; indeed, Mrs. Laudersdale always affected you more by her silence than her speech, by what she was rather than by what she said; and it is only the impression produced on her by this walk with which we have any concern.

The road, narrow and winding in high banks fringed
with golden-rod and purple asters, was at first completely shadowed, — an old, deep-rutted, cross-country road,
birch-trees shivering at either side, and every now and
then a puff of pine-breath drifting in between. After a
time it rose gradually into the turnpike, and became a
long, dusty track, stretching as far as the eye could see, a
straight, dazzling line, burnt white by summer-heats,
powdered by travel. There was no wind stirring; the
sky was lost in a hot film stained here and there with
sulphurous wreaths; the distant fields, skirted by low
hills, were bathed in an azure mist; nearer, a veil of dun
and dimmer smoke from burning brush hung motionless;
around their feet the dust whirled and fell again. Bathed
in soft, voluptuous tints, hazed and mellowed, into what
weird, strange country were they hastening? What visionary land of delight, replete with perfume and luxury,
lay ever beyond? — what region rich, unknown, forbidden,
whose rank vegetation steamed with such insidious poison? And on what arid, barren road, what weary road,—
but, alas, long worn and beaten by the feet of other way-
farers! a road that ran real and strong through this
noxious and seducing mirage!

A sudden blast of wind lifted a cloud of dust from before them and twisted it down among the meadows; the
sun thrust aside his shroud and burnt for an instant on a
scarlet maple-bough that hung in premature brilliance
across the way. The hasty color, true and fine, was like
a spell against enchantment; it was the drop that tested
the virtue of this chemistry and proved it naught.

Mrs. Laudersdale looked askance at her companion,
then turned and met his gaze. Slowly her lashes fell,
the earth seemed to fail beneath her feet, the light to

swoon from her eyes, her lips shook, and a full flush
swept branding and burning up throat and face, stinging her very forehead, and shooting down her finger-tips.
In an instant it had faded, and she shone the pallid,
splendid thing she was before. In that instant, for the
first time this summer, she comprehended that her husband's existence imported anything to her. Behind the
maple-tree, the wood began again; without a syllable, she
stepped aside, suffered him to pass, and hastened to bury
herself in its recesses.

What lover ever accounted for his mistress's caprices?
Mr. Raleigh proceeded on his walk alone. And what
was her husband to him? He did not know that such a
man existed. For him there had been no deadly allure-
ment in the fervid scene; it had stretched a land of
promise veiled in its azure ardors, with intimations of
rapture and certainty of rest. Now, as he wandered
on and turned down another lane to the woods, the
tints grew deeper; his eyes, bent inward, saw all the
world in the color of his thought; he would have affirmed that the bare brown banks were lined in deep-
toned indigo flower-bells whose fragrance rose visible
above them or curled from stem to stem, and that the
hollows in which the path hid itself at last were of the
same soft gloom. But, finally, when not far distant from
the Bawn again, he shook off his reverie and struck another path that he might avoid rencontre. Perhaps the
very sound that awoke him was the one he wished to
shun; at the next step it became more distinct, — a
child's voice singing some tuneless song; and directly a
tiny apparition appeared before him, as if it had taken
shape, with its wide, light eyes and corn-silk hair, from
the most wan and watery of sunbeams. But what had a

child to do in this paradise, thought he, and from whence did it come? Impossible to imagine. Her garments, of rich material, hung freshly torn, it may be, but in shreds; her skin, if that of some fair and delicate nursling, was stained with berries and smeared with soil; she seemed to have no destination; and after surveying him a moment, she mounted a fallen tree, and, bending and swinging forward over a bough, still surveyed him.

"Ah, ha!" said Mr. Roger Raleigh; "what have we here?"

The child still looked in his face, but vouchsafed, in her swinging, no reply.

"What is the little lady's name?" he asked then.

This query, apparently more comprehensible, elicited a response. She informed him that her name was "Dymom, Pink, and Beauty."

"Indeed! And anything else?"

"Rose Pose," she added, as if soliciting the aid of memory by lifting her hands near her temples.

"Is that all?"

"Little silly Daffodilly."

"No more?"

"Rite."

"Rite, — ah, that is it! Rite what?"

"Rite!" said the child, authoritatively, bringing down her foot and shaking back her hair.

"And how old is Rite?"

"One, two, four, twenty. Maman is twenty; — Rite is twenty, too."

"When was Rite four?"

"A great while ago. She went to heaven in the afternoon," was added, confidentially, after a moment's inspection to see if he were worthy.

"Ah! And what was there there?"

" Pitchtures, and music, and peoples, and a great house."

" And where is Rite going now?"

" Going away in a ship."

" Rite will have to wash her face first."

But at this proposition the child flashed open her pale-blue orbs, half-closed them as a sleepy cat does, and, with no other change of countenance to mark her indignation, appeared to shut him out from her contemplation.   Directly afterward, she opened them again, bent forward and back over the swinging, and recommenced her song, as if there were not another person than herself within a hundred miles.   Half-hidden in the great hemlock-bough, this tiny, fantastic creature, so fair, so supercilious, seemed in her waywardness a veritable fay, mate for any of the little men in green, bibbers of dew-drops, lodgers in bean-blossoms, Green-Jacket, Red-Cap, and White-Owl's-Feather.

Mr. Raleigh hesitated whether or not he should remain and watch her fade away into the twilight, wondered if she were bewitching him, then rubbed his hand across his eyes and said, in a disenchanted, matter-of-fact manner, —

" Do you know your way home, child?" and obtained, of course, no reply.   For an instant he had half the mind to leave her to find it; but at once convicted of his absurdity, " Then I shall take you with me," he said, making a step toward her, — " because you are, or will be, lost."

At the motion, she darted past and stood defiantly just out of his reach.   Mr. Raleigh attempted to seize her, but he might as easily have put his hand on a butterfly; she eluded him always when within his grasp, and led him such a dance up and down the forest-path as none other than a will-o'-the-wisp, it seemed, could have woven. All at once a dark figure glided out from another alley and snatched the sprite into its arms. It was a colored nurse, who poured out a torrent of broken French and English over the runaway, and made her acknowledgments to Mr. Raleigh in the same jargon. As she turned to go, the child stretched her arms toward her late pursuer, making the nurse pause, and, putting up her little lips, touched with them his own; then, picturesque as ever, and thrown into relief by the scarlet sack, snowy turban, and sable skin of her bearer, she disappeared. It is doubtful if in all his life Mr. Raleigh would ever receive a purer, sweeter kiss.

He had promised to be at the Bawn that evening, and now accordingly sought the shore, where the Arrow lay, and was soon within the shelter of his own house. The arrangement of toilet was a brief matter; and that concluded, Mr. Raleigh entered his library, an apartment now slightly in disarray, and therefore, perhaps, not uncongenial with his present mood. After strolling round the place, Mr. Raleigh paused at the window an instant, the window overhung with clematis, and commanding the long stretch of water between him and the Bawn, which last was, however, too distant for any movement to be discerned there. Soon Mr. Raleigh turned his back upon the scene that lay pictured in such beauty below, and, throwing himself into a deep arm-chair, remained motionless and plunged in thought for many moments. Rising at last, he took from the table a package of letters from India that had arrived in his absence. Glancing absently at the superscriptions, breaking the seal of one, he re-

placed them : it would take too long to read them now ;
they must wait. Then Mr. Raleigh had recourse to a
universal panacea, and walked to and fro across the
room, with measured, unvarying steps, till the striking
clock warned him that time was passing. Mr. Raleigh
drew near his desk again, took up the pen, and hesitated ;
then recalling his gaze that had seemed to search his own
inmost nature, he drew the paper nearer and wrote.

What he wrote, the very words, may not signify ; with
the theme one is sufficiently acquainted. Perhaps he
poured out there all that had so often trembled on his
lips without finding utterance ; perhaps, if ever passionate
heart flashed its own fire into its implements, this pen and
paper quivered beneath the current throbbing through
them. The page was brief, but therein all was said.
Sealing it hastily, he summoned Capua.

"Capua," said he, giving him the note, "you are to go
with me across the lake now. We shall return somewhere
between eleven and twelve. Just as we leave, you are to
give this note to Mrs. Laudersdale. Do you understand?"

"Yah, Massa, let dis chile alone," responded Capua,
grinning at the prospect of society, and speedily following
his master.

The breeze had fallen, so that they rowed the whole distance, with the idle sail hanging loosely, and arrived only
just as the red sunset painted the lake behind them with
blushing shadows. Mr. Raleigh joined Helen Heath and
his cousin in the hall ; Capua, superb with the importance
of his commission, sought another entrance. But just as
the latter individual had crossed the threshold, he encountered the nurse whom his master had previously met in
the wood. Nothing could have been more acceptable in
his eyes than this addition to the circle below-stairs.

Capua's hat was in his hand at once, and bows and curtsies and articulations and gesticulations followed with such confusing rapidity, that, when the mutually pleased pair turned in company toward the kitchens, a scrap of white paper, that had fluttered down in the disorder, was suffered to remain unnoticed on the floor. The courier had lost his despatch. Coming in from her walk, not five minutes later, Mrs. Laudersdale's eye was caught thereby; stooping to take it, she read with surprise her own name thereon, and ascended the stairs possessed thereof.

What burden of bliss, what secret of sorrow, lay infolded there, that at the first thought she covered it with sudden kisses, and the next, crushing it against her heart, burst into a wild weeping? Again and again she read it, and at every word its intense magnetic strength thrilled her, rapt her from remembrance, conquered her. She seized a pencil and wrote hurriedly: —

"You are right. With you I live, without you I die. You shut heaven out from me; make earth, then, heaven. Come to me, for I love you. Yes, I love you."

She did not stay to observe the contrast between her fervent sentences and the weak, faint characters that expressed them, but hastily sought the servant who was accustomed to act as postman, gave him directions to acquaint her of its reception, and watched him out of sight. All that in the swiftness of a fever-fit. Scarcely had the boat vanished when old thoughts rushed over her again, and she would have given her life to recall it. Returning, she found Capua eagerly searching for the lost letter, and thus learned that she was not to have received it until several hours later.

Perhaps no other woman in her situation could have done what Mrs. Laudersdale had done, without incurring

12

more guilt. There could be few who had been reared in
such isolation as she, — whose intellect, naturally subject
to her affection, had become more so through the absence
of systematic education, — whose morality had been
allowed to be merely one of instinct, — to whom intro-
spection had been till now a thing unknown, — and who,
accepting a husband as another child accepts a parent,
had, in the whirl of gay life where she afterward reigned,
found so little time for thought, and remained in such
mental unsophistication as to experience now her first
passion.

As Mrs. Laudersdale entered her room again, the opposite door opened and admitted that individual the selfishness of whose marriage was but half expiated when he
found himself on the surplus side of the world.

In the meanwhile, Mr. Raleigh was gayly passing the
time with Helen Heath. There were to be some guests
from the town that evening, and they were the topic of
her discourse.

" I wonder if we are never to have tea," said she at
last, looking at her watch.

" I did n't know you were attached to the custom," said
he, indifferently, as he had said everything else, while
intently listening for a footstep.

" Ah ! but I like to see other folks take their bitters."

" Do not even the publicans the same ? "

" You will become a proficient chemist, converting the
substance of my remarks to airy nothings through your
gospel-retorts."

" Oh, I understand your optics as well. You like to
see other folks ; taking the bitters is a different thing.
The tea-bell is a tocsin."

" Pshaw ! *You* don't care to see any one ! But shall

there be no more cakes and ale? Have n't you any sympathy for a sweet tooth?"

"None at all."

"Not even in Mrs. Laudersdale's instance?"

"Mrs. Laudersdale has a sweet tooth, then?" Mr. Raleigh asked in return, as if there were any trivial thing concerning her in which he could yet be instructed.

"I'm not going to tell you anything about Mrs. Laudersdale."

"There comes that desired object, the tea-tray. It's not to be formal, then, to-night. That's a blessing! What shall I bring you?" he continued, — "tea or cocoa?"

"Neither. You may have the tea, and I'll leave the cocoa for Mrs. Laudersdale."

"Mrs. Laudersdale drinks cocoa, then?"

"You may bring me some milk and macaroons."

As Mr. Raleigh was about to obey, his little apparition of the wood suddenly appeared in the doorway, followed by her nurse, — having arisen from the discipline of bath and brush, fair and spotless as a snowflake. She flitted by him with a mocking recognition.

"Rite!" cried a voice from above, familiar, but with how strange a tone in it! "Little Rite!"

"Maman!" cried the sprite, and went dancing up the stairs.

Mr. Raleigh's face, as he turned, darkened with a heavier flush than half a score of Indian summers branded upon it afterward.

"That is Mrs. Laudersdale's little maid?" asked he, when, after a few moments, he brought the required salver.

"Yes, — would you ever suspect it?"

Numberless as had been the times he had heard her speak of Rite, he never *had* suspected it, but had always at the name pictured some indifferent child, some baby-friend, or cousin by courtesy.

"She is not like her mother," said he, coolly.

"The very antipodes, — all her father. — Bless me! What is this? A real Laudersdale mess, — custards and cheese-cakes, — and I detest them both."

"Blame my unfortunate memory. I thought I had certainly pleased you, Miss Helen."

"When you forgot my orders? Well, never mind. Is n't she exquisite?"

"Is n't who exquisite? Oh, the little maid? Quite! Why has n't she been here all summer?"

"She was always a sickly, ailing thing, and has been at one of those rich Westchester farms where health and immortality are made. And now she is going away to Martinique, where her grandmother will take charge of her, bottle up those spirits, and make her a second edition of her mother. By the way, how that mother has effervesced this summer!" continued Helen, as the detested custard disappeared. "I wonder what made her. Do you suppose it was because her husband was away?"

At that instant Mrs. Laudersdale came sailing down the stairs.

A week previously, when, to repay the civilities of their friends in the neighboring city, Mrs. McLean had made a little fancy-party, Helen appearing as Champagne, all in rosy gauzes with a veiling foam of dropping silver lace, had begged Mrs. Laudersdale to give her prominence by dressing for Port; and accordingly that lady had arrayed herself in velvet, out of which her shoulders rose like snow, and whose rich duskiness made her perfect pallor more apparent, while its sumptuous body of color was sprinkled with glittering crystal drops and coruscations; and wreathing her forehead with crisp vine-leaves and tendrils, she had bunched together in intricate splendor all the amethysts, carbuncles, garnets, and rubies in the house, for grape-clusters at the ear, till she seemed, with her smile and her sunshine, the express and incarnate spirit of vintage. To-night, stripped of its sparkling drops, she wore the same dress, and in her hair a wreath of fresh white roses. Behind her descended a tall and stately gentleman. She swept forward. "Mr. Raleigh," she murmured, while her eyes diffused their gloom and fell, "let me introduce you to my husband!"

The blow had come previously. Mr. Raleigh bowed almost to the ground, without a word, then looked up and offered his hand. Mr. Laudersdale comprehended the whole matter at a heart-beat, and took it. Then they moved on toward other friends, whom, while waiting for knowledge of his wife's return from her walk, Mr. Laudersdale had not seen. Mr. Raleigh went in search of Capua, and ere long reappeared.

It grew quite dark; the candles were lighted. Rite slipped in, and, after having flown about like a thistle-down for a while, mounted a chair and put her arms about her mother's shoulders. Then Mr. Raleigh, sitting silently on a sofa, attracted her, and shortly afterward she had curled herself beside him and fallen asleep with her head upon his knee; otherwise he did not touch her. Mrs. Laudersdale stood by an open casement; the servant who had carried her note came up the lawn and spoke to her from without. There was no one in the house, and he had left it on the library-table. The pressure of those tender little arms was yet warm about the

mother's neck; she glanced sidelong at the sleeping child.
" He shall never see that note!" she murmured, and
slipped through the casement.

Accustomed to all rash and intrepid adventure during
this summer, it was nothing for her to unmoor a boat, enter it, and lift the oars, not pausing to observe that it was
the Arrow. Just then, however, a little wind ruffled down
and shook the sail, a wind not quite favorable, but in which
she could tack across and back; she drew in the oars, put
to the proof all her new boat-craft, and recklessly dashed
through the dark element that curled and seethed about
her. She had to make but two tacks in that hour's impetuous progress, before the house rose, as it had frequently done before, glooming at but a few rods' distance,
and loading with odorous breath the air that tossed its
vines ere stealing across the lake. She trembled now,
and remembered that she alone of all the party had always unconsciously evaded entering Mr. Raleigh's house,
had never seen the house nearer than now, and never
been its guest. It was entering some dark, unknown
place; it was to intrude on a sacred region. But the
breeze hurried her along while she thought, and the next
moment the keel was buried in the sand. There was no
time to lose; she left the boat, ascended a flight of stone
steps close at hand, and was in the garden. Low, ripe
greenery was waving over her here, deep alluring shadows
opening around, full fresh fragrance fanning idly to and
fro and stealing her soul away. Beyond, the lake gleamed
darkly, the water lapped gently, the wind sighed and fell
like a fluttering breath. She would have lingered forever, — she dared not linger a moment. She brushed
the dew from the heavy blossoms as she swept on, then
the drenching branches swayed and closed behind her;

she found a door ajar, and hastily entered the first room which appeared.

There were stray starbeams in this apartment; her eyes were accustomed to the gloom; she could dimly discern the great book-cases lining the wall, — an antique chair, — the glittering key-board of a grand-piano that stood apart, yet thrilling perhaps with recent harmonies, — a colossal head of Antinoüs, that self-involved dreamer, stone-entranced in a calm of passion. She had been feverishly agitated; but as this white silence dawned upon her, so strong, yet voluptuous, never sad, making in its masque of marble one intense moment eternal, some of the same power spread soothingly over her. She paused a moment to gather the thronging thoughts. How still the room was! She had not known that music was at his command before. How sweet the air that blew in at the window! what late flowers bore such pungent balm? That portrait leaning half-startled from the frame, was it his mother? These books, were they the very ones that had fed his youth? How everything was yet warm from his touch! how his presence yet lingered! how much of his life had passed into the dim beauty of the place! How each fresh waft from the blooms without came drowned in fine perfume, laden with delicious languor! What heaven was there! and, ah! what heaven was yet possible there!

Something that had flitted from the table in the draught, and had hovered here and there along the floor, now lay at her foot; she caught it absently; it was her letter. To snatch it from its envelope, and so tear it the more easily to atoms, was her first thought; but as suddenly she paused. Was it hers? Though written and sealed by her hand, had she any longer possession therein? Had

she more rule over it than over any other letter that
might be in the room? Absurd refinement of honor!
She broke the seal. Yet stay! Was there no justice
due to him? That letter which had been read long before the intended time, whose delivery any accident might
have frustrated, whose writer might have recalled it, —
did it demand no magnanimity of reply on her part?
Had he now no claim to the truth from her? As she
knew what he never would have told her an hour later,
had she authority to recede from the position she had
taken in response, simply because she could and he could
not? Should she ignobly refuse him his right?

Whether this were a sophism of sin or the logic of
highest virtue, she, who would have blotted out her writing with her heart's blood, did not wait to weigh.

"To him, also, I owe a duty!" she exclaimed, dropped
the letter where she had found it, and fled, — fled, hurrying through all the bewildering garden-walks, down from
the fragrance, the serenity, the bowery seclusion, from all
this conspiring loveliness that tempted her to dally and
commanded her to stay, — fled from this dream of passion, this region of joy, — fled forever, as she thought,
out into the wide, chill, lonely night.

Pushing off the boat and springing in, once more the
water curled beneath the parting prow, and she shot with
her flashing sail and hissing wake heedlessly, like a phantom, past another boat that was making more slowly in to
shore.

"This way, Helen," murmurs a subdued voice. "There
are some steps, Mr. Laudersdale. Here we are; but it's
dark as Erebus. Give me your hand; I'm half afraid;
after that spectre that walked the water just now, these
shadows are not altogether agreeable. There's the door,

— careful housekeeper, this Mr. Raleigh! I wonder what McLean would say. Don't believe he'd like it."

"What made you come, then?" asks Helen, as they step within.

"Oh, just for the frolic; it was getting stupid, too. I suppose we've ruined our dresses. But there! we must hurry and get back. I did n't think it would take so long. He can't manage a boat so well as Roger," adds Mrs. McLean, in a whisper.

"Goodness!" exclaims Helen. "I can't see an inch of the way. We shall certainly deal devastation."

"I've been exploring a mantel-shelf; here's a candle, but how to light it? Have n't you a match, Mr. Laudersdale?"

That gentleman produces one from a little pocket-safe; it proves a failure, — and so a second, and a third.

"This is the last, Mrs. McLean. Have your candle ready."

The little jet of flame flashes up.

"Quick, Helen! a scrap of paper, quick!"

"I don't know where to find any. Here's a billet on the floor; the seal's broken; Mr. Raleigh don't read his letters, you know; shall I take it?"

"Anything, yes! My fingers are burning! Quick, it's the last match! There!"

Helen waves a tiny flambeau, the candle is lighted, the flame whirled down upon the hearth and trodden out.

"I wonder what it was, though," adds Mrs. McLean, stooping over it. "Some of our correspondence. No matter, then. Now for that Indian mail. Here, — no, — this must be it. 'Mr. Roger Raleigh,' — 'Roger Raleigh, Esq.,' — that's not it. 'Day, Knight, & Co., for Roger Raleigh.' Why, Mr. Laudersdale, that's your

12 *   R

firm. Are n't you the Co. there? Ah, here it is, — 'Mrs. Catherine McLean, care of Mr. Roger Raleigh.' Does n't that look handsomely, Helen?" contemplating it with newly married satisfaction.

"Now you have it, come!" urges Helen.

"No, indeed! I must find that Turkish tobacco, to reward Mr. Laudersdale for his heroic exertions in our behalf."

Mr. Laudersdale, somewhat fastidious and given to rigid etiquette, looks as if the exertions would be best rewarded by haste. Mrs. McLean takes the candle in hand and proceeds on a tour of the apartment.

"There! is n't this the article? John says it's pitiful stuff, not to be compared with Virginia leaf. Look at this meerschaum, Mr. Laudersdale; there's an ensample. Prettily colored, is it not?"

"Now are you coming?" asks Helen.

"Would you? We've never been here without my worshipful cousin before; I should like to investigate his domestic arrangements. Needle and thread. Now what do you suppose he is doing with needle and thread? Oh, it's that little lacework that Mrs. —— Sketches! I wonder whom he's sketching. You, Helen? Me? Upside down, of course. No, it's —— Yes, we may as well go. Come!"

And in the same breath Mrs. McLean blows out the candle and precedes them. Mr. Laudersdale scorns to secure the sketch; and holding back the boughs for Miss Heath, and assisting her down the steps, quietly follows.

Meantime, Mrs. Laudersdale has reached her point of departure again, has stolen up out of the white fog now gathering over the lake, slipped into her former place, and found all nearly as before. The candles had been taken away, so that light came merely from the hall and doorways. Some of the guests were in the brilliant dining-room, some in the back-parlor. Mr. Raleigh, while Fate was thus busying herself about him, still sat motionless, one hand upon the sofa's side, one on the back, little Rite still sleeping on his knee. Capua came and exchanged a few words with his master; then the colored nurse stepped through the groups, sought the child, and carried her away, head and arms hanging heavy with slumber. Still Mr. Raleigh did not move. Mrs. Laudersdale stood in the window, vivid and glowing. There were no others in the room.

"Where is Mrs. McLean?" asked Mary Purcell at the door, after the charade in which she had been engaged was concluded.

"Gone across the lake with Nell and Mr. Laudersdale for a letter," replied Master Fred Heath, who had returned that afternoon from the counting-room, with his employer, and now sauntered by.

Mrs. Laudersdale started; she had not escaped too early; but then —— Her heart was beating in her throat.

"What letter?" asked Mrs. Heath, with amiable curiosity, as she joined them.

"Do you know what letter, Mr. Raleigh?"

"One from India, Madame," was his response.

"Strange! Helen gone without permission! What was in the letter, I wonder. Do you know what was in the letter, Mr. Raleigh?"

"Congratulations, and a recommendation of Mrs. McLean's cousin to her good graces," he said.

"Oh, it was not Helen's, then?"

"No."

"My young gentleman's not in good humor to-night,"

whispered Mrs. Heath to Miss Purcell, with a significant
nod, and moving off.

"How did you know what was in Mrs. McLean's letter,
sir?" asked Mary Purcell.

"I conjectured. In Mrs. Heath's place, I should have
known."

"There they come!—you can always tell Mrs. Mc-
Lean's laugh. You've lost all the charades, Helen!"

They came in, very gay, and seemed at once to arouse
an airier and finer spirit among the humming clusters.
Mr. Laudersdale did not join his wife, but sat on the
piazza talking with Mr. McLean. People were looking
at an herbal, others coquetting, others quiet. Some one
mentioned music. Directly afterward, Mr. Raleigh rose
and approached the piano. Every one turned. Taking
his seat, he threw out a handful of rich chords; the instrument seemed to diffuse a purple cloud; then, buoyed
over perfect accompaniment, the voice rose in that one
love-song of the world. What depth of tenderness is
there from which the Adelaide does not sound? What
secret of tragedy, too? Singing, he throbbed through it a
vitality as if the melody surcharged with beauty grew
from his soul and were his breath of life indeed. The
thrilling strain came to penetrate and fill one heart; the
passionate despair surged round her; the silence following was like the hand that closes the eyes of the dead.

Mr. Raleigh did not rise, nor look up, as he finished.

"How melancholy!" said Helen Heath, breaking the
hush.

"All music should be melancholy," said he.

"How absurd, Roger!" said his cousin. "There is
much music that is only intensely beautiful."

"Intense beauty at its height always drops in pathos,

or rather the soul does in following it, — since that is infinite, the soul finite."

"Nonsense! There's that song, Number Three in Book One —"

"I don't remember it."

"Well, there's no pathos there! It's just one trill of laughter and merriment, a sunbeam and effect. Play it, Helen."

Helen went, and, extending her hands before Mr. Raleigh, played a couple of bars; he continued where she left it, as one might a dream, and, strangely enough, the little, gushing sparkle of joy became a phantom of itself, dissolving away in tears.

"Oh, of course," said Mrs. McLean, "you can make mouths in a glass, if you please; but I, for one, detest melancholy! Don't you, Mrs. Laudersdale?"

Mrs. Laudersdale had shrunk into the shadow of the curtain. Perhaps she did not hear the question; for her reply, that did not come at once, was the fragment of a Provençal romance, sung, — and sung in a voice neither sweet nor rich, but of a certain personal force as potent as either quality, and a stifled strength of tone that made one tremble.

> We're all alone, we're all alone!
> The moon and stars are dead and gone,
> The night's at deep, the winds asleep,
> And thou and I are all alone!
>
> What care have we, though life there be?
> Tumult and life are not for me!
> Silence and sleep about us creep:
> Tumult and life are not for thee!
>
> How late it is since such as this
> Had topped the height of breathing bliss!
> And now we keep an iron sleep, —
> In that grave thou, and I in this!

Her voice yet shivered through the room, he struck a chord of dead conclusion, the curtain stirred, she emerged from the gloom and was gone.

Mr. Raleigh rose and bade his cousin good night. Mrs. McLean, however, took his arm and sauntered with him down the lawn.

"I thought Capua came with you," she remarked.

"He returned in a spare wherry, some time since," he replied ; and thereon they made a few paces in silence.

"Roger," said the little lady, taking breath preparatory to wasting it, "I thought Helen was a coquette. I've changed my mind. The fault is yours."

He turned and looked down at her with some surprise.

"You know we have n't much more time, and certainly —"

"Kate!"

"Yes, — don't scold ! — and if you are going to propose, I really think you ought to, or else —"

"You think I ought to marry Miss Heath?"

"Why — I — well — Oh, dear ! I wish I had held my peace!"

"That might have been advisable."

"Don't be offended now, Roger!"

"Is there any reason to suppose her — to suppose me —"

"Yes, there !" replied Mrs. McLean, desperately.

He was silent a moment.

"Good God, Kate !" said he, then, clasping his hands behind his head, and looking up the deep transparence of the unanswering night. "What a blessing it is that life don't last forever!"

"But it does, Roger," she uttered under her breath, —

terrified at his abrupt earnestness, and unwitting what storm she had aroused.

"The formula changes," he replied, with his old air, and retracing their steps.

The guests were all gone. Helen Heath was eating an ice; he bent over her chair and said, —

"Good night, Miss Helen!"

"Oh, good night, Mr. Raleigh! You are going? Well, we're all going soon. What a glorious summer it has been! Are n't you sorry we must part?"

"Why must we part?" he asked in a lower tone. "Where is the necessity of our parting? Why won't you stay forever, Helen?"

She turned and surveyed him quickly, while a red — whether of joy or anger he could not tell — flashed up her cheek.

"Do you mean —"

"Miss Heath, I mean, will you marry me?".

"Mr. Raleigh, no!"

With a bow he passed on.

Mr. Raleigh trimmed the Arrow's sail, for the breeze had sunk again, and swept slowly out with one oar suspended. A waning moon was rising behind the trees, it fell upon the little quay that had been built that summer, and seemed with its hollow beams still to continue the structure upon the water. The Arrow floated in the shadow just beyond. Mr. Raleigh's eyes were on the quay; he paused, nerveless, both oars trailing, a cold damp starting on his forehead. Some one approached as if looking out upon the dim sheet, — some one who, deceived by the false light, did not know the end to be so near, and walked forward firmly and confidently. Indeed, the quay had been erected in Mr. Laudersdale's absence. The water was deep there, the bottom rocky.

"Shout and warn him of his peril!" urged a voice in Mr. Raleigh's heart.

"Let him drown!" urged another voice.

If he would have called, the sound died a murmur in his throat. His eyes were on the advancing figure; it seemed as if that object were to be forever stamped upon the retina. Still as he gazed, he was aware of another form, one sitting on the quay, unseen in shadow like himself, and seeing what he saw, and motionless as he. Would Mrs. Laudersdale dip her hands in murder? It all passed in a second of time; at the next breath he summoned every generous power in his body, sprang with the leap of a wild creature, and confronted the recoiling man. Ere his foot touched the quay, the second form had glided from the darkness, and seized her husband's arm.

"A thousand pardons, sir," said Mr. Raleigh, then. "I thought you were in danger. Mrs. Laudersdale, good night!"

It was an easy matter to regain the boat, to gather up his oars, and shoot away. Till they faded from sight, he saw her still beside him; and so they stood till the last echo of the dipping oars was muffled in distance and lost.

Summer-nights are brief; breakfast was late on the next morning, — or rather, Mrs. Laudersdale was late, as usual, to partake it.

"Shall I tell you some news?" asked Helen Heath.

She lifted her heavy eyes absently.

"Mrs. McLean has made her husband a millionnaire. There was an Indian mail yesterday. Mr. Raleigh read his letters last night, after going home. His uncle is dying, — old, unfortunate, forlorn. He has abandoned everything, and must hew his own way in the world from this day forward. Mr. Raleigh left this morning for India."

When you saw Mrs. Laudersdale for the first time, at a period thirteen years later, would you have imagined her possessed of this little drama? You fancy now that in this flash all the wealth of her soul burned out and left her a mere volition and motive power? You are mistaken, as I said.

II.

WHEN Miss Kent, the maternal great-aunt of Mr. Raleigh, devised her property, the will might possibly have been set aside as that of a monomaniac, but for the fact that he cared too little about anything to go to law for it, and for the still more important fact that the heirs-at-law were sufficiently numerous to ingulf the whole property and leave no ripple to attest its submerged existence, had he done so; and on deserting it, he was better pleased to enrich the playfellow of his childhood than a host of unknown and unloved individuals. I cannot say that he did not more than once regret what he had lost: he was not of a self-denying nature, as we know; on the contrary, luxurious and accustomed to all those delights of life generally to be procured only through wealth. But, for all that, there had been intervals, ere his thirteen years' exile ended, in which, so far from regret, he experienced a certain joy at remembrance of this rough and rugged point of time where he had escaped from the chrysalid state to one of action and freedom and real life. He had been happy in reaching India before his uncle's death, in applying his own clear understanding to the intricate entanglements of the affairs before him, in rescuing his uncle's commercial good name, and in securing thus for himself a foothold on the ladder of life, although that step had not

occurred to him till thrust there by the pressure of circumstances.   For the rest, I am not sure that Mr. Raleigh
did not find his path suiting him well enough.   There was
no longer any charm in home ; he was forbidden to think
of it.   That strange summer, that had flashed into his life
like the gleam of a carnival-torch into quiet rooms, must
be forgotten ; the forms that had peopled it, in his determination, should become shadows.   Valiant vows !   Yet
there must have come moments, in that long lapse of days
and years, when the whole season gathered up its garments and swept imperiously through his memory : nights,
when under the shadow of the Himmaleh, the old passion
rose at spring-tide and flooded his heart and drowned out
forgetfulness, and a longing asserted itself, that, if checked
as instantly by honor as despair, was none the less insuf-
ferable and full of pain, — warm, wide, Southern nights,
when all the stars, great and golden, leaned out of heaven
to meet him, and all ripe perfumes, wafted by their own
principle of motion, floated in the rich dusk and laden air
about him, and the phantom of snow on topmost heights
sought vainly to lend him its calm.   Days also must have
showered their fervid sunshine on him, as he journeyed
through plains of rice, where all the broad reaches whit-
ening to harvest filled him with intense and bitterest loneliness.   What region of spice did not recall the noons when
they two had trampled the sweet-fern on wide, high New
England pastures, and breathed its intoxicating fragrance ?
and what forest of the tropics, what palms, what blooms,
what gorgeous affluence of color and of growth, equalled
the wood on the lake-shores, with its stately hemlocks, its
joyous birches, its pale-blue, shadow-blanched violets ?
Nor was this regret, that had at last become a part of
the man's identity, entirely a selfish one.   He had no au-

thority whatever for his belief, yet believe he did, that, firmly and tenderly as he loved, he was loved, and of the two fates his was not the harder. But a man, a man, too, in the stir of the world, has not the time for brooding over the untoward events of his destiny that a woman has ; his tender memories are forever jostled by cent per cent ; he meets too many faces to keep the one in constant and un-changing perpetuity sacredly before his thought. And so it happened that Mr. Raleigh became at last a silent, keen-eyed man, with the shadow of old and enduring melancholy on his life, but with no certain sorrow there.

In the course of time his business connections extended themselves ; he was associated with other men more in-tent than he upon their aim ; although not wealthy, years might make him so ; his name commanded respect. Some-thing of his old indifference lingered about him ; it was sel-dom that he was in earnest ; he drifted with the tide, and except to maintain a clear integrity before God and men and his own soul, exerted scarcely an effort. It was not an easy thing for him to break up any manner of life ; and when it became necessary for one of the firm to visit America, and he as the most suitable was selected, he as-sented to the proposition with not a heart-beat. America was as flat a wilderness to him as the Desert of Sahara. On landing in India, he had felt like a semi-conscious sleeper in his dream, the country seemed one of phan-tasms ; the Lascars swarming in the port, — the mer-chants wrapped in snowy muslins, who moved like white-robed bronzes faintly animate, — the strange faces, modes, and manners, — the stranger beasts, immense, and alien to his remembrance ; all objects that crossed his vision had seemed like a series of fantastic shows ; he could have imagined them to be the creations of a heated

fancy or the weird deceits of some subtle draught of
magic. But now they had become more his life than
the scenes which he had left; this land with its heats
and its languors had slowly and passively endeared itself to him; these perpetual summers, the balms and
blisses of the South, had unconsciously become a need
of his nature. One day all was ready for his departure; and in the clipper ship Osprey, with a cargo for
Day, Knight, and Company, Mr. Raleigh bade farewell
to India.

The Osprey was a swift sailer and handled with con-
summate skill, so that I shall not venture to say in how
few days she had weathered the Cape, and, ploughing up
the Atlantic, had passed the Windward Islands, and off
the latter had encountered one of the severest gales in
Captain Tarbell's remembrance, although he was not new
to shipwreck. If Mr. Raleigh had found no time for reflection in the busy current of affairs, when, ceasing to
stand aside, he had mingled in the turmoil and become a
part of the generations of men, he could not fail to find it
in this voyage, not brief at best, and of which every day's
progress must assure him anew toward what land and
what people he was hastening. Moreover, Fate had
woven his lot, it seemed, inextricably among those whom
he would shun; for Mr. Laudersdale himself was deeply
interested in the Osprey's freight, and it would be incum-
bent upon him to extend his civilities to Mr. Raleigh.
But Mr. Raleigh was not one to be cozened by circumstances more than by men.

The severity of the gale, which they had met some
three days since, had entirely abated; the ship was laid
to while the slight damage sustained was undergoing repair, and rocked heavily beneath the gray sky on the long,

sullen swell and roll of the grayer waters. Mr. Raleigh had just come upon deck at dawn, where he found every one in unaccountable commotion. " Ship to leeward in distress," was all the answer his inquiries could obtain, while the man on the topmast was making his observations. Mr. Raleigh could see nothing, but every now and then the boom of a gun came faintly over the distance. The report having been made, it was judged expedient to lower a boat and render her such assistance as was possible. Mr. Raleigh never could tell how it came to pass that he found himself one of the volunteers in this dangerous service.

The disabled vessel proved to be a schooner from the West Indies in a sinking condition. A few moments sufficed to relieve a portion of her passengers, sad wretches who for two days had stared death in the face, and they pulled back toward the Osprey. A second and third journey across the waste, and the remaining men prepared to lower the last woman into the boat, when a stout, but extremely pale individual, who could no longer contain his frenzy of fear, clambered down the chains and dropped in her place. There was no time to be lost, and nothing to do but submit; the woman was withdrawn to wait her turn with the captain and crew, and the laden boat again labored back to the ship. Each trip in the heavy sea and the blinding rain occupied no less than a couple of hours, and it was past noon when, uncertain just before if she might yet be there, they again came within sight of the little schooner, slowly and less slowly settling to her doom. As they approached her at last, Mr. Raleigh could plainly detect the young woman standing at a little distance from the anxious group, leaning against the broken mast with crossed arms, and looking out over the weary stretch with pale, grave face and quiet eyes. At the motion of the captain, she stepped forward, bound the ropes about herself, and was swung over the side to await the motion of the boat, as it slid within reach on the top of the long wave, or receded down its shining, slippery hollow. At length one swell brought it nearer, Mr. Raleigh's arms snatched the slight form and drew her half-fainting into the boat, a cloak was tossed after, and one by one the remainder followed; they were all safe, and some beggared. The bows of the schooner already plunged deep down in the gaping gulfs, they pulled bravely away, and were tossed along from billow to billow.

"You are very uncomfortable, Mademoiselle Le Blanc?" asked the rescued captain at once of the young woman, as she sat beside him in the stern-sheets.

"*Moi?*" she replied. "*Mais non, Monsieur.*"

Mr. Raleigh wrapped the cloak about her, as she spoke. They were equidistant from the two vessels, neither of which was to be seen, the rain fell fast into the hissing brine, their fate still uncertain. There was something strangely captivating and reassuring in this young girl's equanimity, and he did not cease speculating thereon till they had again reached the Osprey, and she had disappeared below.

By degrees the weather lightened; the Osprey was on the wing again, and a week's continuance of this fair wind would bring them into port. The next day, toward sunset, as Mr. Raleigh turned about in his regular pacing of the deck, he saw, at its opposite extremity, the same slight figure dangerously perched upon the taffrail, leaning over, now watching the closing water, and now eagerly shading her eyes with her hand to observe the ship which they spoke, as they lay head to the wind, and

for a better view of which she had climbed to this position. It was not Mr. Raleigh's custom to interfere; if
people chose to drown themselves, he was not the man to
gainsay them; but now, as his walk drew him toward
her, it was the most natural thing in the world to pause
and say, —

"*Il serait fâcheux, Mademoiselle, lorsqu'on a failli faire
naufrage, de se noyer*"—and, in want of a word, Mr.
Raleigh ignominiously descended to his vernacular, —
"with a lee-lurch."

The girl, resting on the palm of one hand, and unsup-
ported otherwise, bestowed upon him no reply, and did
not turn her head. Mr. Raleigh looked at her a moment,
and then continued his walk. Returning, the thing happened as he had predicted, and, with a little quick cry,
Mademoiselle Le Blanc was hanging by her hands among
the ropes. Reaching her with a spring, "*Viens, petite!*"
he said, and with an effort placed her on her feet again
before an alarm could have been given.

"*Ah! mais j'ai cru que c'en était fait de moi!*" she
exclaimed, drawing in her breath like a sob. In an instant, however, surveying Mr. Raleigh, the slight emotion
seemed to yield to one of irritation, that she had been
rescued by him; for she murmured quickly, in English,
head haughtily thrown back and eyes downcast, — "Monsieur thinks that I owe him much for having saved my
life!"

"Mademoiselle best knows its worth," said he, rather
amused, and turning away.

The girl was still looking down; now, however, she
threw after him a quick glance.

"*Tenez!*" said she, imperiously, and stepping toward
him. "You fancy me very ungrateful," she continued,

lifting her slender hand, and with the back of it brushing away the floating hair at her temples. " Well, I am not, and at some time it may be that I prove it. I do not like to owe debts; but, since I must, I will not try to cancel them with thanks."

Mr. Raleigh bowed, but said nothing. She seemed to think it necessary to efface any unpleasant impression, and, with a little more animation and a smile, added, —

" The Captain Tarbell told me your name, Mr. Raleigh, and that you had not been at home for thirteen years. *Ni moi non plus,* — at least, I suppose it is home where I am going; yet I remember no other than the island and my —"

And here the girl opened her eyes wide, as if determined that they should not fill with tears, and looked out over the blue and sparkling fields around them. There was a piquancy in her accent that made the hearer wish to hear further, and a certain artlessness in her manner not met with recently by him. He moved forward, keeping her beside him.

" Then you are not French," he said.

" I ? Oh, no, — nor Creole. I was born in America; but I have always lived with mamma on the plantation; *et maintenant, il y a six mois qu'elle est morte !* "

Here she looked away again. Mr. Raleigh's glance followed hers, and, returning, she met it bent kindly and with a certain grave interest upon her. She appeared to feel reassured, somewhat protected by one so much her elder.

" I am going now to my father," she said, " and to my other mother."

" A second marriage," thought Mr. Raleigh, " and before the orphan's crapes are —" Then, fearful lest she should read his thought, he added, — "And how do you speak such perfect English?"

"Oh, my father came to see us every other year, and I have written home twice a week since I was a little child. Mamma, too, spoke as much English as French."

"I have not been in America for a long time," said Mr. Raleigh, after a few steps. "But I do not doubt that you will find enjoyment there. It will be new: womanhood will have little like youth for you; but, in every event, it is well to add to our experience, you know."

"What is it like, sir? But I know! Rows of houses, very counterparts of rows of houses, and they of rows of houses yet beyond. Just the toy-villages in boxes, uniform as graves and ugly as bricks —"

"Brick houses are not such ugly things. I remember one, low and wide, possessed of countless gables, covered with vines and shaded with sycamores; it could not have been so picturesque, if built of the marble of Paros, and gleaming temple-white through masks of verdure."

"It seems to me that I, too, remember such a one," said she, dreamily. "*Mais non, je m'y perds.* Yet, for all that, I shall not find the New York avenues lined with them."

"No; the houses there are palaces."

"I suppose, then, I am to live in a palace," she answered, with a light tinkling laugh. "That is fine; but one may miss the verandas, all the whiteness and coolness. How one must feel the roof!"

"Roofs should be screens, and not prisons, not shells, you think?" said Mr. Raleigh.

"At home," she replied, "our houses are, so to say, parasols; in those cities they must be iron shrouds.

13   8

Ainsi soit il! " she added, and shrugged her shoulders like a little fatalist.

" You must not take it with such desperation ; perhaps you will not be obliged to wear the shroud."

" Not long, to be sure, at first. We go to freeze in the country, a place with distant hills of blue ice, my old nurse told me, — old Ursule. Oh, sir, she was drowned! I saw the very wave that swept her off!'

" That was your servant ? "

" Yes."

" Then, perhaps, I have some good news for you. She was tall and large ? "

" *Oui.*"

" Her name was Ursule ? "

" *Oui ! je dis que oui !* "

Mr. Raleigh laughed at her eagerness.

" She is below, then," he said, — " not drowned. There is Reynolds. Mr. Reynolds, will you take this young lady to her servant, Ursule, the woman you rescued ? "

And Mademoiselle Le Blanc disappeared under that gentleman's escort.

The ordinary restraints of social life not obtaining so much on board ship as elsewhere, Mr. Raleigh saw his acquaintance with the pale young stranger fast ripening into friendliness. It was an agreeable variation from the monotonous routine of his voyage, and he felt that it was not unpleasant to her. Indeed, with that childlike simplicity that was her first characteristic, she never saw him without seeking him, and every morning and every evening it became their habit to pace the deck together. Sunrise and twilight began to be the hours with which he associated her ; and it was strange, that, coming, as she did, out of the full blaze of tropical suns, she yet seemed

a creature that had taken life from the fresh, cool, dewy
hours, and that must fairly dissolve beneath the sky of noon.
She puzzled him, besides, and he found singular contradic-
tions in her : to-night, sweetness itself, — to-morrow, pet-
ulant as a spoiled child. She had all a child's curiosity,
too ; and he amused himself by seeing, at one time, with
what novelty his adventures struck her, when, at another,
he would have fancied she had always held Taj and Himmaleh in her garden. Now and then, excited, perhaps,
by emulation and wonder, her natural joyousness broke
through the usually sad and quiet demeanor ; and she
related to him, with dramatic *abandon*, scenes of her gay
and innocent island-life, so that he fancied there was not
an emotion in her experience hidden from his knowledge,
till, all-unaware, he tripped over one reserve and another,
that made her, for the moment, as mysterious a being as
any of those court-ladies of ancient *régimes,* in whose lives
there were strange *lacunæ* and spaces of shadow. And a
peculiarity of their intercourse was, that, let her depart in
what freak or perversity she pleased, she seemed always
to have a certainty of finding him in the same mood in
which she had left him, — as some bright wayward vine
of Southern forests puts out a tendril to this or that en-
ticing point, yet, winding back, will find its first support
unchanged. Shut out, as Mr. Raleigh had been, from
any but the most casual female society, he found a great
charm in this familiarity, and, without thinking how lately
it had begun or how soon it must cease, he yielded himself to its presence. At one hour she seemed to him an
impetuous and capricious thing, for whose better protection the accident of his companionship was extremely fortunate, — at another hour, a woman too strangely sweet to
part with ; and then Mr. Raleigh remembered that in all

his years he had really known but two women, and one
of these had not spent a week in his memory.

Mademoiselle Le Blanc came on deck one evening,
and, wrapping a soft, thick mantle round her, looked
about for a minute, shaded her eyes from the sunset,
meantime, with a slender, transparent hand, bowed to one,
spoke to another, slipped forward and joined Mr. Raleigh,
where he leaned over the ship's side.

" *Voici ma capote !* " said she, before he was aware of
her approach. " *Ciel! qu'il fait frais !* "

" We have changed our skies," said Mr. Raleigh,
looking up.

" It is not necessary that you should tell me that ! " she
replied. " I shiver all the time. I shall become a little
iceberg, for the sake of floating down to melt off Martinique ! "

" Warm yourself now in the sunset ; such a blaze was
kindled for the purpose."

" Whenever I see a sunset, I find it to be a splendid
fact, *une jouissance vraie, Monsieur*, to think that men can
paint, — that these shades, which are spontaneous in the
heavens, and fleeting, can be rivalled by us and made
permanent, — that man is more potent than light."

" But you are all wrong in your *jouissance.*"

She pouted her lip, and hung over the side in an
attitude that it seemed he had seen a hundred times
before.

" That sunset, with all its breadth and splendor, is
contained in every pencil of light."

She glanced up and laughed.

"Oh, yes! a part of its possibilities. Which proves — ? "

" That color is an attribute of light and an achievement
of man."

" Cà et là,
  Toute la journée,
  Le vent vain va
  En sa tournée,"

hummed the girl, with a careless dismissal of the subject.

Mr. Raleigh shut up the note-book in which he had been writing, and restored it to his pocket. She turned about and broke off her song.

"There is the moon on the other side," she said, "floating up like a great bubble of light. She and the sun are the scales of a balance, I think; as one ascends, the other sinks."

"There is a richness in the atmosphere, when sunset melts into moonrise, that makes one fancy it enveloping the earth like the bloom on a plum."

"And see how it has powdered the sea! The waters look like the wings of the *papillon bleu*."

"It seems that you love the sea."

"Oh, certainly. I have thought that we islanders were like those Chinese who live in great tanka-boats on the rivers; only our boat rides at anchor. To climb the highest land, and see yourself girt with fields of azure enamelled in sheets of sunshine and fleets of sails, and lifted against the horizon, deep, crystalline, and translucent as a gem, — that makes one feel strong in isolation, and produces keen races. Don't you think so?"

"I think that isolation causes either vivid characteristics or idiocy, seldom strong or healthy ones; and I do not value race."

"Because you came from America!"—with an air of disgust, — "where there is yet no race, and the population is still too fluctuating for the mould of one."

"I come from India, where, if anywhere, there is race."

" But, pshaw ! that was not what we were talking about."

" No, Mademoiselle, we were speaking of an element even more fluctuating than American population."

" Of course I love the sea; but if the sea loves me, it is the way a cat loves the mouse."

" It is always putting up a hand to snatch you ? "

" I suppose I am sent to Nineveh and persist in shipping for Tarshish. I never enter a boat without an accident. The Belle Voyageuse met shipwreck, and I on board. That was anticipated, though, by all the world; for the night before we set sail, — it was a very murk, hot night, — we were all called out to see the likeness of a large merchantman transfigured in flames upon the sky, — spars and ropes and hull one net and glare of fire."

" A mirage, probably, from some burning ship at sea."

" No, I would rather think it supernatural. Oh, it was frightful ! Rather superb, though, to think of such a spectral craft rising to warn us with ghostly flames that the old Belle Voyageuse was riddled with rats ! "

" Did it burn blue ? " asked Mr. Raleigh.

" Oh, if you 're going to make fun of me, I 'll tell you nothing more ! "

As she spoke, Capua, who had considered himself, during the many years of wandering, both guiding and folding star to his master, came up, with his eyes rolling fearfully in a lively expansion of countenance, and muttered a few words in Mr. Raleigh's ear, lifting both hands in comical consternation the while.

" Excuse me a moment," said Mr. Raleigh, following him, and, meeting Captain Tarbell at the companion-way, the three descended together.

Mr. Raleigh was absent some fifteen minutes, at the end of that time rejoining Mademoiselle Le Blanc.

" I did not mean to make fun of you," said he, resuming the conversation as if there had been no interruption. " I was watching the foam the Osprey makes in her speed, which certainly burns blue. See the flashing sparks! now that all the red fades from the west, they glow in the moon like broken amethysts."

" What did you mean, then?" she asked, pettishly.

" Oh, I wished to see if the idea of a burning ship was so terrifying."

" Terrifying? No; I have no fear; I never was afraid. But it must, in reality, be dreadful. I cannot think of anything else so appalling."

" Not at all timid?"

" Mamma used to say, those that know nothing fear nothing."

" Eminently your case. Then you cannot imagine a situation in which you would lose self-possession?"

" Scarcely. Isn't it people of the finest organization, comprehensive, large-souled, that are capable of the extremes either of courage or fear? Now I am limited, so that, without rash daring or pale panic, I can generally preserve equilibrium."

" How do you know all this of yourself?" he asked, with an amused air.

" *Certaines occasions me l'ont appris,*" she replied, briefly.

" So I presumed," said he. " Ah? They have thrown out the log. See, we make progress. If this breeze holds!"

" You are impatient, Mr. Raleigh. You have dear friends at home, whom you wish to see, who wish to see you?"

"No," he replied, with a certain bitterness in his tone. "There is no one to whom I hasten, no one who waits to receive me."

"No one? But that is terrible! Then why should you wish to hasten? For me, I would always be willing to loiter along, to postpone home indefinitely."

"That is very generous, Mademoiselle."

"Mr. Raleigh — "

"Well?"

"I wish — please — you must not say Mademoiselle. Nobody will address me so, shortly. Give me my name, — call me Marguerite. *Je vous en prie.*"

And she looked up with a blush deepening the apple-bloom of her cheek.

"Marguerite? Does it answer for pearl or for daisy with you?"

"Oh, they called me so because I was such a little round white baby. I couldn't have been very precious, though, or she never would have parted with me. Yes, I wish we might drift on some lazy current for years. I hate to shorten the distance. I stand in awe of my father, and I do not remember my mother."

"Do not remember?"

"She is so perfect, so superb, so different from me! But she ought to love her own child!"

"Her own child?"

"And then I do not know the customs of this strange land. Shall I be obliged to keep an establishment?"

"Keep an establishment?"

"It is very rude to repeat my words so! You ought n't! Yes, keep an establishment!"

"I beg your pardon, Mademoiselle."

"No, it is I who am rude."

"Not at all, — but mysterious. I am quite in the dark concerning you."

"Concerning me?"

"Ah, Miss Marguerite, it is my turn now."

"Oh! It must be — This is your mystery, *n'est ce pas?* Mamma was my grandmamma. My own mother was far too young when mamma gave her in marriage; and, to make amends, mamma adopted me and left me her name and her fortune. So that I am very wealthy. And now shall I keep an establishment?"

"I should think not," said Mr. Raleigh, with a smile.

"Do you know, you constantly reassure me? Home grows less and less a bugbear when you speak of it. How strange! It seems as if I had known you a year, instead of a week."

"It would probably take that period of time to make us as well acquainted under other circumstances."

"I wish you were going to be with us always. Shall you stay in America, Mr. Raleigh?"

"Only till the fall. But I will leave you at your father's door —"

And then Mr. Raleigh ceased suddenly, as if he had promised an impossibility.

"How long before we reach New York?" she asked.

"In about nine hours," he replied, — adding, in unconscious undertone, "if ever."

"What was that you said to yourself?" she demanded, in a light and gayly inquisitive voice, as she looked around and over the ship. "Why, how many there are on deck! It is such a beautiful night, I suppose. Eh, Mr. Raleigh?"

"Are you not tired of your position?" he asked. "Sit down beside me here." And he took a seat.

"No, I would rather stand. Tell me what you said."

13 *

"Sit, then, to please me, Marguerite, and I will tell you what I said."

She hesitated a moment, standing before him, the hood of her capote, with its rich purple, dropping from the fluttering yellow hair that the moonlight deepened into gold, and the fire-opal clasp rising and falling with her breath, like an imprisoned flame. He touched her hand, still warm and soft, with his own, which was icy. She withdrew it, turned her eyes, whose fair, faint lustre, the pale forget-me-not blue, was darkened by the antagonistic light to an amethystine shadow, inquiringly upon him.

"There is some danger," she murmured.

"Yes. When you are not a mark for general observation, you shall hear it."

"I would rather hear it standing."

"I told you the condition."

"Then I shall go and ask Captain Tarbell."

"And come sobbing back to me for 'reassurance.'"

"No," she said, quickly, "I should go down to Ursule."

"Ursule has a mattress on deck; I assisted her up."

"There is the captain! Now —"

He seized her hand and drew her down beside him. For an instant she would have resisted, as the sparkling eyes and flushed cheeks attested, — and then, with the instinctive feminine baseness that compels every woman, when once she has met her master, she submitted.

"I am sorry, if you are offended," said he. "But the captain cannot attend to you now, and it is necessary to be guarded in movement; for a slight thing on such occasions may produce a panic."

"You should not have forced me to sit," said she, in a smothered voice, without heeding him: "you had no right."

" This right, that I assume the care of you."

" Monsieur, you see that I am quite competent to the care of myself."

" Marguerite, I see that you are determined to quarrel."

She paused a moment, ere replying ; then drew a little nearer and turned her face toward him, though without looking up.

" Forgive me, then ! " said she. " But I would rather be naughty and froward, it lets me stay a child, and so you can take me in keeping, and I need not think for myself at all. But if I act like a woman grown, then comes all the responsibility, and I must rely on myself, which is such trouble now, though I never felt it so before, — I don't know why. Don't you see ? " And she glanced at him with her head on one side, and laughing archly.

" You were right," he replied, after surveying her a moment ; " my proffered protection *is* entirely super-fluous."

She thought he was about to go, and placed her hand on his, as it lay along the side. " Don't leave me," she murmured.

" I have no intention of leaving you," he said.

" You are very good. I have never seen one like you. I love you well." And, bathed in moonlight, she raised her face and her glowing lips toward him.

Mr. Raleigh gazed in the innocent eyes a moment, to seek the extent of her meaning, and felt, that, should he take advantage of her childlike forgetfulness, he would be only re-enacting the part he had so much condemned in one man years before. So he merely bent low over the hand that lay in his, raised it, and touched his lips to that.

In an instant the color suffused her face, she snatched the hand away, half rose trembling from her seat, and sank into it again.

"*Soit, Monsieur!*" she exclaimed, abruptly. "But you have not told me the danger."

"It will not alarm you now?" he replied, laughing.

"I have said that I am not a coward."

"I wonder what you would think of me when I say that without doubt I am."

"You, Mr. Raleigh?" she cried, astonishment banishing anger.

"Not that I betray myself. But that I have felt the true heart-sinking. Once, surprised in the centre of an insurrection, I expected to find my hair white as snow, if I escaped."

"Your hair is very black. And you escaped?"

"So it would appear."

"They suffered you to go on account of your terror? You feigned death? You took flight?"

"Hardly, — neither."

"Tell me about it," she said, imperiously.

Though Mr. Raleigh had exchanged the singular reserve of his youth for a well-bred reticence, he scarcely cared to be his own hero.

"Tell me," said she. "It will shorten the time; and that is what you are trying to do, you know."

He laughed.

"It was once when I was obliged to make an unpleasant journey into the interior, and a detachment was placed at my service. We were in a suspected district quite favorable to their designs, and the commanding officer was attacked with illness in the night. Being called to his assistance, I looked abroad and fancied things wore an unusual aspect among the men, and sent Capua to steal down a covered path and see if anything were wrong. Never at fault, he discovered a revolt with intent to murder my companion and myself, and retreat to the mountains. Of course there was but one thing to do. I put a pistol in my belt and walked down and in among them, singled out the ringleader, fixed him with my eye, and bade him approach. My appearance was so sudden and unsuspected that they forgot defiance."

"*Bien*, but I thought you were afraid."

"So I was. I could not have spoken a second word. I experienced intense terror, and that, probably, gave my glance a concentration of which I was unaware and by myself incapable; but I did not suffer it to waver; I could not have moved it, indeed; I kept it on the man while he crept slowly toward me. I shall never forget the horrible sensation. I did not dare permit myself to doubt his conquest; but if I had failed, as I then thought, his approach was like the slow coil of a serpent about me, and it was his glittering eyes that had fixed mine, and not mine his. At my feet, I commanded him, with a gesture, to disarm. He obeyed, and I breathed; and one by one they followed his example. Capua, who was behind me, I sent back with the weapons, and in the morning gave them their choice of returning to town with their hands tied behind their backs, or of going on with me and remaining faithful. They chose the latter, did me good service, and I said nothing about the affair."

"That was well. But were you really frightened?"

"So I said. I cannot think of it yet without a slight shudder."

"Yes, and a rehearsal. Your eyes charge bayonets now. I am not a Sepoy."

"Well, you are still angry with me?"

"How can I be angry with you?"

"How, indeed? So much your senior that you owe me respect, Miss Marguerite. I am quite old enough to be your father."

"You are, sir?" she replied, with surprise. "Why, are you fifty-five years old?"

"Is that Mr. Laudersdale's age?"

"How did you know Mr. Laudersdale was my father?"

"By an arithmetical process. That is his age?"

"Yes; and yours?"

"Not exactly. I was thirty-seven last August."

"And will be thirty-eight next?"

"That is the logical deduction."

"I shall give you a birthday-gift when you are just twice my age."

"By what courier will you make it reach me?"

"Oh, I forgot. But — Mr. Raleigh?"

"What is it?" he replied, turning to look at her, — for his eyes had been wandering over the deck.

"I thought you would ask me to write to you."

"No, that would not be worth while."

His face was too grave for her to feel indignation.

"Why?" she demanded.

"It would give me great pleasure, without doubt. But in a week you will have too many other cares and duties to care for such a burden."

"That shows that you do not know me at all. *Vous avez mal agi avec moi!*"

Though Mr. Raleigh still looked at her, he did not reply. She rose and walked away a few steps, coming back.

"You are always in the right, and I consequently in

the wrong," she said. " How often to-night have I asked pardon ? I will not put up with it ? "

" We shall part in a few hours," he replied ; " when you lose your temper, I lose my time."

" In a few hours ? Then is the danger which you mentioned past ? "

" I scarcely think so."

" Now I am not going to be diverted again. What is this dreadful danger ? "

" Let me tell you, in the first place, that we shall probably make the port before our situation becomes apparently worse, — that we do not take to the boats, because we are twice too many to fill them, owing to the Belle Voyageuse, and because it might excite mutiny, and for several other becauses, — that every one is on deck, Capua consoling Ursule, the captain having told to each, personally, the possibility of escape — "

" *Achevez !* "

" That the lights are closed, the hatches battened down, and by dint of excluding the air we can keep the flames in a smouldering state and sail into harbor a shell of safety over this core of burning coal."

" Reducing the equation, the ship is on fire ? "

" Yes."

She did not speak for a moment or two, and he saw that she was quite faint. Soon recovering herself, —

" And what do you think of the mirage now ? " she asked. " Where is Ursule ? I must go to her," she added suddenly, after a brief silence, starting to her feet.

" Shall I accompany you ? "

" Oh, no."

" She lies on a mattress there, behind that group," —

nodding in the implied direction; "and it would be well, if you could lie beside her and get an hour's rest."

"Me? I could n't sleep. I shall come back to you,— may I?" And she was gone.

Mr. Raleigh still sat in the position in which she had left him, when, a half-hour afterward, she returned.

"Where is your cloak?" he asked, rising to receive her.

"I spread it over Ursule, she was so chilly."

"You will not take cold?"

"I? I am on fire myself."

"Ah, I see; you have the Saturnalian spirit in you."

"It is like the Revolution, the French, is it not?— drifting on before the wind of Fate, this ship full of fire and all red-hot raging turbulence. Just look up the long sparkling length of these white, full shrouds, swelling and curving like proud swans, in the gale,— and then imagine the devouring monster below in his den!"

"*Don't* imagine it. Be quiet and sit beside me. Half the night is gone."

"I remember reading of some pirates once, who, driving forward to destruction on fearful breakers, drank and sang and died madly. I wish the whole ship's company would burst out in one mighty chorus now, or that we might rush together with tumultuous impulse and dance, — dance wildly into death and daylight.

"We have nothing to do with death," said Mr. Raleigh. "Our foe is simply time. You dance, then?"

"Oh, yes. I dance well,— like those white fluttering butterflies,— as if I were *au gré du vent*."

"That would not be dancing well."

"It would not be dancing well to *be* at the will of the wind, but it is perfection to appear so."

" The dance needs the expression of the dancer's will. It is breathing sculpture. It is mimic life beyond all other arts."

" Then well I love to dance. And I do dance well. Wait, — you shall see."

He detained her.

" Be still, little maid ! " he said, and again drew her beside him, though she still continued standing.

At this moment the captain approached.

" What cheer ? " asked Mr. Raleigh.

" No cheer," he answered, gloomily, dinting his finger-nails into his palm. " The planks forward are already hot to the hand. I tremble at every creak of cordage, lest the deck crash in and bury us all."

" You have made the Sandy Hook light ? "

" Yes ; too late to run her ashore."

" You cannot try that at the — "

" Certain death."

" The wind scarcely — "

" Veered a point. I am carrying all sail. But if this tooth of fire gnaws below, you will soon see the masts go by the board. And then we are lost, indeed ! "

" Courage ! she will certainly hold together till you can hail the pilots."

" I think no one need tremble when he has such an instance of fearlessness before him," replied the captain, bowing to Marguerite ; and turning away, he hid his suspense and pain again under a calm countenance.

Standing all this while beside Mr. Raleigh, she had heard the whole of the conversation, and he felt the hand in his growing colder as it continued. He wondered if it were still the same excitement that sent the alternate flush and pallor up her cheek. She sat down, leaning her head

T

back against the bulwark, as if to look at the stars, and
suffering the light, fine hair to blow about her temples
before the steady breeze. He bent over to look into her
eyes, and found them fixed and lustreless.

"Marguerite!" he exclaimed.

She tried to speak, but the teeth seemed to hinder the
escape of her words, and to break them into bits of sound;
a shiver shook her from head to foot.

"I wonder if this is fear," she succeeded in saying.
"Oh, if there were somewhere to go, something to hide
me! A great horror is upon me! I am afraid! *Seigneur
Dieu! Mourir par le feu! Périssons alors au plus vite!*"
And she shuddered, audibly.

Mr. Raleigh passed his arm about her and gathered her
closer to himself. He saw at once, that, sensitive as she
was to every impression, this fear was a contagious one, a
mere gregarian affinity, and that she needed the prepon-
derating warmth and strength of a protecting presence,
the influence of a fuller vitality. He did not speak, but
his touch must in some measure have counteracted the
dread that oppressed her. She ceased trembling, but did
not move.

The westering moon went to bury herself in banks of
cloud; the wind increasing piped and whistled in strident
threatening through the rigging; the ship vibrated to the
concussive voice of the minute-gun. No murmurs but
those of wind and water were heard among the throng;
they drove forward in awful, pallid silence. Suddenly
the shriek of one voice, but from fourscore throats, rent
the agonized quiet. A red light was running along the
deck, a tongue of flame lapping round the forecastle, a
spire shooting aloft. Marguerite hid her face in Mr.
Raleigh's arm; a great sob seemed to go up from all the

people. The captain's voice thundered through the tumult, and instantly the mates sprang forward and the jib went crashing overboard. Mr. Raleigh tore his eyes away from the fascination of this terror, and fixed them by chance on two black specks that danced on the watery horizon. He gazed with intense vision a moment. "The tugs!" he cried. The words thrilled with hope in every dying heart; they no longer saw themselves the waiting prey of pain and death, of flames and sea. Some few leaped into the boat at the stern, lowered and cut it away; others dropped spontaneously into file, and passed the dripping buckets of sea-water, to keep, if possible, the flames in check. Mr. Raleigh and Marguerite crossed over to Ursule.

The sight of her nurse, passive in despair, restored to the girl a portion of her previous spirit. She knelt beside her, talking low and rapidly, now and then laughing, and all the time communicating nerve with her light, firm finger-touches. Except their quick and unintelligible murmurs, and the plash and hiss of water, nothing else broke the torturing hush of expectation. There was a half-hour of breathless watch ere the steam-tugs were alongside. Already the place was full of fervid torment, and they had climbed upon every point to leave, below, the stings of the blistering deck. None waited on the order of their going, but thronged and sprang precipitately. Ursule was at once deposited in safety. The captain moved to conduct Marguerite across, but she drew back and clung to Mr. Raleigh.

"*J'ai honte*," she said; "*je ne bougerai pas plus tôt que vous.*"

The breath of the fierce flames scorched her cheek as she spoke, the wind of their roaring progress swept her hair. He lifted her over without further consultation, and still kept her in his care.

There was a strange atmosphere on board the little vessels, as they labored about and parted from the doomed Osprey. Many were subdued with awe and joy at their deliverance; others broke the tense strain of the last hours in suffocating sobs. Every throb of the panting engines they answered with waiting heart-beats, as it sent them farther from the fearful wonder, now blazing in multiplex lines of fire against the gray horizon. Mr. Raleigh gazed after it as one watches the conflagration of a home. Marguerite left her quiet weeping to gaze with him. An hour silently passed, and as the fiery phantom faded into dawn and distance she sang sweetly the first few lines of an old French hymn. Another voice took up the measure, stronger and clearer; those who knew nothing of the words caught the spirit of the tune; and no choral service ever pealed up temple-vaults with more earnest accord than that in which this chant of grateful, exultant devotion now rose from rough-throated men and weary women in the crisp air and yellowing spring-morning.

The stray sails had thickened into the flickering forest of shipping at last, and as the moment of parting approached, Marguerite stood with folded hands before Mr. Raleigh, looking sadly down the harbor.

"I regret all that," she said, — "these days that seem years."

"An equivocal phrase," he replied, with a smile.

"But you know what I mean. I am going to strangers; I have been with you. I shall find no one so kind to me as you have been, Monsieur."

"Your strangers can be much kinder to you than I have been."

"Never! I wish they did not exist! What do I care for them? What do they care for me? They do not know me; I shall shock them. I miss you, I hate them, already. *Non! Personne ne m'aime, et je n'aime personne!*" she exclaimed, with low-toned vehemence.

"Rite," began Mr. Raleigh.

"Rite! No one but my mother ever called me that. How did you know it?"

"I have met your mother, and I knew you a great many years ago."

"Mr. Raleigh!" And there was the least possible shade of unconscious regret in the voice before it added, "And what was I?"

"You were some little wood-spirit, the imp of a fallen cone, mayhap, or the embodiment of birch-tree shadows. You were a soiled and naughty little beauty, not so different from your present self, and who kissed me on the lips."

"And did you refuse to take the kiss?"

He laughed.

"You were a child then," he said. "And I was not —"

"Was not? —"

Here the boat swung round at her moorings, and the shock prevented Mr. Raleigh's finishing his sentence.

"Ursule is with us, or on the other one?" she asked.

"With us."

"That is fortunate. She is all I have remaining, by which to prove my identity."

"As if there could be two such maidens in the world!"

Marguerite left him, a moment, to give Captain Tarbell her address, and returning, they were shortly afterward seated side by side in a coach, Capua and Ursule following in another. As they stopped at the destined door, Mr. Raleigh alighted and extended his hand. She lingered a moment ere taking it, — not to say adieu, nor to offer him cheek or lip again.

" *Que je vous remercie !* " she murmured, lifting her eyes to his. " *Que je vous trouve bon !* " and sprang before him up the steps.

He heard her father meet her in the hall; Ursule had already joined them; he re-entered the coach and rolled rapidly beyond recall.

The burning of the Osprey did not concern Mr. Raleigh's business relations. Carrying his papers about him, he had personally lost thereby nothing of consequence. He refreshed himself, and proceeded at once to the transactions awaiting him. In a brief time he found that affairs wore a different aspect from that for which he had been instructed, and letters from the house had already arrived, by the overland route, which required mutual reply and delay before he could take further steps; so that Mr. Raleigh found himself with some months of idleness upon his hands, in a land with not a friend. There lay a little scented billet, among the documents on his table, that had at first escaped his attention; he took it up wonderingly, and broke the seal. It was from his Cousin Kate, and had been a few days before him. Mrs. McLean had heard of his expected arrival, it said, and begged him, if he had any time to spare, to spend it with her in his old home by the lake, whither every summer they had resorted to meditate on the virtues of the departed. There was added, in a different hand, whose delicate and pointed characters seemed singularly familiar, —

"Come o'er the stream, Charlie, dear Charlie, brave Charlie!
Come o'er the stream, Charlie, and dine wi' McLean!"

Mr. Raleigh looked at the matter a few moments; he did not think it best to remain long in the city; he would be glad to know if sight of the old scenes could renew a throb. He answered his letters, replenished his wardrobe, and took, that same day, the last train for the North. At noon of the second day thereafter he found Mr. McLean's coach, with that worthy gentleman in person, awaiting him, and he stepped out, when it paused at the foot of his own former garden, with a strange sense of the world as an old story, a twice-told tale, a maze of error.

Mrs. McLean came running down to meet him, — a face less round and rosy than once, as the need of pink cap-ribbons testified, but smiling and bright as youth.

"The same little Kate," said Mr. Raleigh, after the first greeting, putting his hands on her shoulders and smiling down at her benevolently.

"Not quite the same Roger, though," said she, shaking her head. "I expected this stain on your skin; but, dear me! your eyes look as if you had not a friend in the world."

"How can they look so, when you give me such a welcome?"

"Dear old Roger, you *are* just the same," said she, bestowing a little caress upon his sleeve. "And if you remember the summer before you went away, you will not find that pleasant company so very much changed either."

"I do not expect to find them at all."

"Oh, then they will find you; because they are all here, — at least the principals; some with different names, and some, like myself, with duplicates," — as a shier Kate came down toward them, dragging a brother and sister by the hand, and shaking chestnut curls over rosy blushes.

After making acquaintance with the new cousins, Mr. Raleigh turned again to Mrs. McLean.

"And who are there here?" he asked.

"There is Mrs. Purcell, — you remember Helen Heath? Poor Mrs. Purcell, whom you knew, died, and her slippers fitted Helen. She chaperons Mary, who is single and speechless yet; and Captain, now Colonel, Purcell makes a very good silent partner. .He is hunting in the West, on furlough; she is here alone. There is Mrs. Heath, — you never have forgotten her?"

"Not I."

"There is —"

"And how came you all in the country so early in the season, — anybody with your devotion to company?"

"To be made April fools, John says."

"Why, the willows are not yet so yellow as they will be."

"I know it. But we had the most fatiguing winter; and Mrs. Laudersdale and I agreed, that, the moment the snow was off the ground up here, we would fly away and be at rest."

"Mrs. Laudersdale? Can she come here?"

"Goodness! Why not? The last few summers we have always spent together."

"She is with you now, then?"

"Oh, yes. She is the least changed of all. I did n't mean to tell, but keep her as a surprise. Of course, you will be a surprise to everybody. — There, run along, children; we 'll follow. — Yes, won't it be delightful, Roger? We can all play at youth again."

"Like skeletons in some Dance of Death!" he exclaimed. "We shall be hideous in each other's sight."

"McLean, I am a bride," said his wife, not heeding the late misanthropy; "Helen is a girl; the ghost of the prior Mrs. Purcell shall be *rediviva;* and Katy there —"

"Wait a bit, Kate," said her cousin. "Before you have shuffled off mortality for the whole party, sit down under this hedge, — here is an opportune bench, — and give me accounts from the day of my departure."

"Dear me, Roger, as if that were possible! The ocean in a tea-cup? Let me see, — you had a flirtation with Helen that summer, did n't you? Well, she spent the next winter at the Fort with the Purcells. It was odd to miss both her and Mrs. Laudersdale from society at once. Mrs. Laudersdale was ill; I don't know exactly what the trouble was. You know she had been in such an unusual state of exhilaration all that summer; and as soon as she left New Hampshire and began the old city-life, she became oppressed with a speechless melancholy, I believe, so that the doctors foreboded insanity. She expressed great disinclination to follow their advice, and her husband finally banished them all. It was a great care to him; he altered much. McLean surmised that she did n't like to see him, while she was in this state; for, though he used to surround her with every luxury, and was always hunting out new appliances, and raising the heavens for a trifle, he kept himself carefully out of her sight during the greater part of the winter. I don't know whether she became insufferably lonely, or whether the melancholy wore off, or she conquered it, and decided that it was not right to go crazy for nothing, or what happened. But one cold March evening he set out for his home, dreary, as usual, he thought; and he found

14

the fire blazing and reddening the ceiling and curtains, the room all aglow with rich shadows, and his wife awaiting him, in full toilet, just as superb as you will see her to-night, just as sweet and cold and impassible and impenetrable. At least," continued Mrs. McLean, taking breath, " I have manufactured this little romance out of odds and ends that McLean has now and then reported from his conversation. I dare say there is n't a bit of it true, for Mr. Laudersdale is n't a man to publish his affairs ; but *I* believe it. One thing is certain : Mrs. Laudersdale withdrew from society one autumn and returned one spring, and has queened it ever since."

" Is Mr. Laudersdale with you ? "

" No.   But he will come with their daughter shortly."

" And with what do you all occupy yourselves, pray ? "

" Oh, with trifles and tea, as you would suppose us to do. Mrs. Purcell gossips and lounges, as if she were playing with the world for spectator. Mrs. Laudersdale lounges, and attacks the things of the world with her finger-ends, as if she were longing to remould them. Mrs. McLean gossips and scolds, as if it depended on her to keep the world in order."

" Are you going to keep me under the hedge all night ? "

" This is pretty well! Hush! Who is that ? "

As Mrs. McLean spoke, a figure issued from the great larches on the left, and crossed the grass in front of them, — a woman, something less tall than a gypsy queen might be, the round outlines of her form rich and regular, with a certain firm luxuriance, still wrapped in a morning-robe of palm-spread cashmere. In her hand she carried various vines and lichens that had maintained their orange-tawny stains under the winter's snow, and the black hair that was folded closely over forehead and temple was crowned with bent sprays of the scarlet maple-blossom. As vivid a hue dyed her cheek through warm walking, and with a smile of unconscious content she passed quickly up the slope and disappeared within the doorway. She impressed the senses of the beholder like some ripe and luscious fruit, a growth of sunshine and summer.

"Well," said Mrs. McLean, drawing breath again, "who is it?"

"Really I cannot tell," replied Mr. Raleigh.

"Nor guess?"

"And that I dare not."

"Must I tell you?"

"Was it Mrs. Laudersdale?"

"And should n't you have known her?"

"Scarcely."

"Mercy! Then how did you know me? She is unaltered."

"If that is Mrs. Purcell, at the window,—she does not recognize me, you see;—neither did—both she and yourself are nearly the same; one could not fail to know either of you; but of the Mrs. Laudersdale of thirteen years ago there remains hardly a vestige."

If Mrs. McLean, at this testimony, indulged in that little inward satisfaction which the most generous woman may feel, when told that her color wears better than the color of her dearest friend, it must have been quickly quenched by the succeeding sentence.

"Yes, she is certainly more beautiful than I ever dreamed of a woman's being. If she continues, I do not know what perfect thing she will become. She is too exquisite for common use. I wonder her husband is not jealous of every mote in the air, of rain and wind, of every day that passes over her head, — since each must now bear some charm from her in its flight."

Mr. Raleigh was talking to Mrs. McLean as one frequently reposes confidence in a person when quite sure that he will not understand a word you say.

An hour afterward, Mrs. Purcell joined Mrs. McLean.

"So that is Mr. Raleigh, is it?" she said. "He looks as if he had made the acquaintance of Siva the Destroyer. There's nothing left of him. Is he taller, or thinner, or graver, or darker, or what? My dear Kate, your cousin, that promised to be such a hero, has become a mere man-of-business. Did you ever burn fire-crackers? You have probably found some that just fizzed out, then." And Mrs. Purcell took an attitude.

"Roger is a much finer man than he was, I think, — so far as I could judge in the short time we have seen each other," replied Mrs. McLean with spirit.

"Do you know," continued Mrs. Purcell, "what makes the Laudersdale so gay? No? She has a letter from her lord, and he brings you that little Rite next week. I must send for the Colonel to see such patterns of conjugal felicity as you and she. Ah, there is the tea-bell!"

Mr. Raleigh was standing with one hand on the back of his chair, when Mrs. Laudersdale entered. The cheek had resumed its usual pallor, and she was in her customary colors of black and gold. She carried a curiously cut crystal glass, which she placed on the sideboard, and then moved toward her chair. Her eye rested casually for a moment on Mr. Raleigh, as she crossed the threshold, and then returned with a species of calm curiosity.

"Mrs. Laudersdale has forgotten me?" he asked, with a bow. His voice, not susceptible of change in its tone of Southern sweetness, identified him.

"Not at all," she replied, moving toward him, and offering him her hand quietly. "I am happy at meeting Mr. Raleigh again." And she took her seat.

There was something in her grasp that relieved him. It was neither studiedly cold, nor absurdly brief, nor traitorously tremulous. It was simply and forgetfully indifferent. Mr. Raleigh surveyed her with interest during the light table-talk. He had been possessed with a restless wish to see her once more, to ascertain if she had yet any fraction of her old power over him; he had all the more determinedly banished himself from the city, — to find her in the country. Now he sought for some trace of what had formerly aroused his heart. He rose from table convinced that the woman whom he once loved with the whole fervor of youth and strength and buoyant life was no more, that she did not exist, and that Mr. Raleigh might experience a new passion, but his old one was as dead as the ashes that cover the Five Cities of the Plain. He wondered how it might be with her. For a moment he cursed his inconstancy; then he feared lest she were of larger heart and firmer resolve than he, — lest her love had been less light than his; he could scarcely feel himself secure of freedom, — he must watch. And then stole in a deeper sense of loneliness than exile and foreign tongues had taught him, — the knowledge of being single and solitary in the world, not only for life, but for eternity.

The evening was passed in the recitation of affairs by himself and his cousins alone together, and until a week completed its tale of dawns and sunsets there was the same diurnal recurrence of question and answer. One day, as the afternoon was paling, Rite came.

Mr. Raleigh had fallen asleep on the vine-hidden seat outside the bay window, and was awakened, certainly not by Mrs. Laudersdale's velvets trailing over the drawing-room carpet. She was just entering, slow-paced, though in haste. She held out both of her beautiful arms. A little form of airy lightness, a very snow-wreath, blew into them.

"*O maman! Est ce toi?*" it cried. "*O comme tu es douce! Si belle, si chère!*" And the fair head was lying beneath the dark one, the face hidden in the bent and stately neck.

Mr. Raleigh left his seat, unseen, and betook himself to another abode. As he passed the drawing-room door, on his return, he saw the mother lying on a lounge, with the slight form nestled beside her, playing with it as some tame leopardess might play with her silky whelp. It was almost the only portion of the maternal nature developed within her.

It seemed as if the tea-hour were a fated one. Mr. Raleigh had been out on the water and was late. As he entered, Rite sprang up, half-overturning her chair, and ran to clasp his hand.

"I did not know that you and Mr. Raleigh were acquainted," said Mrs. McLean.

"Oh, Madam, Mr. Raleigh and I had the pleasure of being shipwrecked together," was the reply; and except that Mrs. Laudersdale required another napkin where her cup had spilled, all went on smoothly.

Mrs. Laudersdale took Marguerite entirely to herself for a while. She seemed, at first, to be like some one suddenly possessed of a new sense, and who did not know in the least what to do with it; but custom and familiarity destroyed this sentiment. She did not appear to entertain a doubt of her child's natural affection, but she had care to fortify it by the exertion of every charm she possessed. From the presence of dangerous rivals in the house, an element of determination blended with her manner, and she moved with a certain conscious power, as if wonderful energies were but half-latent with her, as if there were kingdoms to conquer and crowns to win, and she the destined instrument. You would have selected her, at this time of her lavish devotion to Marguerite, as the one woman of complete capability, of practical effective force, and have declared that there was nothing beyond her strength. The relation between herself and her child was certainly as peculiar as anything else about them; the disparity of age seemed so slight that they appeared like sisters, full of mutual trust, the younger leaning on the elder for support in the most trivial affairs. They walked through the woods together, learned again its glades and coverts, searched its early treasure of blossoms; they went out on the lake and spent long April afternoons together, floating about cove and inlet of island-shores; they returned with innocent gayety to that house which once the mother, in her moment of passion, had fancied to be a possible heaven of delight, and which, since, she had found to be a very indifferent limbo. For, after all, we derive as much happiness from human beings as from Nature, and it was a tie of placid affection that bound her to the McLeans, not of sympathetic union, and her husband was careful never to oppress her with too much of his society. Whether this woman, who had lived a life of such wordless emotion, who had never bestowed a confidence, suddenly blossomed like a rose and took the little new-comer into the gold-dust and fragrance of her heart, or whether there was always between them the thin impalpable division that estranged the past from the present, there was nothing to tell; it seemed, nevertheless, as if they could have no closer bond, had they read each other's thoughts from birth.

That this assumption of Marguerite could not continue exclusive Mr. Raleigh found, when now and then joined in his walks by an airy figure flitting forward at his side : now and then ; since Mrs. Laudersdale, without knowing how to prevent, had manifested an uneasiness at every such rencontre ; — and that it could not endure forever, another gentleman, without so much reason, congratulated himself, — Mr. Frederic Heath, the confidential clerk of Day, Knight, & Co., — a rather supercilious specimen, quite faultlessly got up, who had accompanied her from New York at her father's request, and who already betrayed every symptom of the suitor. Meanwhile, Mrs. McLean's little women clamorously demanded and obtained a share of her attention, — although Capua and Ursulé, with their dark skins, brilliant dyes, and equivocal dialects, were creatures of a more absorbing interest.

One afternoon, Marguerite, came into the drawing-room by one door, as Mr. Raleigh entered by another ; her mother was sitting near the window, and other members of the family were in the vicinity, having clustered preparatory to the tea-bell.

Marguerite had twisted tassels of the willow-catkins in her hair, drooping things, in character with her wavy grace and fresh youth, sprinkling her with their fragrant yellow powder, the very breath of spring ; and in one hand she had imprisoned a premature lace-winged fly, a fairy little savage, in its sheaths of cobweb and emerald, and with its jewel eyes.

" Dear ! " said Mrs. Purcell, gathering her array more closely about her. " How do you dare touch such a venomous sprite ? "

" As if you had an insect at the North with a sting ! "
replied Marguerite, suffering it, a little maliciously, to escape in the lady's face, and following the flight with a
laugh of childlike glee.

" Here are your snowflakes on stems, mamma," she
continued, dropping anemones over her mother's hands,
one by one ; — that is what Mr. Raleigh calls them.
When may I see the snow ? You shall wrap me in
eider, that I may be like all the boughs and branches.
How buoyant the earth must be, when every twig becomes a feather ! " And she moved toward Mr. Raleigh,
singing, " Oh, would I had wings like a dove ! "

" And here are those which, if not daffodils, yet

'Come before the swallow dares, and take
The winds of March with beauty,' "

he said, giving her a basket of hepaticas and winter-green.

Marguerite danced away with the purple trophy, and,
emptying a carafe into a dish of moss that stood near,
took them to Mrs. Laudersdale, and, sitting on the foot-
stool, began to rearrange them. It was curious to see,
that, while Mrs. Laudersdale lifted each blossom and let
the stem lie across her hand, she suffered it to fall into
the place designated for it by Marguerite's fingers, that
sparkled in the mosaic till double wreaths of gold-threaded
purple rose from the bed of vivid moss and melted into a
fringe of the starry spires of winter-green.

" Is it not sweet ? " said she then, bending over it.

" They have no scent," said her mother.

" Oh, yes, indeed ! the very finest, the most delicate, a
kind of aerial perfume ; they must of course alchemize
the air into which they waste their fibres, with some
sweetness."

" A smell of earth fresh from ' wholesome drench of

14 *   U

April rains,'" said Mr. Raleigh, taking the dish of white porcelain between his brown, slender hands. "An immature scent, just such an innocent breath as should precede the epigea, that spicy, exhaustive wealth of savor, that complete maturity of odor, marriage of daphne and linnæa. The charm of these first bidders for the year's favor is neither in the ethereal texture, the depth or delicacy of tint, nor the large-lobed, blood-stained, ancient leaves. This imponderable soul gives them such a helpless air of babyhood."

"Is fragrance the flower's soul?" asked Marguerite. "Then anemones are not divinely gifted. And yet you said, the other day, that to paint me would be to paint an anemone."

"A satisfactory specimen in the family-gallery," said Mrs. Purcell.

"A flaw in the indictment!" replied Mr. Raleigh. "I am not one of those who paint the lily."

"Though you 've certainly added a perfume to the violet," remarked Mr. Frederic Heath, with that sweetly lingering accent familiarly called the drawl, as he looked at the hepaticas.

"I don't think it very complimentary, at any rate," continued Marguerite. "They are not lovely after bloom, — only the little pink-streaked, budded bells, that hang so demurely. *Oui!* I have exchanged great queen magnolias for rues; what will you give me for pomegranates and oleanders?"

"Are the old oleanders in the garden yet?" asked Mrs. Laudersdale.

"Not the very same. The hurricane destroyed those, years ago; these are others, grand and rosy as sunrise sometimes."

"It was my Aunt Susanne who planted those, I have heard."

"And it was your daughter Rite who planted these."

"She buried a little box of old keepsakes at its foot, after her brother had examined them, — a ring or two, a coin from which she broke and kept one half — "

"Oh, yes! we found the little box, — found it when Mr. Heath was in Martinique, — all rusted and moulded and falling apart, and he wears that half of the coin on his watch-chain. See!"

Mrs. Laudersdale glanced up indifferently, but Mrs. Purcell sprang from her elegant lounging and bent to look at her brother's chain.

"How odd that I never noticed it, Fred!" she exclaimed. "And how odd that I should wear the same!" And, shaking her *châtelaine*, she detached a similar affair.

They were placed side by side in Mr. Raleigh's hand; they matched entirely, and, so united, they formed a singular French coin of value and antiquity, the missing figures on one segment supplied by the other, the embossed profile continued and lost on each, the scroll begun by this and ended by that; they were plainly severed portions of the same piece.

"And this was buried by your Aunt Susanne Le Blanc?" asked Mrs. Purcell, turning to Mrs. Laudersdale again, with a flush on her cheek.

"So I presume."

"Strange! And this was given to mamma by her mother, whose maiden name was Susan White. There's some *diablerie* about it."

"Oh, that is a part of the ceremony of money-hiding," said Mr. Raleigh. "Kidd always buried a little imp with his pots of gold, you know, to work deceitful charms on the finder."

" Did he ? " said Marguerite, earnestly.

They all laughed thereat, and went in to tea.

III.

Spring at last stole placidly into summer, and Marguerite, who was always shivering in the house, kept the company in a whirl of out-door festivals.

"We have not lived so, Roger," said Mrs. McLean, " since the summer when you went away. We all follow the caprice of this child as a ship follows the little compass-needle."

And she made room for the child beside her in the carriage ; for Mr. Raleigh was about driving them into town, — an exercise which had its particular charm for Marguerite, not only for the glimpse it afforded of the gay, bustling inland-city-life, but for opportunities of securing the reins and of occasioning panics. Lately, however, she had resigned the latter pleasure, and sat with quiet propriety by Mrs. McLean. Frequently, also, she took long drives alone or with one of the children, holding the reins listlessly, and ranging the highway unobservantly for miles around.

Mrs. Purcell declared the girl was homesick ; Mrs. Heath doubted if the climate agreed with her : she neither denied nor affirmed their propositions.

Mr. Heath came and went from the city where her father was, without receiving any other notice than she would have bestowed on a peaceful walking-stick ; his attentions to her during his visits were unequivocal ; she

accepted them as nonchalantly as from a waiter at table.
On the occasion of his last stay, there had been a somewhat noticeable change in his demeanor : he wore a trifle
of quite novel assurance ; his supreme bearing was not
mitigated by the restless sparkle of his eye ; and in addressing her his compliments, he spoke as one having
authority.

Mrs. Laudersdale, so long and so entirely accustomed
to the reception of homage that it cost her no more reflection than an imperial princess bestows on the taxes that
produce her tiara, turned slowly from the apparent apathy
thus induced on her modes of thought, passivity lost in a
gulf of anxious speculation, while she watched the theatre
of events with a glow, like wine in lamplight, that burned
behind her dusky eyes till they had the steady penetration
of some wild creature's. She may have wondered if Mr.
Raleigh's former feeling were yet alive ; she may have
wondered if Marguerite had found the spell that once she
found herself ; she may have been kept in thrall by ignorance if he had ever read that old confessing note of hers :
whatever she thought or hoped or dreaded, she said
nothing, — and did nothing.

Of all those who concerned themselves in the affair of
Marguerite's health and spirits, Mr. Raleigh was the only
one who might have solved their mystery. Perhaps the
thought of wooing the child whose mother he had once
loved was sufficiently repugnant to him to overcome the
tenderness which every one was forced to feel for so beautiful a creation. I have not said that Marguerite was this,
before, because, until brought into contrast with her mother, her extreme loveliness was too little positive to be felt ;
now it was the evanescent shimmer of pearl to the deep
perpetual fire of the carbuncle. Softened, as she became,

from her versatile cheeriness, she moved round like a moonbeam, and frequently had a bewildered grace, as if she knew not what to make of herself. Mr. Raleigh, from the moment in which he perceived that she no longer sought his company, retreated into his own apartments, and was less seen by the others than ever.

Returning from the drive on the morning of Mrs. McLean's last recorded remark, Mr. Raleigh, who had remained to give the horses in charge to a servant, was about to pass, when the *tableau* within the drawing-room caught his attention and altered his course. He entered, and flung his gloves down on a table and himself on the floor beside Marguerite and the children. She appeared to be revisited by a ray of her old sunshine, and had unrolled a giant parcel of candied sweets, which their mother would have sacrificed on the shrine of jalap and senna, the purchase of a surreptitious moment, and was now dispensing the brilliant comestibles with much ill-subdued glee. One mouth, that had bitten off the head of a checkerberry chanticleer, was convulsed with the acidulous tickling of sweetened laughter, till, the biter bit, a metamorphosis into the animal of attack seemed imminent ; at the hands of another a warrior in barley-sugar was experiencing the vernacular for defeat with reproving haste and gravity ; and there was yet another little omnivorous creature that put out both hands for indiscriminate snatching, and made a spectacle of himself in a general plaster of gum-arabic-drop and brandy-smash.

" Contraband ? " said Mr. Raleigh.

"And sweet as stolen fruit," said Marguerite. " Ursule makes the richest comfits, but not so innumerable as these. Mamma and I owe our sweet-tooth and honey-lip to bits of her concoction."

"Mrs. Purcell," asked Mr. Raleigh, as that lady entered, "is this little banquet no seduction to you?"

"What are you doing?" she replied.

"Drinking honey-dew from acorns."

"Laudersdale as ever!" ejaculated she, looking over his shoulder. "I thought you had 'no sympathy with'—"

"But I 'like to see other folks take'—"

"Their sweets, in this case. No, thank you," she continued, after this little rehearsal of the past. "What are you poisoning all this brood for?"

"Mrs. Laudersdale eats sweetmeats; they don't poison her," remonstrated Katy.

"Mrs. Laudersdale, my dear, is exceptional."

Katy opened her eyes as if she had been told that the object of her adoration was Japanese.

"It is the last grain that completes the transformation, as your story-books have told; and one day you will see her stand a statue of sugar, and melt away in the sun. To be sure, the whole air will be sweetened, but there will be no Mrs. Laudersdale."

"For shame, Mrs. Purcell!" cried Marguerite. "You're not sweet-tempered, or you'd like sweet dainties yourself. Here are nuts swathed in syrup; you'll have none of them? Here are health and slumber and idle dreams in a chocolate-drop. Not a chocolate? Here are dates; if you would n't choose the things in themselves, truly you would for their associations? See, when you take up one, what a picture follows it: the plum that has swung at the top of a palm, and crowded into itself the glow of those fierce noon-suns. It has been tossed by the sirocco; it has been steeped in reeking dew; there was always stretched above it the blue intense tent of a heaven full of light,—always below and around, long level reaches of hot shining sand; the phantoms of waning desert-moons have hovered over it; swarthy Arab chiefs have encamped under it; it has threaded the narrow streets of Damascus — that city the most beautiful — on the backs of gaunt gray dromedaries; it has crossed the seas, — and all for you, if you take it, this product of desert freedom, torrid winds, and fervid suns!"

"I might swallow the date," said Mrs. Purcell, "but Africa would choke me."

Mr. Raleigh had remained silent for some time, watching Marguerite as she talked. It seemed to him that his youth was returning; he forgot his resolves, his desires, and became aware of nothing in the world but her voice. Just before she concluded, she grew conscious of his gaze, and almost at once ceased speaking; her eyes fell a moment to meet it, and then she would have flashed them aside, but that it was impossible; lucid lakes of light, they met his own; she was forced to continue it, to return it, to forget all, as he was forgetting, in that long look.

"What is this?" said Mrs. Purcell, stooping to pick up a trifle on the matting.

"*C'est à moi!*" cried Marguerite, springing up suddenly, and spilling all the fragments of the feast, to the evident satisfaction of the lately neglected guests.

"Yours?" said Mrs. Purcell with coolness, still retaining it. "Why do you think in French?"

"Because I choose!" said Marguerite, angrily. "I mean — How do you know that I do?"

"Your exclamation, when highly excited or contemptuously indifferent, is always in that tongue."

"Which am I now?"

"Really, you should know best. Here is your bawble"; and Mrs. Purcell tossed it lightly into her hands, and went out.

It was a sheath of old morocco. The motion loosened the clasp, and the contents, an ivory oval and a cushion of faded silk, fell to the floor. Mr. Raleigh bent and re-gathered them; there was nothing for Marguerite but to allow that he should do so. The oval had reversed in falling, so that he did not see it; but, glancing at her before returning it, he found her face and neck dyed deeper than the rose. Still reversed, he was about to relinquish it, when Mrs. McLean passed, and, hearing the scamper-ing of little feet as they fled with booty, she also entered.

"Seeing you, reminds me, Roger," said she. "What do you suppose has become of that little miniature I told you of? I was showing it to Marguerite the other night, and have not seen it since. I must have mislaid it, and it was particularly valuable, for it was some nameless thing that Mrs. Heath found among her mother's trinkets, and I begged it of her, it was such a perfect likeness of you. Can you have seen it?"

"Yes, I have it," he replied. "And have n't I as good a right to it as any?"

He extended his arm for the case which Marguerite held, and so touching her hand, the touch was more lin-gering than it needed to be; but he avoided looking at her, or he would have seen that the late color had fled till the face was whiter than marble.

"Your old propensities," said Mrs. McLean. "You always will be a boy. By the way, what do you think of Mary Purcell's engagement? I thought she would always be a girl."

"Ah! McLean was speaking of it to me. Why were they not engaged before?"

" Because she was not an heiress."

Mr. Raleigh raised his eyebrows significantly.

" He could not afford to marry any but an heiress," explained Mrs. McLean.

Mr. Raleigh fastened the case and restored it silently.

" You think that absurd ?   You would not marry an heiress ? "

Mr. Raleigh did not at once reply.

" You would not, then, propose to an heiress ? "

" No."

As this monosyllable fell from his lips, Marguerite's motion placed her beyond hearing. She took a few swift steps, but paused and leaned against the wall of the gable for support, and, placing her hand upon the sun-beat bricks, she felt a warmth in them which there seemed to be neither in herself nor in the wide summer-air.

Mrs. Purcell came along, opening her parasol.

" I am going to the orchard," said she ; " cherries are ripe. Hear the robins and the bells ! Do you want to come ? "

" No," said Marguerite.

" There are bees in the orchard, too, — the very bees, for aught I know, that Mr. Raleigh used to watch thirteen years ago, or their great-grand-bees, — they stand in the same place."

" You knew Mr. Raleigh thirteen years ago ? " she asked, glancing up curiously.

" Yes."

" Well ? "

" Very well."

" How much is very well ? "

" He proposed to me. Smother your anger ; he did n't care for me ; some one told him that I cared for him."

" Did you ? "

" This is what the Inquisition calls applying the question ? " asked Mrs. Purcell. " Nonsense, dear child ! he was quite in love with somebody else."

" And that was — ? "

" He supposed your mother to be a widow. Well, if you won't come, I shall go alone and read my L'Allegro under the boughs, with breezes blowing between the lines. I can show you some little field-mice like unfledged birds, and a nest that protrudes now and then glittering eyes and cleft fangs."

Marguerite was silent; the latter commodity was *de trop*. Mrs. Purcell adjusted her parasol and passed on.

Here, then, was the whole affair. Marguerite pressed her hands to her forehead, as if fearful some of the swarming thoughts should escape; then she hastened up the slope behind the house, and entered and hid herself in the woods. Mr. Raleigh had loved her mother. Of course, then, there was not a shadow of doubt that her mother had loved him. Horrible thought! and she shook like an aspen, beneath it. For a time it seemed that she loathed him, — that she despised the woman who had given him regard. The present moment was a point of dreadful isolation; there was no past to remember, no future to expect; she herself was alone and forsaken, the whole world dark, and heaven blank. But that could not be forever. As she sat with her face buried in her hands, old words, old looks, flashed on her recollection; she comprehended what long years of silent suffering the one might have endured, what barren yearning the other; she saw how her mother's haughty calm might be the crust on a lava-sea; she felt what desolation must have filled Roger Raleigh's heart, when he found

that she whom he had loved no longer lived, that he had
cherished a lifeless ideal, — for Marguerite knew from
his own lips that he had not met the same woman whom
he had left.

She started up, wondering what had led her upon this
train of thought, why she had pursued it, and what reason
she had for the pain it gave her. A step rustled among
the distant last-year's leaves ; there in the shadowy wood,
where she did not dream of concealing her thoughts,
where it seemed that all Nature shared her confidence,
this step was like a finger laid on the hidden sore. She
paused, a glow rushed over her frame, and her face grew
hot with the convicting flush. Consternation, bitter con-
demnation, shame, impetuous resolve, swept over her in
one torrent, and the saw that she had a secret which
every one might touch, and touching, cause to sting. She
hurried onward through the wood, unconscious how rapidly or how far her heedless course extended.   She
sprang across gaps at which she would another time have
shuddered ; she clambered over fallen trees, penetrated
thickets of tangled brier, and followed up the shrunken
beds of streams, till suddenly the wood grew thin again,
and she emerged upon an open space, — a long lawn,
where the grass grew rank and tall as in deserted grave-
yards, and on which the afternoon sunshine lay with most
dreary, desolate emphasis. Marguerite had scarcely
comprehended herself before ; now, as she looked out on
the utter loneliness of the place, all joyousness, all content,
seemed wiped from the world.   She leaned against a
tree where the building rose before her, old and forsaken,
washed by rains, beaten by winds. A blind slung open,
loose on a broken hinge ; the emptiness of the house
looked through it like a spirit. The woodbine seemed

the only living thing about it, — the woodbine that had swung its clusters, heavy as grapes of Eshcol, along one wall, and, falling from support, had rioted upon the ground in masses of close-netted luxuriance.

Standing and surveying the silent scene of former gayety, a figure came down the slope, crushing the grass with lingering tread, checked himself, and, half-reversed, surveyed it with her. Her first impulse was to approach, her next to retreat; by a resolution of forces she remained where she was. Mr. Raleigh's position prevented her from seeing the expression of his face; from his attitude seldom was anything to be divined. He turned with a motion of the arm, as if he swung off a burden, and met her eye. He laughed, and drew near.

"I am tempted to return to that suspicion of mine when I first met you, Miss Marguerite," said he. "You take shape from solitude and empty air as easily as a Dryad steps from her tree."

"There are no Dryads now," said Marguerite, sententiously.

"Then you confess to being a myth?"

"I confess to being tired, Mr. Raleigh."

Mr. Raleigh's manner changed, at her petulance and fatigue, to the old air of protection, and he gave her his hand. It was pleasant to be the object of his care, to be with him as at first, to renew their former relation. She acquiesced, and walked beside him.

"You have had some weary travel," he said, "and probably not more than half of it in the path."

And she feared he would glance at the rents in her frock, forgetting that they were not sufficiently infrequent facts to be noticeable.

"He treats me like a child," she thought. "He ex-

pects me to tear my dress! He forgets that, while thirteen years were making a statue of her, they were making
a woman of me!" And she snatched away her hand.

"I have the boat below," he said, without paying attention to the movement. "You took the longest way round,
which, you have heard, is the shortest way home. You
have never been on the lake with me." And he was
about to assist her in.

She stepped back, hesitating.

"No, no," he said. "It is very well to think of walking back, but it must end in thinking. You have no im-
petus now to send you over another half-dozen miles of
wood-faring, no pique to sting Io."

And before she could remonstrate, she was lifted in,
the oars had flashed twice, and there was deep water between herself and shore. She was in reality too much
fatigued to be vexed, and she sat silently watching the
spaces through which they glanced, and listening to the
rhythmic dip of the oars. The soft afternoon air, with
its melancholy sweetness and tinge of softer hue, hung
round them; the water, brown and warm, was dimpled
with the flight of myriad insects; they wound among the
islands, — a path one of them knew of old. From the
shelving rocks a wild convolvulus drooped its twisted bells
across them, a sweet-brier snatched at her hair in passing,
a sudden elder-tree shot out its creamy panicles above,
they ripped up drowsy beds of folded lily-blooms.

Mr. Raleigh, lifting one oar, gave the boat a sharp
curve and sent it out on the open expanse; it seemed
to him that he had no right thus to live two lives in
one. Still he wished to linger, and with now and then
a lazy movement they slipped along. He leaned one
arm on the upright oar, like a river-god, and from the

store of boat-songs in his remembrance, sang now and
then a strain. Marguerite sat opposite and rested along
the side, content for the moment to glide on as they were,
without a reference to the past in her thought, without a
dream of the future. Peach-bloom fell on the air, warmed
all objects into mellow tint, and reddened deep into sunset. Tinkling cow-bells, where the kine wound out from
pasture, stole faintly over the lake, reflected dyes suffused
it and spread around them sheets of splendid color, outlines grew ever dimmer on the distant shores, a purple
tone absorbed all brilliance, the shadows fell, and, bright
with angry lustre, the planet Mars hung in the south, and
struck a spear, redder than rubies, down the placid mirror. The dew gathered and lay sparkling on the thwarts
as they touched the garden-steps; and they mounted and
traversed together the alleys of odorous dark. They
entered at Mr. Raleigh's door, and stepped thence into
the main hall, where they could see the broad light from
the drawing-room windows streaming over the lawn beyond. Mrs. Laudersdale came down the hall to meet
them.

"My dear Rite," she said, "I have been alarmed, and
have sent the servants out for you. You left home in
the morning, and you have not dined. Your father and
Mr. Heath have arrived. Tea is just over, and we are
waiting for you to dress and go into town; it is Mrs.
Manton's evening, you recollect."

"Must I go, mamma?" asked Marguerite, after this
statement of facts. "Then I must have tea first. Mr.
Raleigh, I remember my wasted sweetmeats of the morning with a pang. How long ago that seems!"

In a moment her face told her regret for the allusion,
and she hastened into the dining-room.

Mr. Raleigh and Marguerite had a merry tea, and Mrs. Purcell came and poured it out for them.

" Quite like the days when we went gypsying," said she, at a moment near its conclusion.

" We have just come from the Bawn, Miss Marguerite and I," he replied.

" You have ? I never go near it. Did it break your heart ? "

Mr. Raleigh laughed.

" Is Mr. Raleigh's heart such a delicate organ ? " asked Marguerite.

" Once, you might have been answered negatively ; now, it must be like the French banner, *percé, troué, criblé* — "

" Pray, add the remainder of your quotation," said he, — " *sans peur et sans reproche.*"

" So that a trifle would reduce it to flinders," said Mrs. Purcell, without minding his interruption.

" Would you give it such a character, Miss Rite ? " questioned Mr. Raleigh, lightly.

" I ? I don't see that you have any heart at all, sir."

" I swallow my tea and my mortification."

" Do you remember your first repast at the Bawn ? " asked Mrs. Purcell.

" Why not ? "

" And the jelly like molten rubies that I made ? It keeps well." And she moved a glittering dish toward him.

" All things of that summer keep well," he replied.

" Except yourself, Mr. Raleigh. The Indian jugglers are practising upon us, I suspect. You are no more like the same person who played sparkling comedy and sang passionate tragedy than this bamboo stick is like that willow wand."

"I wish I could retort, Miss Helen," he replied. "I beg your pardon!"

She was silent, and her eye fell and rested on the sheeny damask beneath. He glanced at her keenly an instant, then handed her his cup, saying, —

"May I trouble you?"

She looked up again, a smile breaking over the face wanner than youth, but which the hour's gayety had flushed to a forgetfulness of intervening years, extended her left hand for the cup, still gazing and smiling.

Various resolves had flitted through Marguerite's mind since her entrance. One, that she would yet make Mr. Raleigh feel her power, yielded to shame and self-contempt, and she despised herself for a woman won unwooed. But she was not sure that she was won. Perhaps, after all, she did not care particularly for Mr. Raleigh. He was much older than she; he was quite grave, sometimes satirical; she knew nothing about him; she was slightly afraid of him. On the whole, if she consulted her taste, she would have preferred a younger hero; she would rather be the Fornarina for a Raffaello; she had fancied her name sweetening the songs of Giraud Riquier, the last of the Troubadours; and she did not believe Beatrice Portinari to be so excellent among women, so different from other girls, that her name should have soared so far aloft with that escutcheon of the golden wing on a field azure. "But they say that there cannot be two epic periods in a nation's literature," thought Marguerite, hurriedly; "so that a man who might have been Homer once will be nothing but a gentleman now." And at this point, having decided that Mr. Raleigh was fully worth unlimited love, she added to her resolves a desire for content with whatever amount

15   v

of friendly affection he chose to bestow upon her. And all this, while sifting the sugar over her raspberries. Nevertheless, she felt, in the midst of her heroic content, a strange jealousy at hearing the two thus discuss days in which she had no share, and she watched them furtively, with a sharp, hateful suspicion dawning in her mind. Now, as Mrs. Purcell's eyes met Mr. Raleigh's, and her hand was still extended for the cup, Marguerite fastened her glance on its glittering ring, and said abruptly, —

"Mrs. Purcell, have you a husband?"

Mrs. Purcell started and withdrew her hand, as if it had received a blow, just as Mr. Raleigh relinquished the cup, so that between them the bits of pictured porcelain fell and splintered over the equipage.

"Naughty child!" said Mrs. Purcell. "See now what you've done!"

"What have I to do with it?"

"Then you haven't any bad news for me? Has any one heard from the Colonel? Is he ill?"

"Pshaw!" said Marguerite, rising and throwing down her napkin.

She went to the window and looked out.

"It is time you were gone, little lady," said Mr. Raleigh.

She approached Mrs. Purcell and passed her hand down her hair.

"What pretty soft hair you have!" said she. "These braids are like carved gold-stone. May I dress it with sweet-brier to-night? I brought home a spray."

"Rite!" said Mrs. Laudersdale sweetly, at the door; and Rite obeyed the summons.

In a half-hour she came slowly down the stairs, untwisting a long string of her mother's abandoned pearls, great-pear-shaped things full of the pale lustre of gibbous moons. She wore a dress of white samarcand, with a lavish ornament like threads and purfiles of gold upon the bodice, and Ursule followed with a cloak. As she entered the drawing-room, the great bunches of white azalea, which her mother had brought from the swamps, caught her eye; she threw down the pearls, and broke off rapid clusters of the queenly flowers, touching the backward-curling hyacinthine petals, and caressingly passing her finger down the pale purple shadow of the snowy folds. Directly afterward she hung them in her breezy hair, from which, by natural tenure, they were not likely to fall, bound them over her shoulders and in her waist.

"See! I stand like Summer," she said. "Wrapped in perfume. It is intoxicating."

Just then two hands touched her, and her father bent his face over her. She flung her arms round him, careless of their fragile array, kissed him on both cheeks, laughed, and kissed him again. She did not speak, for he disliked French, and English sometimes failed her.

"Here is Mr. Heath," her father said.

She partly turned, touched that gentleman's hand with the ends of her fingers, and nodded. Her father whispered a brief sentence in her ear.

"*Jamais, Monsieur, jamais!*" she exclaimed; then, with a quick gesture of deprecation, moved again toward him; but Mr. Laudersdale had coldly passed to make his compliments to Mrs. Heath.

"You are not in toilet?" said Marguerite, following him, but speaking with Mr. Raleigh.

"No, — Mrs. Purcell has been playing for me a little thing I always liked, — that sweet tuneful afternoon chiding of the Miller and the Torrent."

She glanced at Mrs. Purcell, saw that her dress remained unaltered, and commenced pulling off the azaleas from her own.

"I do not want to go," she murmured. "I need not! Mamma and Mrs. McLean have already gone in the other carriage."

"Come, Marguerite," said Mr. Laudersdale, approaching her, as Mr. Heath and his mother disappeared.

"I am not going," she replied, quickly.

"Not going? I beg your pardon, my dear, but you are!" and he took her hand.

She half endeavored to withdraw it, threw a backward glance over her shoulder at the remaining pair, and, led by her father, went out.

Marguerite did her best to forget the vexation, was very affable with her father, and took no notice of any of Mr. Heath's prolonged remarks. The drive was at best a tiresome one, and she was already half asleep when the carriage stopped. The noise and light, and the little vanities of the dressing-room, awakened her, and she descended prepared for conquest. But, after a few moments, it all became weariness, the air was close, the flowers faded, the music piercing. The toilets did not attract nor the faces interest her. She danced along absent and spiritless, when her eye, raised dreamily, fell on an object among the curtains and lay fascinated there. It was certainly Mr. Raleigh; but so little likely did that seem, that she again circled the room, with her eyes bent upon that point, expecting it to vanish. He must have come in the saddle, unless a coach had returned for him and Mrs. Purcell, — yes, there was Mrs. Purcell, — and she wore that sweet-brier fresh-blossoming in the light. With what ease she moved! — it must always have been the same grace; — how brilliant she was! Youth just enough tarnished to beguile. There, — she was going to dance with Mr. Raleigh. No? Where, then? Into the music-room!

The music-room lay beyond an anteroom of flowers and prints, and was closed against the murmur of the parlors by great glass doors. Marguerite, from her position, could see Mr. Raleigh seated at the piano, and Mrs. Purcell standing by his side; now she turned a leaf, now she stooped, and their hands touched upon the keys. Marguerite slipped alone through the dancers, and drew nearer. There were others in the music-room, but they were at a distance from the piano. She entered the anteroom and sat shadowed among the great fragrant shrubs. A group already stood there, eating ices and gayly gossiping. Mr. Laudersdale and Mr. Manton sauntered in, their heads together, and muttering occult matters of business, whose tally was kept with forefinger on palm.

"Where is Raleigh?" asked Mr. Manton, looking up. "He can tell us."

"At his old occupation," answered a gentleman from beside Mrs. Laudersdale, "flirting with forbidden fruit."

"An alliterative amusement," said Mrs. Laudersdale.

"You did not know the original Raleigh?" continued the gentleman. "But he always took pleasure in female society; yet, singularly enough, though fastidious in choice, it was only upon the married ladies that he bestowed his platonisms. I observe the old Adam still clings to him."

"He probably found more liberty with them," remarked Mrs. Laudersdale, when no one else replied.

"Without doubt he took it."

"I mean, that, where attentions are known to intend nothing, one is not obliged to measure them, or to calculate upon effects."

"Of the latter no one can accuse Mr. Raleigh!" said Mr. Laudersdale, hotly, forgetting himself for once.

Mrs. Laudersdale lifted her large eyes and laid them on her husband's face.

"Excuse me! excuse me!" said the gentleman, with natural misconception. "I was not aware that he was a friend of yours." And taking a lady on his arm, he withdrew.

"Nor is he!" said Mr. Laudersdale, in lowest tones, replying to his wife's gaze, and for the first time intimating his feeling. "Never, never, can I repair the ruin he has made me!"

Mrs. Laudersdale rose and stretched out her arm, blindly.

"The room is quite dark," she murmured; "the flowers must soil the air. Will you take me up-stairs?"

Meanwhile, the unconscious object of their remark was turning over a pile of pages with one hand, while the other trifled along the gleaming keys.

"Here it is," said he, drawing one from the others, and arranging it before him, — a *gondel-lied.*

There stole from his fingers the soft, slow sound of lapsing waters, the rocking on the tide, the long sway of some idle weed. Here a jet of tune was flung out from a distant bark, here a high octave flashed like a passing torch through night-shadows and lofty arching darkness told in clustering chords. Now the boat fled through melancholy narrow ways of pillared pomp and stately beauty, now floated off on the wide lagoons alone with the stars and sea. Into this broke the passion of the gliding lovers, deep and strong, giving a soul to the whole, and fading away again, behind its wild beating, with the silence of lapping ripple and dipping oar.

Mrs. Purcell, standing beside the player, laid a careless arm across the instrument, and bent her face above him like a flower languid with the sun's rays. Suddenly the former smile suffused it, and, as the gondel-lied fell into a slow floating accompaniment, she sang with a swift, impetuous grace, and in a sweet, yet thrilling voice, the Moth Song. The shrill music and murmur from the parlors burst all at once in muffled volume upon the melody, and, turning, they both saw Marguerite standing in the doorway, like an angry wraith, and flitting back again. Mrs. Purcell laughed, but took up the thread of her song again where it was broken, and carried it through to the end. Then Mr. Raleigh tossed the gondel-lied aside, and rising, they continued their stroll.

"You have more than your share of the good things of life, Raleigh," said Mr. McLean, as the person addressed poured out wine for Mrs. Purcell. "Two affairs on hand at once? You drink deep. Light and sparkling, — thin and tart, — is n't it Solomon who forbids mixed drink?"

"I was never the worse for claret," replied Mr. Raleigh, bearing away the glittering glass.

The party from the Lake had not arrived at an early hour, and it was quite late when Mr. Raleigh made his way through ranks of tireless dancers, toward Marguerite. She had been dancing with a spirit that would have resembled joyousness but for its reckless *abandon*. She seemed to him then like a flame, as full of wilful, sinuous caprice. At the first he scarcely liked it, but directly the artistic side of his nature recognized the extreme grace and beauty that flowed through every curve of movement. Standing now, the corn-silk hair slightly disordered and still blown about by the fan of some one near her, her eyes sparkling like stars in the dew-drops of wild wood-violets, warm, yet weary, and a flush deepening her cheek with color, while the flowers hung dead around her, she held a glass of wine and watched the bead swim to the brim. Mr. Raleigh approached unaware, and startled her as he spoke.

"It is *au gré du vent*, indeed," he said, — "just the white fluttering butterfly, — and now that the wings are clasped above this crimson blossom, I have a chance of capture." And smiling, he gently withdrew the splendid draught.

"*Buvez, Monsieur*," she said; "*c'est le vin de la vie!*"

"Do you know how near daylight it is?" he replied. "Mrs. Laudersdale fainted in the heat, and your father took her home long ago. The Heaths went also; and the carriage has just returned for the only ones of us that are left, you and me."

"Is it ready now?"

"Yes."

"So am I."

And in a few moments she sat opposite him in the coach, on their way home.

"It wouldn't be possible for me to sit on the box and drive?" she asked.

"No."

"I should like it, in this wild starlight, these flying clouds, this breath of dawn."

Meeting no response, she sank into silence. No emotion can keep one awake forever, and, after all her late fatigue, the roll of the easy vehicle upon the springs soon soothed her into a dreamy state. Through the efforts at wakefulness, she watched the gleams that fell within from the carriage-lamps, the strange shadows on the roadside, the boughs tossing to the wind and flickering all their leaves in the speeding light; she watched, also, Mr. Raleigh's face, on which, in the fitful flashes, she detected a look of utter weariness.

"*Monsieur*," she exclaimed, with angry assertion, "*est ce que je vous gêne!*"

"Immensely," said Mr. Raleigh with a smile; "but, fortunately, for no great time."

"We shall be soon at home? Then I must have slept."

"Very like. What did you dream?"

"Oh, one must not tell dreams before breakfast, or they come to pass, you know."

"No, — I am uninitiated in dream-craft. Mr. Heath — "

"*Monsieur*," she cried, in sudden heat, "*il me semble que je comprends les Laocoons! C'est la même chose avec moi!*"

As she spoke, she fell, struck forward by a sudden shock, the coach was rocking like a boat, and plunging down unknown gulfs. Mr. Raleigh seized her, broke through the door, and sprang out.

"*Qu'avez vous?*" she exclaimed.

"The old willow is fallen in the wind," he replied.

"*Quel dommage* that we did not see it fall!"

"It has killed one of the horses, I fear," he continued, measuring, as formerly, her terror by her levity. "Capua! is all right? Are you safe?"

"Yah, massa!" responded a voice from the depths, as Capua floundered with the remaining horse in the thicket at the lake-edge below. "Yah, massa, — nuffin harm

15 *

Ol' Cap in water; spec he born to die in galluses; had nuff chance to be in glory, ef 't was n't. I 's done beat wid dis yer pony, anyhow, Mass'r Raleigh. Seems, ef he was a 'sect to fly in de face ob all creation an' pay no 'tention to his centre o' gravity, he might walk up dis yer hill!"

Mr. Raleigh left Marguerite a moment, to relieve Capua's perplexity. Through the remaining darkness, the sparkle of stars, and wild fling of shadows in the wind, she could but dimly discern the struggling figures, and the great creature trampling and snorting below. She remembered strange tales out of the Arabian Nights, Bellerophon and the Chimæra, St. George and the Dragon; she waited, half-expectant, to see the great talon-stretched wings flap up against the slow edge of dawn, where Orion lay, a pallid monster, watching the planet that flashed like some great gem low in a crystalline west, and she stepped nearer, with a kind of eager and martial spirit, to do battle in turn.

"Stand aside, Una!" cried Mr. Raleigh, who had worked in a determined, characteristic silence, and the horse's head, sharp ear, and starting eye were brought to sight, and then his heaving bulk.

"All right, massa!" cried Capua, after a moment's survey, as he patted the trembling flanks. "Pretty tough ex'cise dat! Spect Massam Clean be mighty high, — his best cretur done about killed wid dat tree; — feared he show dis nigger a stick worf two o' dat!"

"We had like to have finished our dance on nothing," said Mr. Raleigh now, looking back on the splintered wheels and panels. "Will you mount? I can secure you from falling."

"Oh, no, — I can walk; it is only a little way."

" Reach home like Cinderella? If you had but one
glass slipper, that might be ; but in satin ones it is impossible." And she found herself seated aloft before quite
aware what had happened.

Pacing along, they talked lightly, with the gayety natural upon excitement, — Capua once in a while adding a
cogent word. As they opened the door, Mr. Raleigh
paused a moment.

" I am glad," he said, " that my last day with you has
been crowned by such adventures. I leave the Lake at
noon."

She hung, listening, with a backward swerve of figure,
and regarding him in the dim light of the swinging hall-
lamp, for the moment half petrified. Suddenly she turned
and seized his hand in hers, — then threw it off.

" *Cher ami,*" she murmured hastily, in a piercing whisper, like some articulate sigh, " *si vous m'aimez, dites le
moi !* "

The door closed in the draught, the drawing-room door
opened, and Mr. Laudersdale stepped out, having been
awaiting their return. Mr. Raleigh caught the flash of
Marguerite's eye and the crimson of her cheek, as she
sprang forward up the stairs and out of sight.

The family did not breakfast together the next day, as
politeness chooses to call the first hour after a ball, and
Mr. Raleigh was making some arrangements preliminary
to his departure, in his own apartments, at about the hour
of noon. The rooms which he had formerly occupied
Mrs. McLean had always kept closed, in a possibility
of his return, and he had found himself installed in them
upon his arrival. The library was to-day rather a melancholy room : the great book-cases did not enliven it ;
the grand-piano, with its old dark polish, seemed like a

coffin, the sarcophagus of unrisen music; the oak panelling had absorbed a richer hue with the years than once it wore; the portrait of his mother seemed farther withdrawn from sight and air; Antinoüs took a tawnier tint in his long reverie. The Summer, past her height, sent a sad beam, the signal of decay, through the half-open shutters, and it lay wearily on the man who sat by the long table, and made more sombre yet the faded carpet and cumbrous chair.

There was a tap on the door. Mr. Raleigh rose and opened it, and invited Mr. Laudersdale in. The latter gentleman complied, took the chair resigned by the other, but after a few words became quiet. Mr. Raleigh made one or two attempts at conversation, then, seeing silence to be his visitor's whim, suffered him to indulge it, and himself continued his writing. Indeed, the peculiar relations existing between these men made much conversation difficult. Mr. Laudersdale sat with his eyes upon the floor for several minutes, and his countenance wrapped in thought. Rising, with his hands behind him, he walked up and down the long room, still without speaking.

"Can I be of service to you, sir?" asked the other, after observing him.

"Yes, Mr. Raleigh, I am led to think you can," — still pacing up and down, and vouchsafing no further information.

At last, the monotonous movement ended, Mr. Laudersdale stood at the window, intercepting the sunshine, and examined some memoranda.

"Yes, Mr. Raleigh," he resumed, with all his courtly manner, upon close of the examination, "I am in hopes that you may assist me in a singular dilemma."

"I shall be very glad to do so."

"Thank you. This is the affair. About a year ago, being unable to make my usual visit to my daughter and her grandmother, I sent there in my place our head clerk, young Heath, to effect the few transactions, and also to take a month's recreation, — for we were all overworked and exhausted by the crisis. The first thing he proceeded to do was to fall in love with my daughter. Of course he did not mention this occurrence to me, on his return. When my daughter, arrived at New York, I was again detained, myself, and sent her to this place under his care. He lingered rather longer than he should have done, knowing the state of things; but I suspected nothing, for the idea of a clerk's marriage with the heiress of the great Martinique estate never entered my mind; moreover, I have regarded her as a child; and I sent him back with various commissions at several times, — once on business with McLean, once to obtain my wife's signature to some sacrifice of property, and so on. I really beg your pardon, Mr. Raleigh; it is painful to another, I am aware, to be thrust upon family confidences — "

"Pray, sir, proceed," said Mr. Raleigh, wheeling his chair about.

"But since you are in a manner connected with the affair yourself — "

"You must be aware, Mr. Laudersdale, that my chief desire is the opportunity you afford me."

"I believe so. I am happy to afford it. On the occasion of Mr. Heath's last visit to this place, Marguerite drew attention to a coin whose history you heard, and the other half of which Mrs. Purcell wore. Mr. Heath obtained the fragment he possessed through my wife's aunt, Susanne Le Blanc; Mrs. Purcell obtained hers through her grandmother, Susan White. Of course, these good people were not slow to put the coin and the names together; Mr. Heath, moreover, had heard portions of the history of Susanne Le Blanc when in Martinique.

"On resuming his duties in the counting-house, after this little incident, one day, at the close of business-hours, he demanded from me the remnants of this history with which he might be unacquainted. When I paused, he took up the story and finished it with ease, and — and poetical justice, I may say, Mr. Raleigh. Susanne was the sister of Mrs. Laudersdale's father, though far younger than he. She met a young American gentleman, and they became interested in each other. Her brother designed her for a different fate, — the governor of the island, indeed, was her suitor, — and forbade their intercourse. There were rumors of a private marriage; her apartments were searched for any record, note, or proof, unsuccessfully. If there were such, they had been left in the gentleman's hands for better concealment. It being supposed that they continued to meet, M. Le Blanc prevailed upon the governor to arrest the lover on some trifling pretence, and send him out of the island. Shortly afterward, as he once confessed to his wife, he caused a circumstantial account of the death and funeral obsequies of each to reach the other. Immediately he urged the governor's suit again, and when she continued to resist, he fixed the wedding-day himself, and ordered the *trousseau.* Upon this, one evening, she buried the box of trinkets at the foot of the oleanders, and disappeared the next, and no trace of her was found.

"When I reached this point, young Heath turned to me with that impudently nonchalant drawl of his, saying, —

"'And her property, sir?'

"'That,' I replied innocently, 'which comprised half the estate, and which she would have received on attaining the requisite age, was inherited by her brother, upon her suicide.'

"'Apparent suicide, you mean,' said he ; and thereupon took up the story, as I have said, matched date to date and person to person, and informed me that exactly a fortnight from the day of Mademoiselle Susanne Le Blanc's disappearance, a young lady took rooms at a hotel in a Southern city, and advertised for a situation as governess, under the name of Susan White. She gave no references, spoke English imperfectly, and had difficulty in obtaining one ; finally, however, she was successful, and after a few years married into the family of her employer, and became the mother of Mrs. Heath. The likeness of Mrs. Purcell, the grandchild of Susan White, to Susanne Le Blanc, was so extraordinary, a number of years ago, that, when Ursule, my daughter's nurse, first saw her, she fainted with terror. My wife, you are aware, was born long after these events. This governess never communicated to her husband any more specific circumstance of her youth than that she had lived in the West Indies, and had left her family because they had resolved to marry her, — as she might have done, had she not died shortly after her daughter's birth. Among her few valuables were found this half-coin of Heath's, and a miniature, which his mother recently gave your cousin, but which, on account of its new interest, she has demanded again ; for it is probably that of the ancient lover, and bearing, as it does, a very striking resemblance to yourself, you have pronounced it to be undoubtedly that of your uncle, Reuben Raleigh, and wondered how it came into the possession of Mrs. Heath's mother. Now, as you may be aware, Reuben Raleigh was the name of Susanne Le Blanc's lover."

" No, — I was not aware."

Mr. Laudersdale's countenance, which had been animated in narration, suddenly fell.

" I was in hopes," he resumed, — " I thought, — my relation of these occurrences may have been very confused ; but it is as plain as daylight to me, that Susanne Le Blanc and Susan White are one, and that the property of the first is due to the heirs of the last."

" Without doubt, sir."

" The same is plain to the Heaths. I am sure that Marguerite will accept our decision in the matter, — sure that no daughter of mine would retain a fraudulent penny ; for retain it she could, since there is not sufficient proof in any court, if we chose to contest ; but it will beggar her."

" How, sir ? Beggar her to divide her property ? "

" It is a singular division. The interest due on Susanne's moiety swells it enormously. Add to this, that, after M. Le Blanc's death, Madame Le Blanc, a much younger person, did not so well understand the management of affairs, the property depreciated, and many losses were encountered, and it happens that the sum due Mrs. Heath covers the whole amount that Marguerite possesses."

" Now, then, sir ? " exclaimed Mr. Raleigh, interrogatively.

" Now, then, Mrs. Heath requests my daughter's hand for her son, and offers to set off to him, at once, such sum as would constitute his half of her new property upon her decease, and allow him to enter our house as special partner."

" Ah ! "

" This does not look so unreasonable. Last night he proposed formally to Marguerite, who is still ignorant of these affairs, and she refused him. I have urged her differently, — I can do no more than urge, — and she remains obdurate. To accumulate misfortunes, we escaped 1857 by a miracle. We have barely recovered ; and now various disasters striking us, — the loss of the Osprey the first and the chief of them, — we are to-day on the verge of bankruptcy. Nothing but the entrance of this fortune can save us from ruin."

" Unfortunate ! " said Mr. Raleigh, — " most unfortunate ! And can I serve you at this point ? "

" Not at all, sir," said Mr. Laudersdale, with sudden erectness. " No, — I have but one hope. It has seemed to me barely possible that your uncle may have communicated to you events of his early life, — that you may have heard, that there may have been papers telling of the real fate of Susanne Le Blanc."

" None that I know of," said Mr. Raleigh, after a pause. " My uncle was a very reserved person. I often imagined that his youth had not been without its passages, something to account for his unvarying depression. In one letter, indeed, I asked him for such a narration. He promised to give it to me shortly, — the next mail, perhaps. The next mail I received nothing ; and after that he made no allusion to the request."

" Indeed ? Indeed ? I should say, — pardon me, Mr. Raleigh, — that your portion of the next mail met with some accident. Your servants could not explain it ? "

" There is Capua, who was majordomo. We can inquire," said Mr. Raleigh, with a smile, rising and ringing for that functionary.

w

On Capua's appearance, the question was asked, if he had ever secretly detained letter or paper of any kind.

"Lors, massa! I alwes knew 't would come to dis!" he replied. "No, massa, neber!" shaking his head with repeated emphasis.

"I thought you might have met with some accident, Capua," said his master.

"Axerden be ——, beg massa's parden; but such s'picions poison any family's peace, and make a feller done forgit hisself."

"Very well," said Mr. Raleigh, who was made to believe by this vehemence in what at first had seemed a mere fantasy. "Only remember, that, if you could assure me that any papers had been destroyed, the assurance would be of value."

"'Deed, Mass Roger? Dat alters de case," said Capua, grinning. "Dere's been a good many papers 'stroyed in dis yer house, firs' an' last."

"Which in particular?"

"Don' rekerlember, massa, 's so long ago."

"But make an effort."

"Well, Massa Raleigh, — 'pears to me I *do* 'member suthin', — I do b'lieve — yes, dis 's jist how 't was. Spect I might as well make a crean breast ob it. I 's alwes had it hangin' roun' my conscious; do' no' but I 's done grad to git rid ob it. Alwes spected massa 'd be 'xcusin' Cap o' turnin' tief."

"That is the last accusation I should make against you, Capua."

"But dar I stan's convicted."

"Out with it, Capua!" said Mr. Laudersdale, laughing.

"Lord, Massa Lausdel! how you do scare a chile! Didn' know mass'r was dar. See, Mass Roger, dis 's jist how 't was. Spec you mind dat time when all dese yer folks lib'd acrost de lake dat summer, an' massa was possessed to 'most lib dar too? Well, one day, massa mind Ol' Cap's runnin' acrost in de rain an' in great state ob excitement to tell him his house done burnt up?"

"Yes. What then?"

"Dat day, massa, de letters had come from Massa Reuben out in Indy, an' massa's pipe kinder 'tracted Cap's 'tention, an' so he jist set down in massa's chair an' took a smoke. Bimeby Cap thought, — 'Ef massa come an' ketch him!' — an' put down de pipe an' went to work, and bimeby I smelt mighty queer smell, massa, 'bout de house, made him tink Ol' Nick was come hissef for Ol' Cap, an' I come back into dis yer room an' Massa Reuben's letters from Indy was jist most done burnt up, he cotched 'em in dese yer ol' brack han's, Mass Roger, an' jist whipt 'em up in dat high croset."

And having arrived at great confusion in his personal pronouns, Capua mounted nimbly on pieces of furniture, thrust his pocket-knife through a crack of the wainscot, opened the door of a small unseen closet, and, after groping about and inserting his head as Van Amburgh did in the lion's mouth, scrambled down again with his hand full of charred and blackened papers, talking glibly all the while.

"Ef massa 'd jist listen to reason," he said, "'stead o' flyin' into one ob his tantrums, I might sprain de matter. You see, I knew Mass Roger 'd feel so oncomforble and remorsefle to find his ol' uncle's letters done 'stroyed, an' 't was all by axerden, an' couldn' help it noways, massa, an' been done sorry eber since, an' wished dar warn't no letters dis side de Atlantic nor torrer, ebery day I woke."

After which plea, Capua awaited his sentence.

"That will do, — it's over now, old boy," said Mr. Raleigh, with his usual smile.

"Now, massa, you a'n't gwine —"

"No, Capua, I'm going to do nothing but look at the papers."

"But massa's —"

"You need not be troubled, — I said, I was not."

"But, massa, — s'pose I deserve a thrashing?"

"There's no danger of your getting it, you blameless Ethiop!"

Upon which pacific assurance, Capua departed.

The two gentlemen now proceeded to the examination of these fragments. Of the letters nothing whatever was to be made. From one of them dropped a little yellow folded paper that fell apart in its creases. Put together, it formed a sufficiently legible document, and they read the undoubted marriage-certificate of Susanne Le Blanc and Reuben Raleigh.

"I am sorry," said Mr. Laudersdale, after a moment. "I am sorry, instead of a fortune, to give them a bar-sinister."

"Your daughter is ignorant? — your wife?"

"Entirely. Will you allow me to invite them in here? They should see this paper."

"You do not anticipate any unpleasant effect?"

"Not the slightest. Marguerite has no notion of want or of pride. Her first and only thought will be — sa cousine Hélène." And Mr. Laudersdale went out.

Some light feet were to be heard pattering down the stairs, a mingling of voices, then Mr. Laudersdale passed on, and Marguerite tapped, entered, and closed the door.

"My father has told me something I but half understand," said she, with her hand on the door. "Unless I marry Mr. Heath, I lose my wealth? What does that signify? Would all the mines of Peru tempt me?"

Mr. Raleigh remained leaning against the corner of the bookcase. She advanced and stood at the foot of the table, nearly opposite him. Her lips were glowing as if the fire of her excitement were fanned by every breath; her eyes, half hidden by the veiling lids, seemed to throw a light out beneath them and down her cheek. She wore a mantle of swan's down closely wrapped round her, for she had complained ceaselessly of the chilly summer.

"Mr. Raleigh," she said, "I am poorer than you are, now. I am no longer an heiress."

At this moment, the door opened again and Mrs. Laudersdale entered. At a step she stood in the one sunbeam; at another, the shutters blew together, and the room was left in semi-darkness, with her figure gleaming through it, outlined and starred in tremulous evanescent light. For an instant both Marguerite and Mr. Raleigh seemed to be half awe-struck by the radiant creature shining out of the dark; but directly, Marguerite sprang back and stripped away the torrid nasturtium-vine which her mother had perhaps been winding in her hair when her husband spoke with her, and whose other end, long and laden with fragrant flame, still hung in her hand and along her dress. Laughing, Marguerite in turn wound it about herself, and the flowers, so lately plucked from the bath of hot air, where they had lain steeping in sun, flashed through the air a second, and then played all their faint spirit-like luminosity about their new wearer. She seemed sphered in beauty, like the Soul of Morning in some painter's phantasy, with all great stars blossoming out in floral life about her, colorless, yet brilliant in shape and light. It was too much; Mr. Raleigh opened the

window and let in the daylight again, and a fresh air that
lent the place a gayer life. As he did so, Mr. Laudersdale entered, and with him Mr. Heath and his mother.
Mr. Laudersdale briefly recapitulated the facts, and
added, —

"Communicating my doubts to Mr. Raleigh, he has
kindly furnished me with the marriage-certificate of his
uncle and Mademoiselle Le Blanc. And as Mr. Reuben
Raleigh was living within thirteen years, you perceive
that your claims are invalidated."

There was a brief silence while the paper was inspected.

"I am still of opinion that my grandmother's second
marriage was legal," replied Mr. Heath; "yet I should
be loath to drag up her name and subject ourselves to a
possibility of disgrace. So, though the estate is ours, we
can do without it!"

Meanwhile, Marguerite had approached her father, and
was patching together the important scraps.

"What has this to do with it?" said she. "You admitted before this discovery — did you not? — that the
property was no longer mine. These people are Aunt
Susanne's heirs still, if not legally, yet justly. I will not
retain a *sous* of it! My father shall instruct my lawyer,
Mrs. Heath, to make all necessary transfers to yourself.
Let us wish you good morning!" And she opened the
door for them to pass.

"Marguerite! are you mad?" asked her father, as the
door closed.

"No, father, — but honest, — which is the same thing,"
she responded, still standing near it.

"True," he said, in a low tone like a groan. "But we
are ruined."

"Ruined? Oh, no! You are well and strong. So am I. I can work. I shall get much embroidery to do, for I can do it perfectly; the nuns taught me. I have a thousand resources. And there is something my mother can do; it is her great secret; she has played at it summer after summer. She has moulded leaves and flowers and twined them round beautiful faces in clay, long enough; now she shall carve them in stone, and you will be rich again!"

Mrs. Laudersdale sat in a low chair while Marguerite spoke, the nasturtium-vine clinging round her feet like a gorgeous snake, her hands lying listlessly in her lap, and her attitude that of some queen who has lost her crown and is totally bewildered by this strange conduct on the part of circumstances. All the strength and energy that had been the deceits of manner were utterly fallen away, and it was plain, that, whatever the endowment was which Marguerite had mentioned, she could only play at it. She was but a woman, sheer woman, with the woman's one capability, and the exercise of that denied her.

Mr. Laudersdale remained with his eyes fixed on her, and lost, it seemed, to the presence of others.

"The disgrace is bitter," he murmured. "I have kept my name so proudly and so long! But that is little. It is for you I fear. I have stood in your sunshine and shadowed your life, dear! — At least," he continued, after a pause, "I can place you beyond the reach of suffering. I must finish my lonely way."

Mrs. Laudersdale looked up slowly and met his earnest glance.

"Must I leave you?" she exclaimed, with a wild terror in her tone. "Do you mean that I shall go away?

Oh, you need not care for me, — you need never love me, — you may always be cold, — but I must serve you, live with you, die with you!" And she sprang forward with outstretched arms.

He caught her before her foot became entangled in the long folds of her skirt, drew her to himself, and held her. What he murmured was inaudible to the others; but a tint redder than roses are swam to her cheek, and a smile broke over her face like a reflection in rippling water. She held his arm tightly in her hand, and erect and proud, as it were with a new life, bent toward Roger Raleigh.

"You see!" said she. "My husband loves me. And I, — it seems at this moment that I have never loved any other than him!"

There came a quick step along the matting, the handle of the door turned in Marguerite's resisting grasp, and Mrs. Purcell's light muslins swept through. Mr. Raleigh advanced to meet her, — a singular light upon his face, a strange accent of happiness in his voice.

"Since you seem to be a part of the affair," she said in a low tone, while her lip quivered with anger and scorn, "concerning which I have this moment been informed, pray take to Mr. Laudersdale my brother's request to enter the house of Day, Knight, and Company, from this day."

"Has he made such a request?" asked Mr. Raleigh.

"He shall make it!" she murmured swiftly, and was gone.

That night a telegram flashed over the wires, and thenceforth, on the great financial tide, the ship Day, Knight, and Company lowered its peak to none.

The day crept through until evening, deepening into

genuine heat, and Marguerite sat waiting for Mr. Raleigh
to come and bid her farewell. It seemed that his plans
were altered, or possibly he was gone, and at sunset she
went out alone. The cardinals that here and there
showed their red caps above the bank, the wild roses that
still lined the way, the grapes that blossomed and reddened and ripened year after year ungathered, did not
once lift her eyes. She sat down, at last, on an old fallen
trunk cushioned with moss, half of it forever wet in the
brook that babbled to the lake, and waited for the day to
quench itself in coolness and darkness.

"Ah!" said Mr. Raleigh, leaping from the other side
of the brook to the mossy trunk, "is it you? I have been
seeking you, and what sprite sends you to me?"

"I thought you were going away," she said, abruptly.

"That is a broken paving-stone," he answered, seating
himself beside her, and throwing his hat on the grass.

"You asked me, yesterday, if I confessed to being a
myth," she said, after a time. "If I should go back to
Martinique, I should become one in your remembrance,—
should I not? You would think of me just as you would
have thought of the Dryad yesterday, if she had stepped
from the tree and stepped back again?"

"Are you going to Martinique?" he asked, with a
total change of face and manner.

"I don't know. I am tired of this; and I cannot live
on an ice-field. I had such life at the South! It is 'as
if a rose should shut and be a bud again.' I need my
native weather, heat and sea."

"How *can* you go to Martinique?"

"Oh, I forgot!"

Mr. Raleigh did not reply, and they both sat listening
to the faint night-side noises of the world.

16

" You are very quiet," he said at last, ceasing to fling waifs upon the stream.

" And you could be very gay, I believe."

" Yes. I am full of exuberant spirits. Do you know what day it is ? "

" It is my birthday."

" It is *my* birthday ! "

" How strange ! The Jews would tell you that this sweet first of August was the birthday of the world.

> " 'T is like the birthday of the world,
> When earth was born in bloom,' " —

she sang, but paused before her voice should become hoarse in tears.

" Do you know what you promised me on my birthday ? I am going to claim it."

" The present. You shall have a cast which I had made from one of my mother's fancies or bass-reliefs, — she only does the front of anything, — a group of fleurs-de-lis whose outlines make a child's face, **my** face."

" It is more than any likeness in stone or pencil that I shall ask of you."

" What then ? "

" You cannot imagine ? "

" *Monsieur*," she whispered, turning toward him, and blushing in the twilight, " *est ce que c'est moi ?* "

There came out the low west-wind singing to itself through the leaves, the drone of a late-carousing honey-bee, the lapping of the water on the shore, the song of the wood-thrush replete with the sweetness of its half-melody ; and ever and anon the pensive cry of the whippoorwill fluted across the deepening silence that summoned all these murmurs into hearing. A rustle like the breeze in the birches passed, and Mrs. Purcell retarded her

rapid step to survey the woods-people who rose out of
the shade and now went on together with her. It seemed
as if the loons and whippoorwills grew wild with sorrow
that night, and after a while Mrs. Purcell ceased her
lively soliloquy, and as they walked they listened. Suddenly Mr. Raleigh turned. Mrs. Purcell was not beside
him. They had been walking on the brook-edge; the
path was full of gaps and cuts. With a fierce shudder
and misgiving, he hurriedly retraced his steps, and
searched and called; then, with the same haste, rejoining Marguerite, gained the house, for lanterns and assistance. Mrs. Purcell sat at the drawing-room window.

" *Comment?* " cried Marguerite, breathlessly.

" Oh, I had no idea of walking in fog up to my chin,"
said Mrs. Purcell; " so I took the short cut."

" You give me credit for the tragic element," she continued, under her breath, as Mr. Raleigh quietly passed
her. " That is old style. To be sure, I might as well
die there as in the swamps of Florida. Purcell is ordered to Florida. Of course, I am ordered too!" And
she whirled him the letter which she held.

Other letters had been received with the evening mail,
and one that made Mr. Raleigh's return in September
imperative occasioned some discussion in the House of
Laudersdale. The result was that that gentleman secured
one passage more than he had intended in the spring; and
if you ever watch the shipping-list, the arrival of the
Spray-Plough at Calcutta, with Mr. and Mrs. Raleigh
among the passengers, will be seen by you as soon as me.

Later in the evening of this same eventful day, as Mr.
Raleigh and Marguerite sat together in the moonlight that
flooded the great window, Mrs. Laudersdale passed them
and went down the garden to the lake. She wore some

white garment, as in her youth, and there was a dreamy
sweetness in her eye and an unspoken joy about her lips.
Mr. Raleigh could not help thinking it was a singular happiness, this that opened before her; it seemed to be like a
fruit plucked from the stem and left to mature in the sunshine by itself, late and lingering, never sound at heart.
She floated on, with the light in her dusky eyes and the
seldom rose on her cheek, — floated on from moonbeam to
moonbeam, — and the lovers brought back their glances
and gave them to each other. For one, life opened a
labyrinth of warmth and light and joy; for the other,
youth was passed, destiny not to be appeased: if his
affection enriched her, the best he could do was to bestow it; in his love there would yet be silent reserva-
tions.

"Mr Raleigh," said Marguerite, "did you ever love
my mother?"

"Once I thought I did."

"And now?"

"Whereas I was blind, now I see."

"Listen! Mrs. Purcell is singing in the drawing-
room."

> "Through lonely summers, where the roses blow
>   Unsought, and shed their tangled sweets,
> I sit and hark, or in the starry dark,
>   Or when the night-rain on the hill-side beats.

> "Alone! But when the eternal summers flow
>   And refluent drown in song all moan,
> Thy soul shall waste for its delight, and haste
>   Through heaven. And I shall be no more alone!"

"What a voice she sings with to-night!" said Marguerite. "It is stripped of all its ornamental disguises,
— so slender, yet piercing!"

" A needle can pain like a sword-blade. There goes the moon in clouds. Hark! What was that? A cry?" And he started to his feet.

" No," she said, — " it is only the wild music of the lake, the voices of shadows calling to shadows."

" There it is again, but fainter; the wind carries it the other way."

" It is a desolating wind."

" And the light on the land is like that of eclipse!"

He stooped and raised her and folded her in his arms.

" I have a strange, terrible sense of calamity, *Mignonne!*" he said. " Let it strike, so it spare you!"

" Nothing can harm us," she replied, clinging to him. " Even death cannot come between us!"

" Marguerite!" said Mr. Laudersdale, entering, " where is your mother?"

" She went down to the lake, sir."

" She cannot possibly have gone out upon it!"

"Oh, she frequently does; and so do we all."

" But this high wind has risen since. The flaws — " And he went out hastily.

There flashed on Mr. Raleigh's mental sight a vision of the moonlit lake, one instant. A boat, upon its side, bending its white sail down the depths; a lifted arm wound in the fatal rope; a woman's form, hanging by that arm, sustained in the dark transparent tide of death; the wild wind blowing over, the moonlight glazing all. For that instant he remained still as stone; the next, he strode away, and dashed down to the lake-shore. It seemed as if his vision yet continued. They had already put out in boats; he was too late. He waited in ghastly suspense till they rowed home with their slow freight. And then his arm supported the head with its long, uncoiling, heavy hair, and lifted the limbs, round which the drapery flowed like a pall on sculpture, till another man took the burden from him and went up to the house with his own.

When Mr. Raleigh entered the house again, it was at break of dawn. Some one opened the library-door and beckoned him in. Marguerite sprang into his arms.

"What if she had died?" said Mrs. Purcell, with her swift satiric breath, and folding a web of muslin over her arm. "See! I had got out the shroud. As it is, we drink *skål* and say grace at breakfast. The funeral baked-meats shall coldly furnish forth the marriage-feast. You men are all alike. *Le Roi est mort? Vive la Reine!*"

THE SOUTH BREAKER.

THE SOUTH BREAKER.

UST a capful of wind, and Dan shook loose the linen, and a straight shining streak with specks of foam shot after us. The mast bent like eel-grass, and our keel was half out of the water. Faith belied her name, and clung to the sides with her ten finger-nails; but as for me, I liked it.

"Take the stick, Georgie," said Dan, suddenly, his cheeks white. "Head her up the wind Steady. Sight the figure-head on Pearson's loft. Here's too much sail for a frigate."

But before the words were well uttered, the mast doubled up and coiled like a whip-lash, there was a report like the crack of doom, and half of the thing crashed short over the bows, dragging the heavy sail in the waves.

Then there came a great laugh of thunder close above, and the black cloud dropped like a curtain round us: the squall had broken.

"Cut it off, Dan! quick!" I cried.

"Let it alone," said he, snapping together his jack-knife; "it's as good as a best bower-anchor. Now I'll take the tiller, Georgie. Strong little hand," said he, bending so that I did n't see his face. "And lucky it's

16 *

good as strong. It's saved us all. My God, Georgie! where's Faith?"

I turned. There was no Faith in the boat. We both sprang to our feet, and so the tiller swung round and threw us broadside to the wind, and between the dragging mast and the centre-board drowning seemed too good for us.

"You'll have to cut it off," I cried again; but he had already ripped half through the canvas, and was casting it loose.

At length he gave his arm a toss. With the next moment, I never shall forget the look of horror that froze Dan's face.

"I've thrown her off!" he exclaimed. "I've thrown her off!"

He reached his whole length over the boat, I ran to his side, and perhaps our motion impelled it, or perhaps some unseen hand; for he caught at an end of rope, drew it in a second, let go and clutched at a handful of the sail, and then I saw how it had twisted round and swept poor little Faith over, and she had swung there in it, like a dead butterfly in a chrysalis. The lightnings were slipping down into the water like blades of fire everywhere around us, with short, sharp volleys of thunder, and the waves were more than I ever rode this side of the bar before or since, and we took in water every time our hearts beat; but we never once thought of our own danger while we bent to pull dear little Faith out of hers; and that done, Dan broke into a great hearty fit of crying that I'm sure he'd no need to be ashamed of. But it didn't last long; he just up and dashed off the tears and set himself at work again, while I was down on the floor rubbing Faith. There she lay like a broken lily, with no life in her little white face, and no breath, and maybe a pulse and maybe not. I could n't hear a word Dan said, for the wind; and the rain was pouring through us. I saw him take out the oars, but I knew they 'd do no good in such a chop, even if they did n't break; and pretty soon he found it so, for he drew them in and begun to untie the anchor-rope and wind it round his waist. I sprang to him.

"What are you doing, Dan?" I exclaimed.

"I can swim, at least," he answered.

"And tow us?—a mile? You know you can't! It's madness!"

"I must try. Little Faith will die, if we don't get ashore."

"She's dead now, Dan."

"What! No, no, she is n't. Faith is n't dead. But we must get ashore."

"Dan," I cried, clinging to his arm, "Faith's only one. But if you die so,—and you will!—I shall die too."

"You?"

"Yes; because, if it had n't been for me, you would n't have been here at all."

"And is that all the reason?" he asked, still at work.

"Reason enough," said I.

"Not quite," said he.

"Dan,—for my sake—"

"I can't, Georgie. Don't ask me. I must n't—" and here he stopped short, with the coil of rope in his hand, and fixed me with his eye, and his look was terrible—"*we* must n't let Faith die."

"Well," I said, "try it, if you dare,—and as true as there's a Lord in heaven, I'll cut the rope!"

He hesitated, for he saw I was resolute; and I would,

I declare I would have done it; for, do you know, at the
moment, I hated the little dead thing in the bottom of
the boat there.

Just then there came a streak of sunshine through the
gloom where we'd been plunging between wind and water, and then a patch of blue sky, and the great cloud
went blowing down river. Dan threw away the rope
and took out the oars again.

"Give me one, Dan," said I; but he shook his head.
"O Dan, because I'm so sorry!"

"See to her, then, — fetch Faith to," he replied, not
looking at me, and making up with great sturdy pulls.

So I busied myself, though I could n't do a bit of good.
The instant we touched bottom, Dan snatched her, sprang
through the water and up the landing. I stayed behind;
as the boat recoiled, pushed in a little, fastened the anchor
and threw it over, and then followed.

Our house was next the landing, and there Dan had
carried Faith; and when I reached it, a great fire was
roaring up the chimney, and the tea-kettle hung over it,
and he was rubbing Faith's feet hard enough to strike
sparks. I could n't understand exactly what made Dan
so fiercely earnest, for I thought I knew just how he felt
about Faith; but suddenly, when nothing seemed to answer, and he stood up and our eyes met, I saw such a
haggard, conscience-stricken face that it all rushed over
me. But now we had done what we could, and then I
felt all at once as if every moment that I effected nothing
was drawing out murder. Something flashed by the window, I tore out of the house and threw up my arms, I
don't know whether I screamed or not, but I caught the
doctor's eye, and he jumped from his gig and followed me
in. We had a siege of it. But at length, with hot blank-

ets, and hot water, and hot brandy dribbled down her throat, a little pulse began to play upon Faith's temple, and a little pink to beat up and down her cheek, and she opened her pretty dark eyes and lifted herself and wrung the water out of her braids; then she sank back.

"Faith! Faith! speak to me!" said Dan, close in her ear. "Don't you know me?"

"Go away," she said, hoarsely, pushing his face with her flat wet palm. "You let the sail take me over and drown me, while you kissed Georgie's hand."

I flung my hand before her eyes.

"Is there a kiss on those fingers?" I cried, in a blaze. "He never kissed my hands or my lips. Dan is your husband, Faith!"

For all answer Faith hid her head and gave a little moan. Somehow I could n't stand that; so I ran and put my arms round her neck and lifted her face and kissed it, and then we cried together. And Dan, walking the floor, took up his hat and went out, while she never cast a look after him. To think of such a great strong nature and such a powerful depth of feeling being wasted on such a little limp rag! I cried as much for that as anything. Then I helped Faith into my bedroom, and running home, I got her some dry clothes, — after rummaging enough, dear knows! for you 'd be more like to find her nightcap in the tea-caddy than elsewhere, — and I made her a corner on the settle, for she was afraid to stay in the bedroom, and when she was comfortably covered there she fell asleep. Dan came in soon and sat down beside her, his eyes on the floor, never glancing aside nor smiling, but gloomier than the grave. As for me, I felt at ease now, so I went and laid my hand on the back of his chair and made him look up. I wanted he should know the same rest that I had, and perhaps he did, — for, still looking up, the quiet smile came floating round his lips, and his eyes grew steady and sweet as they used to be before he married Faith. Then I went bustling lightly about the kitchen again.

"Dan," I said, "if you'd just bring me in a couple of those chickens stalking out there like two gentlemen from Spain."

While he was gone I flew round and got a cake into the bake-kettle, and a pan of biscuit down before the fire; and I set the tea to steep on the coals, because father always likes his tea strong enough to bear up an egg, after a hard day's work, and he'd had that to-day; and I put on the coffee to boil, for I knew Dan never had it at home, because Faith liked it and it did n't agree with her. And then he brought me in the chickens all ready for the pot, and so at last I sat down, but at the opposite side of the chimney. Then he rose, and, without exactly touching me, swept me back to the other side, where lay the great net I was making for father; and I took the little stool by the settle, and not far from him, and went to work.

"Georgie," said Dan, at length, after he'd watched me a considerable time, "if any word I may have said to-day disturbed you a moment, I want you to know that it hurt me first, and just as much."

"Yes, Dan," said I.

I've always thought there was something real noble between Dan and me then. There was I, — well, I don't mind telling you. And he, — yes, I'm sure he loved me perfectly, — you must n't be startled, I'll tell you how it was, — and always had, only may be he had n't known it; but it was deep down in his heart just the same, and by and by it stirred. There we were, both of us thoroughly conscious, yet neither of us expressing it by a word, and trying not to by a look, — both of us content to wait for the next life, when we could belong to one another. In those days I contrived to have it always pleasure enough for me just to know that Dan was in the room; and though that was n't often, I never grudged Faith her right in him, perhaps because I knew she did n't care anything about it. You see, this is how it was.

When Dan was a lad of sixteen, and took care of his mother, a ship went to pieces down there on the island. It was one of the worst storms that ever whistled, and though crowds were on the shore, it was impossible to reach her. They could see the poor wretches hanging in the rigging, and dropping one by one, and they could only stay and sicken, for the surf stove the boats, and they did n't know then how to send out ropes on rockets or on cannon-balls, and so the night fell, and the people wrung their hands and left the sea to its prey, and felt as if blue sky could never come again. And with the bright, keen morning not a vestige of the ship, but here a spar and there a door, and on the side of a sand-hill a great dog watching over a little child that he 'd kept warm all night. Dan, he 'd got up at turn of tide, and walked down, — the sea running over the road knee-deep, — for there was too much swell for boats; and when day broke, he found the little girl, and carried her up to town. He did n't take her home, for he saw that what clothes she had were the very finest, — made as delicately, — with seams like the hair-strokes on that heart's-ease there; and he concluded that he could n't bring her up as she ought to be. So he took her round to the rich men, and represented that she was the child of a lady, and that a poor fellow like himself — for Dan was older than his years, you see — could n't do her justice: she was a slight little thing, and needed dainty training and fancy food, may be a matter of seven years old, and she spoke some foreign language, and perhaps she did n't speak it plain, for nobody knew what it was. However, everybody was very much interested, and everybody was willing to give and to help, but nobody wanted to take her, and the upshot of it was that Dan refused all their offers and took her himself.

His mother 'd been in to our house all the afternoon before, and she 'd kept taking her pipe out of her mouth, — she had the asthma, and smoked, — and kept sighing.

"This storm 's going to bring me something," says she, in a mighty miserable tone. "I 'm sure of it!"

"No harm, I hope, Miss Devereux," said mother.

"Well, Rhody," — mother's father, he was a queer kind, — called his girls all after the thirteen States, and there being none left for Uncle Mat, he called him after the state of matrimony, — "Well, Rhody," she replied, rather dismally, and knocking the ashes out of the bowl, "I don't know; but I 'll have faith to believe that the Lord won't send me no ill without distincter warning. And that it 's good I *have* faith to believe."

And so when the child appeared, and had no name, and could n't answer for herself, Mrs. Devereux called her Faith.

We 're a people of presentiments down here on the Flats, and well we may be. You 'd own up yourself, maybe, if in the dark of the night, you locked in sleep, there 's a knock on the door enough to wake the dead, and you start up and listen and nothing follows; and falling back, you 're just dozing off, and there it is once

more, so that the lad in the next room cries out, "Who's
that, mother?" No one answering, you're half lost
again, when *rap* comes the hand again, the loudest of
the three, and you spring to the door and open it, and
there's naught there but a wind from the graves blowing in your face; and after a while you learn that in
that hour of that same night your husband was lost at
sea. Well, that happened to Mrs. Devereux. And I
have n't time to tell you the warnings I've known of.
As for Faith, I mind that she said herself, as we were
in the boat for that clear midnight sail, that the sea had
a spite against her, but third time was trying time.

So Faith grew up, and Dan sent her to school what he
could, for he set store by her. She was always ailing,
— a little, wilful, pettish thing, but pretty as a flower;
and folks put things into her head, and she began to think
she was some great shakes; and she may have been a
matter of seventeen years old when Mrs. Devereux died.
Dan, as simple at twenty-six as he had been ten years
before, thought to go on just in the old way, but the
neighbors were one too many for him; and they all represented that it would never do, and so on, till the poor
fellow got perplexed and vexed and half beside himself.
There was n't the first thing she could do for herself, and
he could n't afford to board her out, for Dan was only a
laboring-man, mackerelling all summer and shoemaking
all winter, less the dreadful times when he stayed out
on the Georges; and then he could n't afford, either, to
keep her there and ruin the poor girl's reputation; —
and what did Dan do but come to me with it all?

Now for a number of years I 'd been up in the other
part of the town with Aunt Netty, who kept a shop that
I tended between schools and before and after, and I 'd

almost forgotten there was such a soul on earth as Dan
Devereux, — though he 'd not forgotten me. I 'd got
through the Grammar and had a year in the High, and
suppose I should have finished with an education and
gone off teaching somewhere, instead of being here now,
cheerful as heart could wish, with a little black-haired
hussy tiltering on the back of my chair. Rolly, get
down! Her name 's Laura, — for his mother. I mean
I might have done all this, if at that time mother had n't
been thrown on her back, and been bedridden ever since.
I have n't said much about mother yet, but there all the
time she was, just as she is to-day, in her little tidy bed
in one corner of the great kitchen, sweet as a saint, and
as patient; — and I had to come and keep house for
father. He never meant that I should lose by it, father
did n't; begged, borrowed, or stolen, bought or hired, I
should have my books, he said: he 's mighty proud of my
learning, though between you and me it 's little enough
to be proud of; but the neighbors think I know 'most
as much as the minister, — and I let 'em think. Well,
while Mrs. Devereux was sick I was over there a good
deal, — for if Faith had one talent, it was total incapa-
city, — and there had a chance of knowing the stuff that
Dan was made of; and I declare to man 't would have
touched a heart of stone to see the love between the two.
She thought Dan held up the sky, and Dan thought she
was the sky. It 's no wonder, — the risks our men lead
can't make common-sized women out of their wives and
mothers. But I had n't been coming in and out, busying
about where Dan was, all that time, without making any
mark; though he was so lost in grief about his mother
that he did n't take notice of his other feelings, or think
of himself at all. And who could care the less about

him for that? It always brings down a woman to see a man wrapt in some sorrow that's lawful and tender as it is large. And when he came and told me what the neighbors said he must do with Faith, the blood stood still in my heart.

"Ask mother, Dan," says I, — for I could n't have advised him. "She knows best about everything."

So he asked her.

"I think, — I'm sorry to think, for I fear she 'll not make you a good wife," said mother, "but that perhaps her love for you will teach her to be, — you 'd best marry Faith."

"But I can't marry her!" said Dan, half choking; "I don't want to marry her, — it — it makes me uncomfortable-like to think of such a thing. I care for the child plenty — Besides," said Dan, catching at a bright hope, "I 'm not sure that she 'd have me."

"Have you, poor boy! What else can she do?"

Dan groaned.

"Poor little Faith!" said mother. "She 's so pretty, Dan, and she 's so young, and she 's pliant. And then how can we tell what may turn up about her some day? She may be a duke's daughter yet, — who knows? Think of the stroke of good-fortune she may give you!"

"But I don't love her," said Dan, as a finality.

"Perhaps — It is n't — You don't love any one else?"

"No," said Dan, as a matter of course, and not at all with reflection. And then, as his eyes went wandering, there came over them a misty look, just as the haze creeps between you and some object away out at sea, and he seemed to be sifting his very soul. Suddenly the look swept off them, and his eyes struck mine, and he turned, not having meant to, and faced me entirely, and there came such a light into his countenance, such a smile round his lips, such a red stamped his cheek, and he bent a little, — and it was just as if the angel of the Lord had shaken his wings over us in passing, and we both of us knew that here was a man and here was a woman, each for the other, in life and death; and I just hid my head in my apron, and mother turned on her pillow with a little moan. How long that lasted I can't say, but by and by I heard mother's voice, clear and sweet as a tolling bell far away on some fair Sunday morning, —

"The Lord is in his holy temple, the Lord's throne is in heaven: his eyes behold, his eyelids try the children of men."

And nobody spoke.

"Thou art my Father, my God, and the rock of my salvation. Thou wilt light my candle: the Lord my God will enlighten my darkness. For with thee is the fountain of life: in thy light shall we see light."

Then came the hush again, and Dan started to his feet, and began to walk up and down the room as if something drove him; but wearying, he stood and leaned his head on the chimney there. And mother's voice broke the stillness anew, and she said, —

"Hath God forgotten to be gracious? His mercy endureth forever. And none of them that trust in him shall be desolate."

There was something in mother's tone that made me forget myself and my sorrow, and look; and there she was, as she had n't been before for six months, half risen from the bed, one hand up, and her whole face white and shining with confident faith. Well, when I see all that such trust has buoyed mother over, I wish to goodness I had it: I take more after Martha. But never mind, do well here and you 'll do well there, say I. Perhaps you think it was n't much, the quiet and the few texts breathed through it; but sometimes when one's soul 's at a white heat, it may be moulded like wax with a finger. As for me, maybe God hardened Pharaoh's heart, — though how that was Pharaoh's fault I never could see; — but Dan, — he felt what it was to have a refuge in trouble, to have a great love always extending over him like a wing; he longed for it; he could n't believe it was his now, he was so suddenly convicted of all sin and wickedness; and something sprang up in his heart, a kind of holy passion that he felt to be possible for this great and tender Divine Being; and he came and fell on his knees by the side of the bed, crying out for mother to show him the way; and mother, she put her hand on his head and prayed, — prayed, O so beautifully, that it makes the water stand in my eyes now to remember what she said. But I did n't feel so then, my heart and my soul were rebellious, and love for Dan alone kept me under, not love for God. And in fact, if ever I 'd got to heaven then, love for Dan 'd have been my only saving grace; for I was mighty high-spirited, as a girl. Well, Dan he never made open profession; but when he left the house, he went and asked Faith to marry him.

Now Faith did n't care anything about Dan, — except the quiet attachment that she could n't help, from living in the house with him, and he 'd always petted and made much of her, and dressed her like a doll, — he was n't the kind of man to take her fancy: she 'd have maybe liked some slender, smooth-faced chap; but Dan was a black, shaggy fellow, with shoulders like the cross-tree, and a length of limb like Saul's, and eyes set deep, like

lamps in caverns.   And he had a great, powerful heart,
— and, O how it was lost! for she might have won it,
she might have made him love her, since I would have
stood wide away and aside for the sake of seeing him
happy.   But Faith was one of those that, if they can't
get what they want, have n't any idea of putting up with
what they have, — God forgive me, if I 'm hard on the
child!   And she could n't give Dan an answer right off,
but was loath to think of it, and went flirting about
among the other boys; and Dan, when he saw she was
n't so easily gotten, perhaps set more value on her.   For
Faith, she grew prettier every day; her great brown
eyes were so soft and clear, and had a wide, sorrowful
way of looking at you; and her cheeks, that were usually
pale, blossomed to roses when you spoke to her, her hair
drooping over them dark and silky; and though she was
slack and untidy and at loose ends about her dress, she
somehow always seemed like a princess in disguise; and
when she had on anything new, — a sprigged calico and
her little straw bonnet with the pink ribbons and Mrs.
Devereux's black scarf, for instance, — you 'd have allowed that she might have been daughter to the Queen
of Sheba.   I don't know, but I rather think Dan would
n't have said any more to Faith, from various motives,
you see, notwithstanding the neighbors were still remon-
strating with him, if it had n't been that Miss Brown —
she that lived round the corner there; the town 's well
quit of her now, poor thing! — went to saying the same
stuff to Faith, and telling her all that other folks said.
And Faith went home in a passion, — some of your timid
kind nothing ever abashes, and nobody gets to the windward of them, — and, being perfectly furious, fell to ac-
cusing Dan of having brought her to this, so that Dan

actually believed he had, and was cut to the quick with
contrition, and told her that all the reparation he could
make he was waiting and wishing to make, and then
there came floods of tears. Some women seem to have
set out with the idea that life's a desert for them to cross,
and they 've laid in a supply of water-bags accordingly,
— but it's the meanest weapon! And then again, there's
men that are iron, and not to be bent under calamities,
that these tears can twist round your little finger. Well,
I suppose Faith concluded 't was no use to go hungry because her bread was n't buttered on both sides, but she
always acted as if she 'd condescended ninety degrees in
marrying Dan, and Dan always seemed to feel that he 'd
done her a great injury; and there it was.

I kept in the house for a time; mother was worse, —
and I thought the less Dan saw of me the better; I kind
of hoped he 'd forget, and find his happiness where it
ought to be. But the first time I saw him, when Faith had
been his wife all the spring, there was the look in his eyes
that told of the ache in his heart. Faith was n't very
happy herself, of course, though she was careless; and
she gave him trouble, — keeping company with the young
men just as before; and she got into a way of flying
straight to me, if Dan ventured to reprove her ever so
lightly; and stormy nights, when he was gone, and in his
long trips, she always locked up her doors and came over
and got into my bed; and she was one of those that never
listened to reason, and it was none so easy for me, you
may suppose.

Things had gone on now for some three years, and I 'd
about lived in my books, — I 'd tried to teach Faith some,
but she would n't go any further than newspaper stories,
— when one day Dan took her and me to sail, and we

were to have had a clam-chowder on the Point, if the
squall had n't come. As it was, we 'd got to put up with
chicken-broth, and it could n't have been better, considering who made it. It was getting on toward the cool of
the May evening, the sunset was round on the other side
of the house, but all the east looked as if the sky had been
stirred up with currant-juice, till it grew purple and dark,
and then the two light-houses flared out and showed us
the lip of froth lapping the shadowy shore beyond, and I
heard father's voice, and he came in.

There was nothing but the fire-light in the room, and it
threw about great shadows, so that at first entering all was
indistinct ; but I heard a foot behind father's, and then a
form appeared, and something, I never could tell what,
made a great shiver rush down my back, just as when a
creature is frightened in the dark at what you don't see,
and so, though my soul was unconscious, my body felt that
there was danger in the air. Dan had risen and lighted
the lamp that swings in the chimney, and father first of
all had gone up and kissed mother, and left the stranger
standing ; then he turned round, saying, —

"A tough day, — it 's been a tough day ; and here 's
some un to prove it. Georgie, hope that pot's steam don't
belie it, for Mr. Gabriel Verelay and I want a good supper and a good bed."

At this, the stranger, still standing, bowed.

"Here 's the one, father," said I. "But about the bed,
— Faith 'll have to stay here, — and I don't see — unless
Dan takes him over — "

"That I 'll do," said Dan.

"All right," said the stranger, in a voice that you did n't
seem to notice while he was speaking, but that you remembered afterwards like the ring of any silver thing that has

been thrown down; and he dropped his hat on the floor and drew near the fireplace, warming hands that were slender and brown, but shapely as a woman's. I was taking up the supper; so I only gave him a glance or two, and saw him standing there, his left hand extended to the blaze, and his eye resting lightly and then earnestly on Faith in her pretty sleep, and turning away much as one turns from a picture. At length I came to ask him to sit by, and at that moment Faith's eyes opened.

Faith always woke up just as a baby does, wide and bewildered, and the fire had flushed her cheeks, and her hair was disordered, and she fixed her gaze on him as if he had stepped out of her dream, her lips half parted and then curling in a smile, — but in a second he moved off with me, and Faith slipped down and into the little bedroom.

Well, we did n't waste many words until father 'd lost the edge of his appetite, and then I told about Faith.

"'F that don't beat the Dutch!" said father. "Here's Mr. — Mr. —"

"Gabriel," said the stranger.

"Yes, — Mr. Gabriel Verelay been served the same trick by the same squall, only worse and more of it, — knocked off the yacht — What 's that you call her?"

"La belle Louise."

"And left for drowned, — if they see him go at all. But he could n't 'a' sinked in that sea, if he 'd tried. He kep' afloat; we blundered into him; and here he is."

Dan and I looked round in considerable surprise, for he was dry as an August leaf.

"Oh," said the stranger, coloring, and with the least little turn of his words, as if he did n't always speak English, "the good capitain reached shore, and, finding sticks, he kindled a fire, and we did dry our clothes until it made fine weather once more."

"Yes," said father; "but 't would n't been quite such fine weather, I reckon, if this 'd gone to the fishes!" And he pushed something across the table.

It was a pouch with steel snaps, and well stuffed. The stranger colored again, and held his hand for it, and the snap burst, and great gold pieces, English coin and very old French ones, rolled about the table, and father shut his eyes tight; and just then Faith came back and slipped into her chair. I saw her eyes sparkle as we all reached, laughing and joking, to gather them; and Mr. Gabriel, — we got into the way of calling him so, — he liked it best, — hurried to get them out of sight as if he 'd committed some act of ostentation. And then, to make amends, he threw off what constraint he had worn in this new atmosphere of ours, and was so gay, so full of questions and quips and conceits, all spoken in his strange way, his voice was so sweet, and he laughed so much and so like a boy, and his words had so much point and brightness, that I could think of nothing but the showers of colored stars in fireworks. Dan felt it like a play, sat quiet, but enjoying, and I saw he liked it; — the fellow had a way of attaching every one. Father was uproarious, and kept calling out, "Mother, do you hear? — d' you hear *that*, mother?" And Faith, she was near, taking it all in as a flower does sunshine, only smiling a little, and looking utterly happy. Then I hurried to clear up, and Faith sat in the great arm-chair, and father got out the pipes, and you could hardly see across the room for the wide tobacco-wreaths; and then it was father's turn, and he told story after story of the hardships and the dangers and the charms of our way of living. And I

could see Mr. Gabriel's cheek blanch, and he would bend
forward, forgetting to smoke, and his breath coming short,
and then right himself like a boat after lurching,—he had
such natural ways, and except that he 'd maybe been a
spoiled child, he would have had a good heart, as hearts go.
And nothing would do at last but he must stay and live
the same scenes for a little; and father told him 't would n't
pay, — they were n't so much to go through with as to
tell of, — there was too much prose in the daily life, and
too much dirt, and 't wa'n't fit for gentlemen. Oh, he
said, he 'd been used to roughing it, — woodsing, camping
and gunning and yachting, ever since he 'd been a free
man. He was a Canadian, and had been cruising from
the St. Lawrence to Florida, — and now, as his companions would go on without him, he had a mind to try a bit
of coast-life. And could he board here? or was there
any handy place? And father said, there was Dan, —
Dan Devereux, a man that had n't his match at oar or
helm. And Mr. Gabriel turned his keen eye and bowed
again, — and could n't Dan take Mr. Gabriel? And
before Dan could answer, for he 'd referred it to Faith,
Mr. Gabriel had forgotten all about it, and was humming
a little French song and stirring the coals with the tongs.
And that put father off in a fresh remembrance; and as
the hours lengthened, the stories grew fearful, and he
told them deep into the midnight, till at last Mr. Gabriel
stood up.

"No more, good friend," said he. "But I will have a
taste of this life perilous. And now where is it that
I go?"

Dan also stood up.

"My little woman," said he, glancing at Faith, "thinks
there 's a corner for you, sir."

" I beg your pardon —" And Mr. Gabriel paused, with a shadow skimming over his clear dark face.

Dan wondered what he was begging pardon for, but thought perhaps he had n't heard him, so he repeated, —

" My wife," — nodding over his shoulder at Faith, " she 's my wife, — thinks there 's a —"

" She 's your wife?" said Mr. Gabriel, his eyes opening and brightening the way an aurora runs up the sky, and looking first at one and then at the other, as if he could n't understand how so delicate a flower grew on so thorny a stem.

The red flushed up Dan's face, — and up mine, too, for the matter of that, — but in a minute the stranger had dropped his glance.

" And why did you not tell me," he said, " that I might have found her less beautiful?"

Then he raised his shoulders, gave her a saucy bow, with his hand on Dan's arm, — Dan, who was now too well pleased at having Faith made happy by a compliment to sift it, — and they went out.

But I was angry enough; and you may imagine I was n't much soothed by seeing Faith, who 'd been so die-away all the evening, sitting up before my scrap of looking-glass, trying in my old coral ear-rings, bowing up my ribbons, and plaiting and prinking till the clock frightened her into bed.

The next morning, mother, who was n't used to such disturbance, was ill, and I was kept pretty busy tending on her for two or three days. Faith had insisted on going home the first thing after breakfast, and in that time I heard no more of anybody, — for father was out with the night-tides, and, except to ask how mother did, and if I 'd seen the stray from the Lobblelyese again, was too tired for

talking when he came back. That had been — let me
see — on a Monday, I think, — yes, on a Monday; and
Thursday evening, as in-doors had begun to tell on me,
and mother was so much improved, I thought I'd run out
for a walk along the sea-wall. The sunset was creeping
round everything, and lying in great sheets on the broad,
still river, the children were frolicking in the water, and
all was so gay, and the air was so sweet, that I went lingering along farther than I'd meant, and by and by who
should I see but a couple sauntering toward me at my
own gait, and one of them was Faith. She had on a
muslin with little roses blushing all over it, and she floated
along in it as if she were in a pink cloud, and she'd
snatched a vine of the tender young woodbine as she
went, and, throwing it round her shoulders, held the two
ends in one hand like a ribbon, while with the other she
swung her white sun-bonnet. She laughed, and shook
her head at me, and there, large as life, under the dark
braids dangled my coral ear-rings, that she'd adopted
without leave or license. She'd been down to the lower
landing to meet Dan, — a thing she'd done before — I
don't know when, — and was walking up with Mr. Gabriel
while Dan stayed behind to see to things. I kept them
talking, and Mr. Gabriel was sparkling with fun, for he'd
got to feeling acquainted, and it had put him in high
spirits to get ashore at this hour, though he liked the sea,
and we were all laughing, when Dan came up. Now I
must confess I hadn't fancied Mr. Gabriel over and
above; I suppose my first impression had hardened into
a prejudice; and after I'd fathomed the meaning of
Faith's fine feathers I liked him less than ever. But
when Dan came up, he joined right in, gay and hearty,
and liking his new acquaintance so much, that, thinks I,

he must know best, and I'll let him look out for his interests himself. It would 'a' been no use, though, for Dan to pretend to beat the Frenchman at his own weapons, — and I don't know that I should have cared to have him. The older I grow, the less I think of your mere intellect ; throw learning out of the scales, and give me a great, warm heart, — like Dan's.

Well, it was getting on in the evening, when the latch lifted, and in ran Faith. She twisted my ear-rings out of her hair, exclaiming, —

"Oh, Georgie, are you busy ? Can't you perse my ears now ? "

" Pierce them yourself, Faith."

" Well, pierce, then. But I can't, — you know I can't. Won't you now, Georgie ? " and she tossed the ear-rings into my lap.

" Why, Faith," said I, " how 'd you contrive to wear these, if your ears are n't — "

" Oh, I tied them on. Come now, Georgie ! "

So I got the ball of yarn and the darning-needle.

" Oh, not such a big one ! " cried she.

" Perhaps you 'd like a cambric needle," said I.

" I don't want a winch," she pouted.

" Well, here 's a smaller one. Now kneel down."

" Yes, but you wait a moment, till I screw up my courage."

" No need. You can talk, and I 'll take you at una-wares."

So Faith knelt down, and I got all ready.

" And what shall I talk about ? " said she. " About Aunt Rhody, or Mr. Gabriel, or — I 'll tell you the queerest thing, Georgie ! Going to now ? "

" Do be quiet, Faith, and not keep your head flirting

about so!"—for she'd started up to speak. Then she composed herself once more.

"What was I saying? Oh, about that. Yes, Georgie, the queerest thing! You see, this evening, when Dan was out, I was sitting talkin' with Mr. Gabriel, and he was wondering how I came to be dropped down here, so I told him all about it. And he was so interested that I went and showed him the things I had on when Dan found me,—you know they've been kept real nice. And he took them, and looked them over, close, admiring them, and—and—admiring me,—and finally he started, and then held the frock to the light, and then lifted a little plait, and in the under side of the belt lining there was a name very finely wrought,—Virginie des Violets; and he looked at all the others, and in some hidden corner of every one was the initials of the same name,—V. des V.

"'That should be your name, Mrs. Devereux,' says he.

"'Oh, no!' says I. 'My name's Faith.'

"Well, and on that he asked, was there no more; and so I took off the little chain that I've always worn and showed him that, and he asked if there was a face in it, in what we thought was a coin, you know; and I said, oh, it did n't open; and he turned it over and over, and finally something snapped, and there *was* a face,—here, you shall see it, Georgie."

And Faith drew it from her bosom, and opened and held it before me; for I'd sat with my needle poised, and forgetting to strike. And there was the face indeed, a sad, serious face, dark and sweet, yet the image of Faith, and with the same mouth,—that so lovely in a woman becomes weak in a man,—and on the other side there were a few threads of hair, with the same darkness and fineness as Faith's hair, and under them a little picture chased in the gold and enamelled, which, from what I 've read since, I suppose must have been the crest of the Des Violets.

"And what did Mr. Gabriel say then ? " I asked, giving it back to Faith, who put her head into the old position again.

"Oh, he acted real queer. Talked French, too, — O, so fast! 'The very man!' then he cried out. 'The man himself! His portrait, — I have seen it a hundred times!' And then he told me that about a dozen years ago or more, a ship sailed from — from — I forget the place exactly, somewhere up there where *he* came from, — Mr. Gabriel, I mean, — and among the passengers was this man and his wife, and his little daughter, whose name was Virginie des Violets, and the ship was never heard from again. But he says that without a doubt I 'm the little daughter and my name is Virginie, though I suppose every one 'll call me Faith. Oh, and that is n't the queerest. The queerest is, this gentleman," and Faith lifted her head, "was very rich. I can't tell you how much he owned. Lands that you can walk on a whole day and not come to the end, and ships, and gold. And the whole of it 's lying idle and waiting for an heir, — and I, Georgie, am the heir."

And Faith told it with cheeks burning and eyes shining, but yet quite as if she 'd been born and brought up in the knowledge.

"It don't seem to move you much, Faith," said I, perfectly amazed, although I 'd frequently expected something of the kind.

"Well, I may never get it, and so on. If I do, I 'll give you a silk dress and set you up in a bookstore. But here's a queerer thing yet. Des Violets is the way Mr. Gabriel's own name is spelt, and his father and mine — his mother and — Well, some way or other we're sort of cousins. Only think, Georgie! is n't that — I thought, to be sure, when he quartered at our house, Dan'd begin to take me to do, if I looked at him sideways, — make the same fuss that he does if I nod to any of the other young men."

" I don't think Dan speaks before he should, Faith."

" Why don't you say Virginie ? " says she, laughing.

" Because Faith you 've always been, and Faith you 'll have to remain, with us, to the end of the chapter."

" Well, that 's as it may be. But Dan can't object now to my going where I 'm a mind to with my own cousin!" And here Faith laid her ear on the ball of yarn again.

" Hasten, headsman ! " said she, out of a novel, " or they 'll wonder where I am."

" Well," I answered, " just let me run the needle through the emery."

" Yes, Georgie," said Faith, going back with her memories while I sharpened my steel, " Mr. Gabriel and I are kin. And he said that the moment he laid eyes on me he knew I was of different blood from the rest of the people —"

" What people ? " asked I.

" Why, you, and Dan, and all these. And he said he was struck to stone when he heard I was married to Dan, — I must have been entrapped, — the courts would annul it, — any one could see the difference between us — "

Here was my moment, and I did n't spare it, but jabbed the needle into the ball of yarn, if her ear did lie between them.

" Yes ! " says I, " anybody with half an eye can see

17 *

the difference between you, and that's a fact! Nobody 'd
ever imagine for a breath that you were deserving of
Dan,— Dan, who's so noble he 'd die for what he thought
was right, — you, who are so selfish and idle and fickle
and — "

And at that Faith burst out crying.

" Oh, I never expected you 'd talk about me so, Georgie!" said she between her sobs. " How could *I* tell you
were such a mighty friend of Dan's? And besides, if
ever I was Virginie des Violets, I'm Faith Devereux
now, and Dan 'll resent *any one's* speaking so about his
wife!"

And she stood up, the tears sparkling like diamonds in
her flashing dark eyes, her cheeks red, and her little fist
clenched.

" That's the right spirit, Faith," says I, " and I'm glad
to see you show it. And as for this young Canadian, the
best thing to do with him is to send him packing. I don't
believe a word he says; it's more than likely nothing
but to get into your good graces."

" But there's the names," said she, so astonished that
she did n't remember she was angry.

" Happened so."

" Oh, yes! ' Happened so'! A likely story! It's
nothing but your envy, and that's all!"

" Faith!" says I, for I forgot she did n't know how
close she struck.

" Well, — I mean — There, don't let's talk about it
any more! How under the sun am I going to get these
ends tied?"

" Come here. There! Now for the other one."

" No, I sha'n't let you do that; you hurt me dreadfully,
and you got angry, and took the big needle."

"I thought you expected to be hurt."

"I did n't expect to be stabbed."

"Well, just as you please. I suppose you 'll go round with one ear-ring."

"Like a little pig with his ear cropped? No, I shall do it myself. See there, Georgie!" and she threw a bit of a box into my hands.

I opened it, and there lay inside, on their velvet cushion, a pair of the prettiest things you ever saw, — a tiny bunch of white grapes, and every grape a round pearl, and all hung so that they would tinkle together on their golden stems every time Faith shook her head, — and she had a cunning little way of shaking it often enough.

"These must have cost a penny, Faith," said I. "Where 'd you get them?"

"Mr. Gabriel gave them to me just now. He went up-town and bought them. And I don't want him to know that my ears were n't bored."

"Mr. Gabriel? And you took them?"

"Of course I took them, and mighty glad to get them."

"Faith, dear," said I, "don't you know that you should n't accept presents from gentlemen, and especially now you 're a married woman, and especially from those of higher station?"

"But he is n't higher."

"You know what I mean. And then, too, he is; for one always takes rank from one's husband."

Faith looked rather downcast at this.

"Yes," said I, — "and pearls and calico —"

"Just because you have n't got a pair yourself! There, be still! I don't want any of your instructions in duty!"

"You ought to put up with a word from a friend,

Faith," said I. " You always come to me with your
grievances. And I 'll tell you what I 'll do. You used
to like these coral branches of mine ; and if you 'll give
those back to Mr. Gabriel, you shall have the coral."

Well, Faith she hesitated, standing there trying to muster her mind to the needle, and it ended by her taking
the coral, though I don't believe she returned the pearls,
— but we none of us ever saw them afterwards.

We 'd been talking in a pretty low tone, because mother
was asleep ; and just as she 'd finished the other ear, and
a little drop of blood stood up on it like a live ruby, the
door opened and Dan and Mr. Gabriel came in.   There
never was a prettier picture than Faith at that moment,
and so the young stranger thought, for he stared at her,
smiling and at ease, just as if she 'd been hung in a gallery and he 'd bought a ticket.   So then he sat down and
repeated to Dan and mother what she 'd told me, and he
promised to send for the papers to prove it all.   But he
never did send for them, — delaying and delaying, till the
summer wore away ; and perhaps there were such papers
and perhaps there were n't.   I 've always thought he
did n't want his own friends to know where he was.   Dan
might be a rich man to-day, if he chose to look them up ;
but he 'd scorch at a slow fire before he 'd touch a copper
of it.   Father never believed a word about it, when we
recited it again to him.

" So Faith 's come into her fortune, has she ? " said he.
" Pretty child !   She 'a'n't had so much before sence she
fell heir to old Miss Devereux's best chany, her six silver
spoons, and her surname."

So the days passed, and the greater part of every one
Mr. Gabriel was dabbling in the water somewhere.
There was n't a brook within ten miles that he did n't

empty of trout, for Dan knew the woods as well as the
shores, and he knew the clear nights when the insects can
keep free from the water so that next day the fish rise
hungry to the surface; and so sometimes in the brightest
of May noons they'd bring home a string of those beauties, speckled with little tongues of flame; and Mr.
Gabriel would have them cooked, and make us all taste
them, — for we don't care much for that sort, down here
on the Flats; we should think we were famished if we
had to eat fish. And then they'd lie in wait all day for
the darting pickerel in the little Stream of Shadows above;
and when it came June, up the river he went trolling for
bass, and he used a different sort of bait from the rest, —
bass won't bite much at clams, — and he hauled in great
forty-pounders. And sometimes in the afternoons, he
took out Faith and me, — for, as Faith would go, whether
or no, I always made it a point to put by everything and
go too; and I used to try and get some of the other girls
in, but Mr. Gabriel never would take them, though he
was hail-fellow-well-met with everybody, and was everybody's favorite, and it was known all round how he found
out Faith, and that alone made him so popular, that I do
believe, if he'd only taken out naturalization papers, we
'd have sent him to General Court. And then it grew
time for the river mackerel, and they used to bring in at
sunset two or three hundred in a shining heap, together
with great lobsters, that looked as if they'd been carved
out of heliotrope-stone, and so old that they were barna-
cled. And it was so novel to Mr. Gabriel, that he used
to act as if he'd fallen in fairy-land.

After all, I don't know what we should have done without him that summer: he always paid Dan or father a dol-
lar a day and the hire of the boat; and the times were so

hard, and there was so little doing, that, but for this, and packing the barrels of clam-bait, they 'd have been idle and fared sorely. But we 'd rather have starved : though, as for that, I 've heard father say there never was a time when he could n't go out and catch some sort of fish and sell it for enough to get us something to eat. And then this Mr. Gabriel, he had such a winning way with him, he was as quick at wit as a bird on the wing, he had a story or a song for every point, he seemed to take to our simple life as if he 'd been born to it, and he was as much interested in all our trifles as we were ourselves. Then, he was so sympathetic, he felt everybody's troubles, he went to the city and brought down a wonderful doctor to see mother, and he got her queer things that helped her more than you 'd have thought anything could, and he went himself and set honeysuckles out all round Dan's house, so that before summer was over it was a bower of great sweet blows, and he had an alms for every beggar, and a kind word for every urchin, and he followed Dan about as a child would follow some big shaggy dog. He introduced, too, a lot of new-fangled games; he was what they called a gymnast, and in feats of rassling there was n't a man among them all but he could stretch as flat as a flounder. And then he always treated. Everybody had a place for him soon, — even *I* did ; and as for Dan, he 'd have cut his own heart out of his body, if Mr. Gabriel 'd had occasion to use it. He was a different man from any Dan 'd ever met before, something finer, and he might have been better, and Dan's loyal soul was glad to acknowledge him master, and I declare I believe he felt just as the Jacobites in the old songs used to feel for royal Charlie. There are some men born to rule with a haughty, careless sweetness, and others born to die for them with stern and dogged devotion.

Well, and all this while Faith was n't standing still; she was changing steadily, as much as ever the moon changed in the sky. I noticed it first one day when Mr. Gabriel 'd caught every child in the region and given them a picnic in the woods of the Stack-Yard-Gate, and Faith was nowhere to be seen tiptoeing round every one as she used to do, but I found her at last standing at the head of the table, — Mr. Gabriel dancing here and there, seeing to it that all should be as gay as he seemed to be, — quiet and dignified as you please, and feeling every one of her inches. But it was n't dignity really that was the matter with Faith, — it was just gloom. She 'd brighten up for a moment or two, and then down would fall the cloud again ; she took to long fits of dreaming, and sometimes she 'd burst out crying at any careless word, so that my heart fairly bled for the poor child, — for one could n't help seeing that she 'd some secret unhappiness or other, — and I was as gentle and soothing to her as it 's in my nature to be. She was in to our house a good deal ; she kept it pretty well out of Dan's way, and I hoped she 'd get over it sooner or later, and make up her mind to circumstances. And I talked to her a sight about Dan, praising him constantly before her, though I could n't bear to do it; and finally, one very confidential evening, I told her that I 'd been in love with Dan myself once a little, but I 'd seen that he would marry her, and so had left off thinking about it ; for, do you know, I thought it might make her set more price on him now, if she knew somebody else had ever cared for him. Well, that did answer awhile : whether she thought she ought to make it up to Dan, or whether he really did grow more in her eyes, Faith got to being very neat and domestic and praise-worthy. But still there was the change, and it did n't make her any the less lovely. Indeed, if I 'd been a man, I should have cared for her more than ever : it was like turning a child into a woman : and I really think, as Dan saw her going about with such a pleasant gravity, her pretty figure moving so quietly, her pretty face so still and fair, as if she had thoughts and feelings now, he began to wonder what had come over Faith, and, if she were really as charming as this, why he had n't felt it before ; and then, you know, whether you love a woman or not, the mere fact that she 's your wife, that her life is sunk in yours, that she 's something for you to protect, and that your honor lies in doing so, gives you a certain kindly feeling that might ripen into love any day under sunshine and a south wall.

Blue-fish were about done with, when one day Dan brought in some mackerel from Boon Island : they had n't been in the harbor for some time, though now there was a probability of their return. So they were going out when the tide served — the two boys — at midnight for mackerel, and Dan had heard me wish for the experience so often, a long while ago, that he said, Why should n't they take the girls ? and Faith snatched at the idea, and with that Mr. Gabriel agreed to fetch me at the hour, and so we parted. I was kind of sorry, but there was no help for it.

When we started, it was in that clear crystal dark that looks as if you could see through it forever till you reached infinite things, and we seemed to be in a great hollow sphere, and the stars were like living beings who had the night to themselves. Always, when I 'm up late, I feel as if it were something unlawful, as if affairs were in progress which I had no right to witness, a kind of grand free-masonry. I've felt it nights when I've been watching with mother, and there has come up across the heavens the great caravan of constellations, and a star that I'd pulled away the curtain on the east side to see, came by and by and looked in at the south window; but I never felt it as I did this night. The tide was near the full and so we went slipping down the dark water by the starlight; and as we saw them shining above us, and then looked down and saw them sparkling up from beneath, — the stars, — it really seemed as if Dan's oars must be two long wings, as if we swam on them through a motionless air. By and by we were in the island creek, and far ahead, in a streak of wind that did n't reach us, we could see a pointed sail skimming along between the banks, as if some ghost went before to show us the way; and when the first hush and mystery wore off, Mr. Gabriel was singing little French songs in tunes like the rise and fall of the tide. While he sang he rowed, and Dan was gangeing the hooks. At length Dan took the oars again, and every now and then he paused to let us float along with the tide as it slacked, and take the sense of the night. And all the tall grass that edged the side began to wave in a strange light, and there blew on a little breeze, and over the rim of the world tipped up a waning moon. If there'd been anything needed to make us feel as if we were going to find the Witch of Endor, it was this. It was such a strange moon, pointing such a strange way, with such a strange color, so remote, and so glassy, — it was like a dead moon, or the spirit of one, and was perfectly awful.

"She has come to look at Faith," said Mr. Gabriel; for Faith, who once would have been nodding here and there all about the boat, was sitting up pale and sad, like

z

another spirit, to confront it.   But Dan and I both felt a difference.

Mr. Gabriel, he stepped across and went and sat down behind Faith, and laid his hand lightly on her arm.   Perhaps he did n't mind that he touched her, — he had a kind of absent air; but if any one had looked at the nervous pressure of the slender fingers, they would have seen as much meaning in that touch as in many an embrace; and Faith lifted her face to his, and they forgot that I was looking at them, and into the eyes of both there stole a strange deep smile, — and my soul groaned within me. It made no odds to me then that the air blew warm off the land from scented hay-ricks, that the moon hung like some exhumed jewel in the sky, that all the perfect night was widening into dawn.   I saw and felt nothing but the wretchedness that must break one day on Dan's head. Should I warn him?   I could n't do that.   And what then ?

The sail was up, we had left the head-land and the hills, and when they furled it and cast anchor we were swinging far out on the back of the great monster that was frolicking to itself and thinking no more of us than we do of a mote in the air.   Elder Snow, he says that it 's singular we regard day as illumination and night as darkness, — day that really hems us in with narrow light and shuts us upon ourselves, night that sets us free and reveals to us all the secrets of the sky.   I thought of that when one by one the stars melted and the moon became a breath, and up over the wide grayness crept color and radiance and the sun himself, — the sky soaring higher and higher, like a great thin bubble of flaky hues, — and, all about, nothing but the everlasting wash of waters broke the sacred hush.   And it seemed as if God had been with us, and withdrawing we saw the trail of His splendid garments, — and I remembered the words mother had spoken to Dan once before, and why could n't I leave him in heavenly hands? And then it came into my heart to pray. I knew I had n't any right to pray expecting to be heard; but yet mine would be the prayer of the humble, and was n't Faith of as much consequence as a sparrow? By and by, as we all sat leaning over the gunwale, the words of a hymn that I 'd heard at camp-meetings came into my mind, and I sang them out, loud and clear. I always had a good voice, though Dan 'd never heard me do anything with it except hum little low things, putting mother to sleep; but here I had a whole sky to sing in, and the hymns were trumpet-calls. And one after another they kept thronging up, and there was a rush of feeling in them that made you shiver, and as I sang them they thrilled me through and through. Wide as the way before us was, it seemed to widen; I felt myself journeying with some vast host towards the city of God, and its light poured over us, and there was nothing but joy and love and praise and exulting expectancy in my heart. And when the hymn died on my lips because the words were too faint and the tune was too weak for the ecstasy, and when the silence had soothed me back again, I turned and saw Dan's lips bitten, and his cheek white, and his eyes like stars, and Mr. Gabriel's face fallen forward in his hands, and he shaking with quick sobs; and as for Faith, — Faith, she had dropped asleep, and one arm was thrown above her head, and the other lay where it had slipped from Mr. Gabriel's loosened grasp. There 's a contagion, you know, in such things, but Faith was never of the catching kind.

Well, this was n't what we 'd come for, — turning all

out-doors into a church, — though what's a church but a place of God's presence? and for my part, I never see high blue sky and sunshine without feeling that. And all of a sudden there came a school of mackerel splashing and darkening and curling round the boat, after the bait we'd thrown out on anchoring. 'T would have done you good to see Dan just at that moment; you'd have realized what it was to have a calling. He started up, forgetting everything else, his face all flushed, his eyes like coals, his mouth tight and his tongue silent; and how many hooks he had out I'm sure I don't know, but he kept jerking them in by twos and threes, and finally they bit at the bare barb and were taken without any bait at all, just as if they'd come and asked to be caught. Mr. Gabriel, he did n't pay any attention at first, but Dan called to him to stir himself, and so gradually he worked back into his old mood; but he was more still and something sad all the rest of the morning. Well, when we'd gotten about enough, and they were dying in the boat there, as they cast their scales, like the iris, we put inshore; and building a fire, we cooked our own dinner and boiled our own coffee. Many's the icy winter night I've wrapped up Dan's bottle of hot coffee in rolls on rolls of flannel, that he might drink it hot and strong far out at sea in a wherry at daybreak!

But as I was saying, — all this time, Mr. Gabriel, he scarcely looked at Faith. At first she did n't comprehend, and then something swam all over her face as if the very blood in her veins had grown darker, and there was such danger in her eye that before we stepped into the boat again I wished to goodness I had a life-preserver. But in the beginning the religious impression lasted and gave him great resolutions; and then strolling off and along the beach, he fell in with some men there and did as he always did, scraped acquaintance. I verily believe that these men were total strangers, that he 'd never laid eyes on them before, and after a few words he wheeled about. As he did so, his glance fell on Faith standing there alone against the pale sky, for the weather 'd thickened, and watching the surf break at her feet. He was motionless, gazing at her long, and then, when he had turned once or twice irresolutely, he ground his heel into the sand and went back. The men rose and wandered on with him, and they talked together for a while, and I saw money pass ; and pretty soon Mr. Gabriel returned, his face vividly pallid, but smiling, and he had in his hand some little bright shells that you don't often find on these Northern beaches, and he said he had bought them of those men. And all this time he 'd not spoken with Faith, and there was the danger yet in her eye. But nothing came of it, and I had accused myself of nearly every crime in the Decalogue, and on the way back we had put up the lines, and Mr. Gabriel had hauled in the lobster-net for the last time. He liked that branch of the business ; he said it had all the excitement of gambling, — the slow settling downwards, the fading of the last ripple, the impenetrable depth and shade and the mystery of the work below, five minutes of expectation, and it might bring up a scale of the sea-serpent, or the king of the crabs might have crept in for a nap in the folds, or it might come up as if you 'd dredged for pearls, or it might hold the great backward-crawling lobsters, or a tangle of sea-weed, or the long yellow locks of some drowned girl, — or nothing at all. So he always drew in that net, and it needed muscle, and his was like steel, — not good for much in the long pull, but just for a breathing could handle the biggest boatman in the harbor. Well, — and we 'd hoisted the sail and were in the creek once more, for the creek was only to be used at high-water, and I 'd told Dan I could n't be away from mother over another tide and so we must n't get aground, and he 'd told me not to fret, there was nothing too shallow for us on the coast. "This boat," said Dan, "she 'll float in a heavy dew." And he began singing a song he liked: —

> "I cast my line in Largo Bay,
>   And fishes I caught nine:
>   There 's three to boil, and three to fry,
>   And three to bait the line."

And Mr. Gabriel 'd never heard it before, and he made him sing it again and again.

> "The boatie rows, the boatie rows,
>   The boatie rows indeed,"

repeated Mr. Gabriel, and he said it was the only song he knew that held the click of the oar in the rowlock.

The little birds went skimming by us, as we sailed, their breasts upon the water, and we could see the gunners creeping through the marshes beside them.

"The wind changes," said Mr. Gabriel. "The equinox treads close behind us. Sst! Is it that you do not feel its breath? And you hear nothing?"

"It 's the Soul of the Bar," said Dan; and he fell to telling us one of the wild stories that fishermen can tell each other by the lantern, rocking outside at night in the dory.

The wind was dead east, and now we flew before it, and now we tacked in it, up and up the winding stream, and always a little pointed sail came skimming on in suit.

"What sail is that, Dan?" asked I. "It looks like the one that flitted ahead this morning."

"It *is* the one," said Dan, — for he 'd brought up a whole horde of superstitious memories, and a gloom that had been hovering off and on his face settled there for good. "As much of a one as that was. It 's no sail at all. It 's a death-sign. And I 've never been down here and seen it but trouble was on its heels. Georgie! there 's two of them!"

We all looked, but it was hidden in a curve, and when it stole in sight again there *were* two of them, filmy and faint as spirits' wings, — and while we gazed they vanished, whether supernaturally or in the mist that was rising mast-high I never thought, for my blood was frozen as it ran.

"You have fear?" asked Mr. Gabriel, — his face perfectly pale, and his eye almost lost in darkness. "If it is a phantom, it can do you no harm."

Faith's teeth chattered, — I saw them. He turned to her, and as their look met, a spot of carnation burned into his cheek almost as a brand would have burned. He seemed to be balancing some point, to be searching her and sifting her; and Faith half rose, proudly, and pale, as if his look pierced her with pain. The look was long, — but before it fell, a glow and sparkle filled the eyes, and over his face there curled the deep, strange smile of the morning, till the long lids and heavy lashes dropped and made it sad. And Faith, — she started in a new surprise, the darkness gathered and crept off her face as cream wrinkles from milk, and spleen or venom or what-not became absorbed again and lost, and there was nothing in her glance but passionate forgetfulness. Some souls are like the white river-lilies, — fixed, yet floating; but Mr. Gabriel had no firm root anywhere, and was blown about with every breeze, like a leaf on the flood. His purposes melted and made with his moods.

The wind got round more to the north, the mist fell upon the waters or blew away over the meadows, and it was cold. Mr. Gabriel wrapped the cloak about Faith and fastened it, and tied her bonnet. Just now Dan was so busy handling the boat — and it 's rather risky, you have to wriggle up the creek so — that he took little notice of us. Then Mr. Gabriel stood up, as if to change his position ; and taking off his hat, he held it aloft, while he passed the other hand across his forehead. And leaning against the mast, he stood so, many minutes.

" Dan," I said, " did your spiritual craft ever hang out a purple pennant ? "

" No," said Dan.

" Well," says I.   And we all saw a little purple ribbon running up the rope and streaming on the air behind us.

" And why do we not hoist our own ? " said Mr. Gabriel, putting on his hat. And suiting the action to the word, a little green signal curled up and flaunted above us like a bunch of the weed floating there in the water beneath and dyeing all the shallows so that they looked like caves of cool emerald, and wide off and over them the west burned smoulderingly red like a furnace. Many a time since, I 've felt the magical color between those banks and along those meadows, but then I felt none of it ; every wit I had was too awake and alert and fast-fixed in watching.

" Is it that the phantoms can be flesh and blood ? " said Mr. Gabriel, laughingly ; and lifting his arm again, he hailed the foremost.

" Boat ahoy ! What names ? " said he.

The answer came back on the wind full and round.

" Speed, and Follow."

" Where from ? " asked Dan, with just a glint in his
eye, — for usually he knew every boat on the river, but
he did n't know these.

" From the schooner Flyaway, taking in sand over at
Black Rocks."

Then Mr. Gabriel spoke again, as they drew near, —
but whether he spoke so fast that I could n't understand,
or whether he spoke French, I never knew ; and Dan,
with some kind of feeling that it was Mr. Gabriel's acquaintance, suffered the one we spoke to pass us.

Once or twice Mr. Gabriel had begun some question to
Dan about the approaching weather, but had turned it
off again before anybody could answer. You see he had
some little nobility left, and did n't want the very man he
was going to injure to show him how to do it. Now,
however, he asked him that was steering the Speed by,
if it was going to storm.

The man thought it was.

" How is it then, that your schooner prepares to sail ? "

" Oh, wind 's backed in ; we 'll be on blue water before the gale breaks, I reckon, and then beat off where
there 's plenty of sea-room."

" But she shall make shipwreck ! "

" ' Not if the court know herself, and he think she do,' "
was the reply from another, as they passed.

Somehow I began to hate myself, I was so full of
poisonous suspicions. How did Mr. Gabriel know the
schooner prepared to sail ? And this man, could he tell
boom from bowsprit ? I did n't believe it ; he had the
hang of the up-river folks. But there stood Mr. Gabriel,
so quiet and easy, his eyelids down, and he humming an
underbreath of song ; and there sat Faith, so pale and so

18

pretty, a trifle sad, a trifle that her conscience would
brew for her, whether or no.   Yet, after all, there was an
odd expression in Mr. Gabriel's face, an eager, restless
expectation ; and if his lids were lowered, it was only to
hide the spark that flushed and quenched in his eye like
a beating pulse.

We had reached the draw, it was lifted for the Speed,
she had passed, and the wind was in her sail once more.
Yet, somehow, she hung back.   And then I saw that the
men in her were of those with whom Mr. Gabriel had
spoken at noon.   Dan's sail fell slack, and we drifted
slowly through, while he poled us along with an oar.

" Look out, Georgie ! " said Dan, for he thought I was
going to graze my shoulder upon the side there.   I looked ; and when I turned again, Mr. Gabriel was rising up
from some earnest and hurried sentence to Faith.   And
Faith, too, was standing, standing and swaying with indecision, and gazing away out before her, — so flushed and
so beautiful, — so loath and so willing.   Poor thing !
poor thing ! as if her rising in itself were not the whole!

Mr. Gabriel stepped across the boat, stooped a minute,
and then also took an oar.   How perfect he was, as he
stood there that moment ! — perfect like a statue, I mean,
— so slender, so clean-limbed, his dark face pale to trans-
parency in the green light that filtered through the draw !
and then a ray from the sunset came creeping over the
edge of the high fields and smote his eyes sidelong so
that they glowed like jewels, and he with his oar planted
firmly hung there bending far back with it, completely
full of strength and grace.

" It is not the *bateaux* in the rapids," said he.

" What are you about ? " asked Dan, with sudden
hoarseness.   " You are pulling the wrong way ! "

Mr. Gabriel laughed, and threw down his oar, and stepped back again; gave his hand to Faith, and half led, half lifted her, over the side, and into the Speed, followed, and never looked behind him. They let go something they had held, the Speed put her nose in the water and sprinkled us with spray, plunged, and dashed off like an arrow.

It was like him, — daring and insolent coolness! Just like him! Always the soul of defiance! None but one so reckless and impetuous as he would have dreamed of flying into the teeth of the tempest in that shell of a schooner. But he was mad with love, and they — there was n't a man among them but was the worse for liquor.

For a moment Dan took it, as Mr. Gabriel had expected him to do, as a joke, and went to trim the boat for racing, not meaning they should reach town first. But I — I saw it all.

"Dan!" I sung out, "save her! She 's not coming back! They 'll make for the schooner at Black Rocks! Oh, Dan, he 's taken her off!"

Now one whose intelligence has never been trained, who shells his five wits and gets rid of the pods as best he can, may n't be so quick as another, but, like an animal, he feels long before he sees; and a vague sense of this had been upon Dan all day. Yet now he stood thunderstruck; and the thing went on before his very eyes. It was more than he could believe at once, — and perhaps his first feeling was, Why should he hinder? And then the flood fell. No thought of his loss, — though loss it wa'n't, — only of his friend, — of such stunning treachery, that, if the sun fell hissing into the sea at noon, it would have mattered less, — only of *that* loss that tore his heart out with it.

" Gabriel!" he shouted, — " Gabriel!"   And his voice
was heart-rending.   I know that Mr. Gabriel felt it, for
he never turned nor stirred.

Then I don't know what came over Dan : a blind rage
swelling in his heart seemed to make him larger in every
limb; he towered like a flame.   He sprang to the tiller,
but, as he did so, saw with one flash of his eye that Mr.
Gabriel had unshipped the rudder and thrown it away.
He seized an oar to steer with in its place ; he saw that
they, in their ignorance fast edging on the flats, would
shortly be aground ; more fisherman than sailor, he knew
a thousand tricks of boat-craft that they had never heard
of.   We flew, we flew through cloven ridges, we became
a wind ourselves, and while I tell it he was beside them,
had gathered himself as if to leap the chasm between time
and eternity, and had landed among them in the Speed.
The wherry careened with the shock and the water poured
into her, and she flung headlong and away as his foot
spurned her.   Heaven knows why she did n't upset, for I
thought of nothing but the scene before me as I drifted
off from it.   I shut the eyes in my soul now, that I
may n't see that horrid scuffle twice.   Mr. Gabriel, he
rose, he turned.   If Dan was the giant beside him, he
himself was so well-knit, so supple, so adroit, that his
power was like the blade in the hand.   Dan's strength
was lying round loose, but Mr. Gabriel's was trained, it
hid like springs of steel between brain and wrist, and
from him the clap fell with the bolt.   And then, besides,
Dan did not love Faith, and he did love Gabriel.   Any
one could see how it would go.   I screamed.   I cried,
" Faith ! Faith !"   And some natural instinct stirred in
Faith's heart, for she clung to Mr. Gabriel's arm to pull
him off from Dan.   But he shook her away like rain.

Then such a mortal weakness took possession of me that I saw everything black, and when it was clean gone, I looked, and they were locked in each other's arms, fierce, fierce and fell, a death-grip. They were staggering to the boat's edge: only this I saw, that Mr. Gabriel was inside: suddenly the helmsman interposed with an oar, and broke their grasps. Mr. Gabriel reeled away, free, for a second; then, the passion, the fury, the hate in his heart feeding his strength as youth fed the locks of Samson, he darted, and lifted Dan in his two arms and threw him like a stone into the water. Stiffened to ice, I waited for Dan to rise; the other craft, the Follow, skimmed between us, and one man managing her that she should n't heel, the rest drew Dan in, — it 's not the depth of two foot there, — tacked about, and after a minute came alongside, seized our painter, and dropped him gently into his own boat. Then — for the Speed had got afloat again — the thing stretched her two sails wing and wing, and went ploughing up a great furrow of foam before her.

I sprang to Dan. He was not senseless, but in a kind of stupor: his head had struck the fluke of a half-sunk anchor and it had stunned him, but as the wound bled he recovered slowly and opened his eyes. Ah, what misery was in them! I turned to the fugitives. They were yet in sight, Mr. Gabriel sitting and seeming to adjure Faith, whose skirts he held; but she stood, and her arms were outstretched, and, pale as a foam-wreath her face, and piercing as a night-wind her voice, I heard her cry, " Oh, Georgie! Georgie!" It was too late for her to cry or to wring her hands now. She should have thought of that before. But Mr. Gabriel rose and drew her down, and hid her face in his arms and bent over it; and so they fled up the basin and round the long line of sand, and out into the gloom and the curdling mists.

I bound up Dan's head. I could n't steer with an oar,
— that was out of the question, — but, as luck would have
it, could row tolerably ; so I got down the little mast, and
at length reached the wharves.   The town-lights flickered
up in the darkness and flickered back from the black rushing river, and then out blazed the great mills ; and as I
felt along, I remembered times when we 'd put in by the
tender sunset, as the rose faded out of the water and the
orange ebbed down the west, and one by one the sweet
evening-bells chimed forth, so clear and high, and each
with a different tone, that it seemed as if the stars must
flock, tinkling, into the sky.   And here were the bells
ringing out again, ringing out of the gray and the gloom,
dull and brazen, as if they rang from some cavern of
shadows, or from the mouth of hell, — but no, *that* was
down river !   Well, I made my way, and the men on the
landing took up Dan, and helped him in and got him on
my little bed, and no sooner there than the heavy sleep
with which he had struggled fell on him like lead.

The story flew from mouth to mouth, the region rang
with it ; nobody had any need to add to it, or to make it
out a griffin or a dragon that had gripped Faith and carried her off in his talons.   But everybody declared that
those boats could be no ship's yawls at all, but must
belong to parties from up river camping out on the beach,
and that a parcel of such must have gone sailing with
some of the hands of a sand-droger : there was one in the
stream now, that had got off with the tide, said the Jerdan
boys who 'd been down there that afternoon, though there
was no such name as " Flyaway " on her stern, and they
were waiting for the master of her, who 'd gone off on a
spree, — a dare-devil fellow, that used to run a smuggler
between Bordeaux and Bristol, as they 'd heard say : and

all agreed that Mr. Gabriel could never have had to do with them before that day, or he 'd have known what a place a sand-droger would be for a woman; and everybody made excuses for Gabriel, and everybody was down on Faith. So there things lay. It was raw and chill when the last neighbor left us, the sky was black as a cloak, not a star to be seen, the wind had edged back to the east again and came in wet and wild from the sea and fringed with its thunder. Oh, poor little Faith, what a night! what a night for her!

I went back and sat down by Dan, and tried to keep his head cool. Father was up walking the kitchen-floor till late, but at length he lay down across the foot of mother's bed, as if expecting to be called. The lights were put out, there was no noise in the town, every one slept, — every one, except they watched like me, on that terrible night. No noise in the town, did I say? Ah, but there was! It came creeping round the corners, it poured rushing up the street, it rose from everywhere, — a voice, a voice of woe, the heavy booming rote of the sea. I looked out, but it was pitch-dark, light had forsaken the world, we were beleaguered by blackness. It grew colder, as if one felt a fog fall, and the wind, mounting slowly, now blew a gale. It eddied in clouds of dead and whirling leaves, and sent big torn branches flying aloft; it took the house by the four corners and shook it to loosening the rafters, and I felt the chair rock under me; it rumbled down the chimney as if it would tear the life out of us. And with every fresh gust of the gale the rain slapped against the wall, the rain that fell in rivers, and went before the wind in sheets, — and sheltered as I was, the torrents seemed to pour over me like cataracts, and every drop pierced me like a needle, and I put my

fingers in my ears to shut out the howl of the wind and
the waves. I could n't keep my thoughts away from
Faith. Oh, poor girl, this was n't what she 'd expected!
As plainly as if I were aboard-ship I felt the scene, the
hurrying feet, the slippery deck, the hoarse cries, the
creaking cordage, the heaving and plunging and strain-
ing, and the wide wild night. And I was beating off those
dreadful lines with them, two dreadful lines of white froth
through the blackness, two lines where the horns of
breakers guard the harbor, — all night long beating off
the lee with them, my life in my teeth, and chill, blank,
shivering horror before me. My whole soul, my whole
being, was fixed in that one spot, that little vessel driving
on the rocks: it seemed as if a madness took possession
of me, I reeled as I walked, I forefelt the shivering shock,
I waited till she should strike. And then I thought I
heard cries, and I ran out in the storm, and down upon
the causey, but nothing met me but the hollow night and
the roaring sea and the wind. I came back, and hurried
up and down and wrung my hands in an agony. Pictures
of summer nights flashed upon me and faded, — where
out of deep blue vaults the stars hung like lamps, great
and golden, — or where soft films just hazing heaven
caught the rays till all above gleamed like gauze faintly
powdered and spangled with silver, — or heavy with
heat, slipping over silent waters, through scented airs,
under purple skies. And then storms rolled in and rose
before my eyes, distinct for a moment, and breaking, —
such as I 'd seen them from the Shoals in broad daylight,
when tempestuous columns scooped themselves up from
the green gulfs and shattered in foam on the shuddering
rock, — ah! but that was day, and this was midnight and
murk! — storms as I 'd heard tell of them off Cape Race,

when great steamers went down with but one cry, and the
waters crowded them out of sight, — storms where, out of
the wilderness of waves that far and wide wasted white
around, a single one came ploughing on straight to the
mark, gathering its grinding masses mast-high, poising,
plunging, and swamping and crashing them into bottom-
less pits of destruction, — storms where waves toss and
breakers gore, where, hanging on crests that slip from
under, reefs impale the hull, and drowning wretches cling
to the crags with stiffening hands, and the sleet ices them,
and the spray, and the sea lashes and beats them with
great strokes and sucks them down to death: and right in
the midst of it all there burst a gun, — one, another, and
no more. "Oh, Faith! Faith!" I cried again, and I ran
and hid my head in the bed.

How long did I stay so? An hour, or maybe two.
Dan was still dead with sleep, but mother had no more
closed an eye than I. There was no rain now, the wind
had fallen, the dark had lifted; I looked out once more,
and could just see dimly the great waters swinging in the
river from bank to bank. I drew the bucket fresh, and
bound the cloths cold on Dan's head again. I had n't a
thought in my brain, and I fell to counting the meshes in
the net that hung from the wall, but in my ears there was
the everlasting rustle of the sea and shore. It grew
clearer, — it got to being a universal gray; there 'd been
no sunrise, but it was day. Dan stirred, — he turned
over heavily; then he opened his eyes wide and looked
about him.

"I 've had such a fright!" he said. "Georgie! is that
you?"

With that it swept over him afresh, and he fell back.
In a moment or two he tried to rise, but he was weak as

a child. He contrived to keep on his elbow a moment, though, and to give a look out of the window.

"It came on to blow, did n't it?" he asked; but there he sank down again.

"I can't stay so!" he murmured soon. "I can't stay so! Here, — I must tell you. Georgie, get out the spy-glass, and go up on the roof and look over. I've had a dream, I tell you! I've had a dream. Not that either, — but it's just stamped on me! It was like a storm, — and I dreamed that that schooner — the Flyaway — had parted. And the half of her's crashed down just as she broke, and Faith and that man are high up on the bows in the middle of the South Breaker! Make haste, Georgia! Christ! make haste!"

I flew to the drawers and opened them, and began to put the spy-glass together. Suddenly he cried out again, —

"Oh, here's where the fault was! What right had I ever to marry the child, not loving her? I bound her! I crushed her! I stifled her! If she lives, it is my sin; if she dies, I murder her!"

He hid his face, as he spoke, so that his voice came thick, and great choking groans rent their way up from his heart.

All at once, as I looked up, there stood mother, in her long white gown, beside the bed, and bending over and taking Dan's hot head in her two hands.

"Behold, He cometh with clouds!" she whispered.

It always did seem to me as if mother had the imposition of hands, — perhaps every one feels just so about their mother, — but only her touch always lightens an ache for me, whether it's in the heart or the head.

"Oh, Aunt Rhody," said Dan, looking up in her face with his distracted eyes, "can't you help me?"

"I will lift up mine eyes unto the hills, from whence cometh my help," said mother.

"There's no help there!" called Dan. "There's no God there! He would n't have let a little child run into her damnation!"

"Hush, hush, Dan!" murmured mother. "Faith never can have been at sea in such a night as this, and not have felt God's hand snatching her out of sin. If she lives, she's a changed woman; and if she dies, her soul is whitened and fit to walk with saints. Through much tribulation."

"Yes, yes," muttered father, in the room beyond, spitting on his hands, as if he were going to take hold of the truth by the handle, — "it's best to clean up a thing with the first spot, and not wait for it to get all rusty with crime."

"And he!" said Dan, — "and he, — that man, — Gabriel!"

> "Between the saddle and the ground
> If mercy's asked, mercy's found,"

said I.

"Are you there yet, Georgia?" he cried, turning to me. "Here! I'll go myself!" But he only stumbled and fell on the bed again.

"In all the terror and the tempest of these long hours, — for there's been a fearful storm, though you have n't felt it," said mother, — "in all that, Mr. Gabriel can't have slept. But at first it must have been that great dread appalled him, and he may have been beset with sorrow. He'd brought her to this. But at last, for he's no coward, he has looked death in the face and not flinched; and the danger, and the grandeur there is in despair, have lifted his spirit to great heights, — heights found now in an hour, but which in a whole life long he never would have gained, — heights from which he has seen the light of God's face and been transfigured in it, — heights where the soul dilates to a stature it can never lose. Oh, Dan, there 's a moment, a moment when the dross strikes off, and the impurities, and the grain sets, and there comes out the great white diamond. For by grace are ye saved, through faith, and that not of yourselves, it is the gift of God, — of Him that maketh the seven stars and Orion, and turneth the shadow of death into the morning. Oh, I *will* believe that Mr. Gabriel had n't any need to grope as we do, but that suddenly he saw the Heavenly Arm and clung to it, and the grasp closed round him, and death and hell can have no power over him now. Dan, poor boy, is it better to lie in the earth with the ore than to be forged in the furnace and beaten to a blade fit for the hands of archangels ? "

And mother stopped, trembling like a leaf.

I 'd been wiping and screwing the glass, and I 'd waited a breath, for mother always talked so like a preacher ; but when she 'd finished, after a second or two Dan looked up, and said, as if he 'd just come in, —

" Aunt Rhody, how come you out of bed ? "

And then mother, she got upon the bed, and she took Dan's head on her breast and fell to stroking his brows, laying her cool palms on his temples and on his eyelids, as once I 'd have given my ears to do, — and I slipped out of the room.

Oh, I hated to go up those stairs, to mount that ladder, to open the scuttle ! And once there, I waited and waited before I dared to look. The night had unnerved me. At length I fixed the glass. I swept the broad swollen stream, to the yellowing woods, and over the meadows, where a pale transient beam crept under and pried up the haycocks, — the smoke that began to curl from the chimneys and fall as soon, — the mists blowing off from Indian Hill, but brooding blue and dense down the turnpike, and burying the red spark of the moon, that smothered like a half-dead coal in her ashes, — anywhere, anywhere but that spot! I don't know why it was, but I could n't level the glass there, — my arm would fall, my eye haze. Finally I brought it round nearer and tried again. Everywhere, as far as your eye could reach, the sea was yeasty and white with froth, and great streaks of it were setting up the inky river, and against it there were the twin light-houses quivering their little yellow rays as if to mock the dawn, and far out on the edge of day the great light at the Isles of Shoals blinked and blinked, crimson and gold, fainter and fainter, and lost at last. It was no use, I did n't dare point it, my hand trembled so I could see nothing plain, when suddenly an engine went thundering over the bridge and startled me into stillness. The tube slung in my hold and steadied against the chimney, and there — What was it in the field? what ghastly picture?

The glass crashed from my hand, and I staggered shrieking down the ladder.

The sound was n't well through my lips, when the door slammed, and Dan had darted out of the house and to the shore. I after him. There was a knot sitting and standing round there in the gray, shivering, with their hands in their pockets and their pipes set in their teeth; but the gloom was on them as well, and the pipes went out between the puffs.

"Where's Dennis's boat?" Dan demanded, as he strode.

"The six-oar's all the one not —"

"The six-oar I want. Who goes with me?"

There was n't a soul in the ward but would have followed Dan's lead to the end of the world and jumped off;
and before I could tell their names there were three men
on the thwarts, six oars in the air, Dan stood in the bows,
a word from him, and they shot away.

I watched while I could see, and then in and up to the
attic, forgetting to put mother in her bed, forgetting all
things but the one. And there lay the glass broken. I sat
awhile with the pieces in my hand, as if I 'd lost a king-
dom; then down, and mechanically put things to rights,
and made mother comfortable, — and she 's never stood on
her feet from that day to this. At last I seated myself
before the fire, and stared into it to blinding.

"Won't some one lend you a glass, Georgie?" said
mother.

"Of course they will!" I cried, — for, you see, I had n't
a wit of my own, — and I ran out.

There 's a glass behind every door in the street, you
should know, and there 's no day in the year that you 'll
go by and not see one stretching from some roof where
the heart of the house is out on the sea. Oh, sometimes
I think all the romance of the town is clustered down here
on the Flats and written in pale cheeks and starting eyes.
But what 's the use?   After one winter, one, I gave mine
away, and never got another. It 's just an emblem of
despair. Look, and look again, and look till your soul
sinks, and the thing you want never crosses it; but you 're
down in the kitchen stirring a porridge, or you 're off at a
neighbor's asking the news, and somebody shouts at you
round the corner, and there, black and dirty and dearer
than gold, she lies between the piers.

All the world was up on their house-tops spying, that morning, but there was nobody would keep their glass while I had none ; so I went back armed, and part of it all I saw, and part of it father told me.

I waited till I thought they were 'most across, and then I rubbed the lens. At first I saw nothing, and I began to quake with a greater fear than any that had yet taken root in me. But with the next moment there they were, pulling close up. I shut my eyes for a flash with some kind of a prayer that was most like an imprecation, and when I looked again they had dashed over and dashed over, taking the rise of the long roll, and were in the midst of the South Breaker. O God ! that terrible South Breaker ! The oars bent lithe as willow-switches, a moment they skimmed on the caps, a moment were hid in the snow of the spray. Dan, red-shirted, still stood there, his whole soul on the aim before him, like that of some leaper flying through the air ; he swayed to the stroke, he bowed, he rose, perfectly balanced, and flexile as the wave. The boat behaved beneath their hands like a live creature : she bounded so that you almost saw the light under her ; her whole stem lifted itself slowly out of the water, caught the back of a roller and rode over upon the next ; the very things that came rushing in with their white rage to devour her bent their necks and bore her up like a bubble. Constantly she drew nearer that dark and shattered heap up to which the fierce surf raced, and over which it leaped. And there all the time, all the time, they had been clinging, far out on the bowsprit, those two figures, her arms close-knit about him, he clasping her with one, the other twisted in the hawser whose harsh thrilling must have filled their ears like an organ-note as it swung them to and fro, — clinging to life, —

clinging to each other more than to life. The wreck
scarcely heaved with the stoutest blow of the tremendous
surge ; here and there, only, a plank shivered off and was
bowled on and thrown high upon the beach beside fragments of beams broken and bruised to a powder ; it
seemed to be as firmly planted there as the breaker itself.
Great feathers of foam flew across it, great waves shook
themselves thin around it and veiled it in shrouds, and
with their every breath the smothering sheets dashed over
them, — the two. And constantly the boat drew nearer,
as I said ; they were almost within hail ; Dan saw her
hair streaming on the wind ; he waited only for the long
wave. On it came, that long wave, — oh ! I can see it
now ! — plunging and rearing and swelling, a monstrous
billow, sweeping and swooping and rocking in. Its hollows gaped with slippery darkness, it towered and sent
the scuds before its trembling crest, breaking with a
mighty rainbow as the sun burst forth, it fell in a white
blindness everywhere, rushed seething up the sand, — and
the bowsprit was bare ! —

When father came home, the rack had driven down the
harbor and left clear sky ; it was near nightfall ; they 'd
been searching the shore all day, — to no purpose. But
that rainbow, — I always took it for a sign. Father was
worn out, yet he sat in the chimney-side, cutting off great
quids and chewing and thinking and sighing. At last he
went and wound up the clock, — it was the stroke of
twelve, — and then he turned to me and said, —

"Dan sent you this, Georgie. He hailed a pilot-boat,
and 's gone to the Cape to join the fall fleet to the fish-
'ries. And he sent you this."

It was just a great hand-grip to make your nails purple, but there was heart's-blood in it. See, there 's the
mark to-day.

So there was Dan off in the Bay of Chaleur. 'T was the best place for him. And I went about my work once more. There was a great gap in my life, but I tried not to look at it. I durst n't think of Dan, and I would n't think of them, — the two. Always in such times it 's as if a breath had come and blown across the pool and you could see down its dark depths and into the very bottom, but time scums it all over again. And I tell you it 's best to look trouble in the face : if you don't, you 'll have more of it. So I got a lot of shoes to bind, and what part of my spare time I wa'n't at my books the needle flew. But I turned no more to the past than I could help, and the future trembled too much to be seen.

Well, the two months dragged away, it got to be Thanksgiving-week, and at length the fleet was due. I mind me I made a great baking that week ; and I put brandy into the mince for once, instead of vinegar and dried-apple juice, — and there were the fowls stuffed and trussed on the shelf, — and the pumpkin-pies like slices of split gold, — and the cranberry-tarts, plats of crimson and puffs of snow, — and I was brewing in my mind a right-royal red Indian-pudding to come out of the oven smoking hot and be soused with thick clots of yellow cream, — when one of the boys ran in and told us the fleet 'd got back, but no Dan with it, — he 'd changed over to a fore-and-after, and would n't be home at all, but was to stay down in the Georges all winter, and he 'd sent us word. Well, the baking went to the dogs, or the Thanksgiving beggars, which is the same thing.

Then days went by, as days will, and it was well into the New Year. I used to sit there at the window, reading, — but the lines would run together, and I 'd forget what 't was all about, and gather no sense, and the image

of the little fore-and-after, the " Feather," raked in between the leaves, and at last I had to put all that aside ;
and then I sat stitching, stitching, but got into a sad habit
of looking up and looking out each time I drew the
thread. I felt it was a shame of me to be so glum, and
mother missed my voice ; but I could no more talk than
I could have given conundrums to King Solomon, and as
for singing —— Oh, I used to long so for just a word
from Dan!

We 'd had dry fine weeks all along, and father said
he 'd known we should have just such a season, because
the goose's breast-bone was so white ; but St. Valentine's
day the weather broke, broke in a chain of storms that
the September gale was a whisper to. Ah, it was a
dreadful winter, that! You 've surely heard of it. It
made forty widows in one town. Of the dead that were
found on Prince Edward's Island's shores there were
four corpses in the next house yonder, and two in the one
behind. And what waiting and watching and cruel pangs
of suspense for them that could n't have even the peace
of certainty! And I was one of those.

The days crept on, I say, and got bright again ; no
June days ever stretched themselves to half such length ;
there was perfect stillness in the house, — it seemed to
me that I counted every tick of the clock. In the evenings the neighbors used to drop in and sit mumbling over
their fearful memories till the flesh crawled on my bones.
Father, then, he wanted cheer, and he 'd get me to singing " Caller Herrin'." Once, I 'd sung the first part, but
as I reached the lines, —

> " When ye were sleepin' on your pillows,
> Dreamt ye aught o' our puir fellows
> Darklin' as they face the billows,
> A' to fill our woven willows," —

as I reached those lines, my voice trembled so 's to shake
the tears out of my eyes, and Jim Jerdan took it up himself and sung it through for me to words of his own
invention. He was always a kindly fellow, and he knew
a little how the land lay between me and Dan.

"When I was down in the Georges," said Jim Jerdan ——

"You? When was you down there?" asked father.

"Well, — once I was. There 's worse places."

"Can't tell me nothing about the Georges," said father.
"'T a'n't the rivers of Damascus exactly, but 't a'n't the
Marlstrom neither."

"Ever ben there, Cap'n?"

"A few. Spent more nights under cover roundabouts
than Georgie 'll have white hairs in her head, — for all
she 's washing the color out of her eyes now."

You see, father knew I set by my hair, — for in those
days I rolled it thick as a cable, almost as long, black as
that cat's back, — and he thought he 'd touch me up a
little.

"Wash the red from her cheek and the light from her
look, and she 'll still have the queen's own tread," said
Jim.

"If Loisy Currier 'd heern that, you 'd wish your cake
was dough," says father.

"I 'll resk it," says Jim. "Loisy knows who 's second
choice, as well as if you told her."

"But what about the Georges, Jim?" I asked; for
though I hated to hear, I could listen to nothing else.

"Georges? Oh, not much. Just like any other place."

"But what do you do down there?"

"Do? Why, we fish, — in the pleasant weather."

"And when it 's not pleasant?"

" Oh, then we make things taut, hoist fores'l, clap the hellum into the lee becket, and go below and amuse ourselves."

" How ? " I asked, as if I had n't heard it all a hundred times.

" One way 'n' another. Pipes, and mugs, and poker, if it a'n't too rough ; and if it is, we just bunk and snooze till it gets smooth."

" Why, Jim, — how do you know when that is ? "

" Well, you can jedge, —'f the pipe falls out of your pocket and don't light on the ceiling."

" And who 's on deck ? "

" There 's no one on deck. There 's no danger, no trouble, no nothing. Can't drive ashore, if you was to try : hundred miles off, in the first place. Hatches are closed, she 's light as a cork, rolls over and over just like any other log in the water, and there can't a drop get into her, if she turns bottom-side up."

" But she never can right herself ! "

" Can't she ? You just try her. Why, I 've known 'em to keel over and rake bottom and bring up the weed on the topmast. I tell you now ! there was one time we knowed she 'd turned a somerset, pretty well. Why ? Because, when it cleared and we come up, there was her two masts broke short off ! "

And Jim went home thinking he 'd given me a night's sleep. But it was cold comfort ; the Georges seemed to me a worse place than the Hellgate. And mother she kept murmuring, — " He layeth the beams of His chambers in the waters, His pavilion round about Him is dark waters and thick clouds of the skies." And I knew by that she thought it pretty bad.

So the days went in cloud and wind. The owners of

the Feather 'd been looking for her a month and more, and there were strange kind of rumors afloat; and nobody mentioned Dan's name, unless they tripped. I went glowering like a wild thing. I knew I 'd never see Dan now nor hear his voice again, but I hated the Lord that had done it, and I made my heart like the nether millstone. I used to try and get out of folks's sight; and roaming about the back-streets one day, as the snow went off, I stumbled on Miss Catharine. "Old Miss Catharine" everybody called her, though she was but a pauper, and had black blood in her veins. Eighty years had withered her, — a little woman at best, and now bent so that her head and shoulders hung forward and she could n't lift them, and she never saw the sky. Her face to the ground as no beast's face is turned even, she walked with a cane, and fixing it every few steps she would throw herself back, and so get a glimpse of her way and go on. I looked after her, and for the first time in weeks my heart ached for somebody beside myself. The next day mother sent me with a dish to Miss Catharine's room, and I went in and sat down. I did n't like her at first; she 'd got a way of looking sidelong that gave her an evil air; but soon she tilted herself backward, and I saw her face, — such a happy one!

"What 's the matter of ye, honey?" said she. "D' ye read your Bible?"

Read my Bible!

"Is that what makes you happy, Miss Catharine?" I asked.

"Well, I can't read much myself, — I don't know the letters," says she; "but I 've got the blessed promises in my heart."

"Do you want me to read to you?"

"No, not to-day. Next time you come, maybe."

So I sat awhile and listened to her little humming voice, and we fell to talking about mother's ailments, and she said how fine it would be, if we could only afford to take mother to Bethesda.

"There's no angel there now," said I.

"I know it, dear, — but then — there might be, you know. At any rate, there's always the living waters running to make us whole : I often think of that."

"And what else do you think of, Miss Catharine ? "

"Me ? " said she. "Oh, I ha'n't got no husband nor no child to think about and hope for, and so I think of myself, and what I should like, honey. And sometimes I remember them varses, — here ! you read 'em now, — Luke xiii. 11."

So I read : —

"And, behold, there was a woman which had a spirit of infirmity eighteen years, and was bowed together, and could in no wise lift up herself. And when Jesus saw her, he called her to him, and said unto her, 'Woman, thou art loosed from thine infirmity.' And he laid his hands on her : and immediately she was made straight, and glorified God."

"Ay, honey, I see that all as if it was me. And I think, as I'm setting here, What if the latch should lift, and the gracious stranger should come in, his gown a-sweepin' behind him and a-sweet'nin' the air, and he should look down on me with his heavenly eyes, and he should smile, and lay his hands on my head, warm, — and I say to myself, 'Lord, I am not worthy,' — and he says, 'Miss Catharine, thou art loosed from thine infirmity !' And the latch lifts as I think, and I wait, — but it's not Him."

Well, when I went out of that place I was n't the same girl that had gone in. My will gave way; I came home and took up my burden and was in peace. Still I could n't help my thoughts, — and they ran perpetually to the sea. I had n't need to go up on the house-tops, for I did n't shut my eyes but there it stretched before me. I stirred about the rooms and tried to make them glad once more; but I was thin and blanched as if I 'd been rising from a fever. Father said it was the salt air I wanted; and one day he was going out for frost-fish, and he took me with him, and left me and my basket on the sands while he was away. It was this side of the South Breaker that he put me out, but I walked there; and where the surf was breaking in the light, I went and sat down and looked over it. I could do that now.

There was the Cape sparkling miles and miles across the way, unconcerned that he whose firm foot had rung last on its flints should ring there no more; there was the beautiful town lying large and warm along the river; here gay craft went darting about like gulls, and there up the channel sped a larger one, with all her canvas flashing in the sun, and shivering a little spritsail in the shadow, as she went; and fawning in upon my feet came the foam from the South Breaker, that still perhaps cradled Faith and Gabriel. But as I looked, my eye fell, and there came the sea-scenes again, — other scenes than this, coves and corners of other coasts, sky-girt regions of other waters. The air was soft, that April day, and I thought of the summer calms; and with that rose long sheets of stillness, far out from any strand, purple beneath the noon; fields slipping close in-shore, emerald-backed and scaled with sunshine; long sleepy swells that hid the light in their hollows, and came creaming along the cliffs. And if upon these broke suddenly a wild glimpse of some storm careering over a merciless mid-ocean, of a dear dead face tossing up on the surge and snatched back again into the depths, of mad wastes rushing to tear themselves to fleece above clear shallows and turbid sand-bars, — they melted and were lost in peaceful glimmers of the moon on distant flying foam-wreaths, in solemn midnight tides chanting in under hushed heavens, in twilight stretches kissing twilight slopes, in rosy morning waves flocking up the singing shores. And sitting so, with my lids still fallen, I heard a quick step on the beach, and a voice that said, "Georgie!" And I looked, and a figure, red-shirted, towered beside me, and a face, brown and bearded and tender, bent above me.

Oh! it was Dan!

Cambridge : Stereotyped and Printed by Welch, Bigelow, & Co.